# London's Daughter

## Philip Boast

**HEADLINE**

First published in 1992
by HEADLINE BOOK PUBLISHING PLC

First published in paperback in 1994
by HEADLINE BOOK PUBLISHING

10 9 8 7 6 5 4 3 2 1

ISBN 0 7472 4023 X

Typeset by Keyboard Services, Luton

Printed and bound in Great Britain by
HarperCollins Manufacturing, Glasgow

HEADLINE BOOK PUBLISHING
A division of Hodder Headline PLC
338 Euston Road
London NW1 3BH

Philip Boast is the author of *London's Child* and *London's Millionaire* (previously published as *The Millionaire*), both of which feature Ben London. He is also the author of *Watersmeet*, a West Country saga, and *Pride*, an epic novel set in England and Australia. He lives in Devon with his wife Rosalind and two children, Harry and Zoe.

For my brother
Steve

# THE FIVE FAMILIES OF BEN LONDON
## The Millionaire's Family Tree, 1575—1954

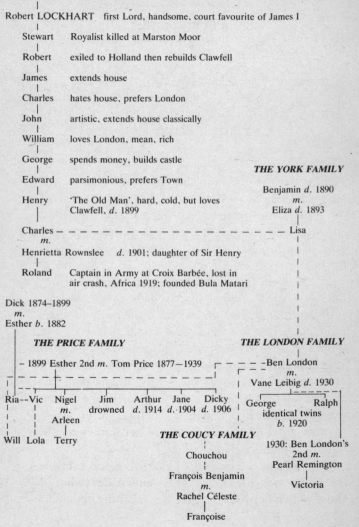

**THE LORDS OF CLEREMONT**

Robert LOCKHART   first Lord, handsome, court favourite of James I

Stewart    Royalist killed at Marston Moor

Robert     exiled to Holland then rebuilds Clawfell

James      extends house

Charles    hates house, prefers London

John       artistic, extends house classically

William    loves London, mean, rich

George     spends money, builds castle

Edward     parsimonious, prefers Town

**THE YORK FAMILY**

Benjamin *d.* 1890
*m.*
Eliza *d.* 1893

Henry      'The Old Man', hard, cold, but loves
           Clawfell, *d.* 1899

Charles — — — — — — — — — — — — — — — — — Lisa
*m.*

Henrietta Rownslee    *d.* 1901; daughter of Sir Henry

Roland     Captain in Army at Croix Barbée, lost in
           air crash, Africa 1919; founded Bula Matari

Dick 1874–1899
*m.*
Esther *b.* 1882

**THE PRICE FAMILY**

— 1899 Esther 2nd *m.* Tom Price 1877—1939

**THE LONDON FAMILY**

Ben London
*m.*
Vane Leibig *d.* 1930

Ria--Vic  Nigel    Jim      Arthur   Jane    Dicky
          *m.*     drowned  *d.* 1914 *d.* 1904 *d.* 1906
          Arleen

George        Ralph
identical twins
*b.* 1920

Will  Lola  Terry

**THE COUCY FAMILY**

Chouchou

François Benjamin
*m.*
Rachel Céleste

Françoise

1930: Ben London's
2nd *m.*
Pearl Remington

Victoria

# Prologue

## Christmas Eve 1946

Pearl's alarm clock rang. She looked across at her husband Ben, his features tense and assertive even in the unconsciousness of sleep, then kissed his naked shoulder and swung her long legs quietly over the edge of their bed, departing without him. Today was *her* day.

Dressing on tiptoe in warm casual clothes and a long scarf, she crept down one side of the marble staircase, the silence of his house clapping momentarily with her footsteps, and made coffee in the intimacy of her own small, homely kitchen. She yawned at her face in the mirror behind the door then groomed her hair, her only vanity, into a pale fan across her shoulders. The excitement of being reunited with her daughter Victoria after these months drove the tiredness out of her mind and she left her cup unfinished.

Outside was the first grey light of London's dawn; the snow was grey, and grey snowflakes whirled slowly down between the grey trees. Lifting her collar and blowing into her hands as she crossed the driveway, Pearl got into her car, turned on the ignition, and thumbed the starter. The motor churned over slowly, then stopped, so she went across and tried Ben's Silver Wraith. As she turned on the ignition, she saw from the corner of her eye the dark figure of a woman waving her arms and running towards her up the drive. Then there was a blinding flash.

Inside London House, Ben woke hearing a woman's voice screaming, 'No! No!' He ran downstairs still half asleep, his bare feet slipping on the marble, hurting his ankle. The fanlight above the doors glowed with a brilliant illumination, casting shadows past him, then the windows blew in around him in a silver cloud and the lights went out.

Ben lifted himself on his hands. His face felt icy cold. He heard the sound of tinkling glass sliding from the skin of his back. He stumbled to the door, hands outstretched, but there was no door. It was completely dark outside and on bleeding feet he slipped down the steps, fell heavily.

'Pearl!' he bellowed. He heard a woman scream. Ben crawled across the scalding wet gravel towards the heat, immersed in black smoke, drowning. He couldn't reach her. 'Help me!' he shouted. 'She'll be all right.'

He felt a hand on his shoulder. 'Pearl!' he hissed, staring up.

'I was too late,' whispered Ria's griefstricken voice. It was the slum girl's hand touching Ben. He looked up into darkness.

Ria knelt beside the kneeling figure. Like a stitched thread, often unseen but always unbroken, holding her life together and giving her hope against the darkest days, her love for Ben London had never wavered. Once she had turned him down because he had everything. Now he had nothing.

'Pearl is dead,' Ria whispered.

Her little girl, Lola, played innocently in the melting snow around the scene of destruction of Ben's life.

The dawn was brilliant, and Ben's eyes were as white as flame.

*Where do you go, when no one will help you, and you have nowhere to go to?*

'Help me!' he roared.

Ria put her arms around his shoulders. Her child threw snowballs into the dying embers.

'I will help you.' Gently, with her fingertips, Ria turned his face to the right, towards his mother Lisa who stood on the top step. 'I will help you.'

Lisa gasped when she saw her son's eyes, and understood. Ben London, always so clearsighted, was utterly blind.

# PART I

## The Fallen Man

Christmas Eve 1946
– 27 December 1946

# Chapter One

*'Help me!'*
*We are alone, and no one on this earth knows*
*us as we truly are.*
*Did you really know your father?*

## 1

Every working day at 8.55 precisely Bill Simmonds's
first job was to drive his employer Ben London to the
London Emporium. Neither 8.54 nor 8.56 was good
enough. Tradition dictated that the drive from the
house on the Mall to the doors of the great store on
Old Bond Street and Piccadilly must take five minutes
exactly, whatever the traffic, without haste and
without delay. That precision was meat and drink to
the pride of a fine chauffeur in a classy uniform. But
such a man was not always what he appeared.

CLANK – *a – clang clang!*

Last night in his single bed, Bill Simmonds had
dreamt of his father, and had become a child again.

CLANK – *a – clang clang* . . . The bell rang again.

'Young' Bill Simmonds sat up white-haired and

naked, his eyes still closed and his face as wrinkled as a monkey's, then sprawled among the greasy sheets of his smelly Wharncliffe Gardens room. He had dreamed of Dad to the flesh, and the experience was still shaking him while he woke.

*Clang . . . clang . . .* The tolling of the Stone Yard bell, remembered from his childhood, accurate enough for Dad to set his watch by, summoned the navvies from Lisson Grove to work in the council depot.

Silence. The only clanging was his hangover; he had a case of the Joe Blakes to be proud of, and his mouth tasted like a street Arab's underpants . . . not that the little street Arabs really wore didies, Dad used to say: they sold them.

'Young' Bill sat limply on the side of the bed, rubbing at his face with his short hairy fingers as though washing it until the shaking stopped. The bell had been in his dream; the old Stone Yard had been a bomb-lot of waste ground since the Blitz, peopled only by Irish ghosts. When he lurched up his foot knocked over like dominoes the line of dark brown bottles arranged as trophies along the dirty carpet, the drained proof of his manhood. He hadn't had a woman here last night so the place was still untidy. The odd creatures struggled to improve him, but he knew what he wanted from them – only the one thing. Alma Hoblin who came from two floors up watered the aspidistras decorating the windowsills for him; God knows why, they didn't need much water or light. Because she fancied him of course; eligible bachelor. He had quite a collection of the bloody things now, even one in the karsy. She was too thin, though, and she wanted to be friends. Bad sign.

A solitary man, he had even cut Ben London's Christmas party for family, friends and employees at the hotel last night. His professional services were Not Required, so he wouldn't go at all. He had his father's temper, all right.

He would have been missed, he reckoned hopefully, people would have wondered if he was well, wouldn't they?

He touched the wet pillow. He must have got well giffed. In his sleep he had cried like a child.

'You're weak as a woman,' he cursed himself.

Five minutes past! Dad had beaten a railwayman's respect for time into his boys, determined they'd make engine drivers as he never had. Bill had failed his father's ambition but he'd never yet been late for work. He stuck today's first Harry Wragg to his pendulous lower lip, went into the kitchen and sat with the karsy door open watching the kettle boil up on the Horseferry hob.

'Young' Bill was fifty-eight years old, but in his dream he had seen Dad brought alive, *re-created*, as a child saw him, complete with that glint in his eye. Even the *feel* of him – like one of those modern paintings, a riot of colour but the more you looked, the more you saw – the achingly brilliant images of a child's dream-memory: Dad red-faced, his white shirt tucked in tight and the pennies glittering coppery eyes on the towpath around him, playing Sunday pitch-and-toss after church with the other Wharncliffe Gardens fathers, their shouts echoing up the wall,

'Penny heads! Penny tails!' and to end the session Dad flipping a few sparkling coppers, turning over and over in the sunlight, into the canal for poor urchins – the Irish street Arabs – to dive and trawl the dark waters for. By 1926, when Ben London had kicked Dad out of his job at the age of sixty-seven, old Bert Simmonds had looked seventy-seven, his cheeks scoured crimson by a lifetime of the wind and sun suffered by drivers of open Victorian carts and Edwardian landaulette limousines, but still wearing his London Emporium chauffeur's cap straight as a die, his badge of pride. His job went to the clever darkie who then took over as head doorman when Hawk died fifteen years ago, and Bill Simmonds was moved up from Delivery to be chauffeur in his father's footsteps. The first thing Bill did was pay homage at the Collingwood Road flat Dad had retired to.

'Remember, my boy,' Dad gave good advice from his tattered armchair, 'yer chauffeur, 'e's as much a public figure as yer 'ead doorman is, a man apart, 'e's got ter be respected or the taxis cut 'im up, and yer can't 'ave *that*, can yer!'

Dad hadn't wished his son good luck, just sat there with that bitter, challenging look in his eye. No one was as good as Dad. He'd never got caught in a jam, he had a sense for traffic flow like a fish's for the currents in water, and a taxi-driver's eye for a gap. No one had known London better than Albert Arthur Simmonds.

'Yes, Dad,' had said 'young' Bill obediently.

'*Yer just like 'im!*' Gloria had shouted long ago. '*Yer 'im ter the life!*'

10

Bill grunted, coming out of the karsy and stirring his tea without washing his hands, but then combing his hair carefully. A man had a private face and a public face.

'*Yer like yer dad ter the life, young Bill!*'

His father, having proudly named his first son Albert after himself, had christened his second son (being girls their elder sisters Gloria and Annie didn't count) William, so Bill the young lad was. Got him confirmed him, too, by old Vezey-Mason at the Emmanuel Anglican Church. A lifetime later Bill happened still to live in the Settlement where once his father had. Apart from that, Bill told himself, he and his father were as different as chalk from cheese, whatever that fat pig Gloria said.

Dad was London-born but Grandad Arthur had had wanderlust (and, it was whispered, a criminal history), and upped from London, 'fer 'is 'ealth', with pretty Elsie and more than a few bob in his pocket. Wealth: such a rumour was useful. In fact he had died itinerant and mad as May-butter, so Dad had started his working life on the hard, cobbled streets of the north among the pigs let out at night to snuffle up the rubbish from gutters and doorways. But Grandma Elsie had a level head on her shoulders and a few coppers laid by, so Dad put every penny of his little inheritance from her into a cab working the Piccadilly station – Piccadilly, Manchester, that is – and some men had grown rich by such investments in the days of the Manchester, Sheffield and Lincolnshire Railway Company. After a brief liaison with a slender young buffet waittress behind the MS & L engine shed (a bragging follies-of-youth wink here from Dad to his boys), he made an honest woman of her, and over the next five years Mrs Simmonds struggled to bring her husband's children into the world, to bring them up proper in the grim two-down with crackling paper in the windows. As the business went from bad to worse there were still happy days to be had at home, Mum always said, with sort of a defiant look at Dad. Then the horse died between the shafts and the replacement had 'blown' lungs, and to cap it off in 1892 little Jack arrived despite all the trouble Mrs Simmonds had took nursing Bill until mother's milk came out of his ears, so they had a new youngest to feed who should never have happened, and Dad couldn't stay his own man. He swallowed his pride for Jack's sake and became an employed worker for the MS & L, one little man among a thousand others.

On 14 October 1895 the MS & L was renamed the Great Central Railway. Almost at once the building of the railway's new Marylebone Station gave employees the chance to move south to London and a new life, and young Bill, who had never seen the metropolis before, remembered hanging from Dad's reins-callused hand in childish awe of the Railway Settlement's vast new yellow-brick buildings – six mansion blocks in all, just the first storey faced artistically in red Suffolk brick, then floor after floor yellow as butter towering to ranks of chimneys fuming against the sky. It was like dying and going to heaven.

Wharncliffe Gardens, five hundred and forty

tenements, two thousand six hundred and ninety (precisely) residents, with glass in their windows, with their own piped water and gas, with their own electricity from behind the four elm trees screening their own Grove Road generating station; two thousand six hundred and ninety proud residents with standards to keep up.

Wharncliffe Gardens, four acres of paved courtyards and flat roofs running north from the Regent's Canal, which entered its mysterious tunnel beneath, like the entrance to an underworld, the Wharncliffe Gardens children running from the playground to watch from the high retaining wall as the bright barges slid into the black mouth below, to be swallowed by the dark. A dark to be kept out. The Settlement was kept spanking-clean by the house-proud women, as proud of their whole community as they were of their own particular mansion blocks and their own little apartments. In the well-planned sunny courtyards above the dark tunnel the well-clothed Wharncliffe Gardens children held hands and sang together, *'We all go the same way home – In the same direction – Oh what a collection – We all cling together like the ivy – On the old garden wall!'*

We all cling together.

*Clang – clang – clang!*

God, what a mess everything was nowadays. Bill thought he heard police bells in the distance, a lighter, higher sound than the heavy clamour of the fire escapes Mr London had driven in the war.

He opened the wardrobe door spotted with greasy fingermarks, and pulled out his immaculate uniform on the hanger. He brushed it, dressed carefully, then examined himself critically in the fly-specked mirror. He brushed the bespoke shoulders again. Bill's eyes pricked as he fitted on his head the chauffeur's peaked cap, yellow and navy blue, the house colours of London Emporium. *We all cling together*.

He hadn't thought, *really* thought, of Dad for years.

Pulling the galoshes over his shoes and snapping the elasticated waterproof cover over his cap, Bill donned a black mackintosh to protect his spotless uniform, and closed the front door of his little ground floor flat carefully behind him, then locked it with three turns of the key, making it safe. Behind the half-drawn curtains and screen of drooping aspidistras a knife remained stuck in a smear of jam, a man's home for him to come back to: dishes piled across the tablecloth, a mixing bowl full of spark-plugs soaking in petrol, Woodbine fag-end stubs like burst insects among the slops in the sink, the bed unmade and bottles empty. A man without a woman.

Neatly turned out as always on the outside, every movement precise, the chauffeur silently descended the three snowy steps. The snow had stopped. Grove Road was a scurrying mass of people in dark make-do clothes, cheap utility cast-offs and recobbled shoes, their heads wrapped in foggy balls of breath. Londoners. They looked cold to the bones because of the fuel shortages; even their daily bread was still rationed. There was no pride in their faces hurrying past him to work as there had been in the war or as Bill remembered from his childhood.

Bill stood alone in the snow. A housewife called an uninterested hallo from the balcony above him, and he looked up at the dirty pile of brickwork, filthy windows, the long perspective of grimy, once-proud wall laced with rusting loo pipes and gutter-drains. The Gardens as it really was.

He crossed into Lodge Road towards the row of lock-up garages, once the Great Central Railway stables – Dad had paid the boys a ha'penny each to go in on Sunday to feed and water the horses, but the railway paid Dad a shilling. Bill stopped at the garage door, staring at the glinting key . . . feeling its promise with a child's intensity, an adult's sense of loss. He had grown up to take Dad's job. To live in Wharncliffe Gardens in Dad's place.

*Yer like 'im ter the life, Bill!*

Now Bill consciously heard the roar of a lorry engine in the distance, a clamouring bell, and looked round calmly; London was full of emergencies. In his childhood bells hadn't been invented for fire escapes, the Met Fire cart with its straining horses rocked clumsily down Grove Road with the crew shouting 'Hi-ya-hi!' He glimpsed a new red fire-engine flash past the entrance to Lodge Road, its urgent appeal dropping an octave as it faded in the distance. Someone else's problem; he was on duty. The morning was vacant again except for the small, lonely figure of Bill Simmonds standing in his black mackintosh against the white snow.

*Did Dad really love us children? Did we really love him?*

The thought lodged in his mind like a nut, spoiling

his pleasure as the garage door swung aside to reveal the dark shape within.

She was beautiful.

Bill Simmonds was in love. That was how he survived.

She wasn't his: not his property, like a child, or a wife. She was his mistress.

'Are you going to be good this morning?' Bill growled.

Although he was in danger of being late he took the yellow duster and groomed the black paint until it held every reflection in perfect colour.

Every owner said the Phantom Three was the finest Rolls-Royce ever built, and maybe that was true, but a fine chauffeur knew what a demanding bitch she really was. That was why Bill loved her, and denied it, every time the garage door swung open: because it wasn't really a car. She had moods and temperament the owner never knew. She could be impossible, then so perfect that Bill forgave her everything. To be her chauffeur was to be privileged.

It was a man's love, but the sort some women would understand: it was a kind of hate. He loved her because she hurt him. She might let him down. She needed pampering with constant attention, those hydraulic tappets wouldn't tolerate any dirt and the timing gears demanded the finest mineral oil at a pressure of one and three-quarter pounds per square inch – no more, no less. A fine chauffeur learned to carry spare plugs and filters, and white linen gloves to keep his hands clean.

Taking off his mac and galoshes he opened the

driver's door, heavy as a swinging vault, lifted himself over the gear-lever into the seat, and thunked the door closed, the outside world now silent, remote. Even Bill's face changed, became immobile in this environment, almost handsome. Meticulously he pressed the foot-pedal that lubricated the suspension and chassis, and allowed time for the engine to warm up before moving off.

Bill Simmonds had started work.

It was dawn in London and the cold sun struck brilliantly across Regent's Park as the Rolls-Royce drew up at the turning from Lodge Road. In the park, hidden from their mother by the bushes, Bill saw a couple of boys pelting a girl with snowballs, and a crapping dog was hauled along by its owner who refused to stop. On the lake the sleeping ducks looked like rugger balls kicked across the icy crust, which was still overflowing a black tongue of water from beneath: last month it had rained for eight days solid. Blinded by the sun despite his peaked cap, Bill Simmonds held up his hand to shield his eyes, and a woman driving an Austin Seven gave way nervously to the imperious gesture.

*Why do you think of your father as though he were dead?*

The Rolls gathered momentum. Wearing his professional expression, or lack of expression, both hands on the wheel in the ten-to-two position, Bill concentrated without appearing to on the lesser traffic swirling alongside him down Baker Street like bits of driftwood; some slower, some faster. Someone overtook him eagerly, but a bus moved to turn right, and the last were first. In Bill's hands the Rolls-Royce maintained her steady, effortless progress. Bill was a chauffeur to his fingertips, he knew it was all in the psychology: the progress of a Rolls-Royce was not that of a car but a ship, accelerating slowly, braking lightly; and he thought of the streets of London channelling the flow of traffic like canals, like the canals of Venice. Bill had never been to Venice. The furthest he had got was day-trips to Brighton with Dad, ices on the Palace Pier and a ride on the Daddy Long-legs railway in the sea to Rottingdean.

Because Dad was still alive, if you called it living. The cradle-to-grave welfare care on the Collingwood Road Estate looked after him in his eighty-eighth year, surrounded by people he did not know and was not capable of knowing. The State nurses had long taken responsibility for him away from his family.

To his amazement Bill found the traffic backed up solid along Constitution Hill: the same old London story, probably he'd never know the cause of it, but now he was in real danger of being late.

Caught out, it took him ten minutes to inch round Hyde Park Corner back to Piccadilly, and he knew for certain he would be late. He rehearsed excuses in his mind: fuel rationing . . . traffic was supposed to be lighter than before the war . . . but Mr London wasn't the type to tolerate excuses. Holding the Rolls in second gear with his right hand almost to forty miles an hour, Bill proceeded along Piccadilly as far as the massive façade of the Emporium, complete with gargoyles, its flags flying above the rooftops. Mike the nightwatchman came out, Bill recognised his battered blue serge cap, but Mike didn't see him. The

news-seller's corner stand carried placards headlined
ZIONISTS STRIKE AT BRITAIN; another proclaimed
IRGUN JEWS EXPLODE J'SALEM HOTEL. The newspapers
fluttered in the old man's hand, again only four pages
long, wartime size, and the tinned meat ration was to
be halved again, Bill saw. A little car nipped out in
front of him, then stalled, and Bill pushed down the
Rolls-Royce's window angrily. The smells and sounds
of London rushed in, dispelling the cocooned silence
inside the car and the rich odour of leather; raw traffic
fumes, the noisy rattle of engines, and beyond
Fortnum and Mason he heard the rapid tolling of the
St James's church bell, St Martin-in-the-Fields slower
and more distant.

Nine o'clock.

*Clang-clang!* Bill pulled over, then turned to the
right along St James's Street, and followed the fire-
engine down to the Mall.

They both turned right again.

'Oh no,' said Bill Simmonds, smelling smoke.

He followed the fire-engine into the driveway of
Ben's house; found it blocked with fire appliances,
hoses uncoiled like canvas snakes, firemen running
clumpingly in thigh-boots and velours, police cars
with flashing lights skewed across the snowy lawns.
For a moment a fire-escape bell clamoured in error,
and Bill recognised it for the sound that had woken
him. He stared, dazed.

A police officer rapped peremptorily on the
windscreen with his white-gloved fist: get it out of
here.

Bill left the Rolls parked across the kerb and stared
at the broken windows of the mansion, at the

19

blackened walls peppered with debris. His mind couldn't comprehend all the destruction: people in uniform everywhere, one of the columns of the portico slumped at an angle, the roof above it drooping and snow and slush sliding down . . . people shouting and running backwards. The busy figures parted, shouting and pushing, to let an ambulance out. Bill walked numbly through the gap: it looked as though he was out of a job, and the thought terrified him. Oake the butler, clad only in pyjamas, strode on bare feet to reassure a group of shivering maids; authoritatively turned back a reporter who was trying to sneak around the side; arranged the removal of a huge incongruous golden coach with classical paintings on the doors from the underground garage. All the time his wife Peggy chased after him, faithful as a dog, holding the slippers that he didn't have time to put on. 'What happened?' Bill kept asking anyone who would listen, then the dirty trails of smoke carried something instantly familiar to any survivor of the Blitz, the nose-catching, acid stink of explosive.

People did not survive explosions.

'Oh, bloody hell,' Bill Simmonds moaned, stopping.

Ben's Silver Wraith looked as though an enormous animal had woken inside it and smashed it open from within. A fireman crouched at the rear of the vehicle with a hose thrust down the petrol filler pipe, high-pressure water spraying back around him in a white fan.

Bill knew the way things went. If Ben London the millionaire was dead, who would look after them?

Without his leadership everything he'd built would go bust and they'd all be on the streets. That was capitalism for you, even under a Labour government. A private chauffeur of almost sixty was on his own, he wasn't a nationalised industry like the Coal Board or the railways that had to be saved, and he wouldn't find another job in these hard times.

And then he saw Lisa.

'Help me!' called Ben London's mother.

Bill looked around him, but everyone else was busy. He trudged over to the tall, silver-haired lady standing by the open rear doors of an ambulance. With earnest faces two ambulancemen were trying to persuade her into it, to slide a blanket over her shoulders, pleading with her to get her feet out of the snow before she caught her death. 'See if she'll listen to you,' shrugged one of the men in a dry voice, chucking the blanket to Bill, before joining his mate lighting up behind the cab.

Bill wasn't Lisa's personal chauffeur, his wage was paid directly by the Emporium. She had her own and he'd already buggered off, wise man. Bill had driven her once or twice and he didn't like her: she had a way of giving orders and expecting them to be obeyed chop-chop, and Bill didn't like being kept on the hop. He was his own man with his own pace.

'All right, are you?' he called nervously. She was older than he but didn't look it, still striking, and she came to him with her hot blue eyes fixed on him alone. The torn hem of her nightdress trailed behind her in the snow. She looked totally vulnerable yet wholly in command, and she was a woman, which

21

confused him. He didn't know how to deal with a distressed woman he couldn't screw.

'Everything's going to be all right,' he told her, and held up the blanket.

'I've lost my son,' she said.

Stress had brought back her native Yorkshire vowels in full force, flat and strong as tea. Her feet were naked and filthy on the churned, sharp gravel; she hadn't even noticed. 'So is Mr London . . .' he said without looking up, hoping she would spare him the word. But she didn't, and he met her eyes, '. . . dead?'

'Pearl were driving to Heathrow to collect her daughter, Victoria, from the Swiss flight,' Lisa told him in her anguish. Men jostled past them. 'Victoria and she was that close, Bill. She were so excited that she couldn't even finish her coffee . . .'

'You'd better sit down before you fall down, ma'am.' Bill caught at her, sure she would drop in a faint.

But Lisa, refusing to cry, pulled her arm away from Bill's hand with contempt.

'Her mother is dead. Her father is blind. How am I to tell Victoria?'

'You can't tell her the truth, ma'am,' Bill Simmonds said.

# 2

Victoria gazed from the huge square porthole at the landscape of snowclouds bumping past the plane, the

note of the twin engines rising and falling irritatingly,
northern France invisible below. The Viking airliner
was in fact a Wellington bomber renovated with every
modern luxury. The man in the seat opposite was
interested in her because she was a schoolgirl, and as
the bumping got worse he kept telling her not to be
frightened. 'The wings are designed to flex,' he
patronised her reassuringly, 'it makes them stronger.'

'I know.' Victoria paid him brief attention. 'My
father was a fighter pilot in World War One. In the
last lot my brother Ralph flew a Hurricane.' Actually
Ralph was her half-brother, Vane's child. But she had
loved him like a brother, closer to him than anyone.
Ralph seducing his girls in the summerhouse. No one
played tennis with Ralph and kept their knickers.

'Shoot down loads of Huns, I expect, did he!'

Victoria bit her tongue. She shook her head.

'I suppose we're going to be friends with them now,'
the man smiled wisely, passing her his bar of
chocolate with an avuncular smile, touching her
hand.

'Ralph was killed.'

'Oh – I'm sorry.'

'It was better that he didn't live.'

The man's face changed, put off by the girl's cold
demeanour. The young could be so very unfeeling,
his face said. He sat back with his eyes closed, and the
plane droned on.

Victoria didn't dare close her eyes in case she
imagined Ralph. He *had* lived, for a little while:
Ralph's twin George, so similar to him in looks and
opposite in nature, couldn't resist telling her. Ralph's

23

plane had gone down burning. 'He was crisped,' George said. She could still hear him saying it, the inflection of George's voice.

Victoria felt more deeply than she could bring herself to show: she dared not imagine the agony Ralph had suffered in those last twenty or thirty hours of his young life. She had been brought up in the war but the horror of war had almost passed her by . . . the man glanced at her sleepily, thinking of her not of his own children. She forced herself to smile innocently, determined to be, while she still wore the school uniform, still childlike.

Only when his mouth slipped open and revealed nasty teeth was she sure he was asleep. She turned to her reflection in the porthole, dropped her lollipop-sucking smile and stuck out her tongue at her blonde Heidi pigtails. As soon as the seatbelt warning was extinguished, she would unbraid them. Her school skirt and blouse would also be discarded: the metamorphosis was at hand. She tucked merrily into the chocolate the man had given her, never travel-sick, her bag full of the other passengers' complimentary Cadbury's bars, export only, still rationed at home. She'd bought some Suchard chocs as well, Pearl's favourite.

Snowspecks peppered the Perspex, outlining her curious, pretty face against the grey wall; the speckles streamed back and were gone. Suddenly the aircraft droned into an immense blue hemisphere of brilliant sunlight and the bumping ceased. Free at last. Victoria's legs in their ghastly black woollen hose were not crossed in the Discipline of Elegance Which

Never Sleeps but stuck straight out beneath the high-backed seat in front of her, and thanks to the delayed flight she'd found time near the hotel to buy the delicious print dress still in its box, a startling tangerine and green with a neckline that was much too plunging; both the colour and the plunging irresistible. She didn't dare even think of wearing it until the Vickers Viking was actually in the air: Madame LaFarge's spies were everywhere – Victoria had glimpsed Lila-May Beaugard chaperoned, groaning, literally to the steps of the DC-4 that would carry her back to Georgia . . . 'All the girls seem so happy at the finishing school, honey,' Pearl had promised last September.

'I'm unimpressed.' Like this, by turning away, Victoria could get whatever she wanted from her mother. 'They're happy because they're obedient. It's a concentration camp.'

'I'm sure you'll enjoy making new friends,' Pearl had begged her wilful daughter, trying to catch her eye, and Victoria had thrilled at her power.

'Daddy wants me to go, not you,' Victoria had sulked.

'Now that's not true.' When hurt, there was steel in Pearl: the hardness that made her beautiful. But Victoria, who had been sent to so many boarding schools – St Joseph's convent, then Roedean School, evacuated during the war to Keswick, far from home – and did not know her mother as well as she thought she did, sailed on.

'I'm unimpressed, Mom,' Victoria accused lightly, 'you're letting him send me away, Mom. You're just a bystander.' She'd stopped, seeing the hurt on her mother's face. Victoria's sharp tongue cut both ways and she had hurt herself too. She admitted tenderly: 'I wish I was as beautiful as you.' She gave the boyish wink and mocking grin that ought to make Pearl laugh.

'I would *never* send you away,' Pearl said simply, straight into Victoria's eyes. 'I never want to tame you. And you are so pretty.'

'Oh, sure, Mom.' Pearl sounded so gushingly American sometimes.

'Buck teeth, squint and all.'

'Mummy, you're goofy!' They hugged, friends again.

'Believe me,' Pearl murmured, 'you will learn to be such a beautiful girl. I do love you.'

But in the end Pearl let her daughter down because she loved Daddy more, had not been able to resist Daddy's will, and Victoria was packed off to the Swiss school.

A convict never returned from prison more joyfully than Victoria did now, or less redeemed. The seatbelt warning light clicked off, and in the cramped space of the Viking's racketing, vibrating, unpressurised toilet compartment she changed from the LaFarge prison uniform of stiff Prussian-blue skirt and cream blouse into her brand new one-piece, its full hem in the latest French fashion several inches below the knee, and neckline plunging from full shoulders *à la poitrine*. It would be chilly at the airport, but Pearl's face would be worth it: her little girl grown up. Mom loved to be sentimental.

26

*Look, Mom – I've learned to be beautiful.*

Staring into the mirror, Victoria released her long blonde hair from the pigtails, combed it with her eyes half-closed in pleasure, and ended with the final luxury, lipstick. Returning to the cabin, she was sure the man in the seat opposite, awoken since she was gone, noticed her. She flashed his attention a brief smile: look at me, you thought I was an ugly duckling but now I'm a swan. But he just smiled tolerantly, seeming almost disappointed. She sat, crossing her legs, and wondered what he meant. Men were a different species from women. There had been no men at Madame LaFarge's, except ground staff, invariably ancient. Even the baker's boy was interesting. The chatter among the girls was exclusively about boys: they dreamed about boys, day-dreamed about them, imagined them constantly, several years older than themselves with names like Alain and Marcel, with strong but gentle hands and kind but firm eyes. Some of the more knowledgeable girls claimed to have lovers, and the head girl in the 1920s was said to have run off with the mayor's son from the village . . . None of these legends was true, but everyone believed in them because they *should* be true.

Victoria hung between two worlds. The man worried her. It was entirely possible he had daughters her own age. Victoria's grin no longer had a child's confidence, she was unhappy without her friends. She stuck her nose in *Vogue* magazine, lapping up the perfect Cecil Beaton photographs, and could not eat another chocolate because of her lipstick.

*I am quite sure Victoria does not know it*, Eugenie

LaFarge wrote in her first end-of-term report, *but I have laid the foundation of a young lady. I look forward to full success next term.*

The British European Airways captain coming back to use the toilet was absolutely gorgeous, but he didn't negotiate the steps over the wing-spar across the cabin with the trained grace of the stewardess, and Victoria was amused that he still wore his peaked cap, even though bent almost double.

'Company rules, I suppose?' she mocked him.

And that made her attractive. He stopped, smiling. 'I'm afraid so.' He was strong-featured with a dark moustache, that pleasant smile. He looked a little like Ralph, that smile very like him. He obviously would have chatted with her for longer, but Victoria looked away.

The stewardess brought coffee, which she refused.

The tiny fields of southern England slid beneath the silver wings. One of the last things Ralph had seen. In June 1942 they would have been green. Now they were bald with snow and looked so cold and lifeless that Victoria shut them out with the glossy pages of the magazine.

The captain, returning past her to the cockpit, paused but said nothing, and a few minutes later the plane began its descent.

## 3

'You can't tell young Miss Victoria the truth, ma'am,' Bill Simmonds was still insisting.

Standing beneath the smoking, peppered frontage of her son's house, Lisa looked down at the dapper little chauffeur without admiration. It seemed to her that every edge about him was sharp, manly, self-contained; even the creases of his trousers sharp as razors with his pride in his job, his sex. Ben, who had seemed to make such a success of his life, inspired this loyalty even from men who were in themselves failures. Lisa knew all about men who failed themselves, did not dare really to love, prisoners who failed their women: long ago she had loved Charles Lockhart all his miserable life for the one beautiful moment between them. And now his son was blind, presumably helpless, taken off to hospital with broken glass in his back like knives.

'I won't lie to her,' Lisa said.

Policemen, ambulancemen, firemen in blue uniforms, workmen with rolled-up shirtsleeves, men from the Gas Board also in blue, pushed past them.

'All you men in your bloody uniforms!' she said.

'You can't tell her the truth,' Bill insisted. 'Come on, I'll get you a good strong cuppa. That's what you need . . .' He wondered what she was thinking.

'His eyes were the first thing I noticed about him.' To Lisa it was dawn on the first day of 1900. She was a frightened dark-haired lass of seventeen, a parlourmaid no older than a schoolgirl, who did not know London, holding her illegitimate baby new-born in her arms by the cemetery gate, swaddled in her bloodied petticoats – and his eyes had flown wide and seemed to stare directly into her own, piercingly blue. The man she loved had deserted her, and Lisa had deserted her baby. She had wrapped him in a warm woollen cloak purchased with the money given by her lover for an abortion, and left her child on the frosty steps of the London Hospital. Left him not to die, but to live.

Yes, but she'd broken her heart. Yes, but by relinquishing him she had found her strength as a woman, *her* own identity, *her* individuality. She had married, but her guilt and certainty in herself destroyed her marriage. She knew men for what they were.

Lisa was a woman alone.

And then, one day in Regent's Park, she'd seen her son. She'd followed him, then hid from him, watching him secretly: enthralled, imperfect, not daring to know him.

Ben London, she dreamed with a mother's pride, was a different man.

She'd learned of his happy childhood with Edith Rumney, a Whitechapel nurse. Edith was a real woman, a kindly soul with the courage to put everything of herself into the child, who thought of herself not at all and gave him his gentle, almost feminine intuition. When she died the boy fell into the hands of rogues, and became the man he was.

But he had known love. Lisa had seen it in the way he walked, in everything about him. But he was not a man to be resisted. For her, he had had the slums she worked in bulldozed and rebuilt as a bright new estate.

All for show. Learning to be like his father who had rejected him, his mother who had deserted him. No man could resist the blood that shaped him.

Bill Simmonds watched the tall, silver-haired lady. You could never tell what they were thinking, the way their minds wandered, bloody aspidistras, you never knew. It was obvious to him what she must do. 'Look, ma'am, tell her at first there's been an accident, her mother's seriously hurt. Only hurt, mind,' he explained gently. 'Then it won't be such a shock when—'

Lisa said implacably: 'Pearl's face was blown off.'

'Oh, Christ,' said Bill in disgust. 'Look, let them take you to the hospital. You're upset.'

'Pearl were the most beautiful woman I ever saw,' Lisa said calmly. 'I don't mean pretty. Something inside her that couldn't be seen. She believed in love.'

Bill shook his head to hear this Lime Grove Studios tripe from a sophisticated woman. He tried to keep her on the rails. 'You *can't* tell Miss Victoria her father is blind just like that. After all, you don't *know* that his eyes . . .' Bill stopped. 'You can't be certain.'

'He had other injuries. The glass . . . I never knew a man had so much blood in him.'

Beneath that calmness she must be hysterical. He considered slapping her. His hands were shaking and he was dying for a fag. 'I'll drive you to the hospital myself!' he said, seeing how he might keep his job. He demanded too loudly, trying to take charge of her: 'Where'd they take him?'

'It wasn't an accident,' Lisa said calmly. 'The gas men say it's gas, and someone else said it's petrol. We all know what it was. Somebody meant to kill my son.'

'Maybe it was one of them unexploded bombs from the Blitz. Come on!'

She stared at him and he felt diminished, but she spoke very quietly. 'Have you never felt guilty about anything, Mr Simmonds?'

31

Bill knew about sin from Vezey-Mason, and how Wharncliffe Gardens was a Protestant island in the sea of the Roman Catholicism of Lisson Grove and the Irish.

She looked at him for a moment longer. He put his hands nervously to his lapels. He couldn't explain about ordinary people to this privileged bitch.

'Yes, drive me to the airport,' Lisa ordered. 'Victoria must be told everything by me personally. I'll never forgive myself if she learns from a newspaper.' She touched her gown as if just realising she was not wearing clothes. 'Have the car ready in five minutes.'

Watching her go, he stuck a Woodbine to his lip. 'Give you five hours if you want,' he muttered, then thought she heard him because she looked back with her torn nightdress trailing behind her, and again he wondered what she felt.

'I remember a man called Simmonds,' she said slowly. 'What was your father's name?'

'Ma'am, Dad called hisself Albert, but everyone else knew him as Bert. He left the firm before your time.'

After a pause she said, 'Were you close to your father?'

'Oh, we were a very close family, ma'am,' said Bill winningly. He looked so self-satisfied that for the first time Lisa felt the stirrings of a sustaining anger.

No one knew better than she that London was a vast and heartless place to those who did not belong. Family held it together, the huge interconnection of aunts, nephews, brothers, cousins. Names changed, faces grew old, new ones were born, but all were part of the web of relationships that was London.

'I feel as though I have lost my son for the second time,' Lisa said. She put her hands over her eyes and wept as though she would die.

Finally, she dried her eyes. Going upstairs to her room, she felt more able to cope. She made herself sit down quietly at her dressing-table for a minute or two, the mirror uncracked, everything in its place as though this was a normal day. Only the faint reminder of smoke tugged at her nostrils, the undertow of grief. She dabbed her cheeks with her wrists, feeling with the delicate insides of her arms how crying had swollen her lips. She pursed them shut, then dressed in any old sensible tweed skirt and a woollen sweater, brushed her hair with a single sweep. That would have to do. She asked the policeman on the landing: 'Is there any more news of my son?'

'It was to the Middlesex Hospital they took him, I believe. That woman with the East End voice insisted on going with him in the ambulance. Wouldn't take no for an answer.'

So Ria, the girl from the Isle of Dogs, had never really been missing from Ben's life, Lisa realised.

'And took her child in with her,' the policeman frowned. 'Not right, showing a little girl a sight like that.'

Lisa buckled on her watch going downstairs, now hurrying, trying to show no sign of her inner turmoil at those wicked shards of broken glass, the Christmas tree with its slashed trunk and frozen yellow sap. She set her face like marble. The maids scurried out of her way in the snow. Bill Simmonds saluted. She got into the car and ordered: 'Heathrow.'

She leaned back with a sigh.

During the drive she saw Bill glance at her only once in the rearview mirror, but knew what he was thinking: *You can't tell her the truth, ma'am.*

Lisa's father had died when she was seven; she remembered vividly the night of her mother's death three years later (but to a child three years was a lifetime), at home in the little village of Blane on the Yorkshire moors. She remembered not with a sense of loss but of growing aloneness, of things beginning to happen to her that she had no control over . . . Growing up was being swept along by events, like a piece of wood in a stream . . . swept into the service of the Lockharts at Clawfell Grange . . . swept later into the arms of Charles Lockhart. Only then, at the age of sixteen and with the baby growing inside her, had she learned to stand on her own two feet. To be alone.

Now Victoria, her granddaughter, was the same age, and must learn too.

Lisa saw that they had left London. The tall green banks of the Staines reservoirs were still pocked with bomb craters from the Luftwaffe's attempts to flood this flat heathland. Heathrow airport now had a brick control tower, and since September a waiting-room had been built between the Nissen huts and Customs tents. Bill parked by the single red telephone box standing forlornly at the roadside.

Lisa opened the car door herself and got out alone.

The plane appeared silently, a speck in the eggshell-blue sky. As it blared overhead, men in brown gabardines suddenly poured out of the waiting-room, leaving the door swinging behind them, reporters cursing the sudden cold, photographers wiping condensation from their lenses. They slithered across the snowy grass towards the plane while it landed, props shimmering then stuttering to a stop.

The stewardess let down the jingling steps from the rear door. Passengers came down blinking and the newsmen seemed almost to attack them in their eagerness. Lisa pushed through the crowd. Victoria appeared in the silver doorway, looking around her shyly, a schoolgirl in a garish hourglass dress, confused and very lost. She saw Lisa and called: 'Home at last!'

One of the newsmen shouted: '*How do you feel?*'

Lisa shoved herself to the steps. Victoria ran down joyously, granddaughter and grandmother embracing as flashbulbs popped for the front page.

Victoria whispered, 'Where's Mummy? Why have you been crying?'

The Rolls-Royce pulled up beside them; thank God for Bill Simmonds. They got in and Lisa drew a deep breath.

'Something unforgivable has happened.' She told Victoria the truth.

## 4

'I don't believe you. It can't be true,' Victoria said numbly. 'She *can't* be.'

'But we think your Daddy is going to be all right,' Lisa reassured her. 'We'll go to him straightaway; he'll want to see you.' She cursed herself. 'I mean, want you near.'

'Don't treat me like a child!' Victoria instructed. She

wouldn't let herself be touched, and Lisa kept her peace in the face of the girl's ferocity, understanding it. 'You know what my father wants,' Victoria asserted, but the older woman made no reply. The young girl was so plainly unsure of herself inside that Lisa's heart went out to her. London suburbs slipped feature-lessly past them in their silent, insulated world of the limousine.

'At least we have each other,' Lisa murmured, waiting for the tears to fall.

'I hate this dress!' Victoria drew her dark eyebrows together, unable to bear the silence any longer. Her reaction to the grief which threatened to overwhelm her was not tears but rage, and Lisa admired her for it. All Victoria's thoughts were of her mother. 'I wore it for her. I'm so ashamed of myself.'

'She would have been pleased,' Lisa said.

'People said she was glossy, empty-headed, not serious.' Victoria glanced across as if for confirmation even of her mother's faults.

'Don't listen to jealous people.'

'But you see, she really loved him.'

'I know. She were a lovely lass and a fine wife to him.'

'It's so unfair.' Still no tears. Victoria dragged at her long blonde hair as if she could make herself ugly, and Lisa felt herself losing control of this situation.

'What's so unfair?'

Victoria murmured unforgivably: 'Her, not him.'

Lisa showed anger. 'I know you don't mean that. You're bound to feel like this at first.'

'*She* never hurt anyone.'

36

Lisa gazed from the window, struggling to forgive Victoria's hardness. If only she herself had not been so weary. 'How well do you know your father?'

'Always him, him,' Victoria lashed out in her grief. 'George asked the same thing when Ralph died. *So you think you know your father?* He said my father stole Ralph's shares in the Emporium. So what? *I* only care about Mummy, and she's—'

'We're all sorry for you.' Lisa tried to provoke the warmth of emotional release, to stem the cold flood of words. Nothing destroyed so much as words. She reached out.

'If I was still in school uniform I could cope,' Victoria complained with trembling lips, then turned away. 'Simone's mother died and they told her in the dormitory, and she didn't even have her proper clothes on. Simone said that was almost the worst thing. It always happens in the worst way, doesn't it.'

'I don't know.'

'It must do.'

The arrogance of youth. 'You can borrow my coat to wear, if you like.'

'Where is it?' Victoria turned back, always practical.

'I think he put it in the boot.'

The girl would not cry. She rocked, dry-eyed, determined, then demanded: 'Was she horribly disfigured?'

Lisa saw the eyes in the rearview mirror glance at her.

'No,' she said. 'Pearl never knew what happened.'

'I'd want to die slowly.'

'You will learn to cope with this, darling.'

'I'd want to feel all my life slipping away and remember everything.' Victoria crossed her long legs, as long as her mother's had been, as graceful and unblemished as if she wore nylons. 'I'd want to say goodbye.' Again Lisa's mind went back to when she herself was sixteen, and she clenched her hands into fists. She saw so much of herself in this girl.

'Your mother loved you,' she said.

'Last September, when my father sent me away to the school and she drove me to the airport, that was the last word I said to her, goodbye.'

'But you can't blame your father.'

'Goodbye to her for ever.'

'But it isn't his fault.'

'Isn't it?' Victoria said unpleasantly. 'Nothing ever happened to my father by accident. He makes everything happen because he *wants* it to. Because all he ever cared about was himself.' She faltered.

'You're too young to understand,' Lisa said hastily. Victoria couldn't comprehend her father's life growing up alone among the people of the Isle of Dogs.

'Himself. That's all men really care about, isn't it?' Victoria smudged her lipstick with the back of her hand.

'I promise you this was an accident.' Lisa looked away from the eyes in the mirror. 'A leaking gas-pipe, or petrol, an electric spark from the ignition—'

'Why don't you tell me the truth?'

'We are very similar, you and I.'

Victoria glared at her grandmother. 'Because of you he was born with nothing. So he wanted everything. Look at all the women he's had.'

Lisa raised her clenched hands.

'So I was right,' Victoria smirked.

'You don't know Ben at all!'

'He doesn't know *me*. He's not really looked at me for years. Mummy was the one who made me happy.'

'You'll see things differently in a day or two.'

'You *would* say that. He had a secret life, didn't he?' She waited for a reply.

Lisa tightened her lips. 'Everyone keeps secrets. Especially from themselves.'

'On the Island of Dogs.' Victoria's clumsiness with the name revealed how little she really knew. 'Even Mummy didn't know about it.'

'If he did have a secret, he would have told her.'

'Would he? Oh, I believe you,' Victoria said harshly.

'For God's sake, cry!' Lisa held her, the sides of their heads touching.

'I can't,' Victoria whispered without moving. 'I want to. You can hear I'm trying. I can't do it just because you want me to. I love her.'

There was nothing Lisa could say. Her granddaughter paused and then said, 'I love Daddy but it's a different love. I've never trusted him.'

The car turned into Mortimer Street. They were close to the hospital now. Victoria rummaged in her handbag, among the long thin bars of Cadbury's chocolate in purple wrappers, and pulled out dark glasses.

'He was always so powerful,' she went on, 'dashing off around the world, everyone saying yes sir around him all the time.' Her mockery was fierce now. 'I had faith in him, I knew he'd always do what he thought was best for me, but it would be what *he* thought was best. I want what *I* want.'

'He needs you.'

'What about *me*? Even my horse couldn't be just a horse, it had come from his own Sultàn. Anyway, like father, like daughter. I'm never going back to that school, whatever he says.'

The car turned into the forecourt of the Middlesex Hospital; newsmen crowded round to impede their progress.

Lisa said gently: 'Are you afraid of seeing him as he really is?'

'I'll wear that coat,' Victoria said. She was glad to get out of the car; she knew the older woman was trying to be kind, but her life was her own. Things had changed since Lisa's day and she'd wanted to make that clear. She was determined to make up her own mind, to make her own decisions, not to be pushed and shoved but to be herself, a modern woman.

*What do you feel?* they were all asking. Everyone demanded feelings of her, demanded she respond – 'Your mother whom you loved is dead,' *what do you feel?* 'Your father is injured, you must feel something': *let us into your heart.*

But she didn't want anyone's help. And right now she didn't know what she felt – frightened, she felt so frightened that she knew she mustn't let go. The kindly chauffeur draped the warm cream and brown coat over her shoulders, the dark glasses protected her eyes from the flashbulbs, hiding the fact that she had not been crying. Newsmen rushed ahead of her to the vantage-point of the steps. She was pushed from side to side by shouted questions but knew she was not expected to say anything. On the top step she stumbled and the hungry cameras clicked like locusts, then the doors of the private Woolavington wing were closed behind her.

Cheap Christmas decorations hung everywhere. She was relieved to see Uncle Cliff, her father's long-time confidant and financial adviser, waiting by the festooned reception desk. Clifford Ford's craggy features were a lifetime older than when she remembered him playing Grandfather's Footsteps with her as a child. 'Thank you for coming, Clifford,' Lisa said, holding out her hand.

'Yes, thanks, Clifford,' Victoria said, aware that she must behave like an adult, glad her eyes were hidden. If she'd called him Uncle Cliff she would have given way.

'I'm so sorry about all this,' Uncle Cliff told her, with genuine sympathy, and shook her hand with his own as dry as paper.

David Jones, the manager of the Emporium, put down the internal phone and came from the desk, grey-haired but still lithe and youthful-looking, no movement wasted, totally efficient and in command in his morning suit and shiny shoes. 'Lisa! This is simply frightful of course. Third floor; he's sleeping. They operated at once, removed significant fragments of glass. The lacerations are mostly superficial, they've made up the blood loss with transfusions.' He noticed Victoria and nodded acknowledgement as they walked across the foyer together. 'You'll want to see him of course.'

'There's no point if he's sleeping,' Victoria shrugged.

'She's very upset,' Lisa said.

'Of course.' David Jones's third *of course*. 'I'll call
the lift.'

Victoria interrupted him: 'You haven't said
about . . .' She blinked.

'Of course it's too early for the eye specialist.'

'I want to see my mother,' Victoria said suddenly,
and he threw her a startled glance. 'I want to see her
more than anyone,' she insisted, and drew her
eyebrows together.

'I'm sure the—' He'd been about to say *the body* –
'I'm sure she's been removed elsewhere by now,'
David smiled.

Bill Simmonds, his peaked cap askew, was failing
to hold the entrance doors closed against the crowd.
'Bloody gutter press!' Victoria heard him swear. A
cleaner mopping the linoleum had stopped to watch
him. ''Ere, give us an 'and,' Bill called, but the
cleaner just leaned on his mop. David Jones hurried
Victoria with his hand on her elbow.

She whispered: 'But what if he's blind?'

'Never mind about that now,' David reassured her.
Victoria looked round fearfully as Bill fell back from
the doors and the newsmen rushed in, the most
youthful at the front slipping on the freshly washed
part of the floor. Old hands at the back spotted their
group and ran towards them beneath the paper-
chains.

'We'll take the backstairs,' Lisa decided. 'David,
Clifford, you stay here and fend them off.' Victoria

followed her into a quiet stairwell, the door slamming and the babble of voices fading entirely as they climbed the dirty concrete flights to the first floor. Victoria stopped.

'But what if he is blind?' she called up.

Lisa, above her, already puffing from her climb, said nothing.

Victoria easily caught her up by the second-floor landing, the older woman now pushing with her hands on her knees. Years ago the miraculous streptomycin had cured her tuberculosis but left a lingering weakness in her joints. Or perhaps that was just age. The echoing business of the hospital enveloped them, suddenly loud as a double door was knocked open here or there, giving glimpses of bright wards or dull corridors, the rattle of pans or the glum backchat of porters pushing stretchers; then more porters pushing trolleys covered with plates – pork with warm gravy today – trailing the smell of boiled carrots past their hairy hands. 'Lunchtime already!' sighed Lisa. She had fallen behind. 'You go on up. My old knees.' She waved Victoria on. 'I'll be all right.'

Her granddaughter hung back but the old woman waved her away.

Victoria climbed alone. The tall collar of the knotted-wool coat caressed her nape soothingly. The stairwell seemed darker, the steps grew gritty beneath her shoes and as the shadows closed around her – even the grimy little wire-meshed windows had ceased at this level – she finally relinquished her dark glasses. The gap around a door glinted above her and

43

she hurried gratefully, found herself blinking at a broad corridor. The door closed on its spring behind her, propelling her gently forward into the light.

Against the wall opposite her a porter leaned with folded arms, waiting for his mate who'd been called away to some other task. His lips were pursed like those of a man longing for a cigarette. Beside him she saw the parked stretcher-trolley in his charge. Beneath the white waterproof sheet lay something.

The porter muttered incoherently to Victoria.

The hand hanging beneath the porter's sheet wore her mother's gold wedding ring.

He looked away from her as his mate returned. The two men chi-hiked with that amiable male hostility that made her want to scream at them, the one having made the other late for his lunch break; both glanced back at her as they wheeled their vehicle off.

Victoria closed her eyes. Her mother was dead, and she would never see her again.

A girl's voice said, 'Can I help you?'

A bright-eyed student nurse was speaking to her. 'Yes,' Victoria said.

The girl raised her eyebrows helpfully.

'I'm looking for my father,' Victoria said.

'That's easy,' said the girl, and pointed.

## 5

The bobby guarding her father's half-open door sat with his helmet propped in his lap, despite his blue and white duty armband. The top button of his monkey-suit was undone, his grey muzzle buried in a mug of tea. Only the flash of his eyes betrayed his relief she wasn't the inspector. Some of the coldness left Victoria as she gained confidence. 'Are you in charge here?'

'Help you, Miss!' he asserted, wiping his top lip.

'I'm his daughter.'

The constable consulted his list with his finger.

'So it wasn't an accident,' Victoria murmured.

'We'll have to wait until Mr London wakes for the answer to that, Miss. You can go in now.'

She went quietly through the doorway into shadows: the curtains drawn, the room was dim, and so small that the ceiling seemed very high above her. An empty chair waited for her by the bed, so Victoria sat in it. A streak of mud marked her coat. Beside her a large bottle of blood, a tube running from it into the bedclothes, hung upside down on a flaking cream-painted pedestal. Beneath the sheet lay the figure of a man, his head so swathed in bandages that she could not recognise him.

She waited, but he did not respond.

'Can you hear me?' she whispered.

His breathing did not change. She could see a little of his hair; her father's hair. They hadn't combed it, or maybe the bandages had messed it up again. There was his strawberry birthmark peeping below. And she recognised his lips now, and the strong line of his jaw was suddenly familiar. She touched her own lips and jaw but they weren't the same: softer, feminine. And he needed a shave. She reached out to touch the difference of his face, then drew back her hand.

'I'm here,' she whispered, finding the courage to stroke his hair. It was a man's hair, fine but surprisingly thick . . . she had not touched his hair since she was a child. She put her hands to her lips.

'Daddy, it's me,' she said. He lay totally unresponsive.

She kissed him.

She realised that she had never known him. She had grown up with everything she wanted, even love; he with almost nothing. She could never have known the real man. His business interests had been so time-consuming that during their every moment together she had fought for his attention, a spoilt child, demanding to be looked at. He didn't oblige, so she'd shut him out, run away as much as sent away. He had known her all too well. But she never knew *him*.

'Can you hear me?' she murmured. No movement but his faint, regular breathing. A strand of cotton-wool was stuck to his roughened chin, she pulled it away; there was no glass of water at the bedside, she must get the nurse to bring some, suppose he woke thirsty? She looked for the call button.

His hand slipped from under the sheet and gripped her own, light as a breath of air.

'Daddy, it's me,' she whispered, elated. She tried to demonstrate to him that she had changed from the child he had last seen. 'I've come back,' she said eagerly.

Then she thought: *Suppose he asks if Mummy is dead?*

His grip on her hand tightened almost imperceptibly. He knew.

46

*Suppose he asks me to unwind the bandages over his eyes?*

'Everything's going to be all right!' she said cheerfully. She was almost crying, the lump in her throat choking her, and put back her head pretending to examine the ceiling.

He wasn't thinking of himself, she was sure of that: her fingers were numb with his strength. Thinking of Mummy, perhaps, of all that he had lost this morning. She couldn't have pulled away from his hand enclosing her own if she had tried.

Or was he thinking of her brother Ralph, lying like this in a room like this, his burned-away flesh beneath the bandages?

'You're hurting my hand!' But his grip did not change. Slowly she realised he wasn't thinking of Ralph or Mummy or anyone else. He was thinking of her. All his attention was on her. The lump rose in her throat again. She was almost crying, determined not to, but the pain was hurting her so much. She clasped her other hand over his, like two people swearing an oath: but still his breathing had not changed. 'I'm here,' she whispered loyally.

His mouth moved.

Suddenly angry voices echoed in the corridor outside.

She leaned close to hear him, then pulled back as her glossy hair threatened to fall over his face, frightened of tickling those bruised, sensitive lips, or of making him sneeze.

'You,' her father said. In the quiet, dark room her father said: '*You.*'

She wanted to ask him what he meant, but instead she heard her tongue whisper, 'Do you love me?'

He did not reply.

Suddenly the door banged open and George, Ralph's brother, breezed in and took charge.

'Is he awake?'

George swept his gaze across young Vicky hanging on to her father's hand at the bedside. Obviously the silly girl thought she must feel griefstricken – nobody knew better how to make people feel guilty than the Old Man. He bent down and kissed her cheek. 'Are *you* all right?' he asked earnestly.

'I thought he said something,' Victoria shrugged, then shook her head.

'Does he know she's dead?' said George, loudly enough. He wore a black suit and buttoned-up waistcoat, black welted shoes made from his own lasts at Lobb's. The only relief from black was his white soft-collared shirt and the gold chain of the fobwatch left him by his maternal grandfather, Georgy Leibig. 'It's you I care about.'

'George, do be quiet now.' Lisa had come into the room behind him. George was easy to hurt, but that made him difficult to put down. He was so vulnerable, like most men, and so at odds with himself that she felt sorry for him; he was expected to be the leader now. If only Ralph had lived. Captured Luftwaffe records for June 1942 confirmed that Ralph was claimed as a kill by *Staffelkapitän* Fritzi Münchener of the *Richtofen Geschwader*, son of the German ace whose life Ben had spared in World War One. George, Fritzi and Ralph had been firm friends in

48

childhood. It was easier for George to blame his father than himself.

'You bloody women,' George laughed affectionately, robbing his words of offence but making them no less hurtful, 'you're always on his side! That's how he always escaped until now.' With a nod of the head George dismissed the conspiracy of women, walked round the bed and stared at Victoria and Lisa with his hands tightly in his pockets. He sighed. 'Well, I suppose it's up to me.' He meant he was back in control of the Emporium. With his father out of the way there was no one to stop him.

'You're such a fool.' Lisa slumped wearily in a chair against the wall. 'How do you feel, Victoria?'

The girl shook her head and Lisa realised how close she was to giving way, how quickly the events of the day were taking their toll on her. She was glad for Victoria's sake that Ria had made herself scarce. This was family business.

'Upset? That's how our father wants you to be, Vicky,' George scoffed. Even now he was aware of his father's presence threatening to dominate him. 'That's how he controls you. He always gets what he wants. He's got you lot summed up.'

'George, don't,' Lisa ordered.

George glared at her then turned to Victoria. 'Don't let him fool you, he never loved anybody!'

For a moment they were like statues; nobody moved. 'What a dreadful family we might become,' Lisa said quietly.

'Oh, have you just realised?' George exclaimed. The two women were so ignorant of the abyss beneath them, all around them, everywhere, where they might fall by taking a single step, that he wanted to scream at them. He forced himself to be business-like. 'There'll be hundreds of arrangements,' he said prosaically, the feature Lisa disliked most about him, 'I'll look after them.'

Still the bandaged figure on the bed did not move.

'He loved my mother.' Victoria's voice was full of pain.

'*She* loved *him*,' George corrected kindly, taking his hand from his pocket and placing it on her shoulder. 'He just loves himself. He's totally self-centred, my dear,' he said, and Victoria, hearing in his cruel words her own voice from earlier, realised how formed by George her youthful views had been, how close she was to being George.

'Not that I blame him,' George added with a man's understanding chuckle.

Victoria felt the tips of her breasts pressing against her dress, the weight of them from her attitude bent over the hand clasped in her lap. Her hair had fallen forward. On the other side of the bed George stood slim and taut, dark hair slicked straight back, his smooth sanguine face still so shiny from the razor it looked *polished*, and she tried to feel all the more aware of her femininity, of her distance from George, to feel instead her closeness to Ben London whose hand moved in her own: she was holding on to him now, squeezing his fingers with her own fingers.

She saw his lips trying to move. She leaned close. 'You'll get better, Daddy. I promise you. Don't try to talk.'

'*You.*' Ben London spoke as if there was no one else here, only her. He let her squeeze his hand.

Then he lifted her hands until her knuckles touched his bandaged head and she was frightened of hurting him. He said in his deep voice: 'Do you understand?'

'I'm here,' George called. 'Yes, of course I understand. I'll look after everything. Come on, ladies, time to go.'

'George, shut up,' Lisa said briskly.

Victoria bent over the bandages, acrid with antiseptic. She was close enough to have touched them with her lips. 'Me?'

Ben London explained nothing more. In her, his daughter, Pearl would live on.

# Chapter Two

## 1

'They're gone now,' whispered the little girl at the keyhole. 'I don't have to be quiet as a mouse any more.'

'Shush,' hissed Ria, 'give 'em time to get away, tons of hush and shush.'

Lola looked round with enormous eyes, a thin child in a threadbare overcoat two sizes too big for her, but said nothing. What with the harsh shadows, Mum looked a sight. The linen room was lit by a single unkind bulb, Mum's hair was all over the place and showed bits of grey at the side too; a net of shadows was thrown down her face, lined with worry and tiredness; but her eyes were still lovely, blue flecked with gold, fierce as fire. Mum was in a state.

'Why were we hiding from the toffs?' hissed Lola in a striking imitation of her mother's voice.

'We're not hiding,' lied Ria, but at least she stopped wringing her filthy hands. 'We were just counting the sheets, weren't we!'

'There's twelve.' Lola could only count to twelve, the number of pennies in a shilling.

'Oh Lord, you've put your mucky fingers on every one,' Ria said glumly. She ran her hands through her hair, leaving dark streaks.

'But who were those people, Mum? The girl was ever so pretty.'

'Well, they were just people,' Ria rallied. 'Flesh and blood, like us.'

'Why were we spying on them?' *Spying* was a word she'd got off the wireless no doubt, what with the falling-out with the Reds.

'You and your questions. Your gob, Miss: upshut it, right?'

'If we're not hiding from them,' Lola continued patiently, '*what* are we hiding from them? Is it our clothes?'

'Did you hear the one about the little girl what was so clever she cut herself on her own tongue?'

'Yes, Mum.'

'And when she smiled her smile went back to her ears.'

Lola held back her curly black hair with the insides of her arms, a curiously delicate gesture, and again put her eye to the keyhole. A nurse bustled in to give the man his medication, took his pulse, yawning and picking her nose because he couldn't see her, murmured a few smiling, comforting words from her bored face, and bustled out.

'It's just it's better this way, right?' Ria murmured guiltily. 'Don't you ever think I'm ashamed, girl. And I've seen much worse than that coat of yours, I'll tell you. When I was your age I didn't have no shoes!' There was more than a trace of pride in her voice.

'Was that when you fell in love?'

Ria didn't reply. Just remembered Ben London, the workhouse boy she'd brought home to see Mum because he didn't have a mum of his own. The child saved from the workhouse by another child. He'd moved in with Vic and her other brothers like a brother. He was the love of her life. But then she remembered Vic screaming: *Did he rape you?* Nothing changed from when you were a child.

Her first baby, Will, Ben London's son, had been born almost too early, when Ria was a slip of a girl of fifteen, lying on newspapers in the humid cellar of Mum's home in Canary Warren on the Isle of Dogs; the first heatwave of the first spring of the Great War. Her second child was born almost too late, a bad marriage and a sour career later, Ria at the age of nearly forty-two, her confinement at the proud little house Vic had got for Mum in Havannah Street. Lola had been born during the bombing raid of 31 July 1941, the same night Vic's warehouse – packed with illicit whisky, but registered by young Terry with war insurance only for the value of molasses – was hit and went up in flames. Lola had been born by the light of the flames and Vic had been wiped out. But so sure was Vic Price's hold on Ben that the millionaire Ben London had paid for all, and Vic, his childhood friend and enemy who had taught Ben to steal, had been saved. That same night, with bomb-blasts fluttering the blackouts, the broken windows sagging against the cheap sticky tape, Ria had lain exhausted with her newborn daughter, Lola, thinking to herself, *I know what love is. This is love. Whoever my baby's father is.*

From the keyhole Lola asked: 'Are we hiding *us*?'

'You give me the shivers sometimes,' Ria swore. 'What have we got to be ashamed of!'

'You're funny in this mood,' Lola said indifferently, sounding just like her grandmother, Esther.

'Oi, you,' Ria warned, then spoiled it by giggling. She felt so guilty and ashamed of everything, and so exhausted, that she could hardly stop. The tears ran helplessly down her cheeks. Lola watched her, interested.

Lola was Ria's pride and joy, her best friend, but something about them was not close: just when they were laughing or joking, thinking they were closest, suddenly there was the abyss. Lola was five and a half years old, but her age was difficult to guess. She was precocious and voluble beyond her years, probably because of the example of the wireless; and rationing meant people ate better than ever they did when Ria was growing up, so Lola was as tall as most girls of seven or eight had been, and better proportioned, already moving with the grace of a dancer – which wasn't so surprising considering her mother's stage career, the happiest time of Ria's life.

Ria struggled to control herself.

There was much of Ria in Lola's eyes of course; they were blue like her mother's, and flecked: but strangely the child's were older eyes, darker, the flecks tawny as old gold. Ria supposed they would lighten with the years. Like most children Lola had her own mind, she insisted on wearing her gypsy-dark hair too long so it was sheer murder to wash, and fining the curls with the lice-comb took forever. 'You'll spoil her,' Esther always warned, and Ria always started, 'I know, Mum . . .' but Esther would plough on, pouring the tea in the little Havannah Street kitchen, or making the indigestible loaves she was so proud of, though Ria was sure the flour contained sawdust like the sausages did. Glumly pounding the dough with her fists on the creaking table then plumping her floury white hands on her hips, she'd say, 'You're a fool for that child, you'll make her vain as what you are.' Then Ria would explain, 'But she's my own little girl.' Esther in the workhouse days – days she was usually merry because she was in the money – had always called Ria *my girl* or *my little girl*. 'Vanity!' Esther snorted nowadays. Since a mistake with bleach scarred her stomach Mum stayed sober as a judge, not an improvement for a dogged widow well into her sixties who liked a tipple; but Ria, since her husband Raymond Trott disappeared, or rather *got* disappeared, had to live with her in Havannah Street, and so an uneasy truce existed between them.

Ria forced herself to stop, realising that Lola's eyes had missed nothing. 'You look awful, Mum,' Lola said gently. 'Your dress is all creased, and so is your face.' She had that frightening way with words.

'It wasn't a very good dress in the first place.' Ria tried to smooth the creases then gave up; her hands were still smudged with soot, her knees where she had knelt – only the second time she had ever entered the grounds of London House – blackened too with dirt, and with brown flecks of blood, not her own. She dropped the ragged hem with a resigned sigh, hiding them. 'The face was all right once. Come on, let's give your chops a quick lick and polish.' She used a corner of one of the folded sheets. 'What a pair we are.'

'I love you, Mummy.'

'Yuch, you horrid little monster. And we're going to have to do something about that hair of yours.' The girl stood on tiptoe, and Ria bent and took a kiss.

Lola looked up at her mother with that odd bright look in her dark eyes. 'You don't look old really.'

'Who, me? I feel old enough for two.'

'You look frightened.'

'Who, me?' Ria repeated.

'You were sad all yesterday evening when we were walking and we saw the golden coach with paintings on the doors, and four white horses.' A child's memory was such a wonderful and terrifying thing.

'Sad!' Ria scoffed. This dress was ruined.

'Then we walked home to the Isle of Dogs because we didn't have the bus fare. You'd spent your last thruppeny piece on a bag of hot chestnuts for us, and they were nice but a bit hard. But later you were frightened.'

'Frightened!'

'Yes, after you heard Uncle Terry's car coming home to Havannah Street in the night. You said you remembered a funny smell, acid, like bath-scale cleaner. I could hear you trying to use the phone, and you've looked more and more frightened ever since,' Lola asserted. 'You have.'

'Those big eyes of yours.'

'It wasn't you who hurt the man, was it?'

'Not this time,' Ria said.

'He'll get better, won't he?'

'He won't get better,' Ria said, and took Lola's place at the door. She was sure Lisa had got Victoria out of the hospital by now, and in any case they'd hear the policeman talking to her if she returned, because she was pretty. Victoria knew nothing of darkness, the secrets that destroyed people's lives, the dreadful power of love, yet today it had been all around her, every moment. Ria checked the keyhole and opened the door a crack, then they crept back into the private room. Lola stood on tiptoe by the bed.

'He's still sleeping.'

'Don't let that fool you.' Ria sat wearily in her muddy dress on the chair, then leaned forward. 'Ben. I'm back.'

Lola shook her head. 'He *is* asleep.'

Ria held her hand beneath his mouth. From his spittle two painkilling pills slipped into her palm. 'You're a silly man,' she said.

'Is he in pain?' Lola asked.

'Yes,' Ria said.

'Poor man!' Lola skipped to the window and pulled aside a corner of the blind, letting a shaft of brilliant sunlight into the room. 'Can he see now?'

'Stop your noise.' Ria winced at the light. 'We'll have to go home in a minute.' She held out her hand and the little girl took it obediently, plunging the room back into darkness.

Hearing them, Ben London moved. 'Ria.'

'I've always been here,' she said. 'You know that.'

There was nothing she could do about Lola overhearing.

'Mum,' Lola giggled, 'do you love him?'

'Only he knows the answer to that.'

'Ria,' Ben London said, 'help me.'

'No one can help you,' Ria said tenderly. 'You made that choice too.' Long, long ago in the days when love won and everything was possible, he had asked her to marry him. She had refused, *because* she loved him, seeing in his success the seeds of his destruction. Because she loved him she had created what she most feared – a life without him – but she had not changed him. A man was what he was.

But it was Lola he reached out for, fumbling. Ria watched her daughter allow her free hand to be taken, a chain linking the two adults.

Lola looked up innocently. 'Mum, who is he?'

Ria had always known this question must come.

'He is your father.'

Slowly she reached out to Ben. *Your* father. It was what Ben believed to be the truth, too. He needed them now. She squeezed her eyes shut, and made the chain of their hands a circle.

'*My father*,' whispered Lola.

# 2

Terry Price waited shyly outside the black iron railings watching the hospital's busy forecourt. He was ashamed of himself for feeling so drained – he had to push his hands deep in his overcoat pockets to stop them shaking. Nothing was worse than showing it.

Ambulances came in, ambulances went out, but the Roller never moved. The natty chauffeur finished polishing and leaned against the Silver Lady puffing a fag behind his cupped hand. The few newsmen still hanging around looked alert every time the hospital doors opened.

So the man was still alive.

Terry hadn't got back to Havannah Street until nearly four this morning, had taken a bath to relax himself, but then tossed and turned sleeplessly in bed until he forced himself to lie motionless on his back, listening to the sounds of the street coming to life: foghorns hooting on the river as the threatened snow began, the milkman's clinking bottles coming closer, clattering outside the door, then the milk-float's chittering fading into silence, turning along West Ferry Road. All this Terry had seen in his mind's eye, recognising the rag-and-bone man's muffled tread going to fetch his horse from the stable, then the creak of his cart setting off for the richer pickings of the West End; street-doors slamming as the lump started for the dock gates, their yawning curses at the snow. At first light, glimmering unnaturally snow-pale across his bedroom ceiling, Terry had pictured his treasured MG tourer parked outside, the work-men pretending to ignore her but glancing at her enviously, her louvred bonnet and leather straps muffled with snow. The same snow would be lying on Ben London's car. He might not try and start it today, or even tomorrow, but Terry had imagined what would happen when he did. He'd been too excited to get it out of his mind.

He'd got up without having slept and dressed casually, but he'd added a foreman's leather waist-coat, doing up all the little buttons for warmth, then an overcoat, hat and scarf. Going out he'd noticed that the milk had already been taken in at Esther and Ria's door. Granny drank a lot of milk for her stomach, and leading away were two pairs of footsteps, one large, one small, soon lost among the workmen's imprints. Terry wiped the snow off the MG and drove up west.

Almost at once he'd realised something had gone wrong.

He followed an ambulance to the Middlesex Hospital, then drove on and parked quietly at the end of Mortimer Street. For a while he merely observed the confusion, not having the nerve to join in, then when things quietened down kept watch from the counter of a small all-day café. The greasy bakelite wireless was propped on a shelf above the serving-hatch, presumably to stop customers stealing it, and the proprietor adjusted the volume with a broom-handle. 'Good for business,' he grunted at the newsmen coming in, but the BBC announced the London explosion 'being investigated by the Gas Board' as only the fourth item, after no news of the British soldiers kidnapped by Irgun terrorists, clos-ures in the cotton industry, coal shortages. So Pearl was dead. The freezing drive in the open car had left Terry's ears blue with cold and he rubbed them with his leather gloves, then with his fingertip wiped condensation from the window, making small clear circles for him to look through.

He was within a couple of weeks of his twenty-first birthday, with perfect white teeth, dark eyes, and a still, listening demeanour that was attractive. Girls liked him because he didn't care about girls, but was kind and attentive in his shy way, and when he fell for the lucky one it would be wholehearted and dependable. He had a lovely quick smile, and there was something dangerous about him. He was Vic's boy, though not his son. He was the son of Vic's brother, Nigel.

Terry had never known his father, or his mother. His mother, Arleen, had died as he was born. Vic had loathed Arleen, and Esther never forgave her for taking Nigel across the river to live in Greenwich. When Nigel was drowned, Vic had taken Terry in.

Terry had come to admire childless Vic with a son's loyalty, obeying him in everything, but also observing him with a stranger's clear eye. Vic taught him everything he knew, but still Nigel and Arleen's blood beat in Terry's veins. Vic was a man of passion, and his passion was the power he wielded among his people. He could never teach Terry that feeling, but Terry longed to learn it as Ben London had, and longed to prove himself to Vic.

*If you know where a man hurts*, Vic had said once, *you know where to hurt him*. In his revenge on Vic's behalf Terry now knew he had killed the wrong person, but the agony of his loss of sight and the loss of the wife he loved would hurt Ben London quite as effectively as death.

Vic would be pleased.

Terry hadn't been able to make his cup of tea last any longer, so he'd gone out and stared through the hospital railings at the Roller that was still there. The chauffeur hurriedly stubbed out his fag, seeing some sign Terry had missed, and drove the car to the steps where a silver-haired lady and a blonde girl appeared – Lisa and Victoria, he gathered from his researches. Then behind them the door opened again, George came out, and Terry pulled down his hat-brim, picking up a discarded newspaper to hide his face. But George, the only one who knew him, was as always concentrating only on himself, listening to himself, talking at Lisa with big gestures like an extrovert, choleric face working. Terry ignored him. Victoria looked sophisticated – you could tell she had been taught how to stand. George had his back to her. She wore an unbuttoned high-collar coat that the wind flapped open, revealing a wicked dress of hues Terry couldn't have bought for love nor money along the Commercial Road, not even the material. George finished his argument, nodded to Victoria like a dismissal, then held his jacket to his sucked-in belly and ran down the steps to his car. Terry read the newspaper as the car turned out past him.

He watched Victoria coming down the steps. They'd taught her how to move and how to hold her hands too: she knew how she was supposed to look. The chauffeur saluted, obscuring her for a moment. He glimpsed her again: the wind had blown her hair over her dark glasses and the expression on her lips had changed slightly, almost a smile. She was hiding how tired she was. She got in the car, then slid across the seat, so Lisa got in the same door and saved the chauffeur a journey. The Roller started down and Terry watched, turning his head without expression as the two women were driven past him, less than six feet away at the closest, but only shadows now behind the glass, one of them putting back her hair. Then the car accelerated away and was gone.

He waited while the newsmen drifted away, watching chill shadows move across the hospital's façade, feeling almost-sad thoughts for Pearl London. He found what he had done very easy to understand; in a way he now owned her. She had been beautiful, but everyone said that of the dead. He'd met her only once, last October at London's Hotel when the leaves were falling golden in Green Park, when Vic from a suitcase had paid back the loan Ben London made him the night of the Blitz firestorm. A quarter of a million pounds in cash, all paid back at peace in the quiet conference room at the top of the hotel. But Terry's watchful eyes had been on Pearl, fancying her in a young man's way. She'd looked kind and reassuring, but she was old enough to be his mother and she wasn't as simple as she appeared – he'd found his mind taking too many pictures of her. Even her smile was complex. There was something hard in her, like biting on tin-foil. Star quality; like Ria in that, Ria who had borne Ben London two children, Pearl only one. But with poor bloody Ria, Terry thought contemptuously, what you saw was what you got. Pearl's surface air of niceness, of being not-quite-serious, had put Terry off: he'd never trust a woman with more to her than he could see . . .

Terry looked up sharply as the hospital doors opened and down the steps hurried two figures. The woman looked like she lived on the streets, her overcoat was filthy and too small, showing the torn hem of her dress beneath it, and she held it closed at her throat where the button had fallen off. Her other hand pulled her little girl after her, the child trying to stamp in the puddles of slush.

Ria and Lola. What were those two doing here? This was earth-shattering news, and Terry knew just what use to make of it. Vic's half-sister going behind his back! This would make Vic sit up, this would get his fire back like in the old days. Terry longed for that above everything. He watched them hail a cab – Ria had money for a cab! – then walked quickly to his car. By the time he reached it, he was running.

## 3

Terry drove down into the East End along Cable Street, into familiar territory: Gronofsky's suits made-to-measure and doing well with the For Sale sign up ready for the move to Golders Green, rows of boarded-up crumbling premises left by those who had already gone, children arriving at the Barnardo's Home queuing outside like little pots waiting to be filled. The owners of the sweatshops wore smart new suits and gold rings, and gilt buckles on their shoes, predators oozing subservience at a whiff of a customer, glossy eels in their warren of endless walls with tiny windows which were as dirty as the brick. Sudden spaces where bombs had fallen, a crouching child earnestly filling a bucket with half-bricks, and on a shard of wall some wag had written in big whitewash letters: HITLER'S SLUM CLEARANCE COMPANY. Chinese flitting in dark doorways like will-o'-the-wisps. On Terry's left as he drove, a train slowly thundered and pulsed towards him at rooftop height, then curved above the road behind him on grimy arches into the Port of London depot. On his right the jumble of tall warehouses hid the river, but he could see it was there: the river's course revealed by the steam-cranes nodding their heads like exotic foreign birds among the smokestacks, the rotting masts with yards crossed and cordage trailing like cotton thread, whirling seagulls as the tide changed, the stink of it. Always there. Without the Thames there was no London.

Ahead of Terry the Old Bull and Bush stood seemingly in the middle of Cable Street, once the site of an abattoir, the ramshackle sheds and pens such places accumulated around them long demolished and never built over, as though the taint remained. Vic had never encouraged building work. He liked the place as it was, and its three storeys had a certain domineering charm, rather like Vic himself.

Here was Terry's real home: where Vic was.

He was astonished not to find a parking place, then remembered it was Christmas Eve and people were blowing their petrol ration, and for the first time in his life had to slant-park beyond the cars, vans and motorcycle-sidecars crowding the road. Bicycles propped against the pub's tiled walls almost blocked the pavement, people were drinking too much and knocking them over. Under the ornate gas-globe, lit only by the sun at this time of day, two sailors exchanged thudding, meaty blows, the smell of blood hanging in the still air, while in the crowd that had gathered slumming girls in fur coats sipped gin-and-lime, and hung on their boyfriends' dinner-suited elbows. The fight ended and the seamen shook hands, wagers were settled amongst the dirty coats at the back of the crowd. Suddenly everyone burst out laughing, even the panting seamen who threw their arms around each other's shoulders like old friends and swaggered good-naturedly back into the pub.

Terry went inside, pushing through the crush. He crooked his finger at Jake, the new barman. 'Where is he?'

'Where's 'oo?' Jake was pig-ignorant. Then the penny dropped. 'Vic's been and gone wiv the kids at the Shadwell 'all, 'e's only got back a minnit.' He pointed out Father Christmas. 'There 'e is! Took my sister's little boy wiv 'im, Jimmy wot 'ad 'is tonsils out, 'e's tickled pink, an' got gave a ice-cream too. Ria and 'er little girl was in fer it but she was out when 'e called for 'er at 'Avannah Street. 'E wasn't 'alf cross. You know what Vic's like abaht Ria; if they wasn't bruvver and sister they'd be man and wife, *I* says.'

'Gimme a perch,' Terry said, and Jake shut up and drew a pint of best.

Around the angle Vic, dressed as Father Christmas, properly fur-trimmed in jovial red clothes with a fluffy white beard, sat on a high bar-stool at the busiest part of the bar, merrily banging his feet on the brass rail to the fiddler's tune, a red nightcap stuck jauntily on his head and its fluffy fur ball swinging. He'd be in a mood as black as thunder he'd missed Ria, Terry knew, but he appeared exuberant with Christmas bonhomie and laughter, clapping his big, stiff hands on the shoulders of Christmas revellers, mostly women attracted by his warmth and strength of personality, Vic playing the life and soul of the party. It was a mystery to Terry how he could care for these worthless, blowsy women older than his mother. There was no drink on the counter in front of him and Terry wondered what Vic was really thinking. Someone pointed to Terry and Vic beckoned him into the magic circle of lipstick smiles and sad eyes. 'Ho ho ho, little boy,' Vic said, with a measuring glance of his eyes, so brown that indoors they looked black.

'Hi hi hi,' Terry said obediently.

'And what do you want for Christmas, little boy?' said Vic, making Terry, who was struggling to assert himself, feel that he *was* a little boy.

'Got a present for *you*.' Terry dropped the newspaper on the counter. Vic read quietly. Deprived of his attention the women drifted away, except one or two stupid or ignorant ones, like Mimsy who had struggled into a sheath dress with a ludicrous orange feather boa, her face almost elastic with nerves and desperation, ready to laugh like a hyena at Vic the great man's merest smile, or doll-shake her head if he should frown. Vic didn't have Father Christmas's beaming rosy-apple cheeks, Vic's cheeks were flat as though he pressed his hands against them. He put down the paper and Terry waited for the expected smile to materialise. The Vic he had once been, home again.

'Gas Board!' Vic said quietly. 'Well, there's a celebration.' But he didn't smile, and his feet had stopped beating time to the music. 'You sleep more when you get older.' Terry, watching his face, held up his hand to the fiddler: shut it. Then Vic said, 'No, let him play.' For the punters he grinned all over his face, banging his feet as merrily as though he were still surrounded by the children, then gave Mimsy a hug and a bussing kiss, and she got everyone joining in again. Meanwhile Vic got down quietly and Terry followed him through into the closed-down room of Trott's Bar.

When the door was shut behind them it was suddenly quiet.

'What have you done, Terry my lad?' Vic growled.

'I thought you'd be pleased,' Terry said cockily.

Vic stared at him. 'It was peace for the first time in my life.'

*Peace*. Terry remembered Vic in the hotel conference room throwing back his debt of a quarter of a million pounds at Ben London. He remembered Vic running away from Ben London, running down the fire escape, running round and round and down like a man possessed. Defeated. At peace.

Now Terry told him: 'You can't really give up, Vic, not you.'

'That's why you did this, is it?'

70

'I owed you everything, Vic,' Terry said simply.

But Vic didn't hug him or even acknowledge his debt to the younger man, just turned away.

Terry followed the broad Father Christmas shoulders amongst the empty seats and tables of the deserted lounge-bar, picking up like a faithful dog the disguise as Vic discarded it, white beard, hat, coat. 'He's finished,' Terry called. 'I did it for you. Welcome back, Vic.'

Undressed, Vic wore a dirty white shirt, stained trousers, and when he tossed away the cheery hat he revealed unwashed hair, grease-black. He had lost his pride. He ran his hands through his hair then frowned at his palms, noticing for the first time how he had not cared for himself, and Terry felt a thrill. '*Welcome back, Vic,*' he whispered.

'Terry, my clever Terry.' Vic wiped his hands. 'All for me.' He rubbed his face. Trade wasn't usually good for much since the war and he'd let the manager, who held the licence, shut up Trott's Bar to keep the saloon and public bars full-seeming and merry. Ted Trott had been the last owner of the pub until his disappearance, as the police believed, abroad, and his late and unlamented son Raymond had married Ria, widowed now for sixteen years; Trott's Bar, though empty, was crowded with memories, cold as cold-storage but kept so clean that the round tables looked to Vic like open mouths crying out for customers. For life. For revenge. Vic hated this room.

'Half a job's no job,' he said wearily.

'All right.'

Vic sat in the corner and placed his hands flat on the gleaming table. The sunlight shining on the etched window-glass behind him, ALES & BITTERS reversed and back-to-front in silvery mirror-image, threw his face into silhouette, his heavy cheeks so sanguine that they seemed black with shadow. 'Even if you kill a man,' Vic said quietly, 'he never dies. They never die, Terry.'

'There's something else you should know,' Terry clinched it. 'I saw your sister Ria leaving the hospital.'

# 4

Vic descended from the pub's side door, past the beer-barrels awaiting the drayman's collection, into the narrow alleyway almost blocked by his Daimler. 'I'm going to Havannah Street!' he called back to Spike.

'Wot, again?' Spike came down the steps on his toes, shrugging on his jacket, still carrying himself like a boxer though he was a widower and his hair was grizzled white. In the war his wife had got a taste for the popular Shakespeares, waiting out beneath the stairs the endless bomb alerts, and one of her dog-eared editions dangled from his hand. He half opened the driver's door but Vic stopped him.

'Not this time,' Vic said.

Spike fell back, paying attention. He took the Woodbine from his mouth. Something had changed. Vic was wearing an overcoat and a suit beneath it for the first time in months, and his face smelled of eau-de-cologne. 'Whate'er you want, guv'nor,' Spike shrugged.

'I want,' Vic said.

He drove down West Ferry Road with the slush flying in pale roaring wings from the wheels of the car, past all the tatty shops tumbledown with decay – they seemed so small and mean now. As a child he remembered them full of promise, a child's whole bright world of opportunity, enormous red apples ranked for the taking outside the greengrocers', gaslights glaring in Kosky's fish shop like magic, and he wouldn't have seen a single person he didn't know by name in those days. Huge numbers of folk had been evacuated or called up during the war, even the mothers and children dispersed, the old tight-knit communities losing their heart and the intricate mass of tiny shops – kept going father-and-son through the generations – being bombed out or moved out, or now simply falling down, condemned by the new building regulations. The authorities said they were appalled by the living conditions the war had exposed, and now Vic knew a new war was being fought here against these people for their own good by their own race: the millionaire developers who erected the New Towns spreading across the fields of Essex. Vic raised his hand from the wheel to familiar faces, or gave a nod of his head through the open window, knowing who owed money and who had an extra husband, or several extra wives, who kept their steps clean and who lived a secret life behind their net curtains; sometimes just narrowing his eyes in bare acknowledgement of someone behind in their payments, aware of his power, but also that it was fading. Like a shark he had to keep moving, keep moving to live. He hadn't changed.

People didn't change, inside. Shops changed and cars changed but people never changed at all. Ria had been born with the heart of a whore and a whore she would remain. He loved her, and that would remain.

Vic slowed, and the wings of slush flopped down as the car crawled around the corner into Havannah Street. The docks had knocked off for Christmas and stevedores and wharfies were spilling out of the pubs, trudging home through the dusk. Vic pulled up outside Mum's house.

He stood on the pavement looking up at the sooty brick, the electric light gleaming in Ria's bedroom window above, her shadow moving across the ceiling. The curtains undrawn and no nets, as though she had nothing to hide. Ria had come home.

But she had been to the hospital. That was what Vic couldn't understand. She had been to see Ben London, incapable of getting him out of her mind. And she had taken Lola with her. Vic smoothed his face with his hands and used his key to open the street-door.

'Vic!' Mum said, caught preening herself at the hall mirror. 'Well what a pleasant surprise, ever so.' Esther had started talking like the middle-class actresses playing working folk on the wireless, and Vic hated it. This horrid false gentility was a lie, but Mum had always believed in it, and so he forced himself to be still. Thank God she was going out,

wearing her brown coat and a purple hat that made
her look ten years sillier. Her eyes were bright and
her cheeks had colour so he knew she'd been at the
Christmas cake for the sherry in it. Poor old Mum;
pleasures got very simple when you were old. God
knows what she would have got up to given free rein.
'I was just popping out for some sugar,' Esther told
him guiltily, 'Christmas isn't a treat without sugar, is
it?' Her hips were broader than ever as she squeezed
past him, and her yellow scarf caught on one of his
buttons. 'Kiss for your old mum!' she said to hide her
embarrassment.

Vic kissed her lips.

'Have you brought Ria's Christmas present?' asked
Esther anxiously. 'Leave it by the tree, there's a good
boy.' In the front room, which whiffed of Christmas
cake like Mum's lips, crumbs speckling the sideboard
where she had scoffed it without a plate, Vic saw her
puny tree standing proudly on the window-table for
the neighbours, cheap sentimental angels wired to its
branches and a few gifts propped against the scrawny
trunk. 'I paid cash,' Esther promised.

'I'll get you a better tree than that,' Vic said.
'Better angels.'

'You are a sweet,' Esther gushed, then he opened
the door for her. 'Well, TTFN!'

'Ta-ta for now,' Vic said, 'don't hurry back.'

'You aren't miffed because Ria was out are you?'
Esther called fretfully from the shadows of the street,
but he shut her out as though he had not heard her,
then stood alone in the hall. Now he could hear the
noises from upstairs: Ria's bedroom door was half

75

open on the landing and he heard her feet thumping on the boards as she moved around, the bang of the wardrobe door, sliding drawers, then silence as she crossed the rug. He listened with his hand over the peeling newel-post.

'I'm a rotten mother,' Ria's voice floated down with a gentleness he had never heard in her before, 'I haven't looked after you enough, have I? You haven't had nothing warm all day.' Vic came upstairs step by step.

'I had a bun at the hospital,' Lola was saying. So everything Terry said was definitely true. Ria had been there.

'Only half a bun.'

'It had currants in it.'

'We'll have tea and cake before we go!' decided Ria, going out of sight to unhook something from the back of the door, and Lola stared straight at Vic arriving on the landing. She didn't move, didn't run to her mother behind the door, just looked at him with that childish innocence in her dark eyes, calling out to him, it seemed to him, to reach out his arms to her. Just the man and the child. But what lies had Ria told her? Ria prattled on behind the door about tea and coats, filling Vic with rage at her empty-headedness. Vic put his head on one side, and so did Lola. She would be a beauty, stick-thin though her arms and legs were now. Her poor thin face. If only Ria would look out for her right. A lovely little gold bracelet or neck-chain, something sparkly.

'Lola,' Vic called.

Ria's voice stopped and she swung the door open, the coat hanging from her hand in front of Vic. The light faded from her eyes.

'Wotcher, Ria,' Vic said. 'I'm back.'

So much about her disgusted him: the cheap Gloria Fox perfume she wore, her dirty dress with the shoulder-straps hanging down her forearms, the top rolled down to her waist revealing her white bra. Her dishevelled hair, no stockings. The voluptuous half-undressed shape of her as she turned, ignoring him like a provocation as he came into the room. The fact that she cared only about herself, had never looked after her children properly, only after herself. Yet her lovely opal-flecked eyes and sensual lips, the shape of her breasts, all the important things were right. Even her selfishness was defiance.

Ria surprised him. She spoke quietly to Lola. 'Go downstairs. Wait for Grandma.' Lola didn't move.

Vic advanced into the room, looking around him.

'What are you doing here, you bastard!' Ria cried suddenly, and tried to close the door on him but Vic was much heavier, so she fell back to the middle of the room, Lola peeping behind her. Vic stopped following. He smiled affectionately, but with Lola there it wasn't the same between them, and when he held out his hands towards the girl she hid her face in Ria's skirt.

'Give your Uncle Vic a kiss,' he cajoled. Lola shook her head without a word. 'Don't she talk at all?' he demanded.

'Don't touch her,' Ria warned.

'You've turned her against me too.'

'Why should she care about you?' Ria looked surprised – pretending, he was sure, in her woman's way, perhaps even from herself. 'Haven't seen you for months!' she scoffed.

'Let her talk.'

'Not to you she don't.'

'What a funny mummy you got,' Vic said, crouching. 'Don't believe a word your mummy says, little Lola. You don't, do you?' he laughed. 'Why shouldn't she kiss her Uncle Vic?' he asked reasonably. 'Let her decide. She's got a mind of her own, hasn't she, girl?' He put out his arms. 'Come on. I'll bring her a present next time.'

'Don't bother,' Ria said.

'What present?' Lola asked.

'Something really special,' promised Vic. 'Sparkly.'

Ria plonked her hand into her daughter's hair. 'Go downstairs, go out back and have a pee,' she said, and guided her round the crouching figure. 'Go on, you haven't for ages. *Right now*.'

Vic looked around Ria's single room, her home, her row of pot plants on the sill, her few Christmas cards on the peeling brown mantelshelf, making an inventory of her threadbare rug and secondhand furniture, dresser, the armchair which shared the bedside lamp. The lumpy bed with the cardboard Woolworth's suitcase on it. Lola's truckle bed nearer the now-cold ashes of the fire.

Ria was outraged. She knelt, now telling Lola very softly: 'Woman's intuition, you know what I mean.'

Lola regarded her. Ria put one finger over the child's lips: 'Go.' Lola ran downstairs, her much-repaired shoes making hardly a sound on the steps, knowing to skip the ones that squeaked.

Ria stood alone with Vic.

'Ria, I don't understand you,' he said simply in the low tones the two used when they were alone together. 'You went to the hospital and saw him.' He wouldn't say the name. 'The bastard.'

'Ben London.' But she didn't ask Vic how he knew where she had been; Vic always knew.

'You, the moment his wife was dead,' Vic said.

'I was too late.'

'And you took Lola with you. That's what I can't forgive.'

'You've never forgiven me for anything!' Ria sparked. 'For not being your brother. That's it, isn't it, Vic, because I'm a woman. Because you can't control me. Because I'm different from you.'

'I had nothing to do with the bomb.'

'Don't be so bloody innocent. You must've put Terry up to it.'

'I swear I knew nothing.' He laid his big hands lightly on her, one on each of her shoulders.

'I don't believe you, don't lie to me,' Ria said uncertainly.

'My whole life is a lie for you.'

But she turned away, pretending, he knew that, pretending she wasn't listening to him, too busy flinging Lola's stuff, her own skirts, smalls, odd shoes, even a small potted plant into that cardboard

79

Woolworth's suitcase on the bed – as though she would ever really dare leave! She was playing up theatrical. Pure Ria. Needing him to stop her, wanting him to. He took her by the wrists to stop her showing off to him, to force her to take him seriously. To touch her.

'Does he still believe that Lola is his daughter?'

Ria met his eyes defiantly: 'That's what I told Lola too.'

She snatched away her arms from him and knocked down the suitcase lid. 'Ria.' He followed her to the little washbasin in the corner, full of dirty water, then watched with a frown as she folded Lola's wet flannel and began dabbing at her own smiling face.

'You've changed,' Vic said.

Kneeling quietly at the end of the narrow backyard, Lola kissed her rabbit goodbye through the wire mesh of his hutch. Thumper was too heavy and floppy to carry far – she wore only her dress because her coat with the big pockets was still behind the door in the room, and she had no string to use as a leash; Thumps couldn't have run fast or far anyway, because he was domesticated and tame. 'Goodbye!' she whispered to the old Dutch rabbit, sire of most of the twitchy-nosed black-and-whites taken home by her friends at the Cheval Street school. She glanced over her shoulder but the scullery door remained shut. 'I got a carrot for your Christmas present,' she confided with the tears trickling down her cheeks, 'it's the one wrapped up in orange paper on the tree. Grandma will unwrap it for you.' She pressed a few potato peelings through for his lunch. 'If I set you free the cats would get you.' Thumper twitched his nose.

A sound from the back of the house; hastily Lola climbed on to the hutch, balanced rockingly, then got one foot and a hand on to the fence and dropped into Mrs Hiscott's yard, the old woman housebound and gazing powerlessly from her bedroom window. Lola waved and cut through to Alpha Road, running so fast across the inner end of Havannah Street that its gloomy perspective was gone in a flash. She turned past the low grey-green bulk of St Luke's church and ran down to West Ferry Road as quickly as her legs would carry her, going so fast into the wind from the river that she wondered if she might fly. The wind gusted its wet, rich odour into her face, the smell of home.

She skidded on the corner and stopped. The lights had come on in the shopfronts along West Ferry Road, illuminating a plodding figure reading the evening paper as she walked. Lola shrank back but Esther looked up. For a moment her face was tragic, mirroring the destruction in the large black-and-white photograph on the front page. Then she said, 'Lola!'

Lola backed away.

'Why haven't you got your coat on?' Esther demanded, approaching. 'What are you doing here?' A wicker basket of shopping hung from her hand and the shadows of passing vehicles hurried across her face. 'Did your mum let you out like this, darling?'

81

She flapped the paper unconsciously as though trying to erase its message from her mind.

'We're going away.' The tears had not melted from Lola's cheeks and Esther reached out as if to touch them.

'But it's Christmas tomorrow,' Esther said despairingly. 'Did your ma put you up to this?'

'We're going away, Mum says, and that's all.' Lola shrank back.

'Well, I'm going to have a word with that mother of yours!' Esther said, colouring. 'Here, you take my scarf. Wrap up.'

Lola snatched the dangling yellow scarf offered by the adult's clumsy hand, dodging back when the hand tried to grab her, wrapping the thick itchy wool around her face so that only her eyes showed, then hugging herself with her arms.

'God knows what gets into that girl,' Esther muttered, 'she's got no right to muck you about like this. She's mad. And this weather too! I'm going to have a serious word with your ma,' Esther decided definitely, 'for your sake.'

'Uncle Vic's there.'

'Hold on here,' Esther instructed, holding out her great seamed hand with its blunt fingers.

Lola shook her head. 'You see,' she said, retreating, 'we're going away where we can be happy.'

'Ria, you're my life,' Vic said, 'I love you.'

He stared at the sloshing water of the washbasin, Ria's naked fingers dipping into it, scooping, turning around themselves as she washed, her rings scattered on the glass shelf. The horror of it: Vic looking after his young brother Jimmy, seeing with a child's clarity Jimmy's little body rolling in the sloshing depths between the West India lock gates where they played, flushed out into the wide river as the gates opened, and the sailor with a gold ring on his finger jamming the hook beneath Jimmy's belt-buckle, and Vic screaming because he thought how it must hurt, then Jimmy's body coming up with the river gushing out of his mouth and eyes where the fish had nibbled him.

Mum's had so nearly been a large Victorian family; all the children sleeping in the same bed, almost all lost.

*Remember*, Vic whispered.

Vic's brothers Arthur and Dicky, dead. Jane, his true sister – Ria was only his half-sister – also dead. Ria lying beside him, warm, until she got her own little corner behind a blanket. The unbearable sadness: Vic remembered Nigel backing to the very edge of Canary Wharf carrying the Jewish shop-keeper Blumenthall on his back, the first man they killed, the man who made their names, the splash of the body into the darkness. Everything Ria knew nothing of: everything done for her. Alan Stark, their neighbour's son, screaming through the handkerchief in his mouth as the tide rose. Nigel, Terry's father, hanging from the side of the rowing-boat in the dark and falling snow with Raymond Trott's hands clamped in rigor mortis around his neck, dragged down into the river by the masonry block, Nigel's fingernails breaking on the wood as he scrabbled and pleaded for Vic to save him. And then finally peace. Nigel's face bubbling quietly down into the black waters. Not forgiveness in his eyes. Understanding.

'Trust me,' Vic told Ria, as she stood at the washbasin.

She dried her face and snapped up the shoulderstraps of her dress, making herself decent. Good.

'I know you better than you know yourself,' Vic said reasonably. 'You hate me because you do feel something for me. I can see your throat beating.'

Ria turned away sharply.

'You don't love Ben London,' Vic said. 'You don't and you never have.'

He smiled confidently, then realised that Ria, combing back her hair, was too calm. She was up to something. His smile faded and he grabbed her suspiciously.

'I'm getting rid of him once and for all.' He stared down into the bitch's eyes, gripping her so tightly that she couldn't possibly escape him again.

'I do hate you.' Ria's face almost touched his. 'I hate everything you are, Vic.'

He stared. 'Lola?' he cursed, 'you bitch!'

He flung Ria from him, scrambling from the room and hurrying downstairs so fast that he fell to his knees across the hall. Going to the rear of the house he knocked aside the kitchen table covered with cakes and pies waiting for sugar, ran down the yard to the airey with its little tilted roof. 'Lola? You in there?' He dragged the door open, then cursed again:

empty. Ria had deceived him. Newspapers fluttered from the pile in the rising wind. He left the plank door swinging and looked around him, then slithered to the rabbit's hutch: footprints in the snow. Poor Lola was gone.

'Ria!' he screamed.

From the house he heard the muffled thud of the front door slamming.

The bitch was doing a runner. Vic took the steps in one and knocked the kitchen table over the other way, the pies falling like shot birds, jam on his shoes, then down the hall he struggled with the front door: locked. It wasn't like Ria to think things out. Someone had planned this for her. Or the cunning bitch was thinking of how someone would have done it: that was how she was one step ahead. Couldn't get that man out of her mind. Damn her, and she had used Lola.

Vic stopped pulling. Had she really gone out or just slammed the door? This was one of her deceits, misleading him again, she was hiding upstairs crouched in the wardrobe, her breasts against her knees, that cunning light in her eyes, waiting for Vic to go out, making a fool of him again in her lust for Ben London. He ran up silently.

Water was swirling from the washbasin, the plug still swinging from the tap, but her rings, except her wedding ring which never came off, remained on the glass shelf. The suitcase was gone from the bed, her coat and Lola's coat gone from the back of the door, but he knew Ria never left home without her rings.

'I know you're here,' Vic said, giving her every chance. He pulled open the wardrobe. Nothing. The speed of his search increasing, he rifled the few dresses remaining as if she might be hiding in them, threw them on the floor: Ria had always loved her dresses. Nothing under the bed. The bathroom empty, then another door: Esther's bedroom still with its double bed as though the old woman could not bear to relinquish memories of all her years of marriage. Beneath it was the perfect hiding place for Ria, exactly the place she would have chosen; but when Vic knelt and peered beneath, grasping for her beneath their mother's bed, his hand encountered nothing but dust.

Ria had gone.

She had taken Lola with her like her own property.

'But you're happy here,' Esther told the little girl earnestly. 'Your ma was happy here when she was a girl.' *Until she brought home the wrong boy*. 'We're a happy family, always have been.'

Lola looked around her alertly on the street-corner.

'Come on.' Esther held out her hand reassuringly. 'Father Christmas might come to you tonight, I reckon.' But Lola was watching the woman who had cut through the Commons Street alley, stood staring back into its dark mouth for a moment, then walked rapidly towards them. Lola recognised that stride: her mother had decided. The Woolies suitcase swung from her hand, not cheerfully but decidedly, and she carried two coats over her other arm. Ria had remembered everything important.

'Here, get warmed up,' she said. Her hair was lovely, her eyes sparkling. Pushing Lola's arms into the smaller coat, she didn't even glance at Esther.

'I can do the buttons!' Lola said.

Ria slipped on her own coat, lifted her hair over the collar with the backs of her hands. 'You can't look me in the eye,' Esther said. 'Why can't you think of someone but yourself?'

'This one's come off.'

'I'll try and sew it later.' Ria snatched it and tried to move Lola past the implacable figure blocking their way. 'I haven't got time, Mum.'

'You and Vic – always did fight like cat and dog!' laughed Esther then, as Ria pushed past, clung on. 'Don't ruin your life,' she urged with a desperate grin made skeletal by the streetlights. 'For Lola's sake.'

How much did Mum really know, or sense? She had said she would never forgive Ben London for being Lola's father, but maybe Mum was just trying to save their family, keep up appearances. That was important. Ria's footsteps hesitated.

'Where's your pride?' Esther said.

'I love Ben and I always have. However he is, whatever, wherever he is.' Ria glanced round with that nasty look in her eye. 'At least I'm not *proud* of being guilty, like some people.'

Esther flushed. 'You can't go back to him this time.'

'I can't hurt Ben any more.'

Esther waved the rolled-up paper. 'It's here in black and white. He's lost his marbles, he's mad. Look! It's in the paper.'

'Even if he is mad,' said Ria, 'my place is with him.' She put her hand between Lola's shoulders to hurry her up.

'*Serious mental condition*,' Esther called after them. 'Don't leave me, I was just telling Lola, we're going to have such a happy Christmas together. Ben's brain-injured by the explosion, darling. Deteriorating condition. Think of Lola. And his eyes. You can't love a blind man. Oh, I'm so sorry for you. But show some sense for once in your life.' Esther dropped her shopping and hobbled after them on her arthritic legs. 'You're just as mad as he is!'

Ria hefted the suitcase, almost a shrug. A bus pulled up at the stop ahead of them and she took Lola's hand in hers, walking faster. Lola skipped joyfully. 'We're going to ride on a bus!'

Esther shouted: 'Ria.'

Then she shouted, 'Ria, I've dropped my shopping . . .'

Vic stepped out into Havannah Street. It was empty.

But over there was the little alleyway known as Commons Street, close by St Luke's, and if she'd cut through there . . . she could be anywhere. No one knew the maze of backstreets and alleys like Ria. But Vic couldn't give up and he ran heavily towards the river with the slush spattering his shoes and trousers, the smell of the river hanging like death over West Ferry Road and the silly cheerful lights going out as the shops shut, the last shoppers going home looking up at him fearfully as they passed.

He stopped, puffing his breath in pale shadows round his head.

And he saw Ria.

She had fooled him.

She passed him in a bus, Lola beside her in the lighted window standing on the seat, looking back. The little figure was still waving as the bus dwindled from view towards the City.

Esther saw him and plodded miserably over. 'It was going to be such a merry Christmas and I was so looking forward to it. It's not been a good year and we were going to eat like pigs.' She'd lost her scarf and was shivering. 'Now this. She's gone wild again.'

Vic put his arms around her and hugged her tight, feeling Mum's warmth through her heavy coat and really needing her for the first time in years.

'Careful, you'll break my old bones,' Esther complained, delighted. 'I've got you back again.'

'I'll look after you, Mum,' Vic promised. 'I'm back with you again. Come on, I'll pick your shopping up. What a mess you've made.'

'You were right about her, Vic.'

'She'll come back, with her tail between her legs, you know Ria,' Vic reassured Mum. 'People like her always do. And I'll be waiting. She's got nowhere to go,' he said with contempt.

'Why did we change buses, Mummy?' Lola asked as they climbed aboard the second omnibus, Ria looking behind her anxiously.

89

'Because.'

'Sixpenny,' the London Transport conductor snuffled over Ria, either with a cold or a hangover, then gave a small fart, or someone did, as he wound the coloured stub out of his machine. 'Pardon. And a thruppenny. Ta.' Lola surveyed him with bright, serious eyes.

'Don't you miss nothing?' Ria asked her.

'I don't know.' Lola had eyes only for the conductor taking fares.

'You're a deep one, you are,' Ria sighed.

Lola said, 'What's going to happen to us?'

'If only I knew the answer to that, girl.'

'Have we said goodbye for ever and ever,' asked Lola as the lights of London swung past the bus, 'is it an adventure?'

'No.' Ria roused herself, for the first time realising how uncomfortable was the suitcase propped across her knees, the bus's luggage cubby already full of cases and an extraordinary folding pram, people taking a few days away for Christmas with family. Everyone wore their Sunday bests and hats, carrying anything valuable where they could see it in their laps, scrawny unrationed turkeys in wicker baskets padded out with a few black bottles of stout, the occasional half-bottle of Johnny Walker jealously guarded. 'No, love, it's not an adventure.'

'It is really,' Lola said, but Ria looked worried so Lola pressed her nose to the streaming glass, the outside world: the lights.

'Don't do that,' Ria fussed, 'you don't know who's been here before.'

'Cable Street.' The conductor eased himself down from upstairs as more passengers swung aboard.

Ria suffered the jolting of the bus, the suitcase cramping her legs.

'Grandma was unhappy and you're unhappy too.'

'We've had better days,' Ria admitted. 'Worse ones, too.'

'Be happy,' Lola said so innocently that for a moment Ria laughed, and Lola hugged her arm. 'At least we're together.' The child stuck her hand in her mum's pocket for reassurance, her fingers encountering a small wrapped package. Her face was transformed by delicious anticipation. 'You're hiding something all crinkly and wrapped up in there!'

'You didn't think I'd forget to nick your Christmas present off the tree as I whizzed out, did you?'

'It *is* an adventure,' Lola said determinedly.

'Everything's an adventure when you're young. There's Tower Bridge.'

'Are we going there?'

'That was long ago when Mummy was young,' Ria murmured.

'Where are we going *now*?'

'On an adventure, of course.'

'That's better. I'm hungry,' Lola said.

'You're always hungry,' Ria tousled her hair fondly, 'I don't know where you put it all. Shit, I think I didn't pack your bloody comb.' She immediately looked more worried about that than anything. 'I must have left my brains behind.' Lola tried again to cheer her up. She persuaded her mother to lay the suitcase on the seat where she could sit on it instead of standing to see out of the window, and Ria rubbed her legs with a sigh of relief, suddenly smiling.

'It's a dream, isn't it,' Lola said, 'riding on a real bus!'

'I wish he'd stop farting,' whispered Ria. 'Try your scarf over your face again.'

'He does it when his machine whirrs. It's not my scarf, it's Granny's scarf.'

'Oh, I know, you don't have to keep telling me everything.'

'He doesn't think anyone notices.' Lola couldn't sit still. 'What's this road now?'

'The Strand.' Ria looked at her hands in her lap. 'I lived here once. In the cellar with the steps down to it, just there.' She pointed without looking. Trott's Nightclub on its foundation of medieval oystershells, its password '*I've slept with Ria!*' a mockery invented by her husband, Ray Trott, who hadn't slept with her, and never did sleep with her as long as he lived.

'Did Daddy live here too?' Lola asked.

In her innocence she meant Ben London. Ria wondered how to lie convincingly, then her tongue ran away with her and she told the truth she had always wanted to believe, the life she never had: Pearl London's life. It was terribly easy to lie to a child, to be perfect.

'We lived in the big house you saw this morning,' Ria lied. 'We had lots of bedrooms and we were so happy. We travelled everywhere but we couldn't

92

always be together, and one day your Daddy came back from Africa.'

'Did he bring me with him like a present?'

'In a way he did.'

'Because he loves you very much?'

'We both love you,' Ria lied reassuringly.

'Are we all going to be together now?'

'Charing Cross station!' the conductor called, 'fare stage.' He whirred his machine for someone getting aboard. 'Pardon.'

'Hang on!' Ria grabbed Lola in one hand and the case in the other, jumping down, and they stood on the wet pavement watching the bus's red tail-light shrinking, then swallowed up by the lights on the gigantic Norwegian Christmas tree soaring from Trafalgar Square.

'Do dreams come true?' asked Lola.

The two figures, the woman with the suitcase pulling the child behind her, hurried across the almost deserted plaza between the fountain pools, then ran up the steps past the drinking fountains marked Metropolitan Drinking Fountain & Cattle Trough Association. 'Can I have hot chestnuts for supper?' Lola asked.

'Anything you want.' Ria had already noticed that all the hot-chestnut men had packed up.

The Haymarket was almost deserted, the rising wind driving scraps of paper along the broad empty thoroughfare as they climbed towards Piccadilly. A Rolls-Royce, the chauffeur cleaning the windscreen with a yellow duster that looked a peculiar colour because of the streetlights, was parked by the steps to

Eros. Incongruously the plinth where the statue should have been standing was bare, the Angel of Christian Charity removed to save him from the bombs, and not yet returned. 'Are we changing buses again?' Lola asked, but Ria shushed her as the chauffeur saw them.

'Miss Ria Price?' he asked, using her maiden name, and she felt as though twenty years had slipped away.

'That's us,' Ria said.

'I'm Bill Simmonds. Mr London's chauffeur.' He held out his hand and Ria shook it. 'Nah, give us yer case, love.' He opened the rear door and Lola scrambled in. 'No feet on the seats!' Bill cautioned. He closed the suitcase in the boot and his two passengers sat without a word, their eyes fixed on the back of his head, every short white hair of which registered his disapproval, as he drove them along Piccadilly.

Ria, however, wasn't to be put down. 'Well,' she demanded, 'any change in his condition, has there been?'

'Mr London's having himself transferred to the Central Eye Hospital in Judd Street.'

Ria worried. Surely that was far too soon.

'What's going to happen to us?' Lola asked.

'I'm just following my orders,' Bill said.

'Do you think he's stuffed?' Lola whispered, and Ria shushed her again.

'For specialist attention, I s'ppose,' Bill said, thawing to the little girl whose eyes caught his in the rearview mirror. Lola stuck out her tongue.

The Rolls cut along a backstreet then turned out

into Park Lane, slowing by a row of attractive
terraced houses then drew to a halt in front of the
hotel. The commissionaire saluted, a porter took
their suitcase. Ria stood looking up at the arch of
brilliant lights: LONDON'S. She looked round, but the
kerb was already empty. They followed the commissionaire into the marble foyer glittering with decorations. One wall was given over to Cartier displays
behind shining plate glass, a mass of flowers on every
table filling the air with exotic perfume even at this
time of year, waiters swept between them balancing
silver trays on their splayed fingers as elegantly as
dancers, moving silently on muffling carpets between
scattered white casual chairs and sofas. At once the
famous concierge, a large black man with nobility
stamped on his powerful features, came round the
desk personally with his hand extended in welcome.
Ria said: 'I'm—'

'We're so glad to see you, again, Miss Price.'

*Again*. Ria coloured, this sort of place spared no
detail in making its guests feel at home, even though
more than twenty years had passed since her ghastly
honeymoon night here with Raymond Trott. Here,
Ria had learned that love need not exist. And the
morning after, she had seen Ben London here again
in this foyer, this very place, *his* place, his brilliant
blue eyes looking straight at her. And realised that
she hadn't got away from him any more than she'd got
away from Vic.

The black man escorted them authoritatively to the
lift. 'Your suite has been prepared,' he advised them.
'You will not be disturbed.'

'Can we have hot chestnuts?' Lola said.

'I will have anything you want,' he laughed, 'personally sent up.'

'Steak,' Ria said suddenly as the lift doors opened on a sumptuous corridor. 'Steak and lobster and chips, and salad with fresh tomatoes. And a bloody big pudding.'

He bowed and they knew it would be done exactly as they demanded. He showed them to their suite, white chairs on a Chinese rug, a bathroom with hot running water that actually steamed, and two double beds in the bedroom. As soon as they were alone Ria threw herself on one bed, rolled over and put her hands behind her head.

'What a relief,' she said, kicking off her shoes. 'This is the life!' The world of Ben London. Ria's face crumpled up and she began to cry. Lola lay beside her holding both her hands clenched in her mother's coat pocket, trying to get her head comfortable in the crook of her mother's arm on the too-soft bed, looking pale and frightened. This was what the room service waiter saw when he arrived, but he flambéed the steaks and popped the champagne giving no sign that he had noticed, and departed without waiting for a tip. He had been paid in gossip.

## 5

Esther was wise. She knew there were bad things in the world, so she wore her smile. She knew this neat pattern of familiar streets and cosy family homes running back from the river was a crust over the darkness of the Isle of Dogs. There was misery to be had behind these bright doors, it would rule her life if she let it. But there were the good things too, kindness and togetherness, the affection of neighbours and the slow intermarriage of the families, new generations blossoming as the old ones withered, and there was an immense satisfaction in being part of this mighty tree with its branches in the sun, the celebration of marriage and birth and passing on, and all its dark roots hidden underground, out of sight. She believed in life as it ought to be. Mrs Morris was dying of a cancer she thought was indigestion, and of course no one told her, but she had never known she had so many friends among her neighbours. Her sons had bought a half-interest in a greenhouse near Chelmsford in Essex and couldn't come back often, but Esther took some mince pies round to the old woman's, the best ones that hadn't visited the kitchen floor when Vic was clumsy, beautifully dusted with mouthwatering sugar. She'd never cared for Mrs Morris much in good health, but everyone agreed that dying – being aware of the darkness – had improved the old biddy no end, and for her last few months she had become almost popular. Coming into the front room Esther found gifts of mince pies on plates along the sideboard, half-opened biscuit tins revealing more mince pies, and Esther knew which Miss Ulcoq had given because they were all cracked and mean on sugar. A large Christmas pudding poked from a box by the chair.

'Well, you've got enough to keep you going, Mrs Morris!' Esther said.

The flock arms of her chair almost obscured the old woman's shrunken form as she struggled up. She wore that long green dress as though she might go out somewhere nice. The room was icy.

'All the years we've known of one another, Mrs Price. Call me Lizzie, go on, why don't you.' In awkward silence they looked around the room. 'Aren't people wonderful – Esther?'

'It's freezing in here.' Esther had hoped for a white Christmas but it was raining again outside, the pavements black and silver. She drew the curtains.

'I can't eat, you see. I thought it would make them keep longer.'

'That fire's no good. Vic will know where to get you another,' Esther said bossily, unable to conceal her pride in her returned son.

'Stay for a sherry.'

'I can't drink. Not that I don't want to be friendly-like.'

'No, I understand. My boys . . .' Lizzie sighed. 'You're so lucky to have Vic. It's all worked out so well for you.'

'Not for want of trying,' Esther said tartly.

'But Ria's gone I hear,' said the old woman with an alert look in her eye. With all her visitors she was the centre of gossip for the street.

'Oh, Ria.'

'She's been such a trial to you, that girl,' Lizzie said cunningly.

'All her life she loved a man who cared nothing for her!' Esther burst out. 'She got no pride in herself, Lizzie, she'd let my house go to wrack and ruin by herself. She don't look after Lola any better. Frankly I'm fed up to the back teeth with her.'

'They're not grateful. Have a pie, go on.'

Esther helped herself to a pie, and Lizzie sipped a small sherry.

'Just a little one then!' Esther said.

When she got back home, the moment she clicked her key in the lock Vic opened the door. 'Did you think I was Ria?' giggled Esther, hugging him impulsively. 'I'm just so happy to have you home.'

Vic needed looking after. He'd never forsaken his mum like the others, never married, always been vulnerable. He had a streak of hardness in him too, like his mum. But she could always get round him.

'Where's Terry?' she demanded. 'Aren't you looking after him?'

'He's busy.'

'Have you sent him to look for Ria?'

'I know where Ria is,' Vic said. 'Money gossips, always has.'

He sniffed her breath, and Esther blushed. She never could hide anything from Vic.

'It was only a little one, dear.'

'Ria will come back and I won't have to lift a finger,' Vic promised her. 'You know Ria.' He found the half bottle left over from the Christmas pudding and held out a glass.

'That's too much!' But Esther gave in. 'To us. To our family.'

'Nice to have you back, Mum,' Vic said, not touching a drop.

Esther wore her smile.

* * *

Vic knew how to hurt. *Half a job's no job*. Stung, Terry had tossed off his beer alone among the deserted tables of Trott's Bar, then gone upstairs to the room he still used. When he left the Old Bull and Bush there was a reassuring weight in the pocket of his overcoat, and people in the crowded public bar got out of his way seeing his confidence. He drove to the Middlesex Hospital, picking up an evening final on the way. Declining mental condition. He threw it away without even checking the racing page.

In the darkness of Christmas Eve, rain beginning to blow in spits on the rising wind, not even the most determined stringer for the Press was going to hang about outside the hospital. By the time the presses rolled again Ben London would be the day before yesterday's news. Terry stood in the doorway of the closed café watching the lighted windows. People started arriving in the hospital forecourt, no one special, visiting hour. From time to time an ambulance arrived or drove away along Mortimer Street and Terry got the feel of the hospital's routine. People were coming out now, visiting hour ending, putting their hands on their hats against the gusting rain. A policeman came out yawning, adjusted his helmet and left without seeing the man watching him from the doorway.

An ambulance arrived, but instead of pulling into the forecourt, Terry watched it turn out of sight around the side of the building. He slipped after it, finding himself in a cobbled delivery area. Rain sheeted across the ambulance's lights as it backed into one of the bays, almost blinding Terry so that he all but knocked over a dustbin. He glimpsed a figure on a stretcher being wheeled into the vehicle; the rear doors slammed at once and Terry ducked behind the dustbins as it pulled away, then ran to his MG. He caught up with the ambulance's tail-lights turning left from Goodge Street.

At the top of the Tottenham Court Road the ambulance turned east along the Euston Road, then turned right again almost opposite St Pancras Station, pulling up by what looked like a private nursing home. Terry read the sign: THE CENTRAL LONDON EYE HOSPITAL, JUDD STREET.

Eye hospital. So he wasn't brain-injured. Ben London knew someone was after him and the rest of it was just disinformation, like in the war. Lies.

Terry drove back to the Old Bull and Bush and phoned Vic. 'He's at Judd Street. No sign of Ria.'

'I know where she is. Tell me if she visits him.'

Terry would do better than that: he'd grab her.

But nothing happened before midnight. Terry returned the next day and watched from the deserted street while everyone else was eating Christmas dinner, and all the next day too, sitting in the car chewing a sandwich while they were finishing off the cold turkey. He wondered about Ben London, wondered what he was going through behind the building's façade, what the man was feeling. It must be terror, Terry reckoned: sheer, numbing terror, lying there alone in the dark, night even during the day, waiting for *him*.

Terry was in no hurry.

He watched families come to visit their relatives in the hospital, some of them each day, a little boy in a school cap despite the holiday, dragged along by his mother who always stopped on the steps to colour his cheeks with a few rubs of her handkerchief, a flustered father and three children who secretly pinched one another, an old spruce military man invariably bearing a small gift, boiled sweets, nuts, just a couple of oranges. There was a voluptuous girl who adjusted her stockings both going in and coming out, thinking everyone must be looking at her seams. But no sign of Ria, and he knew getting Ria was his way back in with Vic.

Once the chauffeur-driven Rolls drew up and Victoria London went quickly into the hospital. No one harassed her this time. She had a lovely walk, almost balletic on her toes, her legs very long and graceful. She stayed only a few minutes so she couldn't be close to her father. But she arrived dutifully on the Friday too, at a different time. A millionaire's daughter didn't bother about visiting hours.

Ria wasn't coming, Terry decided. He phoned Vic.

'He's up to something,' Vic said, but Terry didn't believe it.

On the Saturday Terry stopped off at Covent Garden to buy some flowers, costing a fortune because of the season and the lorry-drivers' strike, half a dozen red, half a dozen white. He parked his car off Judd Street by the telephone exchange, then followed the father and squabbling children into the lobby of the eye hospital, going smoothly amongst them past the desk to the stairs. 'Sorry,' the worried father apologised as they climbed to the first floor. 'It's all Dick Barton with them. I can't do a thing with them if we aren't home in time for the show. Hurry up, children! Lawrence, *don't*.'

They went down the passageway to the left, so Terry, clasping the flowers like a visitor, went right. Nobody stopped him. Because it was quiet now and he was alone, the smell of ether and disinfectant seemed even stronger amongst the bright decorations, toy sleighs tinkling on the draught as he passed. Women's wards, examination rooms, somewhere a wireless tinnily chanting Christmas carols. He prowled upstairs to the next floor.

He had expected the room to be identified by the presence of guards. There were none.

The visitors here were mostly women, beginning to leave, so he pulled back against the wall to let them past. Male wards, this was better. The private rooms must be the other way, and he turned back towards the stairs, then heard footsteps coming up and pretended to examine a noticeboard.

He saw her only from the back as she went away from him, belted cream Burberry matching her long combed-out hair, its fluid blonde sway. He'd recognise that graceful walk anywhere, and for a moment he just watched her. Then he followed Victoria London down the passageway without her knowing, turning right when she turned right, silently following her tapping footsteps, one hand in his overcoat pocket, the other holding the flowers.

Which door would she choose? No policeman on

guard to show which it would be. Victoria hesitated, perhaps realising it too, perhaps feeling disquiet, but she didn't look behind her.

She opened the door to the private room in front of her. The door swung, revealing nothing.

The room was empty. Ben London was gone.

'Bloody hell, she was as surprised as I was,' Terry said into the phone. There was already a queue gathering outside the kiosk and he hunched his shoulders away from them, excluding them. 'She knew nothing about it, I swear it, Vic.'

'She doesn't know him,' Vic said. 'Get to the hotel, fast.'

'Why?'

'That's bloody obvious,' Vic said, 'I'll be there soon,' and there was the sound of the receiver being slammed down.

'Get out of the bloody way!' shouted Terry, catching the fat woman at the head of the queue with the door and venting his frustration on her, then threw back the flowers as he ran past the accusing faces to his car. The drive to Park Lane took three endless minutes in the MG, but he found the hotel quiet, the normal number of people in furs going in and out. Terry watched the gilded commissionaire saluting them beneath the arch of lights, the glass doors behind him reflecting a shining image of Hyde Park, tree branches, blue sky. Terry parked by the terraced houses nearby and stayed in the car. On the pavement pigeons fluffed out their feathers, dry for the first time in days. Suppose Ria had already left? Suppose she was just going to remain hidden in the hotel room? He waited anxiously for Vic to arrive.

Terry stiffened as the Rolls-Royce Phantom III passed him and stopped at the hotel entrance, the chauffeur getting out to open the rear door, and after a minute or two – Terry checking his watch in an agony of suspense – the two figures, the woman and child wrapped in their shabby coats, came hurrying down the steps and climbed into the Roller. They were obviously going to meet Ben London.

'Come on!' hissed Terry, banging his hand on the steering wheel.

He gave up on Vic and followed the imposing black limousine into the traffic around Hyde Park Corner, then saw Vic's Daimler approaching from down East. Terry slammed on the brakes and pulled down the hood, waving frantically. Vic crossed over on foot, both hands in his overcoat pockets, glowered down at Terry in the open car.

'What's the bloody row?'

Terry pointed. 'They're on their way.'

Vic got in. 'There's no hiding place,' he said as Terry drove, 'Ria can't hide from me. She knows it.'

The Rolls crossed in front of Buckingham Palace, then Terry let it draw ahead on the broad expanse of Birdcage Walk, over Westminster Bridge. He pulled closer after the Elephant and Castle, following the twisting roads of suburban south London.

'Don't know this,' Vic said. Terry had never known him in such a mood, lost and angry.

'You left your car door hanging open,' he said.

'So what? I'll report it stolen and the police will drive it home for me.'

The football supporters wore scarves of unfamiliar colours here, foreign territory.

The Rolls kept going south, making intimidatingly smooth progress so that Terry had to keep changing gear to beat the traffic lights. The chauffeur was a wonderful driver, hardly seeming to touch the brakes, using the flow of traffic to his advantage. Terry worried about keeping up if they got into open country, the Roller was probably good for almost a hundred. Both cars were delayed in Brixton, an accident, a car turned over on its roof, Terry right behind the Rolls as they inched past: he could see the top of Ria's head shadowed in the back window, then the Rolls pulled ahead effortlessly on the Brighton road. The low midday sun glared in Terry's eyes across the flatlands but he caught the Roller up in each village.

'If you run out of petrol I'll kill you,' Vic said. 'I want Ria.' There was an angry passion in his voice. 'He's taking her to Brighton. He's doing it to me again.' Terry didn't dare look at him.

'What's he up to?'

Vic said: 'Ben London believes in winning. That's all he believes in. He's telling me he's taking her from me again.'

'He won't get away with it,' Terry said, looking at Vic.

The Rolls swept well ahead of them down the long slope into Brighton, turned by the glittering sea. As it stopped the MG pulled up behind, and Vic got out, an indomitable figure standing on the promenade with his hands in his coat pockets.

Then he said: 'Fooled!'

From the back of the Rolls a woman – not Ria – and a girl – not Lola – were climbing down. The woman took off Ria's old coat and handed it to the chauffeur. She was Peggy Oake, the butler's wife, and the girl was her daughter Anna. They tripped merrily down to the sea and threw stones at the lapping wavelets. Sea-mist was rising. The chauffeur looked at the closed pier disappearing into the fog like a man remembering his childhood, seeing an altogether different scene.

'Ben London thinks he's won,' Vic said. 'But I have his eyes.'

# PART II

## The Ice Palace

27 December 1946 – 21 March 1947

# Chapter Three

*Where do you go, when no one will help you, and you have nowhere to go to?*

## 1

London fog.

Everything had gone, everything had changed. Ria crouched in the back of the parked van which hid her, trying to peer out, but the windscreen revealed only yellow-grey fog. At first the sun had glowed like a pearl in the Saturday afternoon mist, then was swallowed up as the air thickened – the football would be off – and now the ornate, gloomy buildings that had lined the deserted street had disappeared too. 'Don't it pong in here?' Lola sniffed. Despite the cold, the unheated butcher's van reeked of the ghosts of Christmas turkeys that had hung from the rows of hooks above their heads, a penetrating sweet-sour odour like sweat.

Ria shifted uncomfortably. The metal curve of the wheel-arch, the only seat, was unforgivingly cold under her bottom, and she was starting to itch.

Condensation trickled down the thin steel panels. Lola sat on the other side, knees tucked up inside her skirt, regarding her seriously.

'Were they alive?' Lola asked, looking up at the hooks. The nightmares suffered by children.

'No, for the hundredth time. And stop wriggling.'

'My bum itches.'

'Put up and shut up.' Ria was dying to wriggle herself.

'I want to go back to the hotel.' Lola hugged the doll that Ria had given her in the hotel room on Christmas Day. It was a very ordinary wooden doll, one of the thousands home-worked on any London street from Bethnal Green to Southwark, with painted red lips and – the de-luxe touch that had attracted Ria – eyes that opened and closed. It was done with lead weights somehow, but Ria knew as well as Lola that when her eyes were open Dolly was awake, and when they were closed, she was asleep. She was asleep now. Lola sat her up to wake her. 'Don't!' Ria said.

'She's cold.'

'I'm sure Charlie Bookkeeper must be back any minute,' Ria fretted. Lola was bound to start telling her Dolly was hungry soon.

'Where are we?'

'I think it's his law office in Holborn. I recognised the viaduct, it's all legal offices along here, if only we could see them.'

'But why are we waiting?' Lola wailed. The child didn't know a legal office from a viaduct, Ria realised with remorse.

'You've been a good girl, will you just shut your questions?'

Lola said nothing for a long while. 'The fog stinks too.'

'It's a London particular. Smoke.'

'Are we running away from Uncle Vic?'

'I've never run away from anything,' Ria asserted.

'Are you and Daddy going to get married?' Lola said offhandedly but with a knowing, curious eye. Expectant. Excited. Nowadays little girls knew all about marriage, expected it from the wireless, where everyone was married.

'You and me,' Ria said very carefully, 'both of us together, we're going to help Daddy get better.' Another way of saying running away.

'You just want to be with him.'

Ria gave up and scratched. It was worth it. She recognised the look in Lola's eye for her own at that lonely age. Lola was becoming aware of herself. Ria had been only a little older when she first saw Ben London.

'I like Charlie,' Lola said at last.

'Never trust lawyers, darling, or the law.'

'Where are we going?'

'I never did know what Ben was up to!' exploded Ria, and they sat in silence.

'Dolly's hungry,' Lola said.

'Oh, Christ.' Ria searched her pockets. But it was a grey felt coat, not smelling of her, belonging to one of the hotel cleaners perhaps. Holding it out, Charlie had this morning introduced himself in the doorway of the suite where Ria and Lola had been so happy.

He'd been their only visitor, and then things had moved quickly. 'Ria? I'm Charles Bookkeeper, Mr London's solicitor. Call me Charlie. I've got this for you, put it on. Here's Lola's.'

'He knows our names,' Lola had said.

But Ria had been won over by the lawyer's unapologetic smile. 'Daddy sent him.' *Daddy*. The lie rolled so easily off her tongue she was proud of herself. *Daddy*.

'I need your old coats,' Charlie had informed them briskly, 'we haven't got much time. We'll leave by the staff entrance. I have a van waiting.'

'Who is looking after Ben meanwhile?'

'He's alone at my office, of course.' Lawyers didn't work on Saturdays so this was friendship. 'It's time to go.'

Ria had departed the luxurious room, though it had been hers for such a short time, with a nostalgic backward glance. A girl could get used to that sort of life. She saw no one going down the fire escape as Lola, hanging from one hand, skipped the iron steps. It was though the way had been cleared ahead of them. As indeed it had. In the yard the black man guarded a van painted with gilt lettering down the side: *Geo. Stevens, Son & Nephew, Old Bond Street*. 'Everything's going according to plan,' he had reassured them.

'Whose plan?' Ria had demanded. 'Where are we off to?'

'We're just following orders,' both men said together, so that Ria had to laugh at their mutual surprise, the incongruous circle of the gentle po-faced solicitor and powerful Nigerian joined for a moment by her laughter. Then the rear doors were slammed. 'Good luck!'

'Whose orders?' Ria had called, too late.

Charlie wouldn't answer questions as he drove. 'You doubtless know more about him than I.' Was Ben capable of giving orders? Charlie parked in the broad misty street that Ria thought was Holborn, and said he would be just a few minutes. But they had waited here for hours while the fog closed in, and Lola was hungry, and Ria couldn't find anything to eat in these silly pockets. 'I'm sorry, love!'

'It doesn't matter,' Lola said, so Ria knew it did.

At last the door of Charlie Bookkeeper's law chambers opened, illuminating the fog with a yellow electric glow. Two figures crossed the pavement in the failing daylight, one steering the other by the elbow, and the passenger door was opened. Ben London got in. He drew a breath but did not turn round.

'Ria.'

'I'm here,' she said from the back.

'I can hear your teeth chattering.'

'I'm shaking all over.' She touched his shoulder. 'It's really you.'

He turned. 'Oh my God,' Ria said. He looked like Claude Rains in *The Invisible Man*, raincoat with the collar turned up, dark glasses, hat. At least they'd taken his bandages off, but his flesh revealed nothing: until the cuts healed he could not shave.

'It's really me,' he said quietly, and took off the dark glasses. 'See, Ria?'

PHILIP BOAST

But she didn't. Suddenly Ria wondered if she really knew him, this man who'd once been the child with the striking blue eyes. Demanding eyes, the first thing she had noticed about him. That had been a foggy day too, she a grubby little girl bare-footed in a dirty East End street, as old as she'd got fingers on her hands, seeing him dragged through the fog towards the workhouse. Nobody else had seen her, but he'd known she was there. He looked at her and saw *her*. Ria had never forgotten that moment, the most innocent and precious of her life. *I am not alone*, she'd thought, her feet aching on the cold stones, her deepest secret revealed. *He knows that I am special*.

And he needed her.

Now he believed Lola was his child, and Lola believed he was her father.

Ria stared at Ben who could not see her. Two adults with more than half their lives behind them. The magic had gone. Did she know him? As a child she had seen herself in his eyes, his strength. Ben stared past her, helpless, his eyes reflecting the fog, and Ria worried that Lola might be afraid.

'I really am me,' Ben said gently.

Lola gazed enthralled. 'Can't you see anything?'

He turned his head a little towards her voice in the back of the van. Ria watched Lola squeeze her eyes shut. 'Is it as dark as this?' Lola asked, despite Ria's shushing.

Ben laughed. It was so unexpected that Ria jumped.

'Darker than you can imagine,' he said.

'Are we going to have tea now?'

116

Like magic, Ben held out a Mars Bar from his pocket. He thought of everything. Lola snatched it. 'Dolly wants one too.'

'Don't be silly,' Ria tutted quickly, but Ben held out his hand again. Empty air. Ria knew Lola was a few years too old to believe in imaginary Mars Bars, but then the little girl reached her hand obediently into Ben London's. 'Daddy,' she said.

He reached out to touch her hair, but she was no longer there, already crouched back on the wheel-arch eating the sweet, sharing it with the doll in her child's world apart from that of the adults.

Ben held out a Mars Bar in Ria's direction. He didn't say a word.

Charlie Bookkeeper got in and started the engine. Like Lola, Ria wanted to ask where they were going, but she ate her Mars Bar in silence as the vehicle swayed along roads she did not know. It didn't matter where they were going. Ben was running away and they were going with him. Lola cuddled her sleepily, accepting all that happened as perfectly normal as long as she had her mum with her. And her dad. Their heads together, the closeness of their bodies keeping them warm, Ria held her daughter with a fierce possessiveness, never going to let her go, the engine droning steadily now on the straight road. Running away.

'You can't go back to Vic,' Ben said. Of course; he believed Vic had made the bomb. Running from Vic, Ria slept.

'She's asleep,' Charlie Bookkeeper murmured.

'I am the same man,' said Ben London.

\* \* \*

He woke hearing Ria screaming, *No! No!* He had sworn to Pearl that he would never meet the East End girl again, but here she was, her voice echoing from the past. He ran, not away from her, but towards her. A brilliant white glare encompassed him.

*Pearl is dead.*

Ben opened his eyes and saw nothing.

He endured terrible pain, like a man on fire. It was loss.

Part of him hated Ria for being so full of life, for saving him. He saw his pain in colour, red pain. His eyelids were riddled with miscroscopic specks of glass too small to be removed, rubbing his scalded eyes like sandpaper. The specialist had assured him they would work out in time but the soft nerves of the sclera and cornea remembered their agony. He reached up but could not see his hand in front of his face, only feel its pain, the pain of torso and legs and heart, simplifying him like a man in outline drawn by a child's red crayon. One of the knives of glass sent flying by the explosion had penetrated four inches deep into his body, others almost as far, or merely lacerated his naked skin as they whirled past. He was lucky to be alive. *No! No!*

Pearl was dead, the wife he'd loved was dead.

'It's all right,' came Charlie's voice. Of course; he could see Ben's raised hand. The van swung from side to side as if following country lanes. 'They're still asleep. We're lost. This damn fog is everywhere, I didn't want to wake you.' Charlie slowed, then pulled up. 'Are you in any pain?' He had the pills.

'No.'

Ben heard a vehicle drone from right to left in front of them. 'Which way are you going at these crossroads?'

'I think I've been going in circles,' Charlie confessed. 'This damn—'

'What does the sign say?' Ben said coldly.

'Edith again, or Tinwell.' Charlie sounded as weary as a man who'd been driving all night. They must be nearly there.

'Is the signpost leaning to the left?'

'Yes, but—'

'Go right.' Ben listened to the engine labour uphill. 'Turn left through the gates at the top of the hill.'

'How did you know—' Charlie must be giving that quick shake of his head he always did when taking instructions. Ben had first met him many years ago when Georgy Leibig set up the Trust to keep the London Emporium out of Ben's hands, and in those of his own grandchildren, George and Ralph. Charlie and his father before him had been Georgy Leibig's solicitors and Ben had moved quickly to make them his friends. Charlie had worked faithfully in Ben London's interest, and in his shadow, for more than twenty-five years now.

The wheels crunched on gravel. 'Keep to the left past the outhouse,' Ben said.

'Yes, I see it.'

Ben heard the exhaust echo briefly off the outhouse wall. He'd hidden from Ria behind those cracked boards, keeping their promise to Pearl, after Lola was born, never to meet again. Ria had been Ben's world when they were children, he'd loved her with all his heart. But as they grew up she'd invented her own, private picture of him inside herself to fall in love with, not of the man he really was, but a handsome lie as false as the pin-ups some men made of pretty girls. It was Ben who escaped the East End, not Ria, but their son Will had already been conceived. Thirty years later, during the last years of the war when Easton had been used as a convalescent home, Ria had come to visit Will here – poor Will, brain-injured and returned to childhood, sitting in a wheelchair grinning like an idiot, the spittle hanging from his lips staining the precious, pointless volume of Redouté rose drawings given him by his father. Ben had seen – *seen* – Lola here, for the first and only time. A glimpse of her to last him a lifetime. Three years old and cheerfully scuffing her shoes on the stones, red-cheeked from her exertions, Lola had long, black hair which had escaped beneath the navy-blue beret that Ria, getting off the bus, had plonked on her head . . . blue eyes flecked with old gold; Ria's eyes, but deeper, darker. He had kept his promise. Ben's body had ached with the love he couldn't show, but he had remained hidden.

'Which way now?'

'Don't go as far as the stable block, Charlie. Park the van by the steps to the house.'

Charlie killed the motor and Lola's voice came from behind them, waking with a child's instant alertness: 'We're there! Where is it?' She would have been too young to remember being here before.

'Easton Manor,' Ben said. The house had been for

sale all year but not sold in the depressed postwar market. 'It's a beautiful view,' Ben told them, but no one replied, and he realised it must still be dark or foggy.

Ria yawned and he heard her scratching, then making shivering hand-rubbing noises. Ben got down, impatient with her, his feet crunching on the gravel, and opened the van's rear doors. 'Is this home?' chirped Lola.

'No.'

'Wake up, Mum!'

'I am awake,' Ria said. 'This is what I look like when I'm awake.'

'Eek,' Lola said.

'Shut yer face and help me down.' Ria's London accent stood out here, in the dawn wind beginning to rustle faintly across the high treetops, cockerels crowing from time to time on the invisible farmlands, a dog barking far away in the rural emptiness. Their footsteps crossed noisily to him, then Ria was quiet, and Ben knew she was looking up at him, worried by him, trying to add him up. 'Isn't nobody going to tell me where we are?' she said at last. Charlie had gone into the house.

'Easton Manor!' Lola said. 'Can I play?'

'No, Miss, not likely. Hand me down that suitcase of mine.' Ria was asserting command of arrangements. 'Listen, Ben, that Charlie's all right, ain't he? How long have yer known him?'

'Since I stole control of the Emporium from my first wife,' Ben told her, and moved towards the house. He could feel Ria staring after him.

Charlie tapped down the steps. 'I've had a scout round, everything's in order.' He took Ben's elbow when Ben said nothing. 'The heating's on, a man comes once a day to keep the furnace ticking over.' Inside, Ben felt the warm air on his face, setting the blood pulsing like needles again in his unshaven skin. Their voices echoed, the ornaments must have been removed. There had been a chair by the fireplace and he found it as though he could see it, settled back.

'No phone,' Charlie continued. 'I've brought sheets and blankets, and I'll get the village store to send more food up.'

'Don't do that,' Ben said.

'Sorry. How long do you plan to be here?'

'Long enough.'

'We don't think so much of this here hotel of yours,' complained Ria's voice from the hallway.

Charlie Bookkeeper said quietly: 'Ben, we've been friends for a long time.'

'What do you want?'

'Is there any more I can do?' Charlie could not accept he was no longer needed.

'I don't need friends,' Ben said. 'I don't need anyone.'

'Everyone needs someone,' Ria called from the doorway, where she had moved silently, and been listening. He must remember that: every secret must be hidden inside himself. 'Don't be so angry,' she cajoled him, but Ben shook his head. 'Frightened,' she said. 'Empty.'

Charlie gave an embarrassed cough. 'There is a further private matter . . .' He paused, but there was no sound of Ria politely leaving. 'The funeral must take place.'

Ben had known this must come. 'She's dead. Part of the past.'

Ria crossed to him. 'Don't be so hard,' she whispered, close.

'The Coroner has released the . . . Pearl will be laid to rest on January the third,' came Charlie's voice from by the fireplace. 'It's all arranged, you don't have to do anything . . . but you'll want to go . . .'

Ben was silent.

'You can't run away,' Ria said. She knelt beside him, not touching him, just being there.

## 2

*You.*

There was a vacuum in Victoria's life, yet her busy days with Lisa were so different and strange after her remote-controlled childhood in Switzerland, with meetings to decide, arrangements and letters of condolence to be answered, all the hundred-and-one details of such a loss in the family, that at first she was hardly aware of her loneliness. Mary Hannay, Pearl's sister, was travelling in Turkey with her husband, much older than she, in his seventies, and they could not be contacted. 'She was never close to Pearl anyway,' Lisa said unrepentently, 'not since Pearl met Ben.' There were more lists of names Victoria did not know, a thousand and one tiny social emergencies . . . should the American Ambassador be seated directly behind the family? 'Oh, and we'd better send George's timetable to his Emporium office.' Lisa smiled, trying to get Victoria to snap out of it.

Victoria stared at her hands.

*You.*

The nights at London House were long, the milk and soothing talk Lisa brought her at bedtime did not make her sleep, and after her grandmother tiptoed out – treating her like a child! – Victoria lay sleepless with her brain racing.

*What did he expect of her?*

'Penny for them?' Lisa prompted from the lighted doorway.

'I can't put it into words.'

'Goodnight, lass.'

'Goodnight, Gran.' The light went out.

As his only daughter she'd thought she had known her father as well as anyone, privileged to winkle the small extra tokens of love out of him that no one else could expect, the indulgences that were a daughter's birthright: a clothes allowance, riding lessons, a pony at first and then her horse, Pasha. She remembered the bright look in her father's eyes for her, his pride in her when they rode out together on Rotten Row – she was a natural rider as he was – and him on Sultàn letting her pull ahead to win the race. Who else would he have let beat him, but her? Another small token of his love, she saw now. Now it was too late.

Too independent, too selfish, she had never really known him. 'Less of the whip,' he would call, 'let the horse do the work.' But she was driven by the same blood as he.

Now he was gone she realised how much she missed him, and yearned for his return. She had lost her mother but she still had him. But he did not come back that Sunday, or the next day, or the Tuesday, or even phone, and because of this rejection she began to wonder if he had really loved her, his wilful, difficult, adorable daughter, as much as she had thought.

Her childish rebelliousness had been her mother's fault, she decided. Pearl had gushed all her extrovert transatlantic hopes and dreams into her little girl, and spoilt her, Victoria now realised. She blushed – these were night-thoughts, the worst time – remembering what she had made Mummy put up with and how tolerantly Mummy had put up with it: Victoria learning to do moods and sulks to get whatever she wanted, her winning smile when Mummy gave way as she always did. Her father had never been so easy. If he said no that was the end of it. He gave, but he had never let her take. How she had hated that limit on his love, her feeling that she wanted everything and it was his job to provide it.

But now she was not a child. Her life was her own. She could have whatever she wanted. It was limitless.

But she wanted her father. She wanted him to admire her – to *deserve* his admiration. His girl! She had so much to say to him and affection to show on his return, and they would talk all night and she would learn everything, if only he would come back.

But still he did not come back.

What was he demanding of her?

*You.*

She remembered her own hurt, instinctive reply.

*Do you love me?*

There was no answer to a question that asked so much. Victoria's hand still hurt where he had squeezed her.

At first she had roamed the house searching for him, but London House was an empty fortress without him, not a home – not the home she remembered from her childhood. During the day the front rooms echoed with the work of contract glaziers and plasterers in filthy dungarees, scowling men grateful for a job in these depressed times but hating to work the holidays, even on double overtime. When she intruded into an area where they were busy they downed tools and stared at her. Victoria fled to the small quiet rooms at the back of the house, here finding memories of him everywhere, but they were all dislocated, not part of her. She sat on the sofa in the garden room, looking out on the tennis court, and it was dark before tea-time. She sat in the dark.

If he loved her, he would not leave her alone.

The door opened.

But it was only Lisa. She flicked on the standard-lamp in her forthright way, as economical in her movements as a maid, the tea-tray wedged against her hip, then sat in the armchair opposite the sofa and laid the tray on the low table between them. She opened the pot and stirred the tea, pouring it through the strainer into the cups. The old-fashioned routine was reassuring, familiar from a thousand childish tea-times. But this time Lisa made Victoria pick up her own cup and saucer instead of passing it to her.

'He won't be back,' Lisa said.

But the phone hadn't been ringing, and there was no afternoon post today. 'You can't possibly know that.'

'I know him because I know myself.' Victoria merely drank her tea. 'Lass, I'm his mother,' Lisa said earnestly, but did not reach out.

'He'll come back for me,' Victoria frowned.

'I did not come back for him.' Her baby, the steps of the London Hospital.

So it was true, that story about her deserting him. 'He will,' Victoria said uncertainly. 'The funeral—'

'We won't see him on Friday.'

'He loved her!'

'Your father is a man of feelings. He's not perfect, Victoria.'

Victoria thought for a long time. 'You are making your son out to be something . . . something I know my father is not.'

'Whatever happens in childhood happens for ever,' Lisa's mouth turned downwards bitterly, 'and yet it cannot be recaptured.'

'What does he want?'

Lisa was confident. 'Think of yourself, not of him. Your education.'

This was an older woman talking, and Victoria narrowed her eyes.

'Perhaps even university,' Lisa said, warming to her subject, 'learning to help others. To take your place in society.' But these were themes closest to her own heart.

'I'll make up my own mind,' Victoria said.

At last Lisa put out the light. 'Happy 1947.'

Victoria whispered: 'He *will* be there.'

But he did not return on New Year's Day, as she had secretly hoped, nor on the Thursday. And everything was being done for her, everyone was pushing her around, as though, Victoria slowly realised, there was a competition for control of her. God, he'd thrown her to the wolves! Even down to the maid who brought her morning tea at seven, her breakfast tray at seven-thirty, then required Victoria to choose from the clothes she must wear before her steaming bath was drawn by eight. This smart-sharp grey woman of thrice Victoria's age had her instructions from Lisa and, deferential and adamant, was not to be resisted. Lisa knew all about servants, having been one herself. Lisa had never approved of Pearl's easy-going methods, and Victoria was being taken in hand.

'I really do think you should keep on at the École Madame LaFarge,' Lisa suggested.

'I think not,' Victoria said.

'Don't give up. You'll feel differently in a week or two,' Lisa smiled sympathetically.

'It's up to my father,' Victoria said, dry-eyed and determined. But it wasn't up to her father. It was up to her. *You*. She searched for him inside herself, in her feelings. What did he expect of her?

Lisa looked at her and knew the dam holding back those tears must break at the funeral, and then Victoria would come to her.

Bill Simmonds drove them to the funeral. In the suburb of Finchley, a place Victoria had never been,

the cortège parked beside a gravel drive and everyone got out. It was a cheerless chilly day, overcast
and dank, with a hard wind penetrating Victoria's
black veil like bony fingers. Here at the City of
Westminster's St Marylebone cemetery, which she
had never heard of, the body would be laid to rest.
The new American Ambassador, Max Gardner, was
here. Since the dead woman's American parents,
Lowell and Dizzy Remington, were in poor health
and unable to travel from Boston, the service would
be held not in the Episcopal chapel, as they'd have
insisted, but in the stark Dissenters' chapel.

Victoria searched the faces of the crowd. George,
strutting and choleric, was obediently followed by
Clifford Ford, then David Jones the immaculate
manager of the Emporium and his wife Harriet, with
their polished manners and observing eyes which
seemed constantly to be probing for shop-thieves.
Will was not here, living his strange life at Home
Farm looked after by Helen; travel was an ordeal for
them. At the Christmas party only a few days ago,
Lisa had said in the car, Ben London had been a man
in the prime of his power, surrounded by friends. But
even then, she'd noted, Victoria had not been there,
or Bill Simmonds, or . . . doubtless many more. 'His
toast was to absent friends,' Lisa said sadly, '"To
absent friends."'

This crowd were all acquaintances from outside the
family, strangers. Victoria saw no one who mattered.
Ultimately, she realised, her father's life was a
mystery. He was unknown to her. And he was not
here.

She could not believe he could be so uncaring.
A man of feelings! 'Mummy hated the idea of
being buried under the ground, I don't know why,
it was something she dreaded,' Victoria confessed to
Charlie Bookkeeper while the mourners gathered by
the chapel steps. The wind flapped her veil and he
handed her his handkerchief as though he saw
something in her eyes she didn't feel: tears. 'I'm *not*,'
she said, and he replaced the silk in his top pocket
without offence. Victoria studied the lawyer. His
calm, watchful eyes attracted her, though not his
curiosity, his shy, cloistered mannerisms with their
hint of sharpness. Despite his retreating hair, he
retained an appealing boyishness. But most of all he
looked kind. And suddenly Victoria distrusted kind
men, men who hid behind an intrusive masquerade of
concern, pretending they cared. She didn't like the
way he thought he could see into her. She must use,
not be used.

'My father trusts you,' she ferreted.

'He trusts everyone to be themselves: it's the secret
of his success.' A kind, thoughtful outsider might
believe that. Charlie was flawed but genuine, just the
sort of man her father would use.

'You know where he is.'

Through the doorway she could see the coffin
waiting, lying on a draped tabernacle beyond the
pews, and found herself quite unaffected by its shiny
blank wood. The immediacy of the poor white hand
and wedding ring hanging from beneath the hospital
shroud she would always remember, but she realised
she could cope with this slow dance of ceremony. This

was for the living, not the dead; her mother was not really here any more than her father was. It felt colder inside the chapel than outside and she drew back when Lisa went in, so that her grandmother continued alone up the aisle without realising that Victoria was not with her.

'Well, Mr Bookkeeper?'

'You've known me all your life, Vicky, you might at least call me by my name. I thought we were friends.'

She waited. His kindness was supposed to make her break down. He was a good observer, quiet and cool, and would know her father as well as anyone.

'It was your father's explicit instruction that she be cremated,' Charlie explained, 'her ashes not be buried beneath ground. Do you understand?'

But Victoria seized on the fact, not the emotion. 'Then you admit you do know where he is.'

'Yes.' He continued in his honesty: 'But I am afraid that his whereabouts must remain confidential.'

'Even from me, Charlie?'

'Those are my instructions. Why don't you like me today?'

'So he really won't come. He doesn't care.'

'*Because* he cares, don't you understand?'

'No I don't understand! Oh – oh—'

Suddenly the ridiculous thing was happening that she had dreaded; tears running quite uncontrollably down her burning face. Surely the veil would hide them, but Charlie held out that stupid handkerchief; she scrunched it up in her gloved hand, couldn't speak. *You*. She could feel her lips swelling. More tears. 'I'm stupid,' she muttered, dabbing, 'stupid. You must think I'm a prize fool.'

Charlie stared. For a moment in her grief this self-composed young lady had been utterly beautiful, her mother brought back to life.

After the service it was not Lisa that Victoria cut through the crowd to see, but George.

Charlie Bookkeeper wondered how Ben would take the news that Victoria was joining the Emporium – certainly he would forbid it, perhaps even travel down to sort her out, the only person who could control his headstrong daughter who was in some ways so very like him. The girl had taken advantage of the opportunity to buttonhole George and brow-beaten him, always the weak one of the family, into backing her scheme, a *fait accompli* whereby Victoria would not return to the finishing school Lisa had set her heart on. Lisa's parents had been teachers, their belief in organised education survived in her though their faces were forgotten, and the happiest time of Lisa's life had been the unofficial below-stairs education from Miss Bell, the Lockhart family's governess at Clawfell. Now Victoria wanted to throw it all away. George escaped before Lisa could grab him. 'I blame you for this, Mr Bookkeeper,' Lisa warned him in lieu, 'I'm holding you responsible.'

'Oh, it's just some idea her father put in her head.'

'We'll see about that!' Lisa fumed, determined to broach the matter calmly with the girl, but as soon as she'd got Victoria in the back of the car her voice rose. 'Everyone's worked hard to give you your advantages in life. You're only sixteen and that's too young to know your own mind.'

'You were sixteen and you threw it all away. At least I'm not pregnant.'

'That's an ugly thing to say,' Lisa said weakly, her own directness outclassed by Victoria's arrogance. Lisa played her strongest card. 'You can't Come Out as a debutante if you're a shopgirl, you know.'

But Victoria clung to her decision with almost frightening tenacity.

Lisa went to Charlie Bookkeeper's chambers in Holborn belatedly to enlist his support. 'Surely I have the power to force her—'

'Not without her father's consent.' Charlie was grateful for the bulk of his escritoire desk between them, such was the determination in the old woman's personality.

Lisa sat formally, one arm outstretched in black bombazine to the handle of her umbrella, imperious as any Victorian matriarch. 'But it's for her own good and his wishes are unknown.'

'His wish is plainly that she should stand on her own two feet.'

'She's doing it for all the wrong reasons,' Lisa said miserably, 'she won't find her father at the Emporium.'

'Let her make her own mistakes,' Charlie advised. 'You can't help her.'

'I've seen how much harm that attitude can do.'

'More people do harm trying to do good.'

But Lisa couldn't leave it alone, she sympathised too deeply with Victoria in these trying times, trying not only for their own family: postwar London was a far different and more dangerous place than London before the war, she told herself; take the speed of the traffic alone! And nowadays the men lurking in doorways and alleyways were usually criminals, not the honest poor Lisa remembered from the turn of the century, her own youth. The world changed as it turned and, as the old certainties vanished, only convictions sustained one. Victoria had no experience of life, and Lisa dreaded her loss of innocence. Because she cared about Victoria, Lisa went behind her back. George, she decided, was the key.

'I've made my decision!' George said.

'In haste.' They waited for a break in the Piccadilly traffic which raced by in clouds of fumes and drizzle, George stepping impatiently from the kerb towards imaginary gaps then jumping back as horns, their use legal again, blared. Even waiting he rocked back and forth on his heels, unaware of the impression of hesitancy he gave.

'The more you try and make me change my mind' – he laid down the law as they finally crossed the road, Lisa holding up her hand to stop the traffic – 'the more my mind is made up.' He took her elbow possessively. 'Come on in. See what I've done.'

Lisa looked up at the distinctive blue and gold window-canopies of the London Emporium. 'I'm afraid I've never liked this place.'

George shrugged, kissed her cheek with a sigh for her ridiculousness, and the automatic doors hissed closed behind him. Lisa gazed. Once Hawk the head doorman had intimidated this corner, an imperious presence dominating his little patch of polished flag. What a loathsome man he had been, but the place was poorer without him.

David Jones came out without his overcoat – he'd spied her through the glass. 'I know, it's a bit of a business,' he said as he guided her past the Sausage, Potato and Onion shop with its three silver drums of steaming food to the Lyons tea-house further on, she making no effort to shelter him with her umbrella, 'but George has set his mind on it. He's quite extraordinarily fond of her. Have you seen the look in his eyes?' David laughed: 'And since he does control fifty per cent of the shares – effectively one hundred per cent, while Ben is, ah, recovering his strength – George is the boss! I wish I could help you but I'm only the general manager I'm afraid – I only run the place!' he smiled. Lisa never liked men who apologised for taking orders – it was said his wife Harriet ruled the roost at home – but obviously David didn't want Victoria in 'his' store any more than Lisa did, and she realised he might be a useful ally. 'Awful weather, isn't it?' he said, making conversation like a gentleman. He sat her down, then pulled up a chair and ordered a pot of tea from the nippy, slicking the wet from his hair with the palm of his hand. He still looked like a floorwalker. 'Victoria starts at the end of the month, you know.'

'I know.'

'She'll find the work very hard after the easy life she's been used to.'

'Good,' Lisa said, ignoring the implicit sneer in *easy*.

'And the City and Guilds exams are quite demanding.'

'Make sure of it,' Lisa said.

Over in Holborn, as the week passed, Charlie grew increasingly uncomfortable with himself. Several times he looked behind him on the way to work. Nothing! Though he had denied any responsibility for Victoria's actions, which was legally correct, privately he felt guilty about denying help to Lisa, who was obviously genuinely concerned for the girl's future. Charlie would long remember Victoria bitterly weeping at the funeral, deserted by her father, while he remained loyal as a lapdog to his friend, dutifully repeating, 'I have my instructions', like a stuck record.

*Easton Manor on the Northamptonshire border*. It would have been so easy to let slip out. If Ben felt his life was in danger that was a matter for the police, not this running from reality – and then the responsibility for keeping the secret thrown on Charlie's shoulders. Now that the rare excitement of the secret arrangements and clandestine journey was past, Charlie's oldest friend, worry, returned. It was unreasonable of Ben to demand he bear the burden of secrecy alone. Charlie, the son of a solicitor, had been a solicitor all his adult life, and like the Law, ultimately he believed in reason, that reason ordered human affairs.

But Ben would know Charlie felt this.

Nevertheless, he had given Charlie his impossible instructions.

*If I drive up to Easton*, Charlie thought, *what will I find?*

He wrote a letter, c/o The Occupier, to Easton Manor. He allowed seven days for a reply, then eight. Still it did not come. He realised he was no longer in contact with Ben London.

*My father trusts you.*

*No*, Charlie had replied. *He trusts people to be themselves.*

Ben knew what Charlie would do.

So Charlie did it. After several days busy in court on other matters, on Saturday he forsook his usual routine at the Hammam Turkish Baths, instead packed his wife and her mother who was visiting into the Wolseley to make the most of the petrol ration, and drove up to Northamptonshire. 'A day in the country, it's very nice of you, dear,' they said, shivering in their furs despite the heater, wondering what had got into him, 'but where are we *going*?'

'Easton Manor,' he told them briefly. The two women eyed one another significantly. Their Charles rarely used two words where ten would do.

He found the place at once this time. The gates were closed beneath a sky growing heavy and dark with snow, making the house seem very pale behind its nets of bare black trees. He left the car with the engine running for the sake of his mother-in-law's rheumatism, and went down the drive alone.

'Ben? Ben London? Are you here?'

When there was no answer he blew on his fingers and used his key. His posted envelope, c/o The Occupier, was lying untouched on the doormat. So Ben did not know that Victoria's decision was to join the Emporium, did not wish to know. Beside the envelope lay the key that Ben had used to lock the door for the last time. It had been pushed back through the letterbox.

Charlie began to laugh. Ben's departure from Easton Manor had made him safe. Charlie could not betray what he did not know.

Ben London had disappeared even from his last friend, and taken Ria and Lola with him, God knew where.

# Chapter Four

## 1

'I wouldn't have come,' Ria groaned, 'if I'd known life with you was going to be this crummy.' It was the Monday after the arrival of Charlie's legal envelope, the 20th, cold as hell, and Ria couldn't see a single person in sight beyond Ben. He was standing at the roadside like a statue, Lola doing slides past him on the icy tarmac, holding her doll for her, surrounded by the terrible silence Ria endured here, miles from anywhere, only the hiss of Lola wearing out her shoes.

It had been a choice between the devil or the deep blue sea, but it was growing on her that she'd made a dreadful mistake in coming along with Ben. He wasn't at all as she'd imagined him, fighting back, needing her whether he admitted it or not. A bit of style, fighting spirit. But no, he'd changed, he didn't appreciate her like in the old days, didn't treat her like she was special any more. And because *he* didn't feel she was special, *she* didn't. She had to face it, her youth was gone. *Wotcher Ria*: Stanley Kirschbaum's reedy voice, the limelights flaring, the roar of

applause, electricity filling her body, '*May I preesent –*
*Star of the Stage, Shooting-Star of our very own*
*Queen's Music Hall – Ria Price!*' Seventeen, eighteen
years old. Shc had already won and lost Ben London,
his bastard son Will gurgling back home in the crib at
Havannah Street. Oh, the magic of those years.
Youth. And she had thrown them both away. She had
had youth to burn, and now both were lost.

Now they were just like a divorced couple thrown
together again by circumstances, the fires gone cold,
the closeness they had once shared now standing
between them like a wall. He would have been better
off with a nurse.

But he had chosen Ria.

She'd failed him already. No one, least of all her,
could live up to a widower's picture of a woman. She
had failed to take command of the running of Easton
Manor, her big opportunity, as he must have
expected of her. Panicking, she'd just been bossy.
How little he knew of her, the real Ria! She never had
been the genius at housekeeping ordinary women
were supposed to be, she never hoovered in permed
hair and lipstick, like those arch ladies in the domestic
economy films shown at the Glengall Picture Theatre
by the women's clubs or in the advertisements, and
Lily who'd gone on from the Queen's to work for Max
Factor had told Ria the lipstick was actually brown
because it filmed better. Brown-lipped women speaking like duchesses telling her what to do! But how
Esther had lapped it up; she *wanted* to believe in
them. Order. Happiness. Family. Growing old
gracefully.

'That's the only pair of shoes you got!' Ria wailed, and Lola stopped dead.

Ria couldn't hold back an attack of the sniffles: poor houseproud Mum, her little home seemed so far away now on the Isle of Dogs. Warm memories flooded through Ria, Esther trying so hard to be what was expected of her. She'd been first in the road with a Hoover, chucking out the reliable old popping, bubbling gas-copper for the mechanical hot-tub Vic had got her in the thirties when such things were the rage. The sight of the shuddering tub mashing soapsuds and soiled smalls did not fill Ria with joy as the advertisements promised, but rather with a feeling of being exploited, because the bloody things didn't really make any more time, and you couldn't just stop and put your elbows on the table for a friendly chinwag what with all that metallic racket and thumping, not the way you could with a quiet, sociable washboard and mangle by a fireclay Belfast sink. Not that Ria had any woman friends, except Esther at home. That word again.

Ria slept late. She couldn't even get Ben his morning tea on time, or get the bacon to fry crisp for his breakfast, or make him smile. She'd lost the battle. Now they were moving on and Ria felt as useful to Ben as an extra leg.

Lola tugged Ben's cuff. 'Mummy's crying again.'

He didn't offer his handkerchief or anything, or even turn. 'I know.'

'Bloody sympathy,' Ria sniffled, 'just what I wanted.'

'She's really crying, Daddy.'

'I'm not,' Ria muttered. 'I'm bloody angry with myself, that's what.'

He moved his head as though looking down at the little girl, then handed back her doll. 'She's cold, that's all.' It wasn't all and he must know it. She wondered what he was really thinking.

She fell silent, tried to buck herself up. Well, everything had its funny side, didn't it! What a priceless collection the three of them must make thumbing this lift, Ria decided, no wonder no one was stopping for them: a defeated-looking tearful woman in a borrowed overcoat too small for her, the girl in white woollen leggings and an overcoat three sizes too big, and the Invisible Man complete with dark glasses.

'Take those bloody glasses off,' she said.

Ben cocked his head, hearing the engine before any of them, but he didn't put out his thumb. 'It's a car.' Cars didn't slow on the gentle hill. She watched the red tail-lights pass, the only flash of colour, then they shrank below the skyline and everything was grey and black again. Like life with her. They were moving on from Easton Manor because Ria had failed there.

'We're moving because Vic knows of Easton Manor.' Ben spoke as if he'd read her thoughts. 'He knows you, Ria. He knows Will convalesced there during the war. He'll remember you visited him there with Lola. She's cold,' he repeated, then swept Lola effortlessly up and hugged her, dwarfing the child, closer to her than to Ria. It was he who'd thought to find her those leggings. And the too-large overcoat, only Lola's fingertips peeping out of the enormous

arms, was at least warm. Ben got the things that really
mattered right, but he let the rest go. That included
Ria, obviously, she was just tagging along. Lola was
different.

She watched bitterly the growing affinity between
them, Lola's smiling face resting on Ben's shoulder,
the man who had become a stranger to Ria in her
despair: her child squealing with joy as he swung her
round, Lola's hair flying down his back, her eyes
tight-closed in ecstasy. She'd found her father. And
Ria watched helplessly, hating herself; she'd almost
run out of places to hide from herself in this dreadful
landscape bereft of life or warmth. She was so far
from home, from London, everyone she knew and
loved. The warren of passageways and secret entrances where she spent her own childhood, where
everything had been possible. Where she'd met *him*.
They'd been in love and that had explained him. She
hadn't been afraid. Now he was a stranger again. Just
the two figures twirling at the roadside, going
nowhere. 'Ben!'

He stopped and Lola looked round.

Ria's heart almost burst with her secret. *She is not
your daughter*.

Ben put Lola down and, disorientated, walked
blithely into the road, but Lola grabbed his pocket
and turned him towards Ria.

'Yes?' he called.

'Nothing,' she said provocatively, her heart thudding, 'if you don't know I can't tell you.'

'Nothing's nothing with you, Ria.' But his voice
was flat. The old magic between them was gone. He

still needed her but only like he needed a house-keeper, to cook, clean, sew buttons, but once they had been almost husband and wife, when they were young. She wanted him to tear the confession out of her so that she could weep, truly weep. Not this desolation inside as well as out. She couldn't see his eyes.

'Promise me we're going somewhere,' Ria compromised. 'That's all. Be kind to us.'

But he refused. 'You knew me better than that,' he said with contempt. 'I don't know what the future holds.'

'At least promise to Lola, if you don't care about me.'

'Stop playing, Ria.'

'You're just running away,' she jeered. But she took a step towards him.

'You know that's not true.'

'I don't know you. I'm sorry.'

'Not running *from*.' He shook his head as though she'd been born yesterday. 'Running *to*.'

Ria was so cold, so cold through with his gall, that she had to laugh or cry. In the end she laughed. 'I'm still here.'

'We're sticking together!' Lola did a silly child's dance on the ice, swinging the coat's huge arms, drawing attention to herself.

'You mind you don't fall over,' Ria warned. She brushed a piece of fluff from Ben's lapel. 'The two of you are as bad as each other. I thought we were going to stay at that place a little longer, that's all.'

'Easton Manor wasn't home.'

'Is that what you're searching for, Ben?'

He didn't reply.

'London's your home,' she said.

'It's where I was born. Not where I come from.'

They stood in the silence. God, he was keeping her at a distance!

'I used to dream of life with you,' Ria whispered. 'The real you. I don't care if you're just using me. But don't be disappointed in me. I'm not her, Ben. I wish I was, if that would make you happy. Just accept me as I am.' She had to spoil it. 'That's not much, after all!'

He spoke in a low husky voice. 'I've never forgotten you. Even when I was married to Pearl.'

Ria never could leave well enough alone. 'Is that why you hate me now? Because I'm alive?'

'Men are always afraid of women.'

Not running from. Running to, he'd said.

'I'm with you,' she murmured, but she wasn't sure if he'd heard: Lola was shouting.

'Look! Look, there's a tractor coming. Do you think he'll let us ride on the trailer?'

'Ask the Invisible Man,' Ria snorted.

Still she didn't understand him, thought Ria as she clutched the shuddering, jolting nearside of the farm-trailer, the fumes from the Ferguson tractor blowing back over them in stinking blue clouds, watching Ben London impassively seated on a bale of straw with Lola rocking merrily beside him. The workhouse bastard was still enigmatic, hiding himself from her, but Ria quite liked that. His dark glasses were in her pocket, and she regarded him with a certain proprietorial pride. Only a small victory, but her first. 'Told you,' she swanked, 'at least you look a bit more human now.'

The farmer had stopped without speaking. Not attempting to compete with the clattering Ferguson, he merely gazed at Ben then nodded and jerked his thumb at the empty trailer behind him. 'He'll be buying store cattle at Stamford market,' Ben had said. One of the cuts by his mouth had grown infected, a purple scar visible even through his beard.

'You've got it all planned,' she flattered him.

'Have I?' She realised how sad he was, though his face didn't move a muscle.

He added, 'It's market day. We'll pick up another ride there . . .'

'What's the matter?' she said.

'Ria, what do my eyes look like?'

'Oh, Ben!' She crossed unsteadily to him. 'You look fine, you really do.' She didn't know how to touch him; gripped his shoulder. 'You could have asked any time.'

'Yes, of course. Are they white?'

'Blue.'

'The same blue?'

'As always,' she lied.

'I feel I am the same man,' he said. 'That's the worst thing.' Lola held his hand. Ria returned to her seat on the tarpaulin.

The hauliers' strike had been settled, the soldiers were returned to barracks, and with the backlog of trade the market looked chaotic: lorries and trailers unloading and loading braying, bleating, obdurate animals by the stockpens. 'Try and find us a lorry,' Ben said, but Ria had had it up to here with livestock and led Ben among the tacky market stalls, Lola hanging on to the hem of his coat, her eyes enormous to see the piles of vegetables. Half of them she didn't know the names for in these out-of-town accents, Brussels, kale, caulies: Ria was strictly a bangers-and-mash mum. Ben picked out the babble of dour talk around them. 'Everyone reckons there's cold weather coming, they've lifted everything they can from the ground before it locks solid.' He followed one voice, broadest Lincolnshire yellowbelly and the smell of earth, a spud farmer who'd brought in everything out of the clamp his ex-army three-tonner could carry. 'Take you where?'

'North,' Ben said, 'just north.'

They travelled twenty miles that day, sitting three across in the unheated cab, Lola on Ria's lap shifting over with every gear-change: and so their strange journey continued. *But your home isn't in the north*, Ria almost whispered, then said nothing. The farmer's wife gave them plates of fried eggs for supper, a meal worth it just for the expression on Lola's face, who had never seen more than one fresh egg at a time before, great doorsteps of sawn bread, yellow home-churned butter, honey that Lola didn't know what it was, never having had honey before.

Of course everyone thought they were husband, wife and daughter, a charade impossible for them-selves to believe with Ben sleeping on the floor, that emotional wall between them like separate rooms. There was no sign of affection for Ria, or admission that he needed her. She dabbed disinfectant on his face, combing his hair, the silliest little things he couldn't do for himself. It was a humiliation, she knew, for such a man as he had been, and she didn't expect gratitude. She was patient, let him lead.

And still he led them onward, moving on each day with a different name, a journey into anonymity, but Ria was faithful. She didn't ask where they were going, if they were going anywhere, being with him, keeping faith. Ten miles next day, then none at all on Wednesday because of the sleet. Five long miles tramping lanes to the next village, Ria already forgot what it was called, then a long ride with a commercial traveller almost fifty miles up the Great North Road, and being dropped off at a roadside smallholding.

And all the time Ben's depression was growing worse. 'I can't see,' he shouted in his sleep, then she heard him sit up. 'God help me,' whispered his voice, 'I can't see. Are you here?' She reached out into the dark, but the child stirred swiftly beside her, floorboards creaked, and she knew Lola was already holding his hand. She had become very devoted to her Daddy and Ria was all too conscious of how poorly knitted were the clothes she had made for the doll.

Next day was Saturday, and the first snowstorm began, white misery.

A long way to the south, Vic watched the Wolseley do a three-point turn at the gates to Easton Manor, pluming steam from the exhaust because the engine had been left idling so long, the two women had been going soundlessly chatter-chatter behind the glass, never thinking of Vic standing behind the car, never turning round or looking in the mirror, and Vic just standing there, waiting. Then jaunty footsteps sounded on the gravel and from the shadows Vic watched the foolish solicitor return, smiling, shaking his head, empty-handed. So Vic did not seize him. The fool let the gates clang cheerfully closed, got in the car, said something to the women and laughed. Vic watched the car drive away, then went back to his Daimler parked behind the bushes of a gamekeeper's track, and drove to the gates of Easton Manor.

Ben London was no longer here.

But he had been here. Vic could feel it in the cold iron. He pushed the gates wide then drove in.

The sky was so dark with snow that the house, despite its dark, ivy-clad walls, looked pale. Ivy-clad, that was nice. And nice leaded windows too. Vic peered through the letterbox; a dark hallway, stairs with plain Wilton carpet that would show every mark. Vic had a key in his pocket that would open anything. He went inside, let the door click softly shut behind him.

'Ria?'

She'd been here, he could smell her, her cheap perfume, smell her clothes, found a strand of her blonde hair on the antimacassar of an armchair in the living-room. So she had sat to the right of the fire, that had been her place. And Ben London on the left. Close enough for their feet to touch.

Vic clenched his hands in his pockets. He had no key to unlock Ben London; even blind the man was a mystery to him, a man of feelings like himself. A man of instinct, and the only man Vic feared.

The shiv came out of Vic's pocket, the blade glittering between his fingers in the leaden light. Ben London was gone from here as if he had never been, left no mark as if this place had meant nothing to him. But that single blonde strand of Ria's gave him away, and the cheap, potent, unforgettable perfume of her. Vic touched the white lace antimacassar with the tip of his bladed hand. The velvet chairback opened effortlessly, spilling its horsehair insides on to the seat. The vases on the mantelshelf. He knocked them with his left hand one at a time, smashing them before they fell.

Broken, the pottery lay among the cold ashes of the fire, and he kicked it with his shoes. He crossed to the table in the window-bay and broke it, then stopped.

Outside, it was snowing.

Vic hated being alone.

He pulled down the curtains in a heap, then went through to the kitchen trailing footsteps of grey ash. Ria hadn't even bothered to do the washing-up of course, the sink was full of plates still smeared with meat-grease and dried-on mashed potato, bits of reconstituted egg, luridly yellow, a burned-on and boiled-over milk saucepan, a heavy iron frying-pan, blackened, which he picked up and clouted on to the miserable collection, once, then twice more. Then he brought it down as hard as he could, shattering the Belfast sink. The plug swung pointlessly from its chain down the denuded wall.

150

He dropped the frying pan and turned slowly.

On the table remained a half-eaten bowl of porridge, a teaspoon still in it, and the chairseat padded up with a thick cushion, the sort of thing a mother did for her child in a strange house.

Vic called softly, 'Lola?'

He picked up the teaspoon, still smeared from her lips, and put it in his pocket, then went upstairs. How loud his footsteps sounded. He stopped, and even his breathing seemed loud. He waited until he was in control of himself, staring up at the bedroom door at the top of the stairs, just staring, then started up again.

He looked around the vacant bedroom.

'What lies have you told them, Ria?' he called.

Vic lay down on the bed, just lay there without a sound, his shoes all covered with ash.

Ria was the guilty one, not he.

Somewhere during the white misery of the snow-storm, which had reached them earlier in the day since it came from the north, Ben and Ria realised that Lola's doll was missing. The smallholder's daughter had been Lola's age, and they'd gone too far to turn round and steal it back, though Lola didn't seem to mind. She was growing up quickly. When Ben lost his wallet, it was she who found it in the snow. Her eyes followed him everywhere, and Ria didn't want her to grow to trust a man too much. She sat between them at the supper-table while the snow whirled like moths outside the black kitchen window, making sure they were early to bed while Ben stayed up and the old farmer bemoaned the fate of his sheep in this weather. They were well out of cattle country now. On Sunday they struggled only the long, long mile through the featureless, snow-covered terrain as far as the next village, Bawtry, and put up in desperation at the crossroads pub. 'Aye, and what's thy name?'

Ben said, 'Trott.' It was Ria's married name.

That night she whispered: 'Aren't we free?'

There were two single beds in this room, and the fire guttered on its last ounce of coal.

He turned over away from her. It seemed to take hours for the fire to go out.

And so they went on, Ria letting him lead them. She had guessed his quest was leading them nowhere, but she was wrong. The very next day they turned away from their old friend, the Great North Road, which had carried them so far, and struck off into the wilderness of lesser roads. Roadsigns and the names of villages, taken down and stored in council depots during the war to confuse German parachute troops, had not been restored in these very rural areas, or been lost, or perhaps these communities had always been nameless except to the people who knew them. Every crossroads was bare, each nameless village tightly huddled in its dale, the only signs were on the A-road winding through these hills: Manchester. And so they followed Manchester, picking up secondhand clothes and cast-offs along the way: a yellow woolly bobble-hat for Lola to go with her yellow scarf, their thick woollen socks a sudden gift, plucked from the chest of drawers in the untouched bedroom by a farmer's wife whose sons had been lost on the convoys, a pair of discarded seaboots, old farmyard wellies for Ria that came up over her knees and her feet were warm at last. 'I'm never going to take these socks off!' she laughed, but Ben did not respond. 'We look a right pair of down-and-outs,' she said to the mirror.

By nationalised Great Central railway from Manchester Piccadilly, they could be home in a couple of hours. That close, that impossibly far. Because never once had Ben doubted she was loyal to him, never once had he turned without being certain she was there, never once as he spoke into the darkness that surrounded him had he doubted that she was listening.

The wind blew from the west and they tasted the sour coal-smoke of the great industrial conurbation ahead of them, its dull mist drifting in the sky.

'Is that the place?'

'No,' he said, 'we'll go north again.' Ria looked up the wall of white hills in that direction and shivered. Someone had to tell him the truth.

'Where do you think you're leading us, Ben? Because I'm not sure if we can go there, you know?'

He didn't reply. Lola played in the snow, swinging around the bus stop on her arms. Beside the road chuckled a black stream like a single thread in the white desolation.

'Ben, what do you think is around us?' Ria asked gently. 'What do you think you would see?'

'It's early morning,' he said suddenly. 'No, it's dawn. There's a stream, Blane Ghyll, falling past us into an immense green . . . England. A river in the

153

distance, silver under the low sun. Beyond it no end to how far we can see. No end.' He closed his mouth with a snap. 'For me.'

Ria sighed. He knew her so well. 'All right, I won't go running home,' she said. 'I've said I'm with you and I am. You're stuck with me.'

'Both of you,' Ben said.

'Our family,' said Lola, but Ria turned on her furiously, telling her to stop it with her swinging on the bus stop, it was driving her crazy.

'And look at your gloves, you must be deliberately trying to ruin them or what, and oh for Chrissake, my girl, if you've got to wear that stupid bobble-hat why can't you wear it straight . . .' Her tirade died away.

'I can hear the bus!' Ben said, and it was him Lola ran to, not Ria, though Ria held her hand out.

Ben called up in the direction of the driver, 'Are you for Blane?'

'Ask the weather, it were twenty below last night.'

The bus drew up by the deserted Methodist chapel in Blane before dark, and they got down to find a closely cupped village of black stone terrace houses, some whole streets shut up except for a solitary light or two since the Rownslee mills were closed, those enormous black structures dominating the workers' dwellings huddled beneath the white moor. The gritstone walls of the factories had been built for eternity but their roofs already yawned open to the sky. The ghyll that had powered their clanking looms and whizzing shuttles now hissed unimpeded by waterwheels down the culverts beside the main street. So quickly had the money come and gone, but the hills remained. Ice hills beneath a sky full of snow.

It was a hard land.

They stayed at the inn by the school, then set out on foot through the snow that had fallen overnight, climbing beside the Blane Ghyll, soon beyond the net of black drystone walls that the village had thrown out around it. The fresh snow was soft and exhausting to walk through, but Lola followed, jumping playfully in Ben's footsteps. Though now the air was still so that their voices echoed, the windswept hillsides around them were covered in frozen heather like tightly knotted white hair. 'I don't like these ditches,' Ria complained.

'Groughs. Not ditches, they're called groughs.'

'Who told you that?'

'Lisa.'

'Oh my God,' Ria said. 'It's the place you come from!' She ran after the two figures, Lola now leading Ben through the snow. 'Clawfell?'

He pointed up at the white moor. 'Clawfell. My father was Charles Lockhart, eleventh Lord Cleremont of Clere Mount, Blane and Clawfell. And my mother was his parlourmaid.'

'But I thought that place was derelict years ago,' Ria said.

'The past never dies,' he flung back over his shoulder.

As they climbed, the ghyll ran under the ice, muttering at first, then silence enclosed them as it froze on these northern slopes, the moor grey like a breaking wave above them. As the skyline dropped away Ria caught them up, and gasped at what she saw below them.

'Tell me what you see,' Ben said.

But it was Lola who replied, 'It's beautiful.'

And so Lola came to Clawfell Grange.

'Grange means farm,' Ben said, 'this was once a working, fertile bowl in the hills. Fertile compared to the hills. Sheltered, compared to the hills.'

'But it's *beautiful*,' Lola said, and Ben frowned as she spoke, as if he had not understood her. Clawfell Grange had never been beautiful.

'It looks like it's made of ice.' Ria was chilled. Lola knew that Mum was going to stand there in the snow complaining about the cold, drawing attention to herself, which was what she did when she was exhausted and worried. Just like Grandma in that, Lola realised suddenly. 'I'm never going to be warm again as long as I live . . .'

'Mum, it's got frozen ponds and rockets!'

'Turrets,' said both the adults together.

They followed the path outlined by giant humps of snow, boulders laid by Victorian labourers working only with block and tackle, horse and cart and shovel, as markers indicating the line of the holloway in winter. 'Robbie Lockhart was granted these Crown lands when he was ennobled as the first Lord Cleremont,' Ben told them. 'The grange was never a farm again, that business was carried on at the Home Farm. The business of Clawfell Grange was to be a great house. The great house of a great family. And so it became.'

'It *is* beautiful,' whispered Lola, 'I want to play!'

'Hold hands!' Ria ordered. 'You stick with me, girl.'

No smoke rose from the chimneys. No lights burned in the turrets, and the windows were as blank as ice. The thought of Ben's mother Lisa being dragged here when the place was inhabited and powerful, forced to work her fingers to the bone for these aristocrats when she was a child probably not much older than Lola, filled Ria's heart with bleak despair. 'Let's turn round, Ben.' She stopped. 'Let's go home.'

'This is my home. This is where I come from, and now I've come back.'

'Once I dreamed of places like this,' Ria sighed. 'Now I'd settle for warm feet and a cup of cha.' But Lola slipped from her hand and ran beneath the walls, playing whatever games children pretended, her shrill cries squeaking to the enormous silence where the adults stood.

'That's the first time I've heard her play in two weeks,' Ben murmured.

'Oh, stop it. All right, here we are! But I'd be happier if I knew your real reason for coming here. It isn't just because Vic can't find you here, you're not that sort of bloke. Ben, is it because of *me*? Do you feel anything at all for me or am I just a pair of washing hands?' She let the silence between them drag out. 'No, I knew you wouldn't answer that one.' Nothing showed in his featureless gaze. 'What are you thinking, Ben? What goes on in that head of yours?' she demanded. 'You're still a mystery to me, though I suppose I wouldn't have it any other way.'

'But you are a mystery to me, Ria.'

To her it was an extraordinary thing. She stared at

him. Everything about her was gone, her dignity, her hair unwashed, greasy old-gold curls half over her face. She probably smelt like an old dog, too, at least she imagined she did, yet he could still come out with something magical like that. She kissed his cheek. 'There,' she said.

'Splonker!' shouted Lola. 'Wheeee!'

'That was for free.' Ria sniffed the air. 'No smoke, no fumes. No danger of traffic on the streets, and I bet it doesn't even have a phone or a wireless. The natural life. What are you doing to me, Ben?' She tugged him along. 'Come on, Lola, we'll freeze if we stay out here! There's more snow in that sky if I ever saw it.'

'Lola, what do you see?' he called.

The little girl's reply was joyous, free of care. 'A place where I can play! Look at me!' She skidded towards them.

'Hold on,' Ben said, 'we must be near the steps.' Walking backwards with a child's ease, Lola led him up the smooth slope of snow which hid the ten steps, and they found themselves in the hollow space of a porte-cochère, free of snow but bearded with grey ice. 'Here's where the carriages drew up.'

'There's words carved into the stone above the doors.' Lola squinted. The words were difficult.

'Except the Lord buildeth the house,' Ria read aloud, 'they labour in vain that build it.'

'It cost George Lockhart a hundred and fifteen thousand pounds to build this a century and a half ago,' grunted Ben.

'It's a real English castle!' Nothing could dampen

Lola's enthusiasm, her conviction that everything that happened to her was an adventure. 'It's like in the picture books, but smaller.'

'It's a fake castle. James Wyatt Gothic. Everything about it is a fake.'

'Don't say that.' She hugged his hand. 'If only you could see it.'

'A window for each day of the year. They wouldn't resist cannon-shot for an instant. It's a folly, a gigantic folly. The turrets are to hide water-tanks, the battlements don't have anything behind them. The barbican is just stone facing. A shell, that's all.' His voice was so unhappy that Ria was determined to like the place. She understood hiding.

Entering it was like disturbing a tomb. Ben leaned his shoulder against the studded double doors – just who had the family thought they were keeping out? Though he had used the key first Ben still felt he was breaking in, the frost and congealed ice splintering loudly as it gave way. Suddenly he pushed with all his strength and with a bang the door grated open on the tiled floor.

Snowflakes wandered after them into the motion-less gloom. Lola said, 'It's such a sad place, really.' The girl and her mother found themselves pushing aside the shadows, the shutters all closed, the furniture not covered by dust-sheets but let go to ruin by Charles, Ben's father, who had died rejected by his son. 'But now I know I hardly knew my father,' Ben said. 'He died just before the war . . . there was more to Charles Lockhart than I knew how to look for.'

He stood in about the centre of the reception hall, trying to remember it as it had been, to imagine how it looked now. He envisaged the stairs, smelling of damp, in front of him with the portraits rising up one curving wall, probably all dark with dust by now. Charles had always hated this place, his own father's love for these bare bleak Yorkshire hills had taken precedence over everything, even Charles. The boy grew up here almost a prisoner, the privileged prisoner of his father's love: even his unhappy marriage to the wealthy Lady Henrietta Rownslee had been arranged to pay for his father's obsession. When in due course he inherited Clawfell it was Charles's pleasure to let it fall into this decay. With Roland, his only legitimate son, dead in Africa it had been Charles's revenge on his ancient family to deny love, to be the last of his line. Revenge was a dish best eaten cold. He even denied that he loved Lisa, then weakened in the last few moments of his tormented, wasted life, confessing the truth of his feelings for her in her arms; too late, but he did not die alone or unmourned.

His portrait, an aristocrat's clear, invulnerable gaze from a simple gilt frame, would be staring from the stairs in front of Ben, but all Ben saw was darkness and pain.

In the next room Ria tried to wipe the grime from a table with her fingertips, but everything was frozen hard as iron, even the cushions. The whole interior of the house was fixed solid by frost. They couldn't live here, but how could she persuade Ben of that? Through the gloom their breaths hung in puffs of

160

curling vapour, crystallising to make more ice on the furniture. 'Watch you don't get lost,' Ria warned as Lola played.

'I won't!' She pulled on a rope by the fireplace and a bell rang distantly. Ria suddenly felt a ghost might come, responding to her summons.

She turned back. 'When was the last time you was here, Ben?' she called.

She found him at the foot of the staircase. 'The twenty-first of October, 1925.'

'Sorry I asked,' grumbled Ria. 'Why should you remember the exact date? Who were you with?' She clapped her hand to her mouth. 'Me and my big—'

'We watched the shooting stars, orionids, Pearl and I. Clawfell Grange was going to seed even then. Lisa came back here briefly during the war, I believe. Memory lane, the place she had once washed, scrubbed, knew every niche probably. It's a warren of backstairs and corridors used only by servants. This place probably had thirty staff, neither seen nor heard.'

'Lola!' Ria called. 'What are we going to do here, Ben? Burn all this rubbish to keep warm?' She gripped his hand nervously. 'Where's that girl got to?'

'There's some stairs going down over here,' he said.

'No there aren't.' Then, to her delight, Ria saw the door in the panelling, not hidden but discreet, for the use of staff no doubt, so what Ben said must be true: *neither seen nor heard.* A warren of servants. 'Come on,' she said, leading him down the steps descending steeply inside the wall, and they came out in a large whitewashed room, its ceiling curved to support the great weight of the house above.

'Ben, it's a kitchen! There's fireclay sinks and copper pots and pans, and doorways without doors, and nooks and crannies everywhere.' She sniffed. 'Looks in better nick than upstairs, the painted brick's not flaking yet, and the stone floor don't smell. We must be below ground or something, the ceiling's ever so high and there's only little curved windows right at the top.'

'So the kitchen girls couldn't look out and be distracted.'

'What by?'

'Oh, stableboys, I expect. Passionate thoughts.'

'It's too cold for passionate thoughts,' Ria said with a sly glance.

Scampering footsteps came round the central fireplace that obscured most of the next room from Ria, then Lola's face appeared red with excitement. 'Look what I've found!' she beckoned.

Ria went through. For a moment she couldn't speak. She saw an iron cooking range and a scrubbed oak table, and on the table was piled a collection of packages carefully wrapped in greaseproof paper. Ria unwrapped a few with shaking fingers. Bacon. A roundel of cheese. Beside them on the table were stacked cans of corned beef, a jar of sweets, Libby's powdered milk, and in a paper bag she found a dozen brown eggs with feathers still sticking to their shells. There was a five-pound tin of Lipton's tea with a picture of a yacht on it. Carefully wrapped in newspaper, freshly dug carrots lay like orange fingers. Brussels sprouts, potatoes in folded sacking. Omo, bleach, a long bar of red carbolic soap ready to be cut up into chunks and a knife to do it with, the knife point jammed through a folded piece of paper into the soap.

'Do you know what's here, Ben?'

'Through the doorway beneath the bell-registers you'll see a carpeted corridor.' Ria nodded, finding it. 'Along there is the old living quarters for the butler and his family,' Ben said. 'Two bedrooms, a comfortable parlour, a view of the porte-cochère for advance warning of arrivals and to keep tabs on the stable-block. His name was Crane, I believe. He died in London, thirty or forty years ago.'

'You're saying those rooms are ready for us?'

'Look if you don't believe me.'

'Tell me what I see on the table.'

'Bacon, cheese, tea, everything you need.'

Ria shook her head. 'How did you do it?'

'The hospital phone.' But Ria had seen no telephone wires leading to this house, nor any sign of someone living here. 'Blane Post Office sent the telegraph boy to the Home Farm,' Ben said gently. 'Can you see a note in familiar handwriting?'

Ria pulled the knife out of the soap, unfolded the piece of paper with shaking fingers. *Love, Will.*

'My son is here!' Ria cried.

'Our son,' said Ben, taking Lola's hand gently in his fist, 'and our daughter.'

## 2

London. The deserted metropolis, only the smoke moving. Piccadilly frozen like an old-fashioned

Christmas scene between the dark façades of Burlington House and the hotels, even an old horse-drawn dray turning out of Bond Street to make the picture complete, bumping over the banks of shovelled ice from earlier storms, then towing wheel-ruts down the virgin snow towards Piccadilly Circus. The silence was amazing, only the creaking of the axles and the wheezing of the old horse carrying to Victoria's ears, then the hunched-up driver pulling down his muffler and leaning out over the cartwheel, blowing his nose loudly into the snow before slowly hunching back between muffler and cap. Victoria stood on the corner of St James's Street with her vivid blue eyes following the dray into the distance, her attention caught because it was the only thing moving under the smoke, not a car or a cab or a bus in sight. A horse-drawn dray in the centre of London!

Monday 3 February, her first day at work, a month exactly since her mother's funeral. And the more they tried to change her mind, saying she couldn't join the Emporium, the more they stiffened her determination. Victoria could do what her father had done.

She caught a glimpse of herself in a window: that blue. She'd inherited his colour, everyone said so, and the short cold walk from the Mall had burnished her cheeks to a fine glow. She wore a dark blue cape like a nurse's, then under her prussian-blue cap she had clipped back her blonde hair – that colour inherited from her mother's side, surely – and with her strong bone structure she knew that she looked, not severe or powerful – she was too young – but certainly businesslike. Like father, she told herself, like daughter.

Her father started his job in Leibig's Emporium at twenty years of age by the simple expedient of marrying Leibig's daughter Vane, who died just before Victoria was born. She couldn't believe Ben London was a man who had ever really loved his first wife, that would be much too convenient. Old Leibig passed on within a year of the marriage, luckily, but luck was the art every millionaire cultivated: in no time at all Ben renamed the drab, moribund store London Emporium, leapfrogged his trusted David Jones over every opposition to the position of general manager, plunged the place willy-nilly downmarket in a succession of mass-appeal sales and wide-access promotions, and excepting only the Depression years the business had made money hand over fist ever since. Where Ben had been unlucky was in his children.

Even she must have been a disappointment to him, Victoria admitted loyally as she crossed Piccadilly towards the gleaming canopies of the Emporium, the pavements outside swept clear of snow even this early. Dearly though Victoria had grown up adoring her elder half-brother, she was certain Ralph's refusal to work at the Emporium had broken his father's heart; whereas George, the survivor, could not now be kept out. Victoria wondered if she was taking Ralph's place. Was that what her father had meant by '*You*'?

He had no other legitimate heirs apart from her and

George, no one who meant anything to him compared to his family. There was talk of some bastard child in France. And of course there was Will, badly injured in the war, a sad memory from his father's very early life on the Isle of Dogs, whose selfish mother – Ria? – couldn't be bothered to look after him because of her singing career, and so had lost him to Ben, not a man to stand by idly. Poor Ria, never even allowed into London House to see her son. Victoria remembered the strange boy coming and going during her childhood, a gentle undriven lad attending the Slade School of Fine Art without inspiration, the children – including Will himself – well aware he was never part of the family, whatever Daddy wanted. Only Victoria and George carried the London name.

George who now, since he held exactly half the voting shares, was her employer.

She looked round as people appeared on the street, suddenly streaming like black ants from the Green Park Underground. She could hear their buzzing, formless chatter; they seemed so full of life – their red lips twinkling, women putting back their hair and borrowing pins, coats of every colour, the youngsters elbowing one another to make each other slip, pulling each other's scarves, hurrying on: the Tube had been delayed, apparently. Swearing at one another, pushing snow under collars, giggling, scurrying. The men who could afford the luxury wore overcoats, always black, and walked slightly apart. As the extraordinary flood of women, to whom she was instinctively drawn, approached her, Victoria heard them snorting their complaints about the weather, pipes frozen, plenty of nudging jokes about brass monkeys and frozen stopcocks. ''E couldn't get the old cock turned on and I said, that's a change, luv,' one oversized woman in the human flood that swept past Victoria was talking down to her friend, 'better give yer ball-valve a wiggle while yer at it, I told 'im.' She winked at Victoria, thinking she knew her. These women's work had been indispensable during the war and they knew it; the men had returned to their guaranteed jobs to find everything changed, and their promotional prospects not at all as bright as they remembered from the good old days. Victoria marched with the flow, caught by the excitement. A neatly brushed man with a folded umbrella walked beside her but when she said 'hallo' he looked at her like a stranger. Already she'd broken one of the rules. A store must be a place of hierarchies, of wheels within wheels – probably he was in some department or position that still looked down on women. Victoria did not allow herself to feel rebuffed or like a new girl, she was here to learn, and smiled brightly amongst the herd sweeping her towards their routine tasks. To them this was just another Monday morning. But to her it was another world, a wonderful vivacious world without stuffiness or pretence. Freedom. Hurrying on.

Under a redbrick archway, almost a tunnel, they entered a cobbled courtyard ranked with yellow and blue delivery vans, open to the sky but surrounded on every side by grimy walls, part of the store the clients – still the Emporium's quaint term for customers –

never saw. They never saw this chaos: no deliveries this morning, and the chief of Dispatch was red-faced, sweeping both his hands back across his bald head, cursing the council workmen who were not clearing the roads. The large, foul-mouthed woman in a lavender-coloured overcoat came back to Victoria.

'Lost, are yer?' So she looked lost. Victoria learned that lesson.

'It's my first day.' She tried to sound casual, as though she'd known plenty of other first days in her time. 'No, I'm not lost.'

The woman looked ferocious but not unkindly. 'I'm 'Ilda,' she introduced herself heavily, holding out a hand like a ham, ''Ilda of 'Ades.'

Victoria was determined to be surprised by nothing and they shook hands like men. 'How do you do, Hilda from Hades.'

'*Of*, not from, yer silly bint, 'Ades is where I work, not where I bloody comes from.'

'She bloody does and all!' cried someone in the jostling crowd.

'Where is Hades here? Is it a department?'

'Dahnstairs,' Hilda said ominously. 'Don't pay no attention ter that lot. They're envious, because it's warm dahn there. Ooh, it's lovely and warm! Clocked on yet?' Victoria shook her head. 'Yer *are* a green one,' said Hilda. 'There'll be a toll board in yer department too, don't fink they don't know every-think yer do, yer tea-breaks, visits ter stockholding areas, they're all marked up. The code for the karsy is Number Eighty-Four, so yer can talk abaht it in front

of clients without giving offence if yer got ter go.'
Clamping her arm round Victoria's shoulders, she led
her through the crush to the racks of clock-on cards.
'Give us yer name, then, don't stand on ceremony.'

'Victoria.'

'Vicky. Pick out yer card, Vicky.' Hilda's face
changed when she saw the last name on the brown slip
– Christian name written in ordinary script, surname
in capitals.

Victoria was determined not to say *I'm afraid so* in
that superior way like they did in films. 'He's my
father.'

'Poor baa-lamb, I am sorry for yer.' Victoria
flushed, but there was no offence in the big woman's
words, only warm sympathy. 'Yer see, poor cousin
trumps, I was in the same boat myself. My old dad
worked 'ere thirty-one years and, as for me, anything's better'n scrubbing floors and wiping bums, so
the minute the littl'uns upped an' left 'e got me in 'ere,
an' I never looked back.' With a smile for Victoria's
hesitation at the unfamiliar punch-clock, Hilda took
the card in her squodgy fingers and popped it in and
out of the slot. 'There. Now yer clocked on. Yer one
of us.'

But Victoria wondered if she could ever really be
like these people.

Hilda led her down a concrete slope to a subter-
ranean warren below the sales floors, stacked to the
ceiling with boxes and tubs, packers in overalls
pushing sack-trucks and dragging laden trolleys from
a maze of shelving and brown cardboard. 'Heart of
the place!' Hilda bragged proudly, propelling the

169

newcomer across her domain by the sheer force of her enthusiasm. 'No maps provided! This is where everything gets done, stock control, don't let anyone bluff yer different. This place couldn't exist without us. Why, shillybunkins don't organise itself and jump on the shelves by magic, do it! Natchrully we're all at sixes and sevens now what with the weather, and yer'd think the war was still on, the trouble getting stuff sometimes, makes yer cry. We're important 'ere, girl, though they pay us in pennies.' She leaned on a crate in front of Victoria, her gaze steady. 'It's an important job.'

'Yes, I know.'

'When I first started it used ter be buyers dahn 'ere, little men like moles in black suits, dusty order forms everywhere and goose quills, but the telephone's changed all that, they work upstairs now – got windows!' She started unwrapping her muffler, which seemed endless. 'Now it's just us women dahn 'ere. Much better, natchrully. Brains, not brawn. How much d'yer reckon a score of Christmas cakes weigh? Gotter be cunning. Team work. Women are stronger than men.'

'I can see that.'

'Don't yer forget it,' Hilda said, squashing her beret on to the hook, searching with a frown for the end of her muffler.

Victoria heard tip-tapping footsteps on the concrete and a new voice broke in. 'Terrific, you've found your own way in with us. I meant to meet you but I got caught up.' This pert, graceful creature, but too thin, with brown curls softening her pleasantly

sharp features, was someone Victoria knew. Cathy
Jones, David's daughter, was now twenty-two,
having also joined the Emporium at sixteen, and had
worked her way up from junior to senior sales
assistant and, the last Victoria had heard, was buyer
in the handbag department with a staff of three older
women. 'I'm supposed to look after you.' Cathy held
out her hand, thin-boned but warm. Shaking hands
was something women did here, obviously. Then
Cathy spontaneously kissed cheeks. 'Oh, Victoria,
I'm so sad. I just wanted to say how sorry we all – that
tragic accident—'

Victoria was sure they didn't really feel sorry for
her, why should they, though Cathy seemed genuine.

'Thank you.'

'I'm so silly.' Cathy's lips trembled with emotion
and her eyes were bright-edged. There was nothing
false about her personally, Victoria decided, but what
about everyone else? 'I danced with your father at
that wonderful party he gave the night before . . .
none of us guessed what would happen. Afterwards
when I danced with George – I mean—' she hesitated
to show such first-name familiarity in front of Hilda.

'Don't stand on ceremony,' Victoria said, and
Hilda said, 'Ha!' She obviously liked Cathy a lot,
whatever Cathy thought of her.

'While we danced I was saying to George how
beautiful Pearl looked.' Cathy's tears threatened to
overflow. There was more to this emotional display
than just Pearl, Victoria decided, unless Cathy was
one of those girls who believed in beauty. She was
plain enough, it would take a man in love to think she

was pretty. Victoria warmed to her. Cathy was a professional.

'And what did George say?'

'Hc pretended to be angry.' Drunk, Victoria guessed. Cathy continued: 'He said, "Does Ben think all this glitter is worth anything? Who does he think it impresses?" And I said, "It's against the dark. That's all. Against the dark."'

Victoria found herself glancing at Hilda for a reaction. Hilda's mouth had gone down and her eyebrows up: we know what we know, they said. Cathy burned a candle for George?

Victoria said briskly, 'You're the boss, Cathy, just tell me what to do.'

''Scuse, 'scuse!' said Hilda impatiently waving her way past them, 'I can't stand chitter-chattering 'ere all day! Nothing but deadlines 'ere, a shortage on the floor and a delivery to mark in . . .'

There were certainly two sides to Cathy, Victoria noted. Already she was calm and collected again, though pale, and turned to the row of hooks. 'Right, three-two-one, Victoria, that's your number. Three-two-one. Engrave it on your memory. Always hang your hat and coat there.' She tried to smile, then the smile became genuine as they went to the stairs. 'Isn't that a dreadful woman?' Cathy giggled.

'Isn't she!' The two girls climbed upstairs together. Victoria had little opportunity for friendships, but she supposed this was what it was all about, this fleeting closeness. She was pleased that Cathy obviously liked her, and she liked Cathy, quite sure which of them had the stronger personality. But Cathy had six years' useful experience of playing the game of the Emporium's ways. Furthermore Victoria guessed that David Jones, the Emporium's general manager, was a man who brought his work home and that the store had always been part of Cathy's youth in a way it never had been for Victoria.

'My father didn't want you to join the Emporium,' Cathy admitted while they climbed, throwing the words across her shoulder casually, assuming Victoria already knew or that it was of no importance.

'Yes, George insisted on my learning the ropes,' Victoria said, adjusting a few wayward strands of hair then catching up with quick, decisive footsteps.

'My father is simply afraid that your working here might put you in a difficult situation,' Cathy said with the appearance of unfaked innocence. So that was what David had told his daughter. What he wanted Victoria to hear.

'I'm sure we can avoid that,' Victoria said sincerely.

'Oh, *I* know that.'

'I'm here to learn, Cathy. This job's my idea, no one else's.'

'Completing your education. You're the same age I was when I started, you know?'

'Really!'

'Isn't that remarkable. My father was very keen. I'm an only child,' she added, as though that explained everything.

'Where will I be working?'

'With me, of course.' Cathy said. *Of course!* Just like her father. 'He wanted a son, I think.'

'Then you're supposed to keep tabs on me,' Victoria smiled.

'Oh, no!' Cathy seemed naïve about store politics, which Victoria felt an instinctive grip for. 'No more than with any other junior, that is. You won't get special treatment any more than I did.' Only six years to buyer!

They came to the top of the broad stairs on the ground sales floor, a hive of busy activity around the long counters. Below a cavernous ceiling the grid of navy-carpeted walkways radiated towards them from the imposing double-height row of pneumatic glass doors at the faraway entrance, where Old Bond Street turned into Piccadilly. Though darkly tinted, both they and the plate-glass windows along the two exterior walls were today brilliant with the white snowy glare outside, making the interior lights seem yellow and dim.

'It doesn't look so glum usually,' Cathy said. 'We're doing our bit, saving electricity. They say there are going to be power cuts, industry on a four-day week.'

A bell clanged three times and a boy's voice shouted: 'Doors open in ten minutes!'

'There won't be much early trade today,' said Cathy with a practised glance at the weather, 'but the Emporium opens at nine o'clock precisely, trade or not. The doors are tinted so as to be difficult for clients to see through – if they see a store is empty they don't come in. Afraid of getting jumped on by a saleswoman. If they see it's too busy they go somewhere else to avoid the crowds. The inside of the

Emporium is supposed to be timeless. Few clocks, little daylight.'

They watched porters wheeling canvas castor-trolleys, tubs and skips from the service lifts, taking them into the hollow centres of the beeswaxed counters to be unloaded on to the displays by the shopgirls. Ants.

'The Emporium has always had a large proportion of female staff,' Cathy explained, leading Victoria through what at first seemed to be total confusion: workmen and porters and cleaning women weaving around them, never quite knocking into them, all seeming to know one another by the names which flew around Victoria's head like birds; a shopgirl had lost her tin of pins, another found someone else's tape measure; for a few moments as they passed they heard a floorwalker administering a magisterial ticking-off to some hapless drone. Displays that seemed endless unrolled in front of Victoria: cleverly presented rolls and bolts of material one after the other in different varieties, cotton, wool, silk, satin, curtain-velvet; carefully graded arrays of colour and quality that swept the eye forward and made the mouth water.

'The counters are kept clear for measuring,' Cathy said. 'Textured materials are on these purpose-built fixtures where the clients can touch them. The rolls with colourful prints are placed on angled mounts behind the counter where they'll catch the eye from a distance. Furnishing fabrics are put on the back wall, as they're considered purchases and draw clients through the store.'

Victoria stared at the bright silks, cotton prints, nets and taffetas, textured tweeds and flannel, suitings of barathea, serge and gabardine. 'It's amazing!' she exclaimed amid the hubbub. 'I never realised it was such an art! I want to buy it all.'

'Only thirty years ago,' Cathy said, 'the male and female staff worked twelve-hour days, were fined for gossiping or untidiness, ate in separate dining-halls, slept in strictly segregated dormitories on the top floor, and were never allowed out except on Sundays. And then only under supervision.'

'Now everyone arrives by public transport.'

'From east of Aldgate Pump, mostly. Floorwalkers and buyers from the . . . ah . . . semi-detached suburbs of north or south London, of course.' Sounding just like her father again, but the *ah* was almost self-mockery.

'What's on the top floor nowadays?' Victoria asked as they walked.

'Still the Waterfalls restaurant of course, very popular during the war and extremely profitable – the Government set such low fixed prices for meals, but the cover charge could be high as the sky. Administration on the west side of the top floor. On the east, your father's old apartment has never been demolished, though it wasn't used during the war because of the danger of bombs. But the Emporium was never hit.'

'And below that, on the third floor?'

'Empty. No one's got any money, you see, what with the recession and war shortages. One of the golden rules of retailing, Victoria: no holes on shelves. If you haven't got it, don't flaunt it. Better to shut down a whole floor to keep the others busy, because people buy when they see other people buying. Give 'em what they want at a price they can afford, put it in their hands and they're hooked. Human nature.'

'Are people really so stupid?'

'Every fisherman knows that to catch a fish you have to think like a fish.'

'Now you make me sound stupid.'

'Give them what *they* want, not what you think they ought to have. The client comes first.'

As they moved on Victoria flicked her fingers at a glittering display of inexpensive gold-plated watches. 'But some of these things—'

'Lines.'

'Some of these lines – they're awfully cheap quality, aren't they?'

'We never ever say "cheap", Victoria. Those watches turn as fast as we can get them in, guaranteed unconditionally for twelve months. It's a wonderful display.'

'What happens after twelve months?'

'Now you *do* sound stupid! They break, of course. That's what guarantees are for. Clients can pay more upstairs for lifetime watches.' Cathy stopped in a quiet space by a window. 'Victoria, relax,' she said kindly, putting out her hand to pause the younger girl, then crossed her arms lecturingly. 'No one's expecting anything of you, you know. You're not expected to be a genius or be so fantastically brilliant you just come in here and show us how it's done. Ease up. You're just sixteen.'

'You mean I'm a know-it-all.' Victoria's eyebrows had drawn together into a straight line.

'You certainly know your own mind, yes. Terrific.'

'But?'

'You can be happy here, meet people, ordinary people, possibly make friends you'll keep for the rest of your life . . .'

'*But,*' Victoria said.

'But you're a woman. This is a fine place, Victoria, but it's just a store, not a family. You'll want—'

Victoria drew herself up tall. 'Don't tell me what I am supposed to want.'

'You'll get married, have babies.' Cathy clicked her fingers. 'No career.' She touched Victoria's shoulder. 'Just relax a little, that's all I'm saying. Most of London Emporium's employees are women. But only three buyers are women. And above that level of seniority there are no women, only men.'

'Of course men have the experience.'

'Men,' said Cathy laconically, 'have the sex.'

What was unspoken in this conversation, Victoria realised, was that she wouldn't get anywhere because she was Ben London's daughter. The life of an heiress was as constrained as that of a girl without a penny to her name; more so, because no one cared about a pauper, whereas an heiress inevitably attracted attention. In fact, although she was regarded as rich, Ben had always been strict with money and Victoria had little in her own name. While Lisa would dole out money for tuition fees unstintingly, she disapproved of Victoria going it alone, and if Victoria had made up her mind to do so she would have to pay her own way. That naturally – *natchrully*, she heard the in-domitable voice of Hilda echo in her head – natchrully made Victoria more determined than ever to be independent, and she was enraged that Cathy had so soon seen fit to raise an obstacle, however long-term or theoretical it might be, to her career. Victoria stopped. Or had Cathy been *told* to see fit?

'Did my grandmother tell you to warn me off?'

'No,' Cathy jerked out, surprised. 'Are you always so direct? No . . . I think my father as general manager wanted you to have no illusions, but I know he meant it in the friendliest way. Now you mention it, I suppose it was put to me I should have a word . . . yes, I realise that now. You always say what's right in the front of your mind, Victoria, but other people are more . . . sensitive, elliptical.'

*That's one lesson I won't learn,* Victoria thought.

'You're a buyer,' she pointed out. 'I suppose his scheme is that you and I should spend the rest of our lives selling handbags?'

Cathy looked embarrassed. 'Actually I've been promoted . . . sideways. I've been appointed floor-walker of cosmetics and toiletries. It's a much bigger and more complex department.'

'Congratulations on making history,' Victoria said ironically.

'I thought I liked you,' Cathy rebuked her. 'I'm changing my mind. Now you listen to *me*, Victoria.' This delivered in a mild, steely voice that seemed to go on and on, a dressing-down far more effective than shouting, and Victoria almost squirmed to be so caught out: Cathy could be a tyrant. 'We have to work together, don't we?' Vicky almost agreed aloud, *yes*. 'And we will, won't we?' *Yes*. 'Now listen,' Cathy said sweetly, leading the way towards the doors where a few workmen with screwdrivers were making final adjustments to prefabricated glass counters. 'The ground floor of a store, any store, sells certain types of merchandise. People have to pass through it – the lifts and elevators are deliberately placed at the back – to get where they really want to go. And on their way they spend money on things they didn't know they wanted. The little luxuries that catch their eye the moment they come through these doors, the selling-est part of the sellingest floor. In the war that was fabrics for them to run up their own clothes, basic haberdashery, lipstick, cheap useful bits 'n' bobs, the stuff you see here. But times have changed since the Americans won the war for us. We're getting Americanised. What's exciting? Clark Gable, not Robert Donat; hamburgers, not good old SPO.'

'And handbags don't—'

'Handbags don't sizzle.'

Two clangs from the bell. Five minutes.

Above the new plate-glass stands which ranged out from the doors, cheerful illuminated signs were flickering to life, neon names familiar to all: Elizabeth Arden, Helena Rubenstein, Yardley, Gloria Fox, Max Factor, a gleaming area of glass and clean milk-white wood that could not fail to arrest the purse of any woman entering the store. Cathy watched Victoria's face.

'And this was George's very own idea?'

'Well, no,' Cathy said. 'My father's, actually, but of course George approved it.'

So it was David Jones's pet project, and he'd taken the opportunity to put his daughter in charge of it. Yet Cathy was too innocent to see her achievements were not her own.

'It must have cost a fortune,' Victoria said. 'I thought money was so short, currency restrictions and import restrictions and Export or Die, all the big high street stores on their uppers—'

'You see that's the beauty of it!' Cathy said enthusiastically. 'It doesn't cost the store a single penny of capital. These stands are paid for one hundred per cent by the perfumery and toiletry houses. All we do is supply the selling space and the sales staff.'

'Including me?'

'Us.'

Victoria gazed at the displays. What she saw made her feel demeaned. Perfumes, but not Chanel or the high-priced exclusive brands familiar to her from her mother's wrists before the war . . . those expensive luxuries would still be sold upstairs, she guessed, by suitably unctuous matrons in suitably exclusive surroundings to suitably rich clients, a week's wage for a working man in a tiny, beautifully crafted bottle. When there was more money around such things might filter down from the carpeted salons to these mass-market halls of affordable luxuries. 'We're selling what ordinary people want,' Cathy said. She smiled, obviously believing in them herself. 'We're selling dreams.'

And what did ordinary people dream of in this dirty, dull, disorderly old world? Cleanliness. Everything here had a scent, scented soaps, scented face-creams and scented hand-creams and scented shampoos, the smell of cleanliness. And colour, nothing dull, pale pink soap and pastel blue soap for that extra cleanliness. Tubes of toothpaste guaranteed to clean your teeth whiter and toothbrushes guaranteed to last a year. Clark Gable and hamburgers.

'When do I start?' Victoria asked bravely. She had rarely felt more dismayed and intimidated, realising how much she had to learn. From the other girls' nimble fingers she saw that purchases must be wrapped in a certain way and the bow knotted *just so*, that they must not so much crouch as twist-and-bob to take out fresh stock from beneath the counter. She saw them glancing at her under their eyelashes and *knew* that they would hate her, that she would never fit in. Once inside she would never escape from these glaring white stands, all as identical as dice below their splashy neon names, David Jones would make sure of that, and she would be under Cathy's eye all the time. And she would give up.

She would give up and go back to Lisa, who would smile understandingly and pick up the phone to Switzerland.

Cathy held out a full-breasted, tight-waisted jacket in cherry with small gilt buttons and large, almost military padded shoulders. The left breast was embroidered in swirly gold thread with the legend: *Gloria Fox*. Victoria put it on with a sigh, the latest Gloria Fox house style. She looked, she decided, like a cross between a bellboy and a harlot.

'*You can be happy here, meet people, ordinary people, make friends you'll keep for the rest of your life . . .*'

'You look smashing, perfect fit,' said Cathy, although it felt too tight. All the other girls ignored Victoria as she finished up the fiddly buttons and squeezed herself into her tiny compartment of wood and glass, the cheap cosmetics and toiletries ranked on the counter that surrounded her, hemming her in, her own little box where she would stand – or sit nearly standing, so tall was the three-legged stool on whose unyielding rim she perched the outermost curve of her buttocks – for nine hours a day, except thirty minutes for lunch and two ten-minute tea-breaks.

It was very lonely.

Because Victoria had never had friends, she expected everyone to be her enemy. She had been so shifted around between boarding schools that she had no idea of home, of settlement. Soon people saw her loneliness, her fear of being hurt, as hostility and couldn't be bothered to take the time and trouble to break through to her. Her wary certainty that she would be attacked or rebuffed meant that she attacked first, rejecting before she faced rejection.

The other girls on the stands didn't have the chance to make up their minds about her. Victoria's certainty that she was the odd one out made that come true.

She came into the store on a considerable wave of sympathy for her father, which annoyed her. She didn't need anybody's help. There was something of him about her, the eyes of course, and something of his sudden warmth and interest, his obvious personal fascination in *you*, about her smile. But her smile was rare, and so tight it flickered around the edges. It looked deliberately turned on, and the eyes, a touch too strong on a pretty girl, flinched before settling a little too demandingly. Hostile. Confidence to the point of aggression looked good on a man but in a girl it was just aggression, without charm.

'She's not a patch on 'er dad,' opined Watson from the furnace-room, rubbing his bristling forearms as he settled in the canteen, near Hilda. He had a thing starting with her.

'Give 'er time.' Hilda plonked her elbows on the red-check oilcloth tabletop and blew over the steaming mug of tea clamped between her hands.

'Time I were orf,' said Mike the nightwatchman, doffing his cap. 'Good day, all.'

Bill Simmonds gave his opinion. 'There's more going on,' he told them knowledgeably, 'than yer can possibly know.' He now worked as Lisa's chauffeur but that was not nearly a full-time occupation, so he made work where he was still officially employed, at the Emporium. Increasingly George London, who did not drive, used him to come here from his home in Primrose Hill and back again in the evening, taking over his father's well-known routine, nine o'clock sharp.

'Young Bill knows it all!' cackled Watson, yet still Hilda didn't look at him first, and Wattie shut up while she was in this mood. He loved older women, you didn't have to use rubbers.

'Yer don't care what's going on, young Bill,' Hilda was saying, ''ere we are in the Shadow of the Atomic Whatsit, yer meat ration's cut, yer can't 'ardly get beer for love nor money, and there yer are – 'appy!'

'I'm not,' Bill said suddenly. 'No, I'm not.'

'Yer 'appy so long as yer get to drive yer bloody car.' Sometimes Bill drove David Jones nowadays, but she had noticed that he polished the car just as hard.

'I knows more than I says, 'Ilda dear,' said Bill snobbishly, recovering his equilibrium, 'and that's all I says.'

Wattie summed Victoria up in the only term that mattered to the male side of the table. 'She's a good-looker, she is.' He made half-melons of his hands against his chest and flexed his fingers erotically.

But Hilda had got her gums into 'young' Bill and wasn't going to let go. 'Get on with yer, Bill. I reckon yer wouldn't mind driving Joe Stalin about if he paid yer wages – really, wouldn't yer, Bill?'

In the face of this woman's mockery, her contemptuous use of his unadorned name and the titter that followed it round the table, 'young' Bill swallowed the secret that had been about to bloom on the tip of his tongue: his deceitful trip to Brighton with Peggy and her daughter dressed up in disguise, and the man who had followed them just like in the Graham Greene film showing at every Odeon along the New Road, *Brighton Rock*. He finished his tea with dignity and stood up wiping his mouth. 'That was uncalled for, 'Ilda. I got better things ter do.'

''E's upset, yer've upset 'im, 'Ilda,' Wattie said wisely as the door slammed. 'Let me read yer palm,' he winked.

'Geroff.' Hilda was angry. 'None of yer got the faintest idea abaht 'er.' She looked into the faces round the table, the girls still tittering amongst themselves and the men looking attractive but so thick-headed. 'Lor' save us,' she said in disgust, getting back to work. 'She's sad, that's all.' And the door slammed a second time.

But Victoria discovered that she could sell. She loved selling. It was a strange, callous power, selling someone what they wanted. And it wasn't a gift, something she'd been born with – nothing, she had learned, was for free in this life – selling was the product of sheer hard work.

Often when customers – sorry, *clients* – came into the store she could see what they wanted as clearly as if it was written on their faces, and yet what came out of their mouths was often completely different. I wonder if you could help me? They wanted to be persuaded into the rigmarole of purchasing, they wanted to be given confidence. And they wanted to think that they were in control. That *they* would choose. But the girl was helpful, not pushy, *interested* . . . and they *did* end up getting what they wanted.

186

More. What they needed. And the sure confidence that they had been right to make their purchase, even if it did cost a bit more than they thought. But things you really needed always did, didn't they?

So every day the doors opened and Victoria smiled her bright smile for the clients, the one the other salesgirls never saw. With her over-educated maturity and determination to succeed she didn't see the clients coming into the store quite as people, real people with friends and families, shivering and shaking the snow off their shoes by the doors, rather she saw each one as a set of clues. The way they walked, they way they moved their eyes, whether they nipped at the fingertips of their gloves with their teeth as they came down, looking around them curiously, or left the gloves on. Everything was a clue to what would happen next. Gloves-on wouldn't buy, no point in wasting time on them. Dowdy shoes and questionable hat, but well-cared-for face and hands, now *she'd* buy from the conservative 'Palace' range on the counter.

The tarted-up Gloria Fox marketing maiden who regularly visited, with eyes as hard as porcelain, explained that all Gloria Fox cosmetics were sold The Gloria Fox Way, *on* the counter, which had more layers than a wedding cake, but clever lighting and the bright colours of the products themselves made it enticing rather than cluttered. Some lucky girls at stands selling classier names had almost bare counters, and reverently produced samples only on request. But Victoria soon learned who was likely to have her eye caught by her colourful display, and she had her bright smile ready. It touched her eyes, *it* was real and honest. Victoria wanted to sell as much as her prey wanted to buy. Women with fur collars were sure game. Victoria's disappointment when she lost was real. As she got better at her job she needed to win, and sometimes she wanted to shout after a departing back, 'I could have made you look better than that, you know!'

Dowdy shoes and questionable hat had a peaky daughter who begged her mum for one of the brighter lipsticks from the 'Young Princess' range, just introduced. The Gloria Fox people didn't miss a trick when romance was in the air, and the young Princess Elizabeth was in the news because of that handsome Philip Mountbatten and the possibility – and therefore marketing possibilities – of what might happen there in the marriage stakes. Royal Red was this month's colour. 'Aw, be a sport, Mum.' So the poor woman would dig into her purse, and Victoria smiled her smile.

For Victoria, selling became almost as physical a need as buying was for the clients. She loved her job. She lay awake thinking at night how to do better, opportunities she had missed, slicker ways of using samples. Almost an obsession, but it seemed a harmless one. Her own body language and facial language timed to perfection the tiny assertive movement that hooked the client's attention, probably a woman who was bustling past with no intention of buying and her mind fixed on a dozen more important things. Clients were like salmon, they had to be hooked, the invisible bond provoked by that first bait cast by the salesgirl, then her eye-catching counter display. Hook, line and sinker, the dry sale successfully closed.

And then there were nervous people who were unsure of themselves but who wanted the product, people who had already netted themselves and could be drawn in by the salesgirl with her almost-indifference, not-quite-impatience dropped in one or two little drips. 'I just can't make up my mind!' the poor things would bleat, and Victoria would say politely, 'Perhaps this one, madam . . .' which of course was much more expensive, and much more desirable.

But some clients were more strongminded. Perhaps their system was to purchase the least expensive line of an expensive name, and little would divert them from it; they went straight to Daisy or Moira's classy stands, sometimes Jeanette's. Other types believed it was best value to buy from the top of a cheap range, and they'd come to Gloria Fox and snatch the top-line stuff in handfuls, showing off, without caring about what they bought or about Victoria working for what she sold. They were the ones she liked least, they were too easy. But the name of the game was always the same, getting their money.

In her first week Victoria's sales were third by item volume, seventh – bottom – by value. Her second week, as she learned the tricks, saw her at number two by volume, behind Daisy Johnstone and Jeanette whose name was really Jean, and up to fourth by value, although turnover was dropping so low now because of the big freeze. At the start of her third week, when she was determined to lead the pack, the store was struck by what at first seemed to be disaster.

Walking up St James's first thing on Monday morning, her coat buttoned tight against the bitter cold – because she had to look smart in her job Victoria wore sheer Wolsey nylons, not the warmer but ugly woollen hose – she picked her way across the filthy vista of Piccadilly, the disgusting sooty mounds of hardpacked snow chucked up in the losing battle of the shovels, wheel-ruts now set into rails of jagged ice that seemed designed to turn heels and sprain ankles. She stopped in the middle of the road. The Emporium was dark. The power cuts had started.

But the Underground was running as usual. 'They're keeping the power on for the blinking trains,' Daisy complained as they crossed the court-yard, not wearing her muffler over her face in fear the wool would shine her pretty nose, 'but what are we supposed to do when we get here?'

Cathy intercepted them by the cloakroom. 'You're allowed to keep your hats and coats on, it's official. Our turn for the power off today. And maybe tomorrow too, if it gets worse.'

'But it can't!' Moira said.

'How shall we sell without lights?' Jeanette shivered. 'Look at my fingers, they're simply blue already.'

'Suck 'em,' said Hilda, going past.

'It's all right for her!' all five girls said. 'She's got the furnace to keep her warm.'

'Bloody fire's only ticking over enough ter keep yer

bloody pipes from freezing,' glowered Hilda.

'I can understand no electricity for lights,' Daisy complained to Cathy, who looked colder than any of them, 'but no heat seems ridiculous.'

'Bloody furnace got no coal,' Hilda grunted, padded around with enough warm garments to turn her into a greasy-looking snowman, or snow-woman, and her eyes glared out of what they could see of her face. 'Even yer chapel Welsh are digging the mines seven days the week, but there's twenty-foot drifts on the railways and yer points got iced, didn't they? My cousin Bob's a lineman, man and boy, and 'e's been getting double overtime. Pickaxe broke off in 'is 'and, the metal was that brittle, it's the cold.'

'Ten-minute bell,' Cathy said, shivering.

Victoria listened to all this interplay carefully.

'Well I shan't,' Jeanette pouted. 'No one's going to come in today anyway, I mean clients might be stupid but they're not crazy, are they?'

'They're neither stupid nor crazy,' said Cathy, giving Daisy a push to get her going. 'Just get on with it, Jean.' The two girls went up with faces like thunderclouds, followed reluctantly by Moira. Victoria watched with fresh respect for Cathy's professionalism.

'Yer'll see,' Hilda told Victoria, 'Cathy's right, we'll get more people in than ever up there terday. The worse fings get, the more we Londoners make the bloody effort. People say we're knackered by the war. But fighting's in our blood, we'll flock out in droves, yer'll see if I'm not right.'

Victoria found the lifts and escalators eerily silent, only the stairs in use, the dark salesfloor a galaxy of candles. And Hilda was right, morning was busy, the afternoon busier. Soon it seemed not at all strange to be working by candlelight, the warm points highlighting the girls' eyes and hair prettily, although the cheap 'n' cheerful cosmetic colours in the racks looked decidedly odd hues. Clients who had not purchased a particular colour before preferred to examine them in the natural daylight by the windows, but as thefts went up they had to be escorted, a task usually performed by Cathy as the floorwalker, rather than leave a stand unattended. But it was dark by four-thirty, and business tailed off. Cathy was downstairs snatching her delayed tea-break and Jeanette had taken the opportunity to wander from her stand to gossip with Daisy. Moira, out of it at the far end, kept glancing enviously at her friends' whispering lips, audible giggles, but she was stuck with an old woman who wouldn't make up her mind. Victoria worked quietly at her lists, ankles crossed, tongue following the working of her pencil. A man's voice, the first male voice she had heard today, spoke up behind her.

'It's cold enough for the Thames to freeze over.'

'I'm sorry, sir,' she gasped, turning, 'you're the first man I've had today.' He smiled. In her startlement she had come out with the worst possible response. If he was the wrong type she'd not just put her foot in it, she'd jumped in it with both feet, and Victoria felt the heat break over her face. She was flushing bright red. Yet it was perfectly true that all her clients had been women today, so she held her ground, trying to ignore the colour she felt glowing on her cheeks. She wouldn't back down. 'You know what I mean,' she said.

'I know what you mean,' he said seriously. He wore the collar of his overcoat up as though not to be recognised. When she put down her pencil his eyes flashed to her hands, all his concentration on her – not just on her eyes but on everything about her, as though no one else in the store existed. Even so, he didn't put his collar down.

She waited. Men were much more difficult customers than women, very much more difficult to read: they weren't always sensible, and they didn't enjoy shopping. You always had a fair idea what girls were thinking, *how* they thought, how to catch them, what would appeal or not to their femininity and the sort of person they were, and that was why Victoria was successful at selling. But for a girl, selling to men was different. For a start they spoke a different language. They wanted something *popular*, never wanted chic or fashionable which was what girls desired. Men wanted 'light blue' and were not tempted by 'aquamarine'; they wanted their purchases to be well made, distrusting anything eye-catching rather than being drawn to it. There was a sort of opaque remorselessness to men, knowing what they wanted, yet with an unpredictable impulsiveness that made them almost impossible. But they tended to buy the first thing they were presented with. And he was young. . .

She dominated with a smile, unconsciously drawing in her breath, filling herself out a little. 'How can I help you?'

He glanced down. 'I'm a bit embarrassed.'

She watched him without expression. He looked quite personable, but not upper-class and self-centred, his voice was soft not educated, so a man – a *young* man – who worked for his living. 'I work in the City, you see,' he said mildly. Brown eyes, which she had never liked, and flicks of undistinguished sandy hair across his forehead. Realistically, she decided, he couldn't be more than four or five years older than she. But a clerk's wages hadn't bought that lovely navy woollen overcoat, and there was a touch of dandy about him with those matching blue, almost-but-not-quite-black, leather gloves. Aware of himself. Black shoes of course, she could see beneath the counterflap, and pretty dirty, dribbling with melting ice, but anyone's would be. But not much, so she doubted he'd walked even from the Underground: he probably had a car.

'Snap,' she said suddenly. His overcoat was the same shade as hers.

'Oh – yes,' he said, unimpressed. But candlelight made warm points in the brown eyes. Victoria drew back slightly. 'You see . . . my girl—' Victoria didn't help him. Moira had got rid of the old lady and nipped out to join the other girls, holding a clip-sheet to make herself look busy. Cathy wasn't due back for seven minutes; Moira would allow five. Victoria wished they were closer.

'Oh, yes?' she said, echoing him without realising it. 'Your girl?'

He nodded, then shrugged, as if by that she would understand everything.

194

Victoria could not hide her impatience behind the false delicacy that older clients would expect of salesgirls. 'You mean you're in love with her?'

He shrugged again: obviously. Victoria prompted him, 'But she doesn't know it and you want to show her.' Just as there were men shy about purchasing underwear for their wives, some men were intimidated by the unmasculine mystique of perfumes. This young man was a little bit immature, and Victoria felt confident of her superiority. But he had steady eyes. Perhaps he had been playing with her a little. Victoria flushed again and decided she'd better stick to her sales spiel. 'Gloria Fox toiletries and cosmetics are blended from the finest ingredients. . .'

'I'll explain,' he said, leaning his forearms cockily on the only available square of counter-top not occupied by lipsticks, creams and powders, bargain-offer foundation packs and scents in every size and shape, all glittering oddly from the candle in its saucer between them. Victoria crossed her arms sceptically. 'I have a good job in the City,' he said to her secret satisfaction – she'd got him right. 'Actually I'm an insurance actuary. Father's footsteps.'

'I thought actuaries were dull and dusty people,' she said without intending the compliment.

His face didn't move. 'My mother died when I was born.'

'I – I'm sorry.'

He acknowledged her apology with a tilt of his head. 'My father put my name down for the Vaudey Grammar School. But he died too.'

Listening to his voice, she said nothing. She was

vaguely aware that she was wasting time. Her fingers twitched automatically over the papers of a stock clip-sheet.

'At the school there was a girl. But I won't tell you her name, because I can see I'm boring you. I thought some soap.'

'You know her well enough to give her *soap*?'

'I never even spoke to her, I doubt she even noticed me.'

'She probably did.'

'She's not like other girls,' he said simply, and Victoria hid her smile. Little boys! – he reminded her of Ralph. 'Everything about her,' he said. 'Everything.'

'Perfume. Perfume is the perfect gift.'

'The other day I saw her. She'd changed. But not the way she walked. Not the way she touched her hands to her hair. She'd learned so much, she'd learned to be a woman, grown up. Girls learn so quickly to be adult. But I knew her at once. The real things don't change, do they? I followed her.'

'Why didn't you speak to her?'

'Because I'm in love with her. I want her. It's not words we need.'

Cathy was returning from the stairs and Moira flew back to her stand, dropped her clip-sheets that skidded and fluttered in every direction on the highly polished floor. She bent over inelegantly showing the backs of her knees, the twist-and-bob forgotten. But he didn't even glance at the interesting sight.

'Perfume,' Victoria said earnestly. 'I recommend "Evening Mist", or perhaps—'

'Let me smell it,' he said.

She presented the sample bottle between finger and thumb, as she had been taught.

'Put some on your wrist,' he said.

'Oh, I'm not supposed to.'

'No one's looking.'

She pulled back her unglamorous overcoat and squirted the stuff on her exposed skin, over the shadowy pulsing vein just visible beneath her flesh. He leaned forward. She wore her selling smile. '"Evening Mist" is our most popular—'

'No,' he said.

She replaced the cap on the bottle.

'That one over there,' he said. 'The pretty shape. So many whirls on it I can't read it.'

'"Tonight".' It was a product Victoria particularly disliked, so strong that everyone who wore it smelt the same, and if he made her put it on her wrist she would reek of it even after her bath. She held it out to him hoping he would shake his head.

'Try it, please,' he said.

'I'll run out of wrists!' But he neither returned her smile nor dropped his eyes from her own. She sighed, changed hands, and squirted.

He smiled. 'I like that one,' he said, 'what's your opinion?'

He had perfect white teeth, almost too perfect, perhaps that was what irritated her. It was un- reasonable to grumble about a man because he had no fillings. She *wanted* to find some flaw in him, not to have to pay attention to him. He was no fool; he'd used her against herself very cleverly. She wondered if his name was Alain or Marcel. But there was this other girl, and she disliked him because of her. And the way he had made Victoria use her wrists so dispassionately.

'It's great,' she said, rolling several lies into one.

He laughed, and she wondered how much he really cared about this other girl, or about anyone, in fact. She saw right through him.

She turned her back and wrapped up his package, as nimble-fingered with the paper as though she was folding origami, tied the ribbon skilfully, and turned. He held out a ten-shilling note and she gave him a penny change. 'Thank you, sir. Goodbye.'

He left without a word.

'I wondered if you were having trouble with that one,' Cathy said.

'No, not at all.'

Late that night Victoria sleepily decided that the other girl had ginger hair and buck teeth.

The next day, Tuesday, when she returned from work, Lisa held out a package to her. 'This came for you.' Since Victoria had started her job they exchanged no more words than necessary. She went upstairs and opened the package in her room.

She held the bottle in her hand. '*So many whirls on it I can't read it.*'

And his note, slightly chilling – which surely he would not have intended – in its sentiment. He must be lying. Because, of course, no one could really be the most beautiful woman in the world. Certainly not on a nine-and-elevenpence bottle of 'Tonight' perfume.

# Chapter Five

## 1

Ben London lay in darkness. Moving his eyes from side to side, wondering what had woken him, he saw nothing. The bedclothes beneath his body, of which he was so aware, were creased and uncomfortable. He must have been tossing and turning in his sleep, but now he put out his hands carefully and pulled the sheet flat by touch. And lay in the dark.

He was dreaming he was awake.

He wore pyjamas, which he had never done when he was married. Will, snowed in over at Home Farm, was no match for his father's physique even now: they fitted Ben a size too small, the buttons too tight, creasing the material uncomfortably, and wouldn't button over the swell of his chest at all. The trousers were held up by a cord. It was easy to get into these pyjamas by himself with his eyes squeezed shut, like a child's game, doing up the buttons and knotting the cord by touch alone. *I can do this!* he'd shouted at Ria. *It might not be much but I can do this, at least.* He made a mental note, for when he met Will, for Will to put on weight so that his pyjamas fitted properly in future.

But why was it still dark in the room? Ben squinted suspiciously at the shining gap between the drawn curtains, where they didn't quite meet. It was light outside! He'd overslept, that was all!

He jumped up and threw the curtains wide on a magnificent vista of green fields, black and white Friesian cows grazing between bales of hay as yellow as butter, stooks of wheat, a yellow sun in a sky of Maxwell Parrish blue. That blue more blue and beautiful than any other. He could see it was going to be a wonderful day in the Dales, they'd have a picnic. Hastily he shrugged over his shoulders the maroon dressing-gown Ria had left draped on the end of the bed, opened the bedroom door still fresh-smelling with its glossy white paint, painted by Will anticipating their holiday. All the poor lad was good for, this dog-like faithfulness.

*They grow up and are cut down like the wheat.* No doctors could help him.

The corridor was dark, of course. It seemed reasonable because it was windowless, of course he could not see. The kitchen was at the far end. Ben held out his hands in front of him as he walked. He could smell tannin now, tea brewing. Ria was making the morning tea.

But why was Ria here?

Always here.

'*Where am I?*' he whispered in his sleep.

Ria, the cuckoo in his heart.

*Where am I?* He opened his eyes, and he was blind.

*Remember* . . .

He twisted and turned.

There was nothing. He drew in his invisible elbows to his ribs and clenched his invisible fists, cursing himself for these dreams in which he saw so clearly. It was as if his own mind was taunting him, so great was his grief. They were so desperately real. He saw the sky, he saw the fields, he saw the lovely Dales stretching out to the horizon, and far away the silver flash of a river. It was awful, simply awful. He wanted to shriek.

A quiet knock on the door. The smell of the paint – that was real, and the tannin-smell of the tea. 'Come in.' The door creaked open on its hinges; that idiot boy Will had forgotten to oil them while he was painting. It wasn't his fault he was like he was; but Ben's fingers twitched in his frustration, and he was full of anger.

A little girl's voice asked shyly, 'Are you awake?'

'Put the tray down there,' Ben said, and heard her place it on the bedside table as usual.

'Shall I draw the curtains?' Lola asked. She asked this every morning, and every morning he replied the same. Why bother? But still, she did bother.

This morning his reply was different. 'Yes, open them,' Ben said, and listened to the ratcheting sound. Then he asked the most painful question. 'What do you see?'

But she didn't stay by the window, her slippered feet pattered back, her knees bounced on the squeaking bedsprings, and she cuddled him. Blindness had not sharpened his sense of smell any more than it sharpened his hearing or touch, only increased his awareness of them and all he must be missing. There were no trade-offs at all, and she smelled perfectly ordinary, a little girl who'd been eating toast and marmalade.

'It's all white and frozen,' she said. 'It's nothing. You can't see ice.'

'Ah,' he said in his satisfaction.

'Mummy says you can stay in bed all day.' Her hair moved against his face and he knew she had sat back on her heels, was looking at him.

'To me there's no difference between day and night.'

'You're funny.'

'I'm not funny.' He *did* sound self-pitying.

'Mum feels sorry for you,' Lola scoffed, obviously not sharing the feeling. 'That's why she goes to all this trouble – breakfast in bed. She's burnt the bacon again,' she added unsympathetically. 'It's because you said you like it crispy.'

'Your Mum can't cook.'

'She wants to do her best for you.'

'Why?'

'Ask Mum!' She had settled back on her toes but he actually *felt* her shrug, probably a slight movement of the bed; he was sensitive to the smallest vibrations. He rolled over and found the bacon sandwich, bit down hard. 'You're right,' he said.

'You're the only person she's ever cooked breakfast for.'

'I don't know why she bothers.' He picked a burnt

202

crust out of his mouth, tapped it with his fingernail. Lola didn't laugh. What stories had Ria told her?

'She wants to bother,' Lola said tentatively. 'You've always had people to look after you. But it means ever so much to her.'

'I didn't ask her to.'

'Yes you did. You wanted her to come with you. I was so happy she'd found you again. In the hospital you needed her. Now she's come here she's thrown away everything for you, and you're just speaking with words again.'

Ben finished his toast.

'How old are you?'

'You know. Four fingers on one hand and nearly two on the other. Mum says if you put toast crumbs all over the bed it doesn't matter.' This had been a bone of contention between them during the first week or two in the frozen silence of Clawfell, when he had got up for lunch and Ria chattered brightly, clattering the knives and forks, and then the washing-up, as though the cheerful sound would bring him back. She made up his bed during the afternoon while he waited by the kitchen range. He was unredeemed by her routine, finally irritated almost unbearably by it, and stayed in his room.

'Why doesn't it matter about the toast crumbs?'

'It's only you sleeping on them,' Lola repeated cheerfully. 'She says you can lie in your pit. She's not making your bed any more.'

He hugged Lola, her eyelashes against his cheek.

'Don't, your breath's got bacon on it,' Lola told

him, pulling back. 'And you haven't cleaned your teeth in weeks, and I have to clean mine twice a day.'

'This toast was enough to clean them.'

'That's not funny,' Lola insisted. He felt her get off the bed and he didn't want her to go.

'Would you like to see me shave?' he asked suddenly.

'What's shaving?' Lola said, intrigued, and suddenly he realised how little she really knew. Her feelings were astonishingly adult, everything ready in place; but every so often he realised how little she really knew of the world. Brought up by the two women on the Isle of Dogs, she had never even seen a man shave. Suddenly the project was exciting. 'Come on,' he said, swinging his legs over the bedside, 'let's get rid of this beard.' She was quiet, as though she found the idea disturbing. She had never known him without his beard; this one was the only face of his she had known. Removing his face. Understanding, he held her hands gently. 'It won't hurt me,' he promised.

'Can I watch?' She sounded as excited as he now.

''Course you can.'

She led him down to the bathroom with its endless supply of hot water from the range. 'I'll put the light on,' she explained.

He found the basin – the tap was still hot from when Ria had used it earlier – filled it. When he breathed in he could feel the steam. His fingertips felt for the mirror beaded with cold droplets, then the tile shelf beneath it covered with Ria's oddments: toothpaste, a toothbrush and a smaller one, a bottle of something,

a tiny eye-brush . . . Ria had taken it over completely. How long had he been so depressed, to let her
get away with it? He found his shaving gear chucked
underneath a flannel. He worked up a lather with his
shaving brush on the soap and covered his beard.
Lola was utterly silent.

'Are you still here?'

'I'm watching,' she whispered, and he could tell she
was fascinated. He resisted a smile, opened the
straight razor and stropped it. His hands remembered
these tasks flawlessly, but when he raised the blade
near his ear, pulling his cheek flat with his other hand
ready for the stroke, Lola squealed.

'Left a bit!'

When he was finished he splashed the hot water
over his face. 'You look just the same,' she said,
sounding disappointed. 'Can I turn on your bath?
Then I've got to go and get dressed. Mum says I can
go out and play. The snow's not too deep in the yard
round the back.'

'I want you to help me today.'

'Mum said it would be like this,' Lola said glumly.
'She said when you were unhappy you were bad
enough, but if you ever felt better, you'd be
*unbearable*.' That statement had the Ria ring of truth
about it.

'Don't be rude,' Ben said.

'Will you ever get better?' Lola asked.

He chucked the flannel in the direction of her
voice, but she had dodged back to the door and it
splashed harmlessly into the rising bathwater. The
door slammed and he locked it, then undressed. He

inched himself into the hot water, lying back with his eyes closed. His eyes closed as if he were asleep. Will you ever get better?

Without people, he did not know what he felt. He had always been a man who needed life – goods in, goods out – *needed* women around him. Outsiders preferred to think him callous or ruthlessly using women as tools for his own purposes. Of course the opposite was true. Everyone made their own destiny.

But now all that was gone and, alone, he felt no sense of direction, no purpose in his life. Nothing to hold on to. He was blind, with no hope he would regain his sight. Nothing.

The awful dreams, too numerous to bear, of the disappeared world. He saw, in his mind's eye, Pearl's smile spreading from her lips to her eyes.

'You have no light sensation whatsoever,' the specialist had told him, and Ben remembered the smell of cigar-smoke and mohair suit. The vast, cool, kindly fingers probing the sensitive orbits of his eyes. He remembered each finger feeling larger than a banana. A yellow banana. Ben remembered yellow. The Judd Street specialist had murmured in a low aside, to a nurse or someone, 'No reaction to stimulus.'

Ben had demanded loudly, 'Does that mean I'll never see ever again?'

'Ask us in six months. After such major trauma, physiological, psychological—'

Ben had said bitterly, 'Or six years, sometime, never. At least tell me the truth!'

'Bluntly, I'm afraid all your fuses are blown.' *What does that mean?* 'My dear chap,' the specialist had told him, 'you could stare at the sun.'

Being blind was to be in another world.

Ben gripped his hands over the sides of the bath and pulled himself up. His fingers fumbled for the soap dish, found it, and he soaped his invisible body by feel. The movement made a phosphorescent light bloom in his head, yellow-red, slowly rotating like a radar trace, and he clung on to it as it faded. *Don't go.* Cortical vision. His brain imagining that it could still see.

*He* didn't need Ria. His blindness needed her. Needed her even to make his stupid morning tea – how could he even tell how much Lipton's was piled on the spoon, or tell when the kettle was boiling, except by scalding his hand in the steam? He was a millionaire with money to buy anything. But he could not fry his own bacon for breakfast, or even do his own washing. He got out of the bath and hopped on the cold lino, unable to find the bathmat, but fortunately the towel hung over the rail where it belonged, and he was able to dry himself.

Wrapping himself in the towel he returned to his bedroom, once the room of Crane's young children; Ben had an idea both were killed in the First World War. But the boys' two single beds remained, and he slept in the one nearer the door, because he could locate himself by touching the end of the bed before relinquishing his hold on the doorhandle. Once he was past the bed he had the window an arm's length on his right. Four paces brought him to a wardrobe. One door was cold, a mirror. Opening the mirror-door towards him and reaching in, one, two, three drawers down, counted on the handles, the fourth drawer contained his socks. At first he'd worn odd colours that caused Lola no end of fun, but now Ria bundled each pair, assuring him they were identical. Next drawer up, underpants. Above that a drawer of neatly folded vests, untouched, he did not use them, and the top drawer was nothing but lumberjack shirts, in green or red check apparently, but definitely with hard-worn leather elbows and shoulder-tops that his fingers could feel. As he shrugged the shirts on they smelled subtly of another man's sweat – Will's. There came often, to the listening ears of a man who did nothing else all day, the distant ringing of an axe chopping wood beyond the snowdrifts that blocked the main house off from Home Farm. Ria, with longing in her voice to see their son, had spied woodsmoke giving away the farmhouse's position behind the spinney on the far side of the fishponds, where Will lived with Helen. Ria was dying to see him, but Ben was happy enough to be with his thoughts and their daughter, who was whole. He did not like Ria to think about Will.

'Lola?' he called. Her and Ria's bedroom was the next down the corridor, close enough for them to hear him if he called out. Because of the two girls he called it the harem.

'Don't be like that,' Ria had said, and he had laughed.

Now Ben opened the left door of the wardrobe,

selecting – one pair was as good as another – from a row of his trousers on hangers, and on the floor his fingers knocked past the cold rubber of wellington boots and the beaten-up Larson shoes he had arrived in, coming to a pair of clumping steel-toed work-boots. As if he could work! But he mastered the laces.

'Lola!' he shouted. He listened. No reply came.

The humiliating business began again, feeling past the beds, reaching at arm's length for the doorhandle, then brushing the right wall of the corridor with his fingernail, stopping when he snagged the jamb of the next bedroom door, the harem. His voice rose. 'Lola? Ria?' Nothing. He went on with arms outstretched ready to meet the door at the end of the corridor, opened it (the slightly loose-feeling handle on the right, remember, and remember it opened out-wards). He was now in the kitchen, could hear the range murmuring to its flames. 'Ria!' He had been determined not to call out again.

He turned as something fluttered behind him – a piece of paper perhaps – but of course he could see nothing. Probably a draught. He closed the door and walked, sliding one hand along the brick wall, the old whitewash dusting his fingers, and Ria was always on at him about washing his hands, just as she did Lola, making him feel like a delinquent little brother to his girl rather than her father. It must be hard for Ria too. But *she* could see.

'Ria?'

He found the door in the wall, and went upstairs into the house where his ancestors had lived, the proud dynasty whose bastard son he was. His footsteps echoed in the empty space. 'Ria?' He had lost the wall and had to retrace his steps. 'Ria, damn you!' he shouted.

'Got you!' Lola said behind him. 'Who did you think I was?'

'What are you doing there! I nearly jumped out of my skin. Don't be naughty like that again!'

'I'd be frightened too if I couldn't see,' she said reasonably. 'I've been following you with my eyes almost closed.'

'Didn't you hear me calling?'

'I knew you'd be annoyed when you found out. Mum always runs to you the minute you call, but *I'm* not your servant. I nearly lost you on the stairs even with my eyes open. It really was dark, and I was afraid.'

He stopped. No one was as ruthless as children; little savages. She slipped her hand affectionately into his, getting round him with what was undoubtedly a smile, he could *hear* it. 'I'm sorry,' she said beguilingly, then congratulated herself. 'You jumped, didn't you!'

'Lola, for me it's dark all the time,' he tried to explain.

She thought about it. 'But night lasts more than half the day, and's no more dark for you than what it is for us, is it?'

'You're no good for me,' he sighed, tousling her hair.

'Don't,' she said fiercely. 'That's my hair.'

'Just don't surprise me again,' he grinned. He took a step, but she didn't.

'Who did you really think I was, Daddy?'

'You wouldn't understand,' he said.

She led him forward. The resonance of their voices changed and he sensed there was something in front of them, perhaps a window. 'Mum put on her hat and coat and went outside, that's why she didn't come. She was crying.'

'Why?'

'Because she'd said nasty things about you. About you staying in bed and not caring about anything, and she called it your pit,' Lola said with relish. 'It's not your fault,' she said by rote. But her fingers didn't squeeze. It was.

'I didn't know how upset she was.'

'You don't know anything. She's always upset after she's angry.'

'Well, I'm out of bed now,' Ben said irritably.

'There she is!' Lola shouted, and he realised they must be by one of the big leaded windows near the front doors. 'It's too late to say you're sorry.'

Ria was going. A terrible dread gripped Ben's heart. Packed her bags and left. So that was how he felt about her: alone without her. But she would hardly leave Lola behind. He told himself he couldn't look after himself without Ria, that was all. 'Where is she?' he asked calmly.

'She saw Will setting out across the fishponds and she's running to meet him. He's walking on the ice.' Lola's fingers tapped the window and Ben felt her wave. He wondered if in the snowdrifts somewhere below, Ria had turned and waved back at their faces behind the glass.

'What's she doing?'

'She's waving. She's got her coat on and those silly wellies what are too big without her thick socks on. She forgot them, she was so excited. She's borrowed my yellow scarf without asking me and it's fluttering everywhere because of the wind, and the clouds are ever so dark. Is that man really my brother?' For the first time she sounded shy.

'Will? Yes, he's your brother.'

'I thought he was going to be a *boy*, and we could play and everything.'

'He's more than thirty years old. Your mother and I have known each other almost all our lives.'

'Then you must love her very much,' Lola said with a child's sense of priorities, then sounded peculiarly grown-up, a real daughter of the Isle of Dogs: 'Is that why you make her unhappy?'

'Love isn't always like that.' Ben would not forsake Pearl so easily.

'It'd be a cinch to make her happy,' Lola dreamed. 'I wish you'd kiss her. She'd say yuk! But then she'd laugh, wouldn't she, Dad?' He sensed her nodding. She'd decided what she wanted. 'Then we'd all be happy, and I'd know we were all together.' He felt her breath condense on his hand which she was holding, her kiss on his thumb quick and entirely without affectation. 'Everything's going to be all right,' the little girl insisted, sounding so ludicrously determined that he laughed to hide his sadness.

'It's not always such a cinch,' he said.

Lola wouldn't believe it. 'There they are! Mum's got over the snowdrift but she's frightened to go on to the ice, she's holding out her arms. Oh Dad, you'd like it! Isn't she silly! They're together now and she's got her arms around him and she's hugging him. She's so happy she's crying. It's a different sort of crying, isn't it?'

He thought he could hear their little cries of reunion mewling even through the glass. 'Yes,' he said without a smile, 'it is.'

'Wave to them!' Lola cried, 'wave! Dad, *smile!*'

He waved blindly and smiled blindly.

*Who did you think I was, Daddy?*

Lola ran downstairs to greet the brother she had never met, leaving Ben upstairs alone and forgotten in her excitement. Ria and Will were just coming inside, the wind from the south-west bringing a stinging breath of Manchester across the wild moorland. Lola dodged into the shelter of an archway to observe them.

'My little girl's a shy one with strangers, Will!' Ria laughed, lifting her feet out of her snowy boots and padding to the sink to fill the kettle. 'Look at me, now I've got wet feet.' Snow had drifted into her boots almost at once, but such had been her joy at Will's approach that she had not noticed at the time, terrified that the ice would suddenly crack open under his weight and swallow him up. 'Sit down, sit down, go on,' she gestured at the table, she couldn't stop saying something, anything, she was so glad to see him. Will had taken off his cap and come inside, ducking his head beneath the low Victorian lintel just like his father did, except he held his cap in both hands. Was he afraid he would drop it? Will's broad smiling face was polished like an apple, eerily unlined. At first glance – and the eye was pulled to the scar just visible under his hair, pale as a blade sewn across his skull – he seemed simple, childlike. Perhaps that was not the whole truth, because he had not been particularly simple or childish even as a child. Lola watched him wide-eyed.

It was already warm, even hot in the kitchen, but Ria, being sociable, just had to open the range's fire-door, hissing when the cast iron burned her fingers as usual. 'Will I never learn!' Glancing at her children, who paid no attention to her, only to each other, she chucked precious lumps of coal on the fire. She deliberately left the fire-door open so the flames flaunted their illumination cheerfully along the glinting walls, which she had festooned with copper pans, bedwarmers with lovely long handles, rice-steamers and God-knows-what from the cupboards for a homely atmosphere. It was the sort of domestic touch women were expected to love busying them-selves with, though not Ria, but now she hoped Will would notice her effort and like it, though of course he wouldn't say anything. She had sensed at once on the ice he'd retained his father's ability to take in everything at a glance. Then Ria cursed herself for that thought. Ben would never again . . . She so badly wanted everything to be normal, all of them a happy family together, even here in this desolation so far from her familiar streets of London, and she lowered the kettle on to the hotplate feeling her heart would break.

Normally Lola, who always sensed her mother's feelings, would ask, 'What's the matter, Mum?' And Ria would feel free to chat away merrily to her daughter who was far too young to understand.

But now she saw Lola engrossed with Will, and hoped they would be friends. Oh Lord, she was so quick, he so slow. Once they would have been much alike, though dreamy Will had never had that quickness, and now any hope of it had gone for ever. He dragged his footsteps with more than adult slowness. Even his smile was slow, thought out. He looked at the Windsor chair that Ria with her happy blubbery grin was trying to wave him into, then reached out his arm and turned it slightly to face Lola, lowered himself into it and put his elbows on his knees, his unmarked face on the child's level. They surveyed one another seriously, without words. Ria struggled to eavesdrop whilst apparently finding cups and saucers.

'We can play snowballs if you like,' Lola said. Her mother breathed a sigh of relief. Lola liked him.

'Lola. What a beautiful name. What a beautiful little girl you are.' Will held out his hand.

She giggled and looked to her mother, who nodded. 'Don't worry about her, Will, she'll be chattering nineteen-to-the-dozen in a minute.'

Will shook Lola's hand.

'No,' he said, 'she has been talking to her father.'

There was no side to his voice, he was without cares. He tried to speak to Lola again but Ria asked, 'What do you think of my saucepans?'

'You're not allowed to be unhappy, Mum,' Will

215

said. 'Sit down. Talk to me like in the old days.' Ria watched him dab his hand with quick innocence over Lola's face, pretending to catch her nose between his fingers. All the things Ben could never do. Will showed the tip of his thumb between his fingers in mock surprise.

'What is it?' Lola squeaked.

'Your nose!'

Lola clapped her hands over her face with a squeal of delight.

Solemnly he pretended to stick her nose back on and his thumb disappeared.

'Snowballs now!' Lola said.

He turned insistently to Ria. 'Sit down with me.'

'I don't know if I've got the time,' she fretted, but he held out his arm.

Soon with faces red and merry, the three of them sat laughing at ease around the table, swapping family gossip. Helen was well, but she hated the snow, and would have thrown a fit if she'd known Will was going to cross the ice instead of chop wood. 'You look all right, you really do!' Ria cried in her relief, patting Will's glowing cheeks, then holding his hand again on the table. On bad days, she knew from his convalescence, he stayed in his wheelchair, but the migraine attacks were slowly getting better. Lola watched silently.

It was Ria who chattered nineteen-to-the-dozen, of course: she lived in her mouth. Talking was giving, she felt relief so great it was like a physical force draining through her. The strain of these almost silent weeks. 'I've been quiet as a nun, I really have.'

'Why?'

She flicked up her eyes expressively. Upstairs. 'It hasn't been easy for him.'

'Or you. What about you?'

Gratefully Ria relaxed, chancing her arm with the home-made biscuits. 'Mind they don't poison you and I hope you don't break your teeth.' They wolfed the whole plateful, Lola nibbling quietly. 'Come on, say something to your brother,' Ria ordered gaily, confiding in a stage whisper, 'normally I can't shut her up.' Lola's eyes were set on Will's face with the same childish intensity with which she observed her father's every move. Noting everything. But Will was not Ben London. Ria, too, had seen that at once. Will was a really nice person.

There was nothing forced about it: he was nicer than a man. How clever Ria was to think of hanging the saucepans like that, how tasty the biscuits were and she must give Helen the recipe. He was a lovely man, thoughtful and unthreatening. 'Really? They were really OK?' So Ria got more biscuits down in the tin. 'Oh, I just made the recipe up as I went along!' she lied earnestly; she had agonised over the Mrs Beeton. The pages flashed through her mind. Behind every page stood, in her mind's eye, the figure of Ben London. How could she put such disappointment into words? Nothing about being together with him at last was as she had dreamed. There was so much she wanted to confess that every muscle in her body grew tense, she was frightened of throwing the biscuits in every direction when she opened the tin.

Will put his hand over hers. 'Is he very difficult?'

Ria glanced at Lola, who nibbled the biscuit with her ears standing out on stalks. 'Did you leave him alone upstairs?' Ria said in a rising voice.

'OK,' sighed Lola, getting up.

'And don't say OK!'

Lola glanced back. 'I know when I'm not wanted.' That look. Noting everything as children always noted everything.

'*I* said OK,' Ria told her, 'that's different. Come on, give us a kiss.' But Lola ran out of sight upstairs. 'She'll have to go to school, I'll get some peace.'

'Were you a little hard on her?' Will said, putting his hand over Ria's on the table, the oak washed and scrubbed over so many years that the wood had formed whorls like fingerprints.

'I wasn't hard,' Ria said dully. 'I've been banging my head on the wall, and that's hard.' She wasn't meeting Will's eyes now.

'OK,' he murmured reassuringly.

'Where do they get it from?' said Ria in despair. 'I feel so bloody useless and I really don't think I can cope.'

'We're talking about Ben of course?'

'Who else!' sparked Ria aggressively, and anyone but Will would have been startled, but he remained calm. Explored her problem in his stolid way. Ria wished he wasn't so inert, that he'd scream or shout or something. She tried again to relax.

'Mum, did you think it would be easy coming here?'

'I thought it would be worth it.' There. It was said. 'Being together. Maybe I'd take him for a walk in the

218

afternoons, you know, grass and daisies and the little tweety-birds singing in the trees. At least give that to him.' She said doggedly: 'Affection.'

Neither the feel of Will's hand nor his expression had changed, but he was nodding, at least he was listening. 'You're a born romantic, Mum,' he said, surprising her.

Ria wondered if he bedded Helen and thought he must do. She couldn't believe they just went to sleep together and woke up together. She wondered if he was capable of care and passion.

'He hardly talks to me,' Ria said, 'it's as if he's ignoring me to punish me.'

'Maybe you should leave him. Maybe that would be best – for him, as well as for you.'

'No, I couldn't leave him again,' Ria said at once.

'Why not?' asked Will casually.

'Because he's not the one to blame!' Ria admitted. '*I'm* the guilty one. He would have been happier if—' She stopped. *If you'd never been born, Will*, she thought. 'If he'd never met me.'

'Mum, you must feel something for him if he makes you so unhappy.'

'I wish Ben and I were children again,' Ria whispered, 'I wish we could have our time over. I wanted to be married in St Luke's and I wanted to get away from Vic and I wanted to be grown up . . . I seduced Ben to make him marry me, not because I loved him.'

Hurt showed in Will's eyes.

'I hated Vic more,' Ria confessed. 'Ben was the one in love. For him what had happened between us in the

219

night by Tower Bridge was real and genuine, he believed in me. But when Vic found about the child I carried—'

'Me,' Will said.

'You changed everything between me and Vic.'

'I'm glad,' Will said, but Ria shook her head.

'I betrayed Ben because I didn't have the guts to stand up to Vic. Vic made Ben eat his shit, you know. Literally. He'd kill him if he ever came back. All because of me, because . . . oh, I did love Ben. But how could he ever love me after what I'd done to him? How could he ever care anything for me?' She ended tearfully: 'And he doesn't. You'll see he doesn't. He's so cold to me, he hardly talks. He's punishing me.'

'Because you loved him once? Leave him,' Will repeated. 'For his sake as well as yours.'

Ria nodded miserably. 'Because I still love him.'

This was a dreadful conversation, the sort that rubbed the wound more the longer it went on, but Ria was powerless to prevent herself. She pulled her hand away from Will then threw him a haunted look. 'No, Will. Leaving doesn't work. It doesn't solve anything, change anything.'

'Of course, but—'

'I'm still me, aren't I? Wherever I am I've still got me with me, haven't I?' She tried to explain, 'You see, there's more between Ben and me than you can know.'

Will said blandly, 'Isn't that always the case with parents?'

'Stop sounding like one of them lick-it-and-stick-it marriage guidance blokes they got down the council!'

Will obviously struggled to comprehend his mother. After his years at London House in the thirties he probably knew Ben better than she did. 'I didn't realise how strong your feelings for him still were . . .'

'Does it show?' Ria worried about letting herself down. 'I'm living in the same house with him but I can't communicate with him.'

'He must be very difficult.'

'He's impossible.' Ria added in a low voice: 'And there's something more. He frightens me, because after all we've been through I don't think there's anything left between us any more.'

## 2

'Don't let me fall,' Esther said anxiously. 'A rare sight I'd look lying on my blooming arse. At a proper funeral too.'

'You look the bee's knees,' Vic reassured her, though he had been looking at the clouds building in the west, above the river, as he came out of the house. 'Give us a smile.'

Everything in Esther's life nowadays had to be proper: hat, black, pinned. Coat, brushed, and a black satin lining too. Because Vic was back home she had told herself they were the aristocracy of Havannah Street once more, and Esther came out of her front door with her head held high. She didn't half take advantage of him.

'I've got you, Mum,' Vic said, handing her across the slippery pavement to one of the limousines that

Tovey & Sons & Co, Funeral Directors, had queued
at the kerb. What a to-do, said Esther's smile, but a
pleasurable to-do. The church was only a short walk
but Mrs Morris had wanted to go out with style,
having made more friends dying than in her life; and
as a thank-you to the streets for making her last
months bearable, the funeral would not go straight to
St Luke's, in clear view though it was. 'You follow in
the next car,' Vic said aside to Terry. 'No arguing.'
Vic was reasserting his authority over Nigel's boy
these days, and Terry sketched a salute without a
smile. But Vic smiled at Mum and put a rug over her
knees as he settled beside her.

The cortège, in a shameful waste of petrol but a
wonderful morbid show, would trail Mrs Morris's
Armstrong Siddeley hearse – not a proper bier with
black cartwheels and horses with black plumes,
Esther sniffed, but the vehicle was stuffed with plenty
of pricey hothouse flowers and wreaths nevertheless –
following the circuitous route of neighbourly thanks-
giving. The planning of this rite of passage from the
community had given Mrs Morris much peace, from
Havannah Street then up and down Cheval Street,
Tooke Street, Malabar Street, West Ferry Road and
only finally to Strafford Street and back to St Luke's,
almost where the body had started. She had died
content in the knowledge, and Esther understood the
sentiment, that chatty young mums on doorsteps
would wave the tiny bunched hands of their latest
swaddled babies in farewell as the hearse passed, net
curtains would be parted and windows thrown open
to wave her goodbye. And some were. But so many of

the houses were empty now, Esther noticed, the windows were square black eyes, gaudy front doors peeling. And Esther thought there weren't as many children as there used to be. The little beggars used to run all over the place, she remembered, one or two of the braver urchins rattling sticks on the revolving cartwheels until they got a clip round the lughole, but there was none of that now. The docks weren't full of masts either: Esther was surprised by that, she'd not realised it before. Groups of youths hung around waiting for the pubs to open, arrogant and miserable with the cold. Of course everyone as long as she could remember was always saying that the Isle of Dogs was going to the dogs, but in her experience the place had actually got a good deal better than it used to be. Now it seemed to be going downhill again. People grumbled, but people always grumbled, that was what the froth on beer was for. Maybe this time they had something to grumble about . . . those who remained.

Esther held up her gloved hand at the car window. 'Don't do that,' Vic said, 'it makes you look like Queen Mary.'

Esther quite liked the idea. In truth she'd had one or two little ones before departure and she hoped to see another one or two after the service, when the closest friends were to be invited back to the Morris house. The two Morris boys, who'd vanned down from Chelmsford in Moss Bros suits, looked sour about the expenditure, and the house already had an agent's sign outside it. 'Aren't the boys moving back home?' she asked, surprised.

'The council are talking about compulsory purchase on that whole row,' Vic grunted. Esther was alarmed.

The cars turned past a bomb-lot of waste ground where two girls pushed a pram with a laughing toddler in it, weaving at a terrifying pace between the heaps of rubble. 'Tears before bedtime,' said Esther automatically. 'You don't see so many children as in my day.'

'Young families are being moved out.'

'The council can do that too, can they?'

'These days they can do whatever they like. They'll talk and talk and nothing will happen, don't fuss,' Vic yawned.

'Talk about what? What do they want our houses for?'

'Knock them down for council flats.'

Esther couldn't imagine everything gone. 'At least I've got you, dear.'

'Don't fret, Mum.'

'I wish Ria was here, I can't help it,' Esther sniffled into her nice lace handkerchief, a Christmas present from Vic. 'Funerals always do this to me. Funerals and weddings. Ria never did things proper, that's her trouble.'

'We're well off without that vaudeville tart,' Vic murmured. 'Once a tart, always a tart.' Vic's contempt for Ria was frightening. But Ria had done so much to deserve it, Esther told herself, being so full of life, so difficult, taking advantage of her sex. 'All these years she deceived you, Mum,' Vic said.

'Vic, don't,' Esther quavered, 'be gentle today.

224

Look at my make-up.' Strafford Street, nearly there.
She powdered her blotched cheeks frantically.

'All these weeks and she hasn't been in touch, not a
postcard, not a phone call, not a peep,' Vic said in a
voice darkening with rage, and glanced at Esther
without affection, as if he blamed her for Ria's
behaviour. 'It doesn't matter. People expect you to
cry today.' Then he smiled, 'Don't mind my temper,
Mum, it's only because I care about *you* so much.'

The hearse crunched among piles of rotten ice by
the mean single-storey church, built of grey-green
Thames mud housebricks like everything else round
here, dirty and drab in the dank air. Everyone was
heartily sick of the old snow by now, mottled almost
black with sooty specks. 'That's what our lungs look
like inside,' coughed some joker, Denny Hyde the
retired skin merchant. No one laughed. This winter
had hung around for ever, children's games turned
deadly with hardpacked balls of March ice that broke
noses and windows. Everyone was fed up and low
with it, and to cap it all, Esther had overheard talk
that the moment the thaw came the Government
would ban coal fires in houses until next winter. It was
terrible getting old, and she gripped Vic's warm,
black-gloved hand gratefully. One day they'd place
her in here beside Nigel and she'd lie at peace among
her children, including Vic in due course, and maybe
even Ria would come back at the end of her life. And
everyone would be together, and forgiven.

'When she was a little girl Ria dreamed of being
married here.'

'Shut it,' Vic said. He'd seen Betty Stark hanging

around by the wall where the memorial stones were, looking like a woman caught out, trapped by the sudden flurry of activity that she had not expected. By her foot, bombsite weeds had been placed on Nigel's stone, all the poor woman could find, Vic saw – a few snowdrops, ragged things that seeded themselves on the rubble of people's homes. Vic stared at her and she stared back. Now that Pearl London was dead, Betty Stark, who had midwifed Lola and whose hands first touched the baby, was the only outsider who knew the secret of Ria's child. She'd seen it in Vic's eyes. And when Ria cuddled her bundle and promised her newborn infant what mothers always did, that she'd have the world, it was Betty Stark who said, 'But she won't have a father.' Vic would never forgive Betty for that.

'Oh,' waved Esther busily, 'there's Betty Stark!' She bustled over. Vic hastened after her just in case, but the girl would never dare say anything unwise. He fixed her with his eyes, and Betty kept forcing herself to look away from him, smiling for Esther, but her gaze always came back to Vic. 'It is you, Betty?' Esther said.

'Mrs Dempsey now,' Betty said. She was still a strong-looking, attractive woman, but her face was clawed with lines, her top eyelids almost disappeared. She worked hard hours as a cleaner at the London Hospital. Nigel had been the love of her life just as Arleen had been the love of his, and it was Betty's tragedy that he'd never recovered from Arleen's death. So Betty, with a house in Poplar somewhere, still lived and grieved for him. Esther was amazed but touched by the woman's behaviour: no one knew where Alan Stark, Betty's first husband, was buried – but here was his widow still laying flowers on her boyfriend's stone! And Nigel had felt not a thing for her.

'I remarried,' Betty told Vic. 'Mr Dempsey is a Customs Officer at the West India Dock,' she said proudly to Esther, with her strong, vulnerable smile. 'I started a new life.'

'Customs clerk,' Vic said. 'The Official Mr D. knows about the flowers does he, Betty?'

'Oh, I just picked them myself,' Betty said rapidly, anxious to get past.

'Goodbye,' Vic said, holding open the gate.

But from the pavement Betty turned back to Esther. 'Nigel was a kind man.'

After the service the guests went back to Mrs Morris's house in Havannah Street. It was hardly worth getting in the car, and though Esther insisted on riding, Vic walked. He began to suffocate in the little front room full of prattling women: none of them would take off their hats, the sherry was so sweet it clung in the glass and the mince pies were stale. Esther was having a fine time and Terry had got earnest in a corner with the Morris boys, the Essex mafia, just as Vic had told him to. Lads moving out to the new towns took with them many fine family traditions, and market gardening was a good cover. Hitler's bombs had a lot to answer for. London was dissolving, its people planned and organised by official bodies these days, not so much the church or the beat policemen, but plainclothes detectives

227

and clever hygiene regulations. Prying middle-class bureaucrats seemed honestly horrified that a toilet door opened into a kitchen and that the kitchen had no running water. Let them find an 'airey' in the yard and that was the end of you. Rooms of a size, window of a size, people of a size. Everything was against the law. 'One day,' this was one of Vic's favourite jokes, 'they'll regulate the air we're breathing.'

He had to get outside. The air felt sticky with warmth and dark clouds hung overhead. As it began to rain he walked back to the house. Inside – probably against regulations – he'd had a simple doorway knocked through the wall into next door, which Terry would have no use for during his next few months in Essex. When Ria came back, and Vic had no doubt that she would come back, because she was a woman and women always came home, this was where she would come home with his daughter.

3

*Who did you think I was, Daddy?*

Ben turned slowly from the window and, with hands outstretched, launched himself lumberingly across the spacious reception room. He remembered perfectly where the stairs were – he thought. His steel-capped workboots tapped on the tiles, black-and-white chequer squares about a yard, he knew, on each side. His holiday here with Pearl twenty-two

228

years ago remained a clearsighted memory within him, as alive as though it was yesterday, illuminating sudden flashes in his mind with the squeak of a step or door, the echo of his tread making him recollect this black-and-white chequer as vividly as though he saw it, remembering himself sauntering across it in those carefree days: dressed for dinner maybe with a drink dangling in his hand, and Pearl beside him on his elbow, wearing those sapphires that matched her eyes, a sparkly hipless sheath dress, twenties-style. Ben London, stone blind, wearing check shirt and work-boots, stopped. He squeezed his eyes shut as though that could make him stop seeing her.

He must let Pearl die.

He took another step and fell against the stairs. He broke his fall with his hands on the bare wood, sensing the look of the staircase rising above him: its wide wooden curve, balustraded on the inner radius where the stairs were steepest. The gentle incline of the broad steps on the far side was designed to be traversed by elegant ladies in enormous, hooped, early-Victorian dresses, coming and going to the brilliant entertainments once held in these echoing, icy chambers. Bare wood. Were the walls where the portraits had hung also bare? Had they been removed to a place of safety from the damp? He did not think so. He could feel them, the weight of their gaze, the slow tocking of time passing without remorse. The feeling reminded him of the epitaph commonly on headstones in older church-yards, chilling in its smugness. *One day you will be as we.* Once they too had been alive and in love under the sun.

He heard a footstep.

*Who did you think I was?*

He kicked lightly with his foot at the bottom step.

*I'm Vic Price. Remember me.*

'What do you see?' he called to his left. Lola's footsteps skipped from the doorway to the kitchens. He bent down. He'd thought it was Vic Price had found him again, that was what.

'I wasn't trying to creep up on you,' Lola murmured.

'I know,' he whispered.

She chuckled. 'Don't you want to come and meet Will? He's downstairs and we were eating biscuits! He says OK and eats two biscuits at a time but I'm not allowed.'

The last time Ben had seen Will was on the last night of Pearl's life. 'He'll be up when he's ready. Did he bring anything with him?'

'He had a bag with shopping in it.' Lola still called food *shopping*. 'Eggs, big brown ones. I don't think Mr Attlee knows about Will's chickens. A proper crusty loaf not like Mum makes. Cheese and butter, I think Will's cow is a secret too. I want to see Will milk the cow. She's black and white and freezing.'

'Friesian. You can help him when the weather's better.'

'You come too.'

'Do you like Will?'

'Oh, yes!' said Lola joyously. 'But I don't love him.' She took Ben's hand. 'I'll look after you.'

Ben swallowed then cleared his throat.

'Don't pretend to be a big softie!' said Lola, delighted. She turned serious, and Ben knew he was being worked on. They were very similar, he and his daughter. 'You won't let Mum send me to school, will you?' Lola said.

'Big ears.'

'I couldn't help myself,' Lola said daintily. He could imagine her look, and hid his laughter.

'There's a school in the village. I suppose you'll go there.'

She cut to the heart of the matter. 'Did you go to school, Dad?'

'That's different.'

'I'm learning more about you all the time, aren't I?'

He squeezed her hand gently, and repeated, 'Tell me what you see.'

'Pickshures. They go all the way upstairs.' He asked her what they were pictures of. 'Old men.' He let her lead him up a few steps and knew the patch of wall left blank by Cleremont family tradition was in front of them.

'What do you see, Lola?'

She shrugged. 'Nothing.'

'Sometimes what you don't see is the most important thing. There's no portrait of Robert Lockhart, the first Lord Cleremont, is there? Yet he was the most important of all those old men, because he founded the dynasty. Without him there would have been none of us.'

'But they're *old*,' Lola said.

Ben murmured: 'Sons of sons of sons. The male

231

line. The family name is extinct, only its blood lives on, in me. Counting for nothing. I haven't the name, I can't inherit the title.'

'What about girls?' Lola said.

'For centuries these men were successful.'

'Successful!'

'They never married for love.'

'Then what were they successful at?' she asked.

Ben had never really known his father until it was too late. He'd learned the truth of the Lockhart family only when he found Lisa, his mother.

'They survived,' Ben London said.

The Lockharts were Teviotdale Scots, courtiers who, in the spring sunshine of 1603, came south with the Scottish King James to the throne of England. A vain and cunning laird, Robbie Lockhart wagged a silver tongue in his forgotten, handsome face, so much the King's favourite he was showered with royal kisses even in public. 'Flattery, immorality and borrowed money,' Lisa had repeated with rigid distaste, but also with a kind of admiration for the family whose blood flowed in the veins of her illegitimate son. 'The usual basis of a proud dynasty!'

His many enemies called Robbie 'The Undertaker' for his political hatchet-work, but his reward was one of the sixty lay peerages created by his grateful monarch. Given charge of the starch monopoly, Lord Cleremont with the King's indulgence and his own purloined revenues bought these lands at Clere Mount, Blane and Clawfell, not quite the Teviotdale remembered of old Robbie's youth, but half-way. *Half-way* also summed up the family's circumstances when Parliament declared the monopoly void a few years later. Name they had, land they had, pride they had, money they did not have. After Robbie died, his house, fortified as a Royalist redoubt in a district mostly supporting Parliament, was burned in the Civil War and his portrait destroyed. His son Stewart, a Cavalier and fine swordsman, was killed later by gunshot at Marston Moor.

'Sixteen forty-four,' chanted Lola excitedly, 'the Battle of Marston Moor!'

'How did you know – you can't even count.' Ben frowned, 'Did you learn that rhyme at your Cheval Street School?'

'There!' Lola scoffed dismissively. 'No, at hop-scotch.' From the way she tugged him on he knew school was still a sensitive subject. 'Is that one Stewart?' she said quickly, adding, 'Shall I tell you about him? He's got fancy clothes and a big hat with a feather in it.'

'His son Robert escaped to Holland but their lands and holdings were confiscated. He had only his family pride to sustain him.' The stairs creaked under them as Lola led him up. 'Stewart had been extravagant, proud, touchy, always in debt. Robert was fierce and narrow, but honest, and amongst the "butterboxes" of his Dutch exile he learned the lesson of poverty. When his estate was returned to him under the Restoration, he rebuilt the house on a solid founda-tion of wool exports to his Dutch contacts from Leyden. "Wool built this house."'

'But he's got a hard face like stone,' Lola said. 'And only his house and hills behind him.'

233

'The house and hills that he loved.'

'But what about his wife? Why aren't his wife and children painted in the picture too? It would have been nice,' Lola said, 'I would have liked to see them. But I expect they'd have worn funny clothes too, wouldn't they?'

'Love was not considered necessary to a successful marriage,' Ben explained. 'Most people don't know their families – our great-grandparents are unknown perhaps, even their life and times mysterious; our grandfather's sisters are lost to us with the changing of their names, women disappearing from the bloodline as if they were unimportant, and coming into new families from nowhere. The blood remembers, but our brains forget. Our history isn't written down, our portraits aren't painted, so our children and our children's children cannot really know themselves, what blood shapes them, what forces move them.' He stopped, sensing someone there. Or perhaps it was just Lola's silence that alerted him. 'Will?'

'You heard the stair creak,' Will said. Ben reached out into the dark and, feeling his arms taken, embraced his son. He said nothing. It was all in his grip. The step squeaked as Lola sat down and watched them.

Ben kept his hand on Will's shoulder. 'I'm glad you're not in that wheelchair.'

Will laughed cheerfully. 'Same old father! You never accept that some of us don't have quite your determination. Don't let him bully you, Lola.'

'She was showing me the portraits.'

Will pointed. 'Robert. Dutch gables on the house.'

'Will paints pictures,' Ben explained, 'he knows about such things.'

'These are in an awful mess,' Will said reproachfully. 'Damp . . . it's a shame. You're not going to leave them to rot where they are?'

Ben didn't answer.

Will's voice lost its slowness, filled with enthusiasm. 'Let's go up a few steps, Lola.' She scrambled eagerly to her feet. 'This is Robert's son James, who extended his father's house, but from misplaced filial duty, in his father's memory, not love for it. Bit of a rakehell. James was not the country gentleman he had been born to be! The gambling, extravagant side had come out in him, he couldn't help himself. He spent little time here. And *his* son, Charles –' a few steps more – 'hated the place. He preferred London.'

'But he knew his duty,' Ben said. 'Home, land, name. Each Lord Cleremont with Lord Cleremonts standing behind him. The child's duty was to continue the great name of their family. The eldest son must marry and produce a male heir. Nothing else mattered. *That* was how they succeeded. They knew who they were. *There* was their name coming down through history. Whether in London or Clawfell they were masters of their blood.'

'Prisoners,' Will said.

'Ultimately. But for hundreds of years they were successful.'

Will shrugged, a shrug his father could not see. 'This painting of Charles's son John is by Gainsborough . . . ice has cracked the varnish. John was of the generation that loved Clawfell, added a

235

portico and wings, picturesque gardens . . . His son William loved London, a miser burning brown coal in his fireplace on an income of a hundred thousand a year. John's grandson, George, loved the moors and wasted his inheritance building Clawfell into a fake castle.'

'There you have it,' Ben said, 'one generation moving to London, the next rediscovering the cleansing gales of Clawfell, a genetic metronome ticking back and forth down the generations. None of them ever realised how formed and dominated they were by their blood, despite all their interest in bloodstock.'

'And no girls,' said Lola sadly. 'Didn't they happen?'

'A person can live a life here,' Will said, 'and no one would ever know.'

They had almost reached the top of the stairs and were hidden by the ascending curve of the balustrade from below. Down there, out of sight, Ria paused in the doorway and rested one hand on the icy wood, the other in the pocket of her skirt, listening to their voices floating down.

'Yes, the Cleremont ladies must have had daughters.' The rough, raw edge of emotion in Ben's voice surprised Ria. He was grieving for Pearl – sometimes Ria felt that Ben's memory of that elegant, fantastic lady, who'd had everything so bloody easy in her life, was more alive to him than she was. Just her bloody *memory*, for God's sake. Ria brushed a few strands of hair out of her eyes: good old Ria. 'They and their fleeting lives,' Ben said sadly, 'their feminine hopes and desires, their eyes and smiles, their passing years. A few bits of faded sewing, embroidered samplers, scraps of childish handwriting, their forgotten names, almost nothing remains. How can we know what had meaning for them? Their lives are unrecorded. Invisible. Gone. Just like the lives of ordinary folk.'

*No, it's not like that at all,* Ria wanted to say. *It's all worth it.*

'Everything changed,' Ben said, 'when the family became impoverished. Then the women were put to work. Edward, the ninth Lord Cleremont, my grandfather who loved London, wed his youngest daughter by his second marriage, Diana, into the wealthy Prideau banking family for obvious reasons. My own father Charles was married to Henrietta Rownslee, also for her money.'

Will murmured, 'But he loved Lisa, your mother.'

'His affair with her destroyed him.'

Ria came quietly upstairs. No one could move with less fuss than Ria when she wished. Her skirt whispered around her legs. *I'm Ria Price. I'm special,* she heard herself chanting in her head. Will had his back to her, and Lola, who saw her, said nothing.

'I wish you'd let me clean these pictures,' she heard Will saying.

But Ben shook his head. 'They're all I have. Lisa hardly remembers her own parents, nothing at all of her grandparents. Who am I?' He pointed blindly. '*They're* who I am.'

'All this in your life I never knew of,' Ria said.

'Neither does Vic,' Ben said.

*Oh my God*, thought Ria, *he hasn't changed at all*.

Lola broke into the silence. 'Look!' she yelled with a laugh, pointing, then running downstairs with her skirt flying so that Ria almost shouted out, her heart in her mouth, sure the little idiot would trip and roll over and over to the bottom and get up crying and grazed, making more work. Ria kept a small bottle of iodine stashed downstairs but Lola was a bear about anything stinging. Once in desperation at home, Lola screaming over a cut knee, Ria had slapped on some pungent white industrial disinfectant nicked from Corporation supplies by her friend Pat, who cleaned the public lavs opposite the Seamen's Institute and at Island Gardens. Lola had never trusted antiseptics after that stinging experience. Ria would be in for another bloody battle of wills, twenty minutes just getting Lola to tolerate a dab from the cotton wool, then endless fuss, and Ria getting more frayed and fraught than ever, and Ben's lunch to cook, and his sheets to change, and she'd hardly slept last night for worrying about him and how she was behaving. She felt like she carried suitcases under her eyes. And she might lose her temper and really *scream* at the child she loved so much. Because she loved her. Only then would Lola understand and agree to go quiet, allow the necessary dabbing to be done.

'Lola, yer bloody idjit!' Ria roared, anger the only way she had of showing her love. Maybe it would be best if she let Will handle Lola, who'd cooperate with him because he was calm and unruffled, watching Lola's hair-raising descent with a mild expression. But it wasn't Will's elbow she had snatched at instinctively. It was Ben's.

But Lola didn't fall. She jumped the last two steps nimbly and her small figure skipped to the broad windows. She stood on tiptoe, her elbows braced on the sill. 'Look – it's raining!'

Grey water streamed down the glass. Outside the snow pocked, began to smear, then dark runnels appeared between the drifts and flowed downhill.

'Now Will won't have to walk home across the ice,' Lola said.

'I'm going to come back and clean those pictures,' Will promised.

'Come back anyway,' Ben told him when they were saying farewell after lunch, Ria's rubbery fried eggs on a whitish fried slice. He lent Will his own coat against the downpour.

'See you tomorrow,' Ria called from the sink then, very quietly, glancing at Ben out of the corners of her eyes, gave up trying to scrub the burnt-on egg from the frypan: what the eye didn't see the heart wouldn't grieve over. She put Lola in the bedroom for her siesta like Mr Churchill did, shoes off, sheets up to her chin, eyes closed, a quick kiss, and left the door ajar because Lola hated it closed. Ria came back to the kitchen where Ben had rolled up his sleeves at the sink, finishing off Ria's trial of strength with the pan. He was still a magnificent figure of a man, the leather patches on the check shirt suited him, showing off his broad shoulders – but why had she instinctively thought him shrunken in stature, simply because he was sightless and needed her help? Surely that ought to make her care for him more, but that wasn't the way she felt. His forehead bobbed within an inch of the dark oak wallcupboards whose height was gauged for the reach of short Victorian serving-girls. Ria watched him work, not sure what she was thinking. Waiting. He banged his forehead and cursed, sending soapsuds flying from his hands as he held them to his head.

'Iodine!' Ria laughed.

He gave the offending cupboard a whack from his fist, scattering the white puffs of foam from his knuckles. But then he grinned at her, *exactly* at her, and said, 'That's the first time I've heard you laugh.'

'What?'

'Really laugh,' he said.

'I'll try and oblige you with a giggle or two more often, sir.' She examined his forehead on tiptoe. 'You'll live.'

'You've been very glum, Ria.'

He was making her feel guilty for what was *his* fault! She dropped back off tiptoe. 'You've been very difficult.'

'You wouldn't be worth it otherwise.'

It was the nearest he'd come to saying a thank-you for all she'd been through, and not much of a thanks either. Ria seized on something else to grumble about. 'I'm almost your prisoner here.'

'Not of me.'

'Of the weather, anyway.'

'You can leave when you like.'

'I won't leave!' Ria gave up. 'It's just I'm so bloody tired I don't know what to do, you've been driving me up the wall. There's Lola sticking to you like a blooming limpet, I hardly never get to see her to myself, and she won't eat unless you eat. She gets up early to take your bloody breakfast in and I have to get up early to cook it so she has an excuse to fawn over you and I've had it up to here . . .'

He gently closed the door to the corridor, leaving clumps of bubbles on the brass handle. She realised she had been almost shouting; Lola might wake. 'Don't give up.' Ben held out his hands like the start of a dance. What did he mean? For an instant Ria felt silly enough to take them in her own hands. That eerie blue gaze: he knew exactly where she was by the sound of her breathing.

'Towel,' he said. His dripping hands.

'I ought to throw it at you,' Ria said. But she didn't.

He wiped his hands, then felt for the range and hung the towel over the drying rail. 'Ria?'

'What now?'

'You're the best mum she could have had,' he said.

'Good God.' Ria tossed her head back impatiently.

'Don't push your luck. You heard.' Again she had detected that strange cutting edge of feeling in his voice. The word *mum* that came so naturally to her, that he treated with such wonder. He looked so tall and mature, ruthless to himself in his self-confidence, and possibly he would be to her, yet there it still was: the little boy somewhere inside him, his innocence, and that tone of his that took Ria back years. She could see the children in the cellar at Canary Warren: Esther putting down her blood-spattered knife by the chopped meat Vic had stolen, her welcome of the

241

lonely boy Ria had found. 'My name's Esther, but you can call me Mum.' Ria's own mother. And Vic throwing his arm around Ria's shoulder, thwarting his mother's welcome in almost the same breath. 'This is Ria. She's my sister. I love her.'

Ria blinked herself back to the present. The past was past. She arranged the towel neatly over the rail.

'I'm glad you shaved that beard off.'

'It's an improvement?'

She thought it transformed him. He put out his hand on the back of the Windsor chair and sat down. It had transformed him into the boy she had loved, the man she had rejected. 'No! Not much of an improvement!' she heard herself say, then was irritated with herself for sounding so flippant and false. No one knew – *had* known – what she really felt better than he.

'What do I really look like?' he asked.

'Like you.' She sat opposite him at the table. 'Ben, you'll let me stay, won't you?'

'You've never been much good at lying,' he said.

What an arrogant bastard he could be. Ria itched to tell him so but held the tip of her tongue between her teeth. 'I think Lola likes me, don't you?' he asked conversationally.

'If you could see her, you'd know it was much more than that!'

He nodded. 'I wanted to hear it from you.'

'You love her, don't you, Ben?'

'Of course I do,' he laughed. 'I'm her father.'

'Well,' Ria said, 'she loves you too.' Her fingernail

traced a pattern in the tabletop's veined wood. Lola
was not his daughter. But how could she ever tell him
so? If she did not, however, she was almost as bad as
Vic. She kept her mouth shut.

She broke her nail, painfully.

'I'll stay as long as you want,' she said desperately.
'I don't want things to be the way they were between
us.'

'Don't want?'

'I mean I know they can't be.'

He shrugged. 'That's a different thing.'

'I preferred you the way you were when you were
hurt,' she said viciously.

'I do need you.' But he made no move to reach out
to her, although he must have heard her hands on
the table. Ria bit off the hangnail. Once she'd had
beautiful nails, when she was on stage. Ben London
began to laugh. 'Ria,' he said with affection. He put
his hands on the table but she moved hers away
sullenly. 'I promised Pearl I'd never meet you again. I
kept that promise. I even hid from you. But I'm not
hiding from you now.'

'Put those down, you won't get round me that way,'
Ria said.

He could tell she was staring at his eyes.

'You really are ruthless,' she murmured, 'you just
manipulate me.'

'I had a good teacher, Ria. You always knew what
you wanted and you always got it.'

'I didn't get you,' she said. 'Not the way I wanted
you, I didn't.'

He said nothing. The most powerful things were said in no words. Ria put one of her home-baked biscuits between his fingers. 'Present,' she said.

But still he said nothing. Friends was never what they had been.

# PART III

## The Undertow

March 1947 – May 1948

# Chapter Six

*Are you happy?*
*Yes, I'm happy!*
*Then why couldn't she see his face?*
*She had won; she had thrown away not her life,*
*but her old life.*

## 1

The snow had melted, but still it rained. Often Lisa tried to persuade Victoria to take a taxi to and from work, at least for the walk home in the dark, and not, it turned out, just to keep her dry. 'You hear such stories nowadays!' Victoria tolerated this nagging but wouldn't listen, saying her walk was only a five-minute stroll down St James's Street, London's Clubland. Finally she openly scorned her grandmother's too-often repeated advice. 'There's so much about London you don't know,' Lisa reproached her. 'You young people are always so sure you know it all. You never know who might be watching you.'

'I can look after myself,' Victoria snapped impatiently. 'I'll carry an umbrella, if that makes you happier.'

'It's not that . . .' The usual row started. 'You just want to get your own way, Victoria! And don't be insolent!'

'Why don't you want me to be happy?' Victoria stormed. 'I just want to be happy and you're stopping me all the time.'

'I'm not. I'm really not, baby. It's for your own good.'

'I'm going up to my room,' Victoria said. That was how it always ended, with Victoria's gramophone crooning some ghastly record behind a closed door upstairs. Victoria's victory.

Downstairs Lisa, undefeated, tried to hide her misery. Not being able to help was worst. The young would be young, she told herself. A grandmother was not the same as a mother or a father, not at all, and the harder Lisa tried to be, the more she failed. She had been young once. She had abandoned her baby and she wanted Victoria to be the child she had never brought up as her own. She knew she had so much to give Victoria but after these difficult weeks Lisa realised she would not prevail. She saw Ben's hand in this. He never did anything without meaning it.

Blinded, lying shocked and agonised in that hospital bed, he had been thinking, deciding, and known what he must do. Deliberately he'd given Victoria what she had always wanted: to be free. He understood her desire for the freedom, with all its perils, that he'd known at her age. She was free to do whatever she wished. To achieve, or to fail. To learn discipline, or run wild. Ben loved Victoria so dearly that he had let her go.

Lisa knew from her own bitter youth – and as she grew older those distant memories drew closer and flowered more vividly in her mind – that nothing in the world could be more wonderful, or more dangerous, than love.

Even, she supposed, a father's love for his daughter.

And still it rained.

Victoria didn't see the man with brown eyes again, but she didn't need to. If he fancied her enough to keep trying that was up to him. She was happy either way, a modern girl for the modern world, 'going places' as everyone said, not one of those cloistered, fainting, milksop ingénues she'd been brought up on who inhabited the Madame LaFarge Library of Literature, boring everyone to death with their coy tears and simpering machinations for the marriage kiss from Mr Right and happiness ever after. And a dozen children no doubt. That wasn't happiness. The world had turned.

Victoria thought everybody thought like herself. But she knew older people were incapable of understanding.

Today everything was new and fresh. The war had broken down the class barriers that already seemed ridiculous in the thirties' films Victoria remembered from her childhood, which seemed incredibly long ago. Imagine, middle-aged men actually wearing evening clothes to queue for the cinema stalls at black-and-white films – hardly any Technicolor 'movies'! – and, simpering beside them, their pampered women spruced up like poodles with *déjà-vu* Victorian fashions – bustle-bows, and crinoline shifts 'underneath' for God's sake! The men whose subservience and appeasement had started the war, the women whose daughters wore overalls in the war-production factories.

Lisa tried to tell Victoria all this had happened before, this shocked *never again* feeling even after the First World War, more than a lifetime ago, long before Victoria was born; that even then people had dreamed the same dreams, a land fit for heroes to live in . . . It had all gone sour, all into the dole queues. Victoria tried to make the old lady comprehend that this time it would be different. The future was a clean slate that would be written by the young. And she was part of it. Intoxicated by it. Working for it. All the great stores employed girls nowadays. She tried to communicate her enthusiasm to Lisa.

'Don't blame your father too much,' Lisa said over supper. 'I know you miss him terribly.'

Victoria told the truth. 'I'm glad he's gone. He's renounced the way of life that brought about his destruction. Thank God the Government are taking everything into public ownership. None of this will be left after the Inheritance Tax. Like this huge house built for one man's ego and only the two of us using it. I just want to be ordinary.'

Lisa laughed at such pouting, silly-sounding radicalism, then remembered herself, and it seemed like only yesterday. 'Don't be offended. I wasn't laughing at you.'

But her white hairs were bound to be an unwelcome intrusion into a young life. However wise an old lady's intentions were, everything was happening to Victoria for the first time. Nothing compared. While Lisa nibbled her dessert Victoria went up to her room and played over and over 'They Say It's Wonderful', and 78s of Frank Sinatra singing with the Tommy Dorsey Band.

Victoria had no illusions about love. She kept the silly bottle of perfume on the dressing-table, unopened, where she could see it. It would be a laugh if she saw him in the shop again, she wouldn't let on she'd received his cheeky gift and his eyes would be disappointed. She was free, so was he, they were both adults and she felt entirely in control of him. An insurance actuary could only ever be a diversion, and a man who thought he could impress her with a bottle of the Fox Pharmaceutical Company's 'Tonight' was barking so completely up the wrong tree that she liked him. She was way ahead of him.

But he didn't come back.

The longer he left it coasting the more she was interested – not in him, of course, but in the adult game she was playing for the first time. Once or twice walking to work, but *only* once or twice, she was sure she was looked at, and the interest, or just the anticipation, spiced her routine. She was curious. But suddenly she lost hope and in her despair convinced herself he'd found someone else. His loss! It rained almost every day. The springtime electricity cuts were longer than ever, as if the power stations were exhausted by their winter effort. Meanwhile

Piccadilly was often dark, as in the wartime blackout, as though peace had never come. And in the evening Victoria listened to her gramophone.

Lisa, incredibly for her age Victoria thought, hit the nail on the head. 'Each generation in its turn thinks *it* discovered sex.' It was Sunday morning and Lisa nodded through the window to the youngsters walking arm-in-arm, eye-to-eye amongst the daffodils of St James's Park, feeding the ducks from white paper bags. 'Anything for an excuse to be together, eh?' Victoria was embarrassed by this blatant trawling for clues but Lisa ploughed on. 'They're glad it's raining so they can huddle under a single umbrella!' It was as if she was observing a comedy of manners, not something desperately serious.

Finally Lisa sat down as though she wanted Victoria to.

'Once I was like you,' Lisa said sadly. Victoria, who remained standing, failed to respond, refused to believe she had something in common with her domineering grandmother. Too many years lay between them.

With Victoria away at work all day, Lisa was helpless. Bearding George again was no good. George would let Victoria get away with whatever she wanted. He'd wrap himself around her little finger if she told him to. 'She's done awfully well, hasn't she?' he said when they bumped into one another on Piccadilly. 'I'm very proud of her, Lisa, and so should you be. My mother

Vane took a close interest in the running of the Emporium, as you know.'

'No, I never met her, she was before . . . before I rejoined my family.'

George smiled broadly, his authority established. 'Oh yes, your good works in Chelsea, wasn't it? Well, precedent, you see. Their names even begin with the same letter. V,' he added helpfully. 'Must rush! Bye.' He kissed her cold, powdered cheek confidently and crossed through the traffic with a spring in his step. Nothing to do with the season bringing forth the buds on the plane trees . . . or was it?

Later Lisa arranged to bump into David Jones, her ally.

'That's George for you!' David said, when she'd explained.

'Couldn't you possibly have a word with him about Victoria? Her job is making life dreadfully difficult and it's been almost two months.'

'I couldn't speak to George at the moment,' David said firmly.

Lisa changed her tack. The days were beyond her influence, but the evenings . . . she wished Victoria would go to more parties. But Victoria knew what sort of stuffy parties Lisa had in mind, every guest vetted by the social class of his or her parents, invited by RSVP stiffy. This *répondez s'il vous plaît* way meant a girl could meet only young Oxbridges, guaranteed suitable. Young men of the class who knew in their blood that a girl wore a good perfume or none at all. Men who could not possibly drop an aitch, except in an 'otel. Victoria spurned most invitations and gradually their number tailed off.

So Lisa decided to be young. The BBC had restarted the television transmissions abandoned during the war, so she purchased a Baird set in a magnificent walnut case, and held a 'television party', the coming thing with up-to-the-minute hostesses. She tried to get Victoria interested in the arrangements, seats giving everyone a good view of the little screen, soft lighting, an ashtray to every hand, and 'television snacks' of hot savouries and small individual cakes that could be eaten without interrupting viewing. Transmissions lasted only an hour or two, and most people turned up wearing evening dress. Victoria yawned.

Afterwards Lisa attempted a heart-to-heart over a mug of Horlicks. 'They're not all bad, you know,' she opened.

Victoria had developed an effective technique of not answering at once. She blew a little steam from her mug, then sipped the froth. 'Bad? Did I say they were?'

'What do you think you want?'

Victoria sipped without looking up. 'Nothing.'

'You're pretending too much. There must be something.'

'Nothing.' The harder Lisa pressed, the more Victoria denied it. She did not want her father back. She even denied the anger in her.

'If you're determined to be like that, I can't help you.' Lisa went up to bed without saying goodnight.

The truth was that for Victoria work was simply a

far more interesting place than home. There were girls her own age, and though they could never be her close friends, because of who she was, here through their busy tea-break gossip in the canteen Victoria glimpsed the web of relationships denied her at home, eavesdropped and secondhand though they were. Here was Hilda sitting like a stone totem wrapped in scarves and mufflers, her varicose legs stuck into an enormous pair of sheepskin-lined wellingtons, mourning Wattie's almost-cold furnace. The faithful, limping Wattie, relegated to menial tasks with the cooling of the fires, fetched Hilda's unflinching figure mugs of tea with his hands mottled from chilblains, and probably his feet too, by his painful walk. It was their own little kingdom down there. 'Fings,' Wattie confided one day to Bill Simmonds, with a glance as Victoria came down to leave her hat and raincoat, 'fings is going from bad ter worse. I'm worried about 'Ilda ter be frank.' He nodded over his shoulder. 'It's 'er delicate lungs.'

'Nothink about that woman's delicate!' Bill said, rinsing his valeting sponge and chamois-leather before returning the bucket to the Gents'. 'Just because she don't let yer paw 'er. They don't compare ter a car, women don't. Women don't 'ave to worry about the salt on the roads, but a car does. And I'll tell yer somethink else, mate. A good motor is more faithful than a woman.'

'What do yer know about it?' Wattie said belligerently, but he looked worriedly at Hilda.

''E takes that bloody car to bed with 'im,' Hilda said.

'I'm kept warm, don't worry,' said 'young' Bill, his eye on the clock. It was time to get to Primrose Hill to collect George, and he fitted the elasticated waterproof covering over his chauffeur's cap because he would have to get out there to hold open the car door for his master – one of his several masters, because David Jones liked to arrive at eight. 'A bachelor's life is a merry one,' he said jauntily.

'Looking at you prime examples of the male sex, I've got to admit . . .' Hilda turned from the men and winked at Victoria, trying to get her to smile, to lose that defensive, expressionless look the girl wore when she thought no one was looking at her. 'Well, Vicky, looking at them lot it's no wonder we're unfaithful, is it!'

'Now then, 'Ilda, don't be fickle,' Wattie ordered. 'Yer know what side yer bread's buttered on.'

'You think too 'ighly of yerself,' Hilda said, with emphasis.

Wattie limped away looking miserable, and Hilda resumed her stone pose. Bill drove his Rolls-Royce out to get it dirty again in the rain, saluting Victoria as he went. She was still the boss's daughter, however hard she tried to grease her way in with them on their level.

'Don't mind me, luv,' Hilda told her with a sigh, relaxing now the men were gone. 'I was born this way. Never let them get to yer heart. They'll break yer sure as eggs is eggs.'

'But you had children,' Victoria said impulsively.

'Of course, didn't have no choice in my day.' Hilda laughed, then looked surprised. 'I loved *them*, yer see? Didn't always like their father in particular.' She put her head on one side. 'Nah, yer a strange one, yer listening but I'm not getting through to yer, am I? Yer've got ter learn ter see yerself as they see yer. To them yer soft and succulent, under a hard shell, but they like that. Any man – I know them all right, Lord be witness to my suffering – they'd fall fer that pretty doll's face yer got.'

'Would they?'

'Poor bitch. I dunno why I like yer, there's something in yer like biting on tin-foil,' Hilda said. 'Just like yer dad. Yer even look like 'im, in yer way. But yer not like 'im really. Yer 'ard all through, there's no softness in yer. 'E always knew when to give a little.'

Victoria laughed. 'When I need a job I'll know who to come to for a reference.'

'It's no bloody compliment, girl. Yer'll bring yerself nothing but grief. Yer clever and yer got that clever smile, and yer young, but use it too much yer'll wear it out.'

Victoria wouldn't let go. 'What did he have that I don't?'

'Magic, that's all. There was none of us didn't fall in love with him a little bit.' She called after Victoria, 'Now, yer don't take me friendly chit-chat unfriendly-like, do yer?'

Victoria hurried upstairs, her lips pressed tight, her shoes tip-tapping.

'She ain't one of us,' Wattie said, shaking his head.

'Yer right,' sighed Hilda. 'She's so lonely. Not like us at all.'

* * *

The ten-minute bell was ringing as Victoria paused near the top of the stairwell then walked calmly up the last few steps. The noise almost made her cringe. This was the face of the store never seen by clients, this busy, bustling uproar, someone she knew hurrying by with a wave, the lifts being recommissioned now the power cuts were ended, the pneumatic doors stuck open and engineers working at them with spanners and curses, a few girls yawning or chatting while the supervisors weren't looking, porters' trolleys rumbling down the walkways between the island communities of counters and departments. The floats were being put in the tills with change from brown paper bags stamped *London and South-West Bank* with green stain. Miss Trant, one of the grey-haired kindly ladies who were the backbone of the Emporium, quietly showed a new girl how to present a display of moulded French glassware, largest items at the back, the lights angled just so to burnish cheap stuff with a bit of glitter. Atop a further counter a girl balanced, pulling a nylon stocking over a mannequin's leg, giving the curvaceous plaster thigh (no longer chaste unrealistic wickerwork) a friendly slap as she jumped down with a flash of her own plump legs. Lucy – juniors always started off on a first-name basis – had joined only this week and obviously still found dressing and undressing the limbs amusing, as well as the admiring glances from the men at Belts & Ties. Victoria wondered how such a giggly girl would stand the boredom after a month or two. Mrs Lehaye's frown was already bearing down towards that lively spirit, though the girl was clearly a quick and nimble worker.

'Good morning, Mrs Lehaye.'

'Good morning, Miss Victoria.' Rigid cordiality from the old dragon.

Victoria passed counters piled high with rolls of material, some beautiful tartans just in but probably too late for the season, she thought. Mr Hull's ordering had gone awry again. She waved and he twiddled his fingers. In the next section snooty-looking fashion mannequins were decked out in slope-shouldered summer dresses with tiny feminine waists, but so full in bust and skirt that the smallest cost twelve ration coupons. One Jean Jolie dress advertised in foot-high neon was made with the wonder material Rayon.

Beyond the windows everything was grey, sheeting rain; people queuing beneath the canopies for buses that didn't come. But inside the store, everything was brilliant.

She saw David Jones and smiled politely. The morning-suited manager, his grey hair gleaming above his unlined face, aftershave-tight, approached her between the counters. 'Victoria, stop.' To her amazement, he tapped his watch. 'You're late.'

She had no excuses ready as anyone else would have done. 'Oh, am I?'

He wasn't amused. 'Yes, Victoria, you are.'

She still thought he was joking. 'I'm sorry, David—' something moved in his eyes. 'Mr Jones, I'm sorry, it won't happen again.' She decided that she didn't like his hair.

'See that it doesn't happen again,' he ordered, 'won't you!' Again he tapped his watch.

Outraged, Victoria walked away. She'd caught him in a mood. Her cheeks felt hot and she knew she had coloured. Daisy smirked and put one hand on her hip. Victoria had got what was coming to her.

But when she looked behind her, David Jones was chatting to some of the other girls, and he smiled at Betty. Victoria frowned. She alone was his enemy, it seemed.

She ignored them and turned on her stand lights, trying to occupy herself with the details that had become her life. The Fox bellboy jacket that had been the theme for the last quarter had been replaced by a more feminine shape in spring green; the company again changed salesgirls' outfits – as it had prewar – in line with the seasons; russets for autumn, warm cherry-reds and golds for Christmas, green for springtime, something light but not clinical for summer, and certainly never that unkind yellow which made most girls' skin look as sallow as if they suffered from a tropical disease. The new hourglass look she wore packaged the way the product was sold as well as each item of the product itself. Victoria knew lunch-hour and the last half-hour before closing would be her busiest times; young pretty office-girls arriving often in parties of three or four, enjoying splashing out their new earnings beneath the glamorous lighting and large soft-focus photos of Kay Francis, the Hollywood star, reprinted *Vogue* covers and colour advertisements featuring the Gloria Girls.

Victoria kept glancing at David Jones but he ignored her. She wondered what had changed.

Moira called to Victoria, 'Have you seen Cathy Jones this morning?'

'Isn't she in?'

'Cathy's cold again, isn't it,' gossiped Daisy, arranging the lipsticks, glancing up wickedly from the corners of her eyes.

'I didn't know she wasn't well.' The others tutted impatiently, not noticing Victoria's preoccupation.

'Ill,' Daisy smirked. 'Poor Cathy.'

'Time for a few puffs.' Moira lit a Passing Cloud, furtively showing it off to the other girls.

'It's you-know-what,' Daisy said. 'Look out, "Casey" Jones again.'

Moira snorted, but stubbed the cigarette out and they all looked busy.

'No, it really absolutely is,' Jeanette said when he'd passed. 'You know what Cathy's like. One of nature's innocents.' Obviously not a recommendation, and the girls shook their heads. 'She's making a most frightful fool of herself you know!' Jeanette said disapprovingly, delighted.

'Lucky her,' Moira said. 'I wish I was.'

'You mean Cathy's got a boyfriend?' Victoria interrupted.

They squealed with laughter. 'Don't know about that! It's not like that at all!'

'What is it?'

'Oh!' they said, 'it's *love*.'

For the last time the bell rang, nine o'clock

precisely. As the great glass doors were unlocked for business the Rolls drew up outside and the chauffeur got down, protected from the rain by a waxed cape and a waterproof over his peaked cap. Saluting at the car's rear door he opened an umbrella with a smooth, one-handed flourish and sheltered George London to the doorway. 'Six o'clock,' George said.

'Six o'clock sharp, very good, sir.'

In the store George looked around him beaming, then did something unusual. He bounded down the short flight of steps and talked to the staff. 'Raining again,' he exclaimed, broadcasting but trying to be liked. His face was veined though he was not yet thirty years old, and as he turned to Victoria his short terse lips sought to be jolly. 'Hallo! Busy at work?' Before she could answer he said, 'Good!' Victoria realised that she had never really thought about him before – you didn't *think* about members of your own family, you just accepted them, warts and all. Hadn't she only started *thinking* about poor George's stylish twin brother Ralph when he was gone, dead? Now something more had changed in George's life, she realised. Victoria found herself summing her half-brother up as though she were selling to him, looking coldly into him to gauge and exploit his picture of himself, his fears and desires – and suddenly it was easy, she saw clear past his façade. George was vulnerable.

'I like to see you working here,' he told her. She was the only one he made eye contact with, and Victoria realised he genuinely liked her, liked seeing

her here. 'Enjoying it? Yes, of course you are.'
Without his support, Victoria realised that she
probably could not have remained at the store, yet it
was unlike George to hold his ground on anything,
least of all against Lisa's wishes. Yet he defied her for
Victoria. What a ninny she had been not to see that
her presence was in George's interest, diluting the
influence of David Jones. David didn't dare stand up
to George yet – but he had sidelined Victoria, isolated
her by putting her on this silly stand outside the
mainstream of the store's life under Cathy's authority, her watchful eye. Did David's ambition, now Ben
London was gone, include his own daughter? You bet
it did.

David Jones appeared at George's elbow. He
ignored Victoria. 'Good morning, Mr London.'
Victoria busied her hands tying ribbon bows. She got
through hundreds each day, one for each package
costing more than five shillings, a rhythm her fingers
remembered flawlessly while she eavesdropped.

'This is Jeanette . . . Daisy . . .' said David, but
George didn't move from Victoria. Didn't take his
eyes off her.

Was George a match for his manager? Victoria
wondered. Yes, because George held half the shares
in the store, real power. But George had failed
before, and Ben had long ago persuaded – bullied, as
George believed – the dying Ralph into bequeathing
*him* the second, crucial half of the voting stock.
George could never be free of his father, those shares
hung over him like a bludgeon.

'I hear you've settled in nicely,' George said to Victoria. 'My mother, Vane,' he told David, 'she loved this place too, back in its great days. Yes, and she was a fighter. Vane fought for all this tooth and nail.' He sighed. 'But of course she was a woman. And in those days women . . .'

'It was a very sad time for us all,' David Jones said.

So that was what George felt. Victoria looked at her half-brother almost with affection. She had never liked him, they were too different, but now suddenly she had the insight that George was shy. He was arrogant and withdrawn because he was painfully shy, and now he was showing this painful friendliness for the same reason. Nothing genuine, all as false and cheap as the cunning display-fronts that made mass production look like a million bucks. But people too? She wondered if his exuberance was because he had been drinking.

'I have one or two concepts that perhaps we could talk over,' David murmured. 'Sir, the third floor—'

Did George trust David Jones? Victoria wondered.

'Nice to see she's got some colour in her face,' George said, and David's mouth smiled in Victoria's direction. Of course George trusted him. George was a fool.

The two men walked away and Cathy arrived immediately afterwards. Her bus had broken down and she'd had to walk, she told the girls. She heard the news of George's visit with indifference. Only Victoria noticed that her shoes were dry. Perhaps she had changed them.

264

* * *

After work Victoria threw on her waxed cape and waterproof hat, joining the throng of girls streaming across the courtyard, then was left suddenly alone as they turned right for the Green Park Underground. She hesitated on the kerb, the rain sheeting around her, then a deliberate movement caught the corner of her eye. Her young man leaned against the brilliantly lit rectangle of an Emporium window, haughty mannequins in summer fashions behind him, their illumination drawing a line down his profile. God, he'd worked that out. He was full of himself, wasn't he? It was dry under the canopies but he was wearing the collar of his raincoat up, silver beads of water still trickling down the exposed underside of the lapels. So he'd been waiting in the rain, and dodged back when he saw her come out.

He beckoned.

Victoria ignored him, looking for a gap in the traffic. There wasn't one. 'It's dry under here,' he called.

She crossed to the central island, then weaved to the far side, though a bus honked her down, much closer than she'd thought. An old lady tugging a shopping trolley turned down St James's Street and Victoria kept close to her. The wheels span faster and the old lady kept her head down. Victoria was frightening her, but there were plenty of people around, businessmen and civil servants coming and going to the various exclusive clubs that lined this street, and a Riley police car cruised past.

She looked over her shoulder. He'd crossed the road and stood by the Fire Alarm on the corner, making no further move to follow her. She took a few more steps. No movement from him, this was as far as he was going. She waited, then took a step back towards him: he came forward a pace. They met outside White's Club, the genteel lamps glowing in the rain-starred bow windows.

'You see into people, don't you?' he said. 'I can tell from the way you're looking at me. Your eyes.'

'I see right through you,' she put him down, but her attention had been arrested by his flattery.

'I've been rehearsing all the right things to say. I got it all planned, Victoria.'

'How did you know—'

His reply was obvious. 'Because that's what the other girls call you.' He said ruefully, 'Don't pretend you didn't even notice me watching you. Of course, girls like you have to be properly introduced,' he sneered.

'I don't even know your name.'

'Terry,' he smiled. He held out his hand. 'Terry Price.'

She was hooked, he could see it plain as pie. Terry played her gently, keeping his hand out, palm up, a sneer on his lips but a smile in his eyes. He glimpsed her tongue hesitating between her pretty lips: she might jump either way. She decided not to back down, and shook his hand like a man would, a positive shake, not just lying it in there ladylike. He held her for a further moment with the lightest of touches, almost between finger and thumb, then let go before she did, and knew he'd got her.

'I don't like that hat,' he grinned, then winked at her. 'I'm not joking. Makes you look severe. But it's none of my business.'

She sparked: 'I don't care what you think.' She was working the hook deeper into herself, doing his work for him. He had to admire her spirit.

'I think of *you* all the time,' he said honestly. Actually he thought about *having* her all the time, but it was near enough to be no lie. She had been about to walk away, playing up to his insult about the hat, which he really didn't like, but she stopped.

'Do you really?'

'Yeah?'

'Think of me all the time?'

He replied with simple masculine sincerity. 'The way you walk, your smell, I love the way your hair moves. She moves. Everything about you is a she. She sways like this.' He twisted his body in a tiny sensual movement, provoking a flicker of her smile. He stopped at once. 'That's why I don't like that hat,' he said earnestly, 'I don't like you to wear *her* up. Concealing yourself.'

'I have to in the store,' she said absently, 'rules.'

'That's it then, not your fault.' He shook his head and so did she unconsciously, all her concentration on him. He took her elbow with that lightest touch so that she hardly realised he was moving her on, then he fell into step beside her. 'I won't walk you home,' he said. 'Just as far as Little St James's Street. You can leave me there.' He took her hand crossing to the traffic island by King Street.

She said, 'Do you behave like this with lots of girls?'

'Find out their names and where they live and send them gifts of perfume? None,' he said, and she believed him. 'None.'

He relinquished her hand, but she clung on as he suddenly crossed in front of a van, running four strides to his three in her tight skirt. They were beneath the streetlamp at the corner of Little St James's Street and he pulled his hand away. 'There. As I promised.'

'What?'

'Your street. Bye.' But he didn't walk off, just left her hanging there.

'Perhaps I'll see you again?' she said. He shrugged, maybe, plainly bored. She said, 'Are you really just an insurance actuary?'

The best lies were closest to the bone, all but true, impossible to forget. 'Been posted to Essex,' he said truthfully, 'that's why you haven't seen me, if you cared.' He could see she cared now. 'I advise how much it will cost people to insure their premises, businesses. Small restaurants.'

'It sounds interesting,' she said, so he held back from her a little more.

'Bloody boring. Can't wait to get home.'

She didn't want him to go. He could see it aching in her eyes. 'Where's home?'

She wouldn't have lasted five virtuous minutes east

of Tower Bridge. 'London,' he said impatiently, and looked at his watch, nice and flashy. 'I get a day free now and then.'

'When?'

'When I want.'

'I come down here every day, except Sundays.'

'Oh, maybe Sundays are my favourite day.'

The lamp threw sudden shadows down her face. '*Au revoir*,' she sulked.

'Ta-ra.'

Without looking back, because he knew she'd be watching, and she'd wave, and he'd either have to wave soppily or ignore her, he walked out of sight to Jermyn Street. It wouldn't take long to get her between the sheets, best to leave her alone now. He was a bit sad she was so easy. He picked up his car outside Cox's Hotel, under the disapproving eye of the commissionaire, and drove down East. Vic wanted people to think of him as the big boss who knew everything, controlled everything. Not quite. That was a nice warm thought over a few beers, almost as nice and warm as the erotic fantasy of Victoria which Terry cuddled to sleep alone at the Old Bull and Bush later that night. He had used the Havannah Street house on the Isle of Dogs much less since Vic had knocked the door through the wall. Vic wanted his family around him, close, depending on each other, helping one another, harking back to a golden nostalgia for his happy childhood, living with Mum just as in the old days. But did Vic really like her? Love her, yes, but *like* her? Terry, too, was supposed to be part of Vic's sentimental happy family like a son, except Terry wasn't having that. Beneath it all, there in that little house, was the dark terrible undercurrent of Vic mourning for Ria like her disappearance was really her death. Missing Lola, too. Poor Vic, Terry thought, at the top of the heap, all alone in a crowd of people. The children he didn't have.

## 2

Esther plodded down to the shops. Now that Vic was back home shopping was a treat again. There were one or two old scores to settle – not that she was the type to hold grudges, heaven forbid. But as it happened she'd not forgotten which butcher had fobbed her off with offal and kept nothing under the counter for her during the war years, and made up weight with fat or gristle. Esther knew all the old tricks, having been a workhouse cook, and knew what humiliation felt like in her shopping basket, and having to carry it home to her family whatever it smelt like.

But now she was looking after Vic, it was known that Vic was looking after her, and Esther shopped with her head held high again and steel in her eye. She remembered which grocer had sold her rotten eggs against her ration card then wouldn't exchange them for fresh. She'd been on her uppers then, grateful for anything they had over, but now Esther recalled each tiny slight against her pride, although she had not an ounce of vindictiveness in her, it was alien to her nature. But for her there was now absolutely no more waiting at the end of the greengrocer's queue while Tommy Land's more favoured customers were helped first. These days Esther went in last and came out first, and no more soggy bits on her veggies either. And she got given those special treats slipped into her basket. A fabulously rare grapefruit for Vic's breakfast, no charge. A beautiful slice of ham for Vic's lunch, a wink, no charge. Jim Snell the butcher gave her a fat pig's trotter to boil up for that sweetest, tenderest meat to be winkled out from between the toes, and all the succulent jelly. Esther most enjoyed bestowing her custom on Yacobsen, whose father in his old age had fled the Nazis and taken over the derelict Blumenthall premises. Now his son Eli was old himself. Fawningly he dry-rinsed his hands from the moment the bell tinged and Esther's blunt bulk loomed in the doorway, his body thin as old rope kinking back and forth between the marble cheese counter and the butter counter and the preserved-meat counter as he served her needs personally, then dry-rinsing till the moment the bell tinged, operated by his very own shaking hand on the doorhandle, to salute her departure. It was thin Yacobsen wearing his baggy white apron like armour who'd been tricky about the eggs. 'Forget and forgive, that's my motto,' Esther had told him generously after Vic's return, then accidentally dropped the whole dozen from the brown paper bag after she'd paid for them. 'It's my fault, myself I blame,' Yacobsen said, his hands rolling over themselves like little frightened animals, 'those paper bags are my mistake.' Forever afterwards he gave her a baker's dozen to make up, confirming to Esther that her rosy view of humanity was the right one.

Even the May weather had come good, smutty leaves unfolding on the one or two trees. A few yellow canaries, not as many as in the great old days when the street was a-flutter with their preening and trilling, had been put out in their cages while the spring-cleaning proceeded vigorously behind the open front doors, but not so many of them either, people weren't so houseproud. Dirty windows; rubbish left lying by the step, carpets weren't taken out and beaten. Esther took the opportunity to look in at the Tooke Arms on the corner of Maria Street, empty though it was except for oldsters. Herbie Turner's wife Ada poured her a little one and popped it on the slate, none of that 'Refusal May Offend' nonsense here. So Esther availed herself of one or two little ones more because the first was *such* a little one – Ada being a second wife and new – then picked up her shopping and waddled genially to Harry Baggs's for a nice piece of fried cod for Vic's lunch, and a pickled onion to go by it. When she got home it was a beautiful sunny afternoon, really hot, and she realised how late she was. Time had a way of disappearing when Esther was feeling so happy, and it was quiet upstairs. Vic had already started his nap. He'd taken over Ria's room to leave next door free for Terry and office work, the arrangement which had worked so well with Nigel in the old days. In a very real sense Nigel's spirit was still alive, and for a moment Esther hesitated at the foot of the stairs with her heart beating for her lost children.

'Bought you some nice fish, dear,' she quavered at the closed door.

Vic lay quiet. At last her footsteps creaked down the hall to the kitchen and he heard a plate rattle as it was taken from the cupboard, rustling paper – Harry Baggs wrapped his fish in the *Telegraph*, got job-lots of returned copies through his brother who worked as a loader in Fleet Street – then the oven door clanged shut. '*Sssh*,' Esther talked to herself.

Vic lay fully clothed on Ria's bed behind the closed door, his shoes laced up, the curtains open. Occasionally a seagull drifted across the glaring sky. He knew he wouldn't sleep; he never managed deep sleep in the afternoons. He used the time for business thoughts, which basically meant thinking how to use people. But he kept thinking of Ria. Suppose she came back? He tried to get his mind around to Terry and the Chelmsford end of the business. But suppose Ria did come back? That was almost the worst torture he could imagine, yet he longed for her return. He would hurt her too. He would make her care.

But dear little Lola's birthday was in a couple of months, and Vic would never harm a hair of her head, his own flesh, his own blood. Vic daydreamed what he would buy her – yes, Ria had brought her back here, because here was home . . . their smiling faces, all forgiven, and him hiding his pain by not looking at Ria, not giving her an excuse to go for him, softly softly catchee monkey . . . all happy together again as they had been when they were children, innocent as children. As Vic dozed even his little brother Jimmy was there, dead for forty years.

And there was Lola, his daughter just as he had last seen her, her face smudged with the dirt that Ria's flannel had missed, her poor unwashed hair hanging in greasy black coils, strange dark eyes flecked like Ria's with old gold, yet Lola's own way of putting her head on one side to look at you curiously. Not at all like Ria, that. Ria was always selfish, always thinking of herself.

God, how he missed his little girl!

Vic's eyes flicked open. Not knowing where Lola was being held was worst.

Having Charlie Bookkeeper, the solicitor, followed had turned up nothing but a lot of office-watching, a routine swelter and icy douche at Hammam's Turkish Baths each Saturday morning, and attendances at magistrates' courts that brought back unnerving memories for his informants. Back in January Terry had been sure that Ben London's daughter, Victoria, knew nothing of her father's impending disappearance – she had arrived at the hospital to find him gone – and only because of that certainty had Vic left her and the grandmother alone. If he had suspected for one minute that they were implicated he would have had the secret out of them. Women, he knew, were infallibly curious creatures, they always wanted to know what was none of their business, that was the way they were made. Suffering they doubtless were, Lisa and Victoria; bound to be a lot of strain, plenty of tension there, but Vic appreciated the ruthless cunning of his enemy: it was common sense Ben hadn't told them where he was, the only way to keep them safe.

Vic was sure Lola wasn't in London, he would have known by now. He had his feelers out and he would have heard something echoing down the spider's web of streets and street-markets, pubs and hotels, brothels and doss-houses and back alleys, bus drivers and cabbies and the boys in blue in their fancy cars. Even Ria could not hide from him for very long here.

But Ria had disappeared as thoroughly as though she was dead.

And Lola? Vic despaired. Ria had already proved she was a bad mother.

He got up, sweating in his suit, and filled the washbasin with cold swirling water. He loosened his tie and splashed his burning face. Seeing strong-featured Betty Stark at St Luke's a couple of months ago had bothered him – Betty Dempsey as she now was, married to the Customs twerp. Her son by Alan Stark, Vic couldn't remember his name, tall serious lad, had been killed at the very end of the war. That was the end of the Stark line, thank God, they'd never come to much. Alan had been weak; he'd beaten Betty more than was good for him, the marks had showed. She must have known it had suited Vic to put Alan out of his misery, not how exactly . . . but Vic knew. Those old warehouses built up over the river were a maze of pilings and cross-girders underneath, and not even Vic could stop the rising tide, any more than he could stop the bubbles rushing around the handkerchief in a drowning man's mouth. Despite her suspicions of Vic's guilt, or because of them, Betty had respected Vic afterwards, obviously even wanted him with a part of herself, the way Vic knew women always want a strong man, and he despised them for it. So when Vic had ignored her she got hot for Nigel instead, second best. But love? She didn't love Dempsey, she was just looking after number one. It was Nigel she still loved, his memory she treasured.

What had Vic seen in her eyes, that day at the funeral? Knowledge. Betty knew who Lola was. With Pearl dead and Ria out of the way, Betty was the only one who *did* know.

Her unforgivable remark about Lola had cut at Vic's heart like a knife. *She won't have a father.* Vic stared at his eyes in the mirror for a few moments, then straightened his tie.

He heard Mum's footsteps plodding past the stairs and went down. What an ox she was. He found her in the front room, smiled and kissed her cheek. 'Darling!' she said. She'd been drinking again, probably a sherry or two at the Tooke Arms, or port; Esther had never lost her old-fashioned taste for gin but her stomach couldn't take it. 'I've kept your fish warm in the oven,' she said earnestly.

'What are you sitting here for then?'

She fetched his plate shimmering with heat on a tray. She'd flamed the gas too high and the batter had glazed. He picked at a few mouthfuls. Esther tutted and took a big bite of her fish to encourage him. 'Have you fed that rabbit today?' he asked, putting his head on one side.

'Don't go on at me about that little thing, there's a dear.'

'It's Lola's, right? When she comes back I want everything just the same as the day she left.'

'Yes, dear.'

'That's better.' He prodded the fish with his fork. 'This is cod. It's a dirty fish.'

'Well, it tastes all right,' Esther bleated. 'I chose it myself, you always liked it before. I only did it for you.' The photographs of the royals along the sideboard had been replaced with little, patiently sewn Christian homilies willed to her by the grateful Mrs Morris, lovingly decorated with lambs and little fluffy clouds in pink knotted wool, and long-haired shepherds kneeling with gold-thread haloes over their heads.

Vic knew he ought to put his arm round Esther's shoulders and calm her down, but instead he found himself pointing at the cheap frames with his fork. 'God looks after those who look after themselves.'

Esther's mouth turned into a thin, determined line. 'Nigel's in heaven,' she said, and as always Vic was surprised at the toughness she could summon up. He put down his tray on the floor and wiped his lips with his handkerchief. 'He's waiting,' Esther said, 'waiting for us.'

'Rubbish.'

'Waiting.'

'You believe what you like,' Vic said, furiously. Arleen had loved Nigel too. Betty Stark still loved his memory. Who would weep for Vic if he died?

'Vic, I didn't mean to upset you,' said Esther

277

pathetically, and he knew he had won, as always. By now there was no satisfaction in it.

'It's all right, Mum,' he said tolerantly.

'You're so worried about Ria, aren't you?'

He shook his head. 'He doesn't really love her, Mum, she's always been a fool for him. It's Lola I'm worried about. She's so young.'

'Ria wouldn't let her come to any harm.'

'Oh, you know what she's like! She hasn't got a thought in her head sometimes.'

'Still, Ria is your sister,' Esther said. 'You'd forgive her.'

'My half-sister,' said Vic.

He got up and kissed Esther's cheek, he had to get out of the house, but Esther said, 'Stop.' She summoned her toughness, gripping his wrist tight. 'Sit down, Vic.' She pointed at his chair. He stared at her then sat impatiently.

'What is it now, Mum?'

'I know you haven't always been a good boy,' she said tediously, 'but your heart's in the right place, Vic, and you're my own flesh and blood. I've supported you through thick and thin and you've been good to me. You've been a good boy to your mum,' she said tearfully.

'Bit busy for this today, Mum.'

'Listen to me, Vic. I told you all this before, many times I know, when you were all young. You always laughed, all you children did, rolled around you did. Kids is cruel.' Her voice had changed; she was remembering back to the last years of the last century. 'My first husband, Dick, he kept a pub. Them was great days, him cock of the walk. Everyone in our street up Poplar fancied him. I was lucky. He had lovely eyes, blue and gold. You'd fall in love with him for his eyes. And he could hold a whole egg in his mouth, lips closed, nothing that man couldn't do, and he was virile all night. I was sixteen but he was much older, mid-twenties. I always liked older men, see,' she tried to joke. 'Ria's Dad, he was. She was born after he died. After I'd married Tom quick-smart.'

Vic knew what was coming, though he hadn't heard the tale for years, not since the Canary Warren days. 'Yeah, Dick was proud of his strength, and he bust his gut hefting a beer-barrel, didn't he?'

'Peritonitis,' Esther wept. 'I got the doctor in and he said it was peritonitis. Dick was sort of going rotten inside and bubbling up, and I had to pay the doctor and the pub wasn't bringing in any cash – customers didn't like the thought of him upstairs. The screaming too, you wouldn't think a man had so much screaming in him. Can't blame them. I didn't even know I was pregnant. Stupid, I was being sick all the time. Dick never knew he'd live on in Ria, he went into the dark alone. Him slowly dying on our double bed, swelling up like a balloon inside his white flannel nightshirt, screaming to burst. I do wish I'd known to tell him.'

She stopped. Vic wondered what they had found quite so funny about this as children. Perhaps because Mum only let it out when she was incapably drunk, sozzled to the eyebrows and tears of grief streaming down her cheeks, drunk and tragic and inconsolably

279

funny. She didn't drink like that now, whatever she'd had earlier had worn off, and the tears in her eyes didn't fall.

'You had to deflate him to get him in his coffin,' Vic said gently.

'That wasn't quite the truth, darling. He was alive. He was in such agony with it he asked me to go down to the kitchen, get the short sharp knife we used to make our pies – we was famous for our pies – and prick him with it. So I went down there and then I came back and I did it.'

'Christ, Mum,' Vic said.

'And he died a few hours later with my arms around him, comfortable-like.'

'What happened then?'

'The usual stuff, the brewery put me on the street. I found I was pregnant, put my head on Tom's shoulder and told him the daughter I had – I always knew she'd be a girl – was *his* child. That's how Ria came into the world, and Tom never knew the truth. Now you know why I believe in forgiveness. It makes the world go round, Vic, none of us is unstained, life's not possible without forgiveness.' She said suddenly: 'What an awful place it is!'

Vic thought about Betty Stark.

# 3

As soon as he was comfortably installed back in the boardroom with its long walnut table, one of George's first decisions had been an odd one, though characteristic of him. He decreed that heating systems in the Emporium would no longer be fired by coal but by gas. Coal supplies had been troublesome last winter and promised the same again, yet the change was an expensive one for little real return. George simply believed in having what was best for the Emporium. Removing the chimneys opened up extra selling space, but they had more than enough of that already – the entire third floor remained closed. The system would be installed by June, the height of summer. Above the gargoyles grimacing from the ornate roof-cornices, the rows of smoke-churning Victorian chimney-stacks became also inert and merely decorative. 'If only everyone would do this!' George exclaimed when David Jones raised the matter.

'At a cost of twenty-five thousand pounds to our company,' David pointed out mildly. *Our*, not *your*.

George lived with it. 'If everyone would do this we'd have clean air in our metropolis.' He promised that no employee would suffer for the change. Mike the janitor was retiring – he was certainly the wrong side of seventy – and George insisted that Watson, made redundant from the furnace room, take his place. David sighed. Of course Wattie would stand on his pride, he'd serviced that bloody boiler man and boy, and he'd never change to a night job at his age, let alone one far from Hilda. David decided to sack him, but the union wouldn't allow it. So Mike had to be asked to carry on for a little longer and Wattie was given a non-job in the stockroom. When George interfered, this was the sort of time-wasting nonsense

that came across David's desk. Happening to pass
Cathy, his daughter, on the stairs, because they were
alone David stopped her, putting his hand on her
arm. She was such a slim, pert girl, reminding him
only a little of Harriet at her age; she was so quick. It
was impossible to mistake her happiness. 'You're
looking lovely. I've never seen you more radiant,' he
said.

Cathy smiled. 'I thought we were being so
discreet.' She wore a ring on her finger, tasteful and
understated. George had chosen it.

'My clever girl.'

She paused. 'You make me sound so . . . *calculat-
ing*.'

'Of course I didn't mean to. And I know it isn't, on
your part.' They both knew who they were talking
about: Mummy. Cathy's mother Harriet, who had
worked at the Emporium before she married David,
had always been ambitious for her husband and, now
her husband's career had stalled, for her daughter.
Finally, Cathy had left home, renting a small bedsit in
St John's Wood, though one carefully vetted by
Harriet, who had turned up on the doorstep with a
giant bottle of Dettol disinfectant and a new toilet
seat still in its brown paper wrapping. But St John's
Wood was a tedious journey from Wimbledon Hill.
After a sigh and a tear for Ben London's tragic
accident, Cathy's mother had turned her attention to
the practical consequences, turned her energies from
her daughter back to her husband. Just as she had in
their early days, she pushed and prodded David into
assertiveness, insisting on the small but desperately

important symbols of status: the chauffeur-driven limousine that picked him up at eight o'clock, and increasingly her use of it during the day. Her cook's wages were paid by the Emporium, it was David's plan to reopen the Food Hall that had once been such a feature of the establishment, and of course lines must be tested for quality. Their gardener was also paid for on some such excuse. But if George knew about David's perks he considered them unimportant. He had another matter on his mind. Her name was Cathy.

And meanwhile Cathy felt trapped between contradictions: her mother's ambition, her father's mannered subtlety, her own busy and worthwhile job working with Victoria and the other girls and, outside the Emporium, her relationship with her boss. She was perfectly helpless in the grip of enormous, chaotic emotions that no one else could understand. 'I *knew* about you and him before you did!' Harriet had claimed to Cathy one Sunday at home, patting her seat to be sat beside. '*I* saw you dancing with George the night of the party, and what did I see? The stars in your eyes.'

Cathy half stood up again. 'And his?' she asked anxiously.

'Simply up to his knees in quicksand, my dear.' She'd meant in love, but George had also been drunk, Cathy remembered. A desirable man who was drunk became an unappealing creature, but with George the opposite was true. She found him much nicer after a glass of claret than when sober, the nervousness unlocked from his tongue, his anger and bitterness evaporating to reveal the vulnerable man beneath. With her, George wasn't weak, he was *nice*. He could be very funny, his eye for caricature reduced her to tears of laughter – he had the Turkish waiter who served coffee at the Trocadero down to a T. The first time she had danced with George, really come close to him, was at Ben London's party. At first George kept up his nastiness as a conscious shell, keeping everyone out, including her, with his boorish monologue. But he began to trust her. While they danced she winkled her way into him and when it was very late he danced with his eyes on her, pretending no more to be someone he was not; he was sweet and kind and made her feel graceful. George had made Cathy feel special that evening. It had ended with horror, the bomb and the death of Pearl London who had been so beautiful, but that was not why Cathy would remember it for ever. She had found George London.

Over the last few months, with her, his drinking became gentle, almost ceased. All his defences were down with her. To the month he was five years older than she. Her intelligence was sharper, quicker than his, yet he had his droll humour that she could never reproduce or predict. Something in him had suffered before he met Cathy, and where she was organised, he lived by instinct and impulse. He had never recovered from having a twin brother who had been loved, who dominated him and stunted his emotions, and Cathy thought maybe she would never mean much to George. Gradually, just friends, they'd drift

284

apart. But one evening at the New Theatre, something Shakespearian with Alec Guinness, George was
all thumbs and nervousness getting her to their seats
which banged up and down, the old George again,
embarrassing her, short-tempered and carping with
the usherette, complaining straight back at people in
the other seats, everyone but Cathy. To cap it, in the
taxi taking her back to St John's Wood, he started
arguing the fare with the cabbie. 'Suit yourself,
chum!' the cabbie swore, throwing on the brakes with
a piercing squeal and dumping them by the roadside
in the pouring rain. As they watched the single tail-
light disappear George was so enraged and mortified
that Cathy had to laugh at him through the raindrops
streaming from the brim of her hat.

'I've waited all evening for the right moment to give
you this,' George said. 'I'm going to do it anyway.' It
was the ring, and he slipped it over her finger. 'It
doesn't mean anything.' Of course it did. He kissed
her nervously and she slid her fingers around the nape
of his neck. A bus pulled up beside them. Goodness,
they were at a bus stop, and everyone downstairs was
staring at them. 'Come on, make up yer minds,' the
conductor yawned. They rode alone on the top deck
to Primrose Hill, imagining everyone talking about
them below and not caring about it. George's house
was modest, with yellow shutters that looked green
and underwatery in the streetlights. George disappeared upstairs and found her a dressing-gown, a
ghastly male paisley which he brought down to the
lounge, leaving her alone to change by the fire. There

was a rug in front of the sofa and Cathy worried what might happen, she didn't want to say no to him in case she lost him, but she wanted him to hold her. The illicitness of being with a man in his house overnight, or for at least part of the night, frightened her. There was something rather experienced about George, of course men had to be. He came back carrying tea in servants' mugs because he couldn't find the cups, and she was annoyed with him because she would probably have found them in a trice, and told him so. But nothing could spoil George's pleasure. They talked and murmured in front of the fire while their clothes dried. With morning the windows turned grey and Cathy knew she was in love. And George? Who knew a man's heart? Later, Bill Simmonds drove them both to the Emporium, letting George out then dropping her round the back. And that was how she arrived with dry shoes, a fact Cathy was sure Victoria noticed, if not the extra ring.

Victoria didn't seem to understand the power of love, that everything in Cathy's life was changed and wonderful. Cathy came to dread sitting by Victoria in the canteen, her tongue frozen, even with the other girls, by Victoria's presence with her long blonde hair in a ponytail, her dark eyebrows drawn together, Victoria's unsmiling unfeeling mouth going about its business of eating and drinking and talking, sometimes even to Cathy, but not about anything that mattered. Not about the desperately important things. Soon even the boiled-vegetables and reheated-roast smell of store dinners, Cathy's main meal of the day, filled her with dismay seeing Victoria there at the long table with a space beside her. Cathy would turn back at the door. She hated being guilty about loving George, but that was what Victoria by her silence, her refusal to acknowledge Cathy's emotions, much less wish her well, was making her feel. Cathy got hungry on sandwiches. The water in the ladies' loo was wonderfully hot these days and after meals the girls tended to linger by the basins; it was one of her jobs to move them on. One day when lunch was finished Victoria was last, trying to scrub some indelible ink from one of her nails. Cathy stood behind her, arms crossed. 'I think it's time we cleared the air, don't you?'

Victoria glanced up but the mirror was steamy. 'Just a minute,' she promised.

'That's enough of that!' Cathy lost her temper. 'You've made what you think of me quite plain, thank you! I've had enough. I don't care if you are the great Ben London's daughter—'

'Wait—'

'Don't you wait me!'

Victoria looked Cathy in the eye. 'What are you talking about?'

Cathy faltered. 'Me and George. You know I've fallen for George.'

'So that's why you've been acting so oddly!' Victoria laughed. 'Our dear George – and you? It's really true?'

'Why else would I shout at you!'

'So you *are* head over heels for him. That's really all there is to it?'

'Him too,' Cathy said pertly.

287

Could Cathy truly not see how her father was using her? Victoria wondered. If an ordinary girl like Cathy was going out with George, the boss, riding in his car, perhaps spending the night with him – which would explain her dry shoes the other morning – Victoria knew what it really meant. She didn't believe in love. Whatever Cathy herself believed – and she seemed so pathetically genuine – Victoria knew that David and Harriet Jones were scheming to move their daughter in at the top. Victoria realised she couldn't trust anyone in the store. What upset her most was that she had wanted to like Cathy, who had seemed so dedicated and professional at her job, best of them all.

'It's love,' Cathy told her simply.

Victoria held out her dripping hands and hugged Cathy with her elbows, putting on an act. 'How could I know unless you told me?' She really hadn't noticed the ring and Cathy didn't like to draw attention to it. 'Tell all! How long has this being going on?'

Cathy instantly forgave everything. 'Time seems to move so slowly when you want to be together. Oh, Vicky, I thought you disapproved, or were upset.'

'How could I be when you hadn't told me!' Victoria dried her hands and saw Cathy's ring at last. 'Oh, it's *lovely*.'

'It doesn't mean anything, you know . . .'

'It's a nice bit of stuff though,' Victoria said blindly.

'Are you sure you really didn't guess about us? And I thought everything was so . . . different,' Cathy said, chagrined. 'I thought everyone knew. A couple of months is forever. Victoria, one day you'll find out—'

'Actually, I do have a boyfriend, you know.'

'Oh, Victoria, you've got to be so careful.'

'It's nothing serious.'

Cathy was delighted. 'But that means it *is*.'

'Don't make a fuss.'

'It's not that pilot you talked about, is it?'

'Of course not.'

'Tell all!'

'Well,' said Victoria, then opened the spring-loaded door and threw back over her shoulder: 'All I can tell you is, he's totally infatuated!' Then she was gone and the door slammed. Cathy shut her eyes and touched her ring, thinking of herself.

Terry wasn't infatuated, of course, and neither was Victoria, it was no big deal between them. Suddenly he'd be there, that was all, like a cat.

'You're like a cat too,' he said, as if he met her by chance instead of deliberately driving all the way down from Chelmsford to hold her hand for five minutes.

So he did think about her a little, maybe, when they were not together.

Victoria liked Terry, liked the way he turned up without being asked, didn't try and get too close to her, kept their meetings clean of demands and desires. It was the opposite from trying to tie her down, he wasn't interested in anything deep. He liked her, liked talking to her for herself, liked walking her home – as far as Pall Mall, anyway. He wanted to be her friend, her friend who held her hand, it meant nothing. All through the spring she never knew when

289

he'd be there, suddenly appearing beside her crossing Piccadilly. It only happened once or twice in the first few weeks, but it was enough for her to get to know him. She started looking for him every day, gradually expecting him. Starting to think about him even when she walked home alone, as she nearly always did, always looking forward to the next time he would be there. The way he held her hand across the road, then kept hold of her as though he'd forgotten to let go, curling his fingers around hers. Soon she curled her fingers even when he wasn't there, remembering. His intimate, sensual talk of their first meeting made more of an impression in her memory than at the time. *The way you walk. Everything about you is a she,* he'd said. Victoria imagined what he saw, and knew she'd see him again.

The evenings were light now. He was good-looking, for a start, and he was always cheerful to see her. In June the sunlight still streamed between the buildings and he wore a dark suit conservatively cut, though the pinstripe was daring, and a 'snap-brim' hat. She told him to take it off and he did, obediently. 'You've got lovely brown eyes,' she told him.

'You've got cats' eyes,' he sighed impatiently. 'Victoria Siamese cat.'

'Don't talk such rubbish!' But then she asked, 'Do you really drive all that way just to see me for three minutes?'

'Aren't you worth it?'

She thought it was terrific. 'You don't really want to be friends, do you?' Victoria said.

'No,' he agreed, and squeezed her hand.

290

Because of his insurance work Terry got an unlimited petrol allowance. Moira's boyfriend and even Jeanette's who was an accountant had to travel by public transport. Victoria kept quiet about her boyfriend with a car; Lisa would have been furious. Anyway, Victoria had discovered Terry herself, she was going to keep him to herself, and he showed no more inclination than she to meet the old folks. As they walked Victoria and Terry never talked about their families, only themselves. Once he took her almost the length of Pall Mall to Trafalgar Square before turning back.

And then she didn't see him for weeks. She walked home slowly, she dragged her feet; she even waited by the Fire Alarm as though he might turn up late. Next time she would suggest buying a bag of crumbs and they could feed the pigeons together in Trafalgar Square, sit together on one of the benches for a while before she had to go home. But each evening she walked down St James's Street alone. The year had passed its peak but was growing warmer, and she wore her yellow summer dress with rayon, her sheer nylon stockings.

Suddenly the red MG roadster pulled up beside her and Terry looked up at her, leaning across to hold open the passenger door. 'Get in.'

It was so easy for him, and she was furious and upset. 'Where have you been?'

'Getting in or not?' He ignored the stalled traffic behind him, put on dark glasses against the low sun. 'Special treat, don't worry.'

'But I was on my way home.'

291

'We aren't going far, worrier! You can phone Granny from the pub.'

'I'm not worried!' she said indignantly. 'What pub?'

'Coming or not?' he sighed, bored.

She got in, pulling her knees almost to her chin to get her high heels over the awkward sill, then leaned back in the bucket seat and he gunned the motor ahead of the traffic along Pall Mall. The slipstream pulled at her clothes and she kept her one hand in her lap, holding down her hair with the other. But the speed was thrilling. 'Tell you what,' he said, 'I'll get you genuine Wolsey nylons half the price of those.'

'From those awful spivs selling them out of suitcases? No thank you.' She put both hands on her legs and let her hair fly.

He looked at her admiringly, scattering the pigeons in Trafalgar Square, then turned left and cut through the backstreets, parking half on a busy pavement. 'Soho,' he said, swinging her out. She made him wait, brushing her hair. 'You look better with it like that,' he said. 'Come on!' The lane was very narrow, crowded with colourful restaurants and cafés, but she wondered if he would really try to take her in a pub, she'd never been in one. When she hung back Terry grinned cockily, grabbing her hand as she tripped across the unfamiliar kerbs and broken paving, entrances to wonderful-looking winding alleys and mysterious passageways. Everyone here was cheery and noisy. There was a jostling untidy warmth to the crowds that was missing in St James's, less than a mile away: poverty and wealth living cheek by jowl in

London . . . she felt as if, having travelled hardly any distance, she had suddenly been transported, pulled by Terry's hand, back to the chaotic streets of the metropolis fifty or a hundred years ago, swarmingly friendly and exciting, where everyone knew everyone else. Gaudy foreign types nodded to Terry, acknowledgements were grunted by men unloading canned goods from a van, even the weary barrel-organ man looked round with the monkey crouched on his cap, and Terry flicked the monkey sixpence, which it nipped suspiciously with its teeth before dropping it in the box. Victoria laughed aloud.

'Everyone knows you,' she said tenderly, and Terry shrugged. He knew from Vic it depended how you looked at people. All Terry knew was he'd swept Victoria off her feet.

Some names were familiar to her, Gaudin's fashionable L'Escargot restaurant in Greek Street, and she glimpsed the spire of St Martin-in-the-Fields through a shabby gap between walls that almost touched overhead: single-room windows with tradesmen still working behind the glass, jewellers' faces distorted by magnifying lenses, tailors shuffling tape measures through their chalky hands, shoemakers among piles of wooden lasts, musical instrument makers, watchmakers, leather workers, workers whose trade she could not guess, cats slipping through piles of rubbish that reached half-way up the walls, and above them Greek and Italian housewives calling cheerfully to each other from first-floor windows, stretching lines of laundry between them to catch the last of the sun.

'Like it? Glad you came?' Terry challenged her.

'Let's just walk. I don't want a drink.'

'It's a romantic sort of place, all right,' he acknowledged. 'What's the matter?'

'I thought you lived in the East End.'

'Yes, darling.' He sounded insulted, but she grinned, loving the way he said *daarlin*. 'All foreigners, this. My guardian, I mean my ex-guardian, has property interests here. All these old leases are expiring. It's a good work, see, otherwise the little tradesmen get shut up.' Terry came to the pub doorway and laid his arm against it, holding the dark red door open for her.

'Can't we go to a café or somewhere?'

'Why on earth?'

'All right,' said Victoria, and went inside without a tremble.


Terry had to admit he really did admire her for that, because Soho must have seemed very strange to Victoria, but she didn't let it show. She was a fighter, but she was at a disadvantage and he was well on top of the situation. This was her first time out and he guessed she was worried because she was under drinking age – she couldn't know some of the saucy dabs in the corners were thirteen or fourteen, but there was a good sprinkling of old dears with character. Victoria, he guessed, thought she'd be arrested or chucked out, but she went to the bar cool as you please. Privileged bitch; he felt a stab of anger, everything was so easy for her. She was lovely and self-confident yet pathetic at the same time, because she knew so little of London, the real London, that she was easy prey. But that was only fair, evened out the scales. He could do what he wanted with her. But now, he realised, he wanted her to love him.

In fact this was a respectable joint. Soho had fallen under C Division at West End Central since the Vine Street and Marlborough Street police stations had been amalgamated. Now there were five hundred coppers falling over one another's feet. He was about to reassure her, but he saw she didn't want that: he'd smelt her warmth as she went by him in the doorway. He studied her form at the bar, the paleness of her throat. A couple of one-armed gaming machines in the corner paid rent to the law, but she didn't even know they were illegal. The man leaning his elbows on the counter from the stool beside her was One-Ton Johnny, a detective-inspector in the Met who took bribes in multiples of one hundred pounds. Victoria hardly glanced at him. Why should she?

'You can phone from here,' Terry said, very aware of her.

She shook her head. 'We aren't staying long enough to phone. One drink then you'll take me back.'

If so, he wouldn't get to touch her tonight. 'Up to you.' He ordered a vodka and lime for her, a perch for him. She listened, fascinated, as he pointed out people he knew. She wouldn't believe One-Ton was a policeman; Terry pointed out Italian Alec and Snowball, Jack Spot, men said to be disreputable types. 'I read it in the newspapers. Everyone knows.' There were stars in her eyes; the glamour of it.

Suddenly Terry stopped, sat looking at her. *Don't you see into me at all?* he suddenly wondered.

'I'll take you home,' he said, pushing back the table, destroying at a stroke the evening he had planned, leaving their drinks unfinished, and hurried her back to the car for her own good.

They rode in silence. He pulled up on the corner of Little St James's Street, but she didn't get out.

'What's the matter?' she said. 'What have I done?'

'It's not your fault.'

'Have I disappointed you?' Her face was less than four inches from his.

'I've changed my mind about you, that's all,' he said.

But she saw the heat in his eyes and she waited to be kissed. She wouldn't let him go.

Terry kissed her then leaned across and opened her door. She climbed out and slammed it. He revved the engine and she followed him with her eyes until the car turned out of sight along Piccadilly.

He'd be back.

# Chapter Seven

## 1

'Tra-la-la!'

Ria groaned as Lola's cheerful trumpet noises approached. With eyes stuck closed with sleep she fumbled for her daughter's Mickey Mouse alarm clock, rattled it, then got one eye open and squinted at its cheerful face. Mickey's left hand was pointed to the nine, his right hand at twelve. Surely the alarm hadn't gone off. It couldn't be nine o'clock! *Tra-la-laaa!* The door was flung open and Ria peered at the figures, one tall, one small, that arrived by her bed. 'Good morning!' Lola greeted her with a kiss. Then she whispered behind her, 'Dad . . .'

'Good morning,' Ben echoed in a butler's unctuous tones. 'Madame's breakfast.'

'Strewth, it's not morning already, is it?'

'I did it!' Lola said, taking the clock and wiggling the switch to show how it was done. 'I turned the bell off like that.'

'But it's *your* birthday,' Ria mumbled.

'But your special treat,' Ben said. 'You deserve a special day.'

'Breakfast in bed!' said Lola. Ben came forward holding the tray like Jeeves. Lola had even hung a white linen napkin over his arm for that final professional touch.

'I haven't got time for this,' Ria muttered, 'that isn't really the time is it? Tell me I haven't overslept?'

'You're tired,' Ben said in his own voice. 'We're showing you some respect. Long overdue.'

'I'm not tired!'

'Don't argue,' he ordered. 'You've been looking after us far too well, Ria, and you are tired.' His words were kindly meant, but his plastic-looking smile tugged Ria's heart.

Mentally, it seemed, he now accepted the fact of his blindness. Ben's facial expressions had become deliberate, almost artificial-looking. His eyelids drooped lazily as though he was half asleep. Although he could now look after himself quite well, Ria suspected he needed her more than before. He answered her suspicion with his own words: 'We need you too much to let you collapse.' Sadly Ria realised that he was growing to accept his condition. Certainly he was no longer fighting it as he had: there was no more talk of the finest specialists being called in. And for months she hadn't seen him try that odd, compulsive habit of his first months here, covering his eyes with his hands then snatching them away to stare at a light, even the sun. He had given up hope of miracles.

'Ben,' Ria said, then shook her head. Nothing. There was so much she wished she could do. And undo.

Lola flung the curtains wide and sunlight flooded through the open window. It was the last day of July. The song of a stonechat warbled from somewhere over the moor, the cow lowing as Will returned her to the grazing near the ponds. 'That's Gladys,' Lola said. She tried to click her fingers as Ben had taught her, but he heard something anyway and bent down with the tray as arranged. 'That's your orange juice,' Lola explained to her mother, 'we couldn't find sugar for the porridge—'

'Left of the sink,' Ria said, reaching for the bed-jacket she'd bought in the village.

'Told you!' Lola admonished Ben. 'I did the talking and he did the reaching up,' she confided to Ria, 'but he wasn't much good.'

'He always had difficulties taking instruction,' Ria responded gravely.

'She's never had any difficulty talking,' Ben said.

'She's a chatterbox.'

'So,' Lola said brightly, 'we made your porridge with salt.' She still wouldn't let Ria take the tray: she had a mind of her own, Ria's girl. 'You'll be disappointed in the fried eggs. He broke the yolks on every one.'

'God, how many did you let him try?'

'We don't give up easily,' Lola said.

'Stop prattling,' Ben said. 'Let Madame eat.'

'Orange juice first.' Lola allowed the tray to be placed on the bed.

'Are you going to watch every mouthful?'

'Come on,' Ben said, and Lola took his hand.

'We're going to mix her birthday cake. Find a use for those eggs.'

'Don't let him make a mess,' Ria told Lola through a full mouth, then called her back and hugged her. 'Thanks a million. Happy birthday, darling.'

'Clawfell Cake with sultanas,' whispered Lola. 'We found six candles. Big ones.'

Fondly Ria watched her go, then nibbled luxuriously. Ria didn't care about food, but Ben did, much more than he used to. Another change. Lola must have told him when he should turn the eggs, and together they'd got the toast the right shade of brown. Ria took bigger mouthfuls, finally rampaging through her breakfast. So this was what it was like to be a lady of leisure. She leaned back and fiddled her fingers at the enforced inactivity. Her nails were a mess. There was no such thing as the romance of motherhood, most days she worked like a skivvy. She did it because she wanted to, but her days had fallen into a very humdrum routine here in the healing peace and quiet of Clawfell. She'd expected Ben to organise Will ten hours a day with odd jobs around the place, but he hadn't, another sign that Ben was slowing down. What interest could a vegetable garden hold for a blind man? Why bother picking a few bunches of nice flowers to put on the windowsills? Ria made him come along but it was a bit of a chore, and he obviously didn't really want to do it – perhaps disliked to, and by now she suspected he only went along with her homegrown therapy for her sake. *His* therapy for *her* sake. Ria sat without moving in bed. She was so lonely.

It was true that she'd been a little tired, maybe. She couldn't help feeling that Ben wanted something from her – something more than she was giving. He knew her better than she knew herself. She started filing her blunted nails: they used to be so lovely and long. *You've got everything you've ever wanted, given that it's an imperfect world*, she told herself. *The man you wanted to love you, your children, a roof over your heads, safety*. So why wasn't she happy?

Ben was right. She needed a special treat. Ria gave up on her nails and decided on a good hot bath and a thorough overhaul. Her two helpers would be running out of enthusiasm by now and probably expected her to get the lunch, but that was their hard luck. She took a long bath and a shampoo, and emerged feeling like a different woman.

She looked at herself naked in the bedroom mirror. Bloody hell. What a lousy mirror it was.

Pulling back her chilly wet hair with her fingers, she stuck out her tongue. Good old Ria! It wasn't the mirror's fault, of course, it was her. She looked great; she would have preferred a few years knocked off the slate, but so would everyone; she was an attractive, vivid woman with plenty of life in her, still naughty. Why did she carry an ugly mental picture of herself? She made her eyes sparkle, her smile vivacious, and she knew how to move with the seamless grace of an actress – as she did now, touching her fingers to her lips and holding them out to the encore of an invisible audience, her presence on stage seeing nothing beyond the lights, hearing nothing but the applause.

Welcome to motherhood.

Ria told herself she had been born with something missing. The lack was something inside her, where it couldn't be seen; only she felt it. When they were young Ben London had sensed her loss and understood her, fallen in love with her, but everyone grew up. Ria would always want more. Always want whatever she couldn't have, or she shouldn't have, she would always be unhappiest when she had most to be happy for, like now. Her childhood dreams, some of them anyway, had come true, and that was more than many people got. But now she was free she didn't want to be free. Now she was in the company of the man she wanted he didn't seem so much.

She told herself Ben London was growing old because he ignored her in the only way that mattered to her. He was afraid to love her, simply take her in his arms. Without his earlier rage to sustain him his blindness was wearing him down prematurely. He had softened, he was nice to her and she was nice to him but Ria knew that wasn't nearly enough. With the passions cooled between them he didn't nearly take the place of her old life. She was homesick. Back home she couldn't have slept past nine o'clock without knowing it! – the clattering milkman, busy traffic, old Frank and Babs across the road arguing, their front door slamming to lock one or the other out, cue for an argy-bargy conducted between the pavement and the bedroom window followed by a weepy reconciliation. And there'd be the mums popping round to Ria, dropping off their kids to play with Lola while they ran down the shops maybe, children's laughter in the house, the Land twins with a few bits of lettuce filched out the back of their dad's greengrocery for the rabbit, feeding him scraps through the wire, screaming with delight when Thumper ate on his back legs, and the funny moustache-twirling way he cleaned his whiskers afterwards. In her mind's eye Ria could see it all, and missed every little bit of that life.

'Ria,' Ben said from the doorway.

Ria jumped, scandalised. But of course she could have been dressed in Arctic furs for all he knew. She stood in front of him naked and he didn't comprehend.

'What do you want, Ben?'

'Lola doesn't know where the unset honey is. Neither do I.'

'Oh, what does the cake matter?' Ria said, looking down at herself, the water beaded on the tips of her breasts and between her legs . . . she might as well be on the moon as far as he was concerned, and when she shook her head sudden droplets scattered from her hair, trickling in icy caresses down her back. There he was, fully dressed and uncomprehending, greasy to the elbows with butter and flour, floury fingermarks scrawled over his shirt and trousers, a broad-shouldered man doing the cooking instead of eating and complaining, and suddenly Ria hated him for trying to take over her job. 'I'll find it for you!' she said roughly. 'Give me a minute.'

'Tell me where it is,' he said reasonably, 'we'll manage.'

'My hair's still wet,' Ria cried. The tears fell down her face. 'Just get out and leave me alone.'

He held out his hands: good old Ria, all pelting rain then beaming sunshine. But perversely Ria avoided his touch and he couldn't hear the whisper of any dressing-gown or slippers, couldn't follow her. 'Ria?' He turned his head in the wrong direction.

'Go away,' Ria said. 'I'm busy.'

'You know better than this.'

'Do I? You don't even let me give you presents.' She accused him on the spur of the moment: 'I wanted to make that cake with Lola.' That wasn't exactly true; she meant she'd saved Lola from Vic and now she felt her little girl slipping away. She'd best shut up before her frustration made her say something really stupid. He always knew when she was lying. That voice full of feeling had made her a wonderful singer, but with him she was a lousy actress. As soon as she opened her mouth she gave everything away. She had never been able to hide from him. Hadn't a little part of her, deep down, hidden away, welcomed Pearl's death, grabbing any excuse to be with Ben and recapture her lost youth and might-have-been? But Ben never forgave and never forgot, and the ghost of Pearl London still stood between them. 'I'm sorry, Ben. This is difficult for me.'

'I do know,' he said, taking Ria's dressing-gown from its hook on the back of the door and tossing it to her before he left. 'I can hear you shivering.'

Ria dressed and went through the kitchen pulling on her fawn coat, doing up the wooden buttons with determination though it was still a fine day outside. Ben was by now mixing sultanas into the mess in the bowl which Ria ignored. 'Where are you going?' Lola piped up.

'Down the village. We're going shopping. You'd better wear your coat too, just in case.' The moors were never less than bleak, and even in summer mists descended without warning. Ria pulled on her outdoor shoes by the door.

'I'm not coming,' Lola said.

'Stop arguing for once.'

'But this is my cake.'

'Ria?' Ben called. 'It's all right,' he told Lola, 'you don't have to go if you don't want to.'

'You mind your own business,' Ria said shortly, and wished Lola was close enough to grab her hand.

'I've arranged she's going to Home Farm,' Ben called. 'Will's letting her watch him paint.' When Ria ignored him he added, 'It's Helen's day for driving into the village. If you're so set on going shopping, do you want a lift?'

'I can walk very well by myself, thank you.' Ria went out. Ben's hand knocked against her shopping basket left standing in its usual place.

'What about my cake?' Lola said, and made a sucking noise with her finger, sampling the mixture. 'More honey.'

'You'll turn into a bee,' he said fondly. 'Don't sneak it all before it's cooked, you'll get stomach-ache.' He knew what she was doing and rapped the bowl with the mixing-spoon.

'Missed. It's my birthday. You love my mum, don't you?' Lola said as he stirred. The funny, childlike way she phrased it made him grin: my mum. 'She says your name in the nights sometimes. That's why she's miserable.'

'I love both of you,' Ben replied.

'Dad.' She stood on a chair and cuddled him.

'But you see, love isn't easy. It's hard.'

'Is that why you're sending me to school next term?'

'You're growing up, Lola.'

'Mum doesn't want me to start school,' Lola said wisely. 'She doesn't want to lose me.'

'We won't,' Ben said. 'That's a promise.'

'Lose me to you,' Lola said.

Ria took her ear from the door.

Miss Parkinson's school had been Ben's idea. The whole education system had been revised root and branch at the end of the war, apparently, and Lola could no longer escape the supervision of the local authority. She had done one term as an infant at the Cheval Street school on the Isle of Dogs, but nothing since, and now at the start of the new academic year, Ben had decided it was safe for her to go to school in Blane. No one there knew Mr London. The Leat Road primary school was a scramble of quaint quarters built with Rownslee largesse on the site of the old Cleremont school, at the junction with the High Road. 'Bit of a dump,' Ria had sniffed, guiding Ben inside, 'high railings.' The headmistress was Miss Parkinson, a deep-voiced jocular woman with a firm handshake.

'Pleased to meet you, Mr – ah—'

'Mr Trott,' Ben had said, and given Ria's guiding

hand such a warning squeeze that she squeaked. 'This is Mrs Trott, and our daughter, Lola.'

Miss Parkinson's brother, Mr Parkinson, was headmaster of the adjacent High Road grammar school, and he dropped by, smelling of tweed and pipe-smoke, his handshake as firm as his sister's, with whom he lived. 'Our mother, God rest her soul, was head cook at the Grange for many years,' ruminated this avuncular soul. Threatened with closure by the declining textile industry and the dwindling population of the village, the two school premises had been run together, though separated by a wall and maintaining separate playgrounds, and each new pupil to boost the school roll was greeted by the principals with open arms. 'I'm sure the lass will be most happy here.'

'I don't think she—' Ria had said, but Ben said smoothly, 'I agree, I think Lola will be very happy here.' So Ria let him have his way. But she had hated him taking the name of the dead Raymond Trott, who had been her husband.

*She's safe*, Ben had whispered, but Ria could not shuck off her entire life so easily. As she walked the gritstone track to Blane, the waters of the leat chuckling beside her along the hillsides, she realised that obviously Ben – Mr Trott! – had not allowed Lola to come with her because he didn't quite trust Ria's loyalty. Once, when they were children, she had betrayed Ben to Vic. He wouldn't give her a second chance.

And yet, she realised, as she came among the

houses and stepped on a proper pavement, a second chance to betray him was exactly what he was giving her. There was a coin-operated telephone in the post office. All she had to do was lift the handset, put her money in the slot and ask the operator to give her a London number, listen until it was answered, and press button A.

But she had no plans to go to the post office. She stopped off at the store and bought a skipping-rope with red wooden handles for Lola.

In the grocer's she tried to think of anything else she wanted so she could look good arriving back at Clawfell, but she hadn't brought her basket or a shopping list. Shopping hadn't been on her mind at all.

Ria knew why she had come. She'd better check the post office in case any letters had arrived. That was a silly excuse for going there, because no one ever wrote to them. Ben sometimes posted letters, or even made calls to Charlie Bookkeeper from the anonymous post office phone, but they never received letters because no one knew they were here.

So she really had no excuse at all to go into the post office.

She went inside. The telephone, complete with a small mirror in a chromed frame, was on the wall by the counter. The dour postmistress glanced at her through the wire and tightened her mouth. Ria smiled back. Her heart was thudding, and she waited until the woman occupied herself with forms. Ria lifted the black bakelite handset and pressed it to her ear.

Though the phone was modern the exchange was not and she dialled TRU.

'Trunk operator, what number please?'

'London, East.' Ria gave the number. She opened her purse on the pay-box and pushed coins into the slot. After a few moments she heard the irregular purring of a telephone bell ringing on the Isle of Dogs. It stopped. Mum's voice in her ear.

'Hallo, Esther Price speaking.'

Ria pressed button A and with the rattle of the accepted coins everything fled her mind. All she could think of was home.

'Oh, Mum!'

At home, Ria knew, the telephone was kept on the sideboard in the front room, by the pictures of the royals, an engagement photograph of the Princess Elizabeth and Philip Mountbatten in the place of honour by now. All this was conjured for Ria out of Mum's voice, and Ria saw Mum standing stooped over the phone the way she did, wearing the dark yellow-brown dress and woollen stockings that hid her veins, her feet pushed comfortably into cherry-red slippers. Her fingers would be playing anxiously with the telephone cord. Mum.

'That's not you is it, Ria?'

'How are you, Mum?'

'Oh my God I can't believe it, it's her. Where are you, darling? Are you coming home today?'

'Are – are you all right?'

'I'm fine, I'm marvellous, dear, when are you coming home?'

Ria closed her eyes. *I can't tell you where I am and I'm never coming home, Mum.* Her silence must have seemed like a fault on the line because Esther's voice rose frantically: 'Hallo? Hallo? Hallo?'

'We're all right, Mum. We're in good health and Lola sends her love. Kisses.'

'Tell me you're almost home.' Esther had got wise to the line and let the silence stretch out. 'Tell me.'

'I can't.'

'This is awful, you've missed Vic, he'll be so disappointed. I told him you might ring but he didn't believe me. I said it's Lola's birthday today, Ria might bring her back home, you never know your luck. I got something special in the fridge on the off-chance. Your favourite, and kidney too. Darling? Vic's so worried about you, he wants to know where you are, he wants to help. Are you close, dear? He's in an awful state, he does miss you, and you know how fond he is of Lola. Ria, really it's not fair of you to do this . . . I'm getting old . . .' She was in full flood. Her voice dwindled as Ria took the handset from her ear.

Ria hung up.

# 2

'Ria is dead to me,' Vic said.

'But Lola isn't,' said Betty Stark. She had always been a woman who spoke her mind and she saw no reason to curb her tongue. But the confidences of such a man as Vic were not a privilege to be taken lightly, and Betty – it wasn't just the gin and fizzy water – was tinglingly aware of the compliment he paid her. She touched her palm to her hair, still brown and curly. He'd caught her almost at her worst, trudging down the ten steps of the London Hospital, tired, tying her headscarf with work-roughened hands. 'What a coincidence,' Vic had said, not fooling her for a moment, 'isn't that a chance?' He'd just stood there in front of her, until Betty had to look round to see if they were being watched. But Whitechapel High Street was far enough from the West India Dock where her husband Mr Dempsey worked for the word not to get back.

'How long have you been watching me?' Betty asked, but she knew the answer. He'd kept an eye on her since that day at the funeral when he'd caught her putting flowers on Nigel's grave.

'Let's have a drink,' Vic said. 'Old times.'

'I don't mind if I do,' Betty said, 'it's better than waiting for the bus.' Betty wasn't afraid of Vic. She loved the way he commanded respect, she'd been aware of him all her life, and the ride in his big car was an appreciated change to her dull routine nowadays. Not that the good old days had really been very good. She'd never found the man to live up to her; a man who married a strong woman became a weak creature. It was Nigel, Vic's brother, who'd opened her eyes to all she'd missed – the first man she'd met to treat her as a real person rather than just a receptacle for cock-of-the-walk braggadocio. The only man she'd loved.

She was silent during the drive to Cable Street.

Outside the pub Vic turned off the engine. 'You don't like me at all, Betty.'

What did he want, sympathy? 'That's not for me to judge,' Betty told him straight out.

'Ria was to blame as much as me.'

Betty just wanted to get in the pub. This invitation back to the Old Bull and Bush was a trip down memory lane for her. She'd often met Nigel here and the place never seemed to change – a lick of nicotine-coloured paint from time to time but never its smell of beer, bare boards and plush. Old feelings and emotions swirled up like vapour as she sat at the table. Nigel's table. Vic didn't ask her what she wanted to drink. Gin-and-splash. Nothing slipped Vic's memory, not one thing.

But Nigel had been everything a man should be: Betty had witnessed his love for Arleen. He had been so clever and organised, yet a loving and kind man too, and when Arleen died he'd doted on the baby that lived, Terry, as caringly as a mother. Betty had often seen him in Island Gardens, the young mums snatching a fag and a moment off on the park benches, contemptuous of his softness, a man pushing a pram. But Betty had dreamed of taking Arleen's place. And so she had comforted him, hoping as Arleen's memory faded, Nigel's love would find a home in her. But he had remained faithful to Arleen's memory. Betty understood the force of that now. What a fool she had been. And yet being a fool had been the most wonderful time of her life. She had sat beside Nigel, like this, at this ringmarked table, many times; now the smell of the beeswax brought the past to life in sudden flashes, the taste of the gin fizzing in her mouth, even Vic's presence bringing back Nigel to her.

'Are you sleepy?' Vic demanded.

Betty pinched herself. 'It's been a long day.' Vic leaned close and grinned at her.

'Got me worked out, Betty?'

'I wouldn't want to do that, Vic.'

'No, you couldn't,' he laughed. 'Hair of the dog?'

'You're trying to get me tipsy!'

'Forget about Ria, she's dead to me. And Lola . . . do you believe in that repentance stuff, Betty?' He didn't wait for her answer. 'I sincerely repent,' Vic said. He'd been careful to give Betty just the one drink before starting in on her, but she wasn't used to it and it showed. 'You don't know me as nosily as you think you do,' Vic told her seriously. 'People forget good turns. I looked after you after Stark left you on your ownsy. Don't be ungrateful. Peace?'

'Well, I don't know.' She looked at him doubtfully. Vic getting his way was very intimidating.

'Go on, have another one,' he urged.

'No.'

'I'll drive you home now if you like.'

'In front of the whole of Poplar High Street!'

Vic raised his finger to the barman. Another. 'Nosy neighbours, eh?'

'Don't even think about it.'

'I'm that bad, eh?'

'You're having me on,' she said uncertainly, really looking at him for the first time. Vic wasn't like Nigel at all. 'You're twisting my words.'

He bunched his shoulders powerfully, looking at her with amusement dancing in his eyes. 'Your Mr Dempsey wouldn't mind us, from what I hear.'

'Vic, don't talk like that.'

'Not the sort of man to object. Quiet sort, white collar, clean hands.'

'He looks after me all right. He's all right.'

'That's all? I heard he works longer hours than you do. Loves pushing his pen more than his you-know-what.'

'That's none of your business!' She had outrage in her voice, but she didn't get up.

'Keeps his missus on a short leash, does he? Keeps an eye on you.'

'He's got nothing to be jealous about, I can tell you!'

'He should have,' Vic said in a quiet, deep voice. He pushed her glass into her hands, but she didn't drink, just stared at his hand touching hers. 'He should have.'

'Don't be wicked, Vic.'

'Don't pretend, Betty.' He took his hand away and she sipped her drink automatically, released. 'There's really so much more to you than you show, isn't there, Betty?'

'Vic, don't.'

'What is there in your life that's so worthwhile, Betty?'

That was a dreadful question to ask, he knew. They never faced up to it.

'Look at the time,' Betty said, getting up, 'I haven't bought his tea yet, I must get a move on.'

'Off you go,' he said without looking at her.

'Ta-ra, Vic.' She hesitated, then snatched up her bag.

'Want me to walk you to the bus?' he called, but she had fled, leaving only a lingering scent of Lysol disinfectant. He grunted with amusement, knowing he'd got her. He'd have to look for somewhere they could use. Finishing his drink, he handed his glass to Jake at the bar and drove to Havannah Street. As soon as he turned the key in the lock he knew something had happened.

Esther was flapping. 'Ria phoned!'

Vic still didn't believe it. 'Why should she phone you?'

'You know what Ria's like, she's so sentimental. It's Lola's birthday. I knew Ria would phone today,' Esther drove home the point for the pleasure of getting one over Vic, 'I was waiting. You should have thought of it,' she said self-importantly.

'Did you speak to Lola?'

'Oh.'

'Then where are they?'

'It was just Ria phoned.'

'Where from?'

Esther retreated into the front room.

'Darling, I was in such a panic, and then I tried to get you at the Old Bull and Bush but they said you'd gone—'

'*Where was Ria phoning from?*'

Esther subsided into the chair shaking her head. She didn't know. Probably she hadn't even thought to ask. Vic could have kicked her.

'Did you hear anything in the background? Lola crying?'

'Ria said she and Lola were healthy.'

'*Healthy!*' screamed Vic. 'God knows what that bastard's done to them.'

Esther sat with her hands in her lap. She stared at the embroidered homilies arranged along the sideboard, shutting Vic out. *Whatsoever a woman soweth, that shall she also reap*. She'd at last had her bunions done by Dr Hall and her feet could tolerate shoes all day. She was wearing a summer dress printed with scarlet poppies and her hair was permed tight. The new curtains she'd chosen were an everglaze chintz also with a poppy design, which was why Vic had brought home the dress for her, so that she matched. He hated any sort of change.

Vic dropped into the other chair, put his head in his hands, and they sat there alone in the front room.

# 3

The moment Ria put the phone down she had known, in a way she couldn't have put into words, that something had changed for ever. Ben had made her change it. When she cut off her mother's voice, Ria had crossed her Rubicon. She could no longer turn back. She had left her old life behind and Ben had made her do it.

She'd done it for him. Now it was up to Ben to deserve her.

Her hands were shaking. When by force of habit

she pressed button B in hope of rejected coins her thumb skidded off the chrome. Ria took her purse off the pay-box and headed for the door. Helen was waiting there. 'I always do that too,' she said. 'It's gambling really.'

She was a pretty girl, devout, and devoted to Will. She wore wellington boots and an agricultural woollen skirt and stood no nonsense from anyone. *She wouldn't last five minutes with Ben!* Ria told herself. Born in Chelsea's Collingwood Road slums, Helen had no children of her own and had worked as Lisa's assistant among the needy children of the district. Down one side of her face lay a strawberry birthmark which fascinated Lola, and when they first met the little girl had caressed it with her fingers. Helen was on the church committee and Ria wondered if she had persuaded Will, genial and childlike, to say his prayers before bed. She had confessed to Ria in her friendly yet unconfiding way: 'Most people carry their disfigurements inside them, where they are hidden, Ria. With me, what you see is all there is.' *You've got a high opinion of yourself*, Ria had thought, but the two women accepted their differences. Helen had done more for Will after his injury during the war than Ria ever could.

'I guess Ben told you to check up on me,' Ria said, coming outside into the sunlight and birdsong over Leat Road.

'Why should he?' Helen laughed, and Ria was stunned by such innocence. 'He's too busy baking that cake. I went over to the main house to see if there was any shopping you wanted but you'd already gone.

He gave me this.' She held out Ria's shopping basket as they went down the steps to the truck.

Ria couldn't be bothered with it. 'Let's go home,' she said.

Ten minutes' drive in the rattling, battered vehicle brought them to the farm. Helen hooted the horn in the yard and Lola waved then ran down from the barn Will used as a studio. Ria picked her up and whirled her round. 'You'll make her dizzy,' Helen said.

'Good,' said Ria, as Lola tugged her inside the barn.

'Look, he's painting!'

Will was sitting beneath the studio windows let into the south roof, a figure glowing in a pool of strong natural light. In his lap was a portable board, thick watercolour paper drummed to it with brown sticky paper. Working faster than Ria could have believed, he was building up colour with translucent washes of pure watercolours. 'Number twelve brush,' Lola confided in a whisper, and Will moved the board expertly for the colours to run. He snatched a piece of sponge and dabbed a tree against the sky: Ria felt his excitement and knew Lola did too, but Helen stood apart, a yearning witness. She had pushed him so hard into expressing this talent and now it excluded her. Will reversed the brush and scratched out something that displeased him, not aware of the people quietly watching him, or the glaze of perspiration on his face.

'He has to work fast,' Lola whispered. 'Number two brush for the cottage, he's got to know his colours.' To Ria's amazement Lola knew the names too, alizarin crimson, chrome yellow, quick as a trice. Ria saw how rich her daughter's life was, the astonishing, uncontrollable rate the child acquired knowledge. 'Mixing Paynes grey and burnt umber,' Lola muttered, 'almost black.' Helen went away to make the tea and returned. She exchanged her wellingtons for shoes and sat reading a magazine.

Will finished with a sigh.

'You're a silly boy,' Helen said tenderly, 'you'll strain yourself. Have you had your nap?'

Will looked at them vaguely, coming back from wherever he had been.

'He hates people looking at his work,' Helen said, though it was she who had first shown his paintings to buyers. She patted his shoulder peremptorily. 'Time for rest.'

Will saw Ria. 'Hallo, Mum,' he said in a slightly slurred voice, getting up with stiff joints. 'I was showing Lola . . . I hope she wasn't bored.'

'She doesn't miss a trick,' Ria said, leaning down. 'Let's have a butcher's.'

'He doesn't—' Helen repeated.

''Course you can, Mum,' Will said. 'It's finished.'

Ria stared. 'It's here,' she murmured, 'except the truck's here in the yard now. And the flowers outside the cottage aren't—'

'He remembers it all,' Lola said proudly, 'it isn't summer. It's spring, in the picture. It's the first time I came over after the snow had gone and I was playing outside.'

'I just hope we can sell it,' Helen said.

'This is Lola's birthday present,' Will said gently. 'For her, from me. Mine. Lola's picture.'

'Oh, Will, you are a sweet. You've got a real talent.'

'The talent that my grandfather threw away,' Will said.

Along one wall he'd propped the ten gloomy portraits removed from around the staircase at the Grange, the ten generations of the Lockhart family whose stern likeness had survived down the centuries. Will had started the process of patiently removing the layers of grime, soot, and discoloured varnish from the crazed surfaces. With the dark weight of years removed from them the faces looked pale and dull, merely flat. Cartoons shorn of authority without the patina of time. 'It'll take me years to finish them,' Will said.

'No more work today,' insisted Helen.

Ria walked back to the Grange with Lola skipping the rope beside her. 'Salt, pepper, mustard, *vinegar*,' she chanted, a children's rhyme older than the hills. Smoke trailed from one single chimney: the fire in the range. Going downstairs, Ria saw the cake waiting on the kitchen table.

'Tra-la,' Ben announced, having heard their footsteps, then dropped the match as it burned his fingers. 'How'd I do?'

He had been right, Ria saw. The cake did matter. One look at Lola's face was enough for Ria: once the millionaire had given his women gifts of rubies and presents beyond price, but the child's expression was magical, the look a mother locks into her heart for ever. The birthday cake he'd baked for Lola was huge and ungainly. There would never be another one like it, crumbled on one side where it had stuck getting it out of the cake-tin – the largest tin a complete Victorian kitchen had to offer, which was large indeed – the top peppered with indentations where anxious examinations had been conducted with a skewer to tell if it was properly cooked, then gosh-pink icing liberally but erratically applied. Six tall candles adorned the top, one of them crooked, two of them red and the rest white. It looked like a confection dreamed up by a blind man, but one with his heart in the right place.

'Does she like it?' Ben whispered. 'What do you see?'

'The candles shining in her eyes,' Ria smiled.

Lola hugged them both. 'This is the most wonderful day of my whole life,' she said, and made a wish.

'Is she asleep?'

'Like a babe.' Ria sighed and sat on her knees beside him on the sofa. The butler's sitting-room was small but she had made it comfortable. There was a thrift shop in the village and she'd hung a few cheap prints on the walls, views of Manchester, hansom cabs, trams outside Manchester Piccadilly. 'What was Lola's wish, d'you reckon?'

'She probably wished the cake tasted as good as it looked.'

Ria snorted. 'It wasn't half bad.'

He held her hand. There was always so much more between them. Impulsively she turned to face him.

'Ben, when I was in the village I telephoned Havannah Street,' she confessed.

'Did you speak to Vic?' The sudden ferocity in his blind eyes frightened her.

'He wasn't in.'

'Did you want to speak to him?'

'No,' Ria said. She had plucked up courage to tell him one truth, but there were so many others she couldn't tell him: he did not know of the worst thing Vic had done to him, that Lola was Vic's child, that Ria's false seduction of Ben almost seven years before had been a lie to hide that truth. Now she thought it might break him. Nor could he know that the bomb that killed Pearl had been set by Terry, not Vic. These were the two secrets Ria still kept.

Ben said, 'What did you tell Esther?'

'Goodbye. Goodbye.'

He reached out, touched her face, his fingers tracing the line of her forehead, eyebrows, cheeks, the tip of her nose.

'I am so sorry, Ria.' He took her hand in his.

'It's all behind me, all in the past.' She looked at him anxiously.

He smiled. 'I trust you with my life.' He kissed her hand. 'I just did.'

She had forgotten the little ring on her finger. She was still Mrs Trott.

# Chapter Eight

## 1

The supposedly reliable Mrs Feynton, who had taken over Cathy's old job in the Emporium's classy handbag department, finally admitted she had fallen pregnant at the age of thirty-four when, by the end of October, the truth could no longer be hidden. She was walking like a sack and even the clients noticed. In the store's unwritten constitution this was an act of treason, it being a truism of the trade that shoppers do not willingly purchase goods from a pregnant sales-woman. Maeve Feynton was dismissed without notice and her job put up for grabs. Cathy took her mother's advice not to return to her previous post, but half a dozen others snatched at this unexpected opportunity for advancement. Victoria bided her time. Playing the field – the others thought only of themselves – she reckoned it was odds-on that David Jones would offer Jeanette, who had worked that department before, the job on the second floor. Second favourite must be Daisy, the budding career girl – her longtime fiancé had just walked out on her – who put her name forward because she wanted more than a change, and cosmetics was not a department with much clout in the Emporium's internal power structure. There were others who applied: they couldn't resist the sound of a starting-gun for any number of reasons, women like Miss Purves from Children's Shoes who was rumoured to hate children, also-rans like Mrs Somebody-or-other from one of the little departments at the back of the store, and bringing up the rear a bevy of hardworking no-hopers without distinction or seniority, such as Lucy, whose bubbling spirits had been flattened by Mrs Lehaye, earnest Mandy who attended nightschool to improve herself, and the happy-go-lucky Barbara, who couldn't quite be discounted because David Jones was known to have an eye for a girl with a saucy smile. The interview was to be held on the first Thursday in November.

Jeanette didn't bother to hide her jealousy when she learned that Victoria had put her name forward. 'Naturally you'll romp home at the interview!' she complained.

'I'll stand just the same chance as the rest of you,' Victoria asserted, 'or less probably. You all know what Jones thinks of me.'

'Come on, dears,' boomed Hilda cheerfully, 'Vicky's put 'er finger bang on it there wiv old Casey Jones.' Even the others had to admit the truth of that. Their mood brightened, and Victoria felt a sudden fear that she really would lose.

Without her father's support, her natural advantage of birth was starting to work against her. She thought carefully what to do, then moved swiftly.

During her lunch hour Victoria breezed up to George's office suite on the top floor as if she owned the place, and gave his new secretary the family smile. 'Is he in?'

'But I'm afraid Mr Ford is with him—'

'Uncle Cliff,' smiled Victoria as the door was opened for her, and offered her cheek to be kissed by the old man, the company's financial director. On clear days these fourth-floor offices had fine views south across the rooftops to St James's Park. George's corner office overlooking Old Bond Street and Piccadilly held a picture-postcard view to Piccadilly Circus, but not today: the open window was a wall of throat-catching, swirling, grey-green fog, stinking of Pool spirit – the headlamps glowing like pearls on the cars below, crawling at less than walking pace between Mayfair and Soho – and trapped smoke. 'If only everyone followed our example,' George said, inhaling, 'and gave up coal.'

Clifford gathered his papers. 'I was just going,' he said. He nodded politely to Victoria and said goodbye to George.

'We've decided to go ahead with the Food Hall,' George began importantly, coming round his desk and fussing Victoria into a chair. He waited for a moment as if expecting a reply, but Victoria gave him none. Everyone knew the Food Hall was David Jones's scheme. 'And we shall refurbish the Waterfalls restaurant,' said George a little more firmly. So that was his idea.

'Oh? Did the Waterfalls ever make money?'

'The restaurant was a fashionable meeting-place,

Victoria, and it brought people into the store. Stylish, in its day.' Having sat her down, he fussed at her to get up again and opened a side door. Leading her along the corridor, he showed her the gutted, echoing space that had been the Waterfalls, designed by Marcus Rumney's flawed genius. A few steps led them up to an incongruous twenties-style fountain, its bowl scattered with a debris of screwed-up newspapers and lollipop sticks. Their shoes crunched on shards of marble, and they stepped over a broken mermaid.

'I'd value your opinion,' George said shyly.

'It sounds a wonderful idea!' Victoria said. 'The store needs vision.'

'Do you think so? All they talk about is cash flow and return on capital. But I'm sure of it!' George said with more confidence. 'A few lords' ladies, and county women up for the day—'

To Victoria the sound of that clientèle rang more of the year 1900 than the present day, but she knew George's picture of what he must live up to from the store's golden age had been formed by his mother. Vane had worshipped Georgy Leibig, captain of the store in those turn-of-the-century days, whose blood flowed in George's veins. Selling, however, had taught Victoria always to swim with the tide.

'It sounds so exciting!'

'That's what I told Clifford and David.'

'David Jones would swear black was white to do you down,' Victoria said casually.

'Would he?'

George was so innocent that he infuriated her. He had such faith in himself and such self-confidence that could not see, as Victoria could, that he was surrounded by enemies. He was trusting in all the wrong ways: trusting his own judgement, trusting Cathy, trusting David, trusting Victoria. He thought his own self-interest was everybody's. 'I'm sure you're right,' he said sadly. 'I just wish everyone would pull together and share my vision.'

'I'm sure they will.'

'I know you hold the interests of the store at heart, Victoria, as I do.'

'Yes, indeed I do, George.'

She turned and he followed her back to his office. Victoria sat hiding her impatience – her lunch-hour did not last forever.

'I suppose there is a reason for this visit,' he said.

'The vacancy left by Mrs Feynton.'

A number of wooden figurines, unmistakably female and of impressive workmanship, adorned the surfaces of George's office. All had been hand-worked from hardwood, dark mahogany, lignum vitae as black as a Zulu princess, teak and some beautiful pale-veined woods Victoria did not recognise, all smoothed to a gloss as fine as porcelain. George turned one delicately in his blunt fingers. Most people assumed his collection was purchased, but each one came from his own unstylish, inartistic hands. No male figures, not one. Tiny and perfect, the figurine George played with had been carved with Cathy's face, Victoria noticed.

'The interview is to be held on Thursday,' Victoria said. 'I'd like the job.'

'It's yours.'

Victoria noticed that one figure, about a foot high, in pride of place by the inkwell, had been turned from a wood as pale as ivory. An evening gown, furs, one pixie hand held out. The expression on her wooden face was determined, yet indescribably gentle. George's mother. So this was how George saw her. By all accounts the woman had had a will of iron. It was her heart that was of wood.

'Anything more I can do for you?' George said.

'What about the interview?'

George shrugged. 'We can hold it for appearances' sake if you like. If that would make your position easier.'

'No,' decided Victoria. 'Let them see. I want it to be absolutely clear to them how I got this job.'

Victoria London got the job because she was Ben London's daughter and because she was prepared to manipulate George, which Cathy was not. And, Cathy knew, George had wanted to help Victoria because in her he saw something of his mother, Vane. 'She was unlucky too,' George said briefly. 'Well, I don't have to stand by this time and watch it happen. I can do something for her.'

'Victoria won't be grateful,' Cathy advised.

'People never are,' sighed George, 'that's the way we're made.'

So Victoria took over her new job. Almost at once there was tension between her and George. They both confided in Cathy, since she was the friend of each, each using her as a conduit to the other for their views. 'George hates fake glitter,' Cathy let drop to Victoria during the January sales. 'He wants to take the store upmarket.' Victoria took down the glitter but it was plain to Cathy that all Victoria's instincts were for mass-selling, turning stock fast and efficiently. The names of the so-called eternal brands held no magic for her: the opposite. She seemed determined to debunk them as if the store could start afresh, as her own life had. No names, no past. But she had not hesitated to benefit by the use of her own name. It was a love-hate relationship with herself, and Cathy saw how unhappy Victoria was.

She confided to Cathy that she hated the cloying smell of the leather from which the handbags, apart from the very cheapest, were made. It permeated the department and she suffered for every hour she passed there. But these confidences decreased as Victoria's self-confidence grew. Cathy knew that Victoria thought she slept with George, and felt offended by this assumption. But because of it, she began to feel she ought to, and then to feel guilty about not doing so. Was the failure her fault? Did it mean George didn't love her? Or was Victoria just a virgin who wanted Cathy to lose her virginity in Victoria's stead? There was a kind of hot, intrusive light in Victoria's eyes sometimes, Cathy thought.

Having her own department meant Victoria had a phone on the store's internal system. One evening, just before closing, the wall handset rang and Victoria picked it up. 'Yes?'

Terry's voice. 'It's me.'

She held her lower lip between her teeth, excited.

'I knew you would,' she said. The department was quiet except for one of Lucy's clients paying, and another two 'just looking'.

'Missed me?' Terry's voice demanded.

'You're so full of yourself,' she responded fondly. 'Have you learned to behave?'

'I can't get you out of my mind, Victoria.' He knew how to get her going. 'Now then, don't look so superior.'

'Do I?' she taunted him. 'Why haven't I heard from you?'

'Business.'

'You're excused.'

'Have mercy,' he said, a little roughly. Then, 'You obsess me.'

'I hope so,' she grinned, turning to the wall so that the clients should not see her eager expression, putting back a strand of hair from her forehead.

'I love it when you do that.'

She stared at the phone suspiciously. It had buttons only for internal departments. 'Terry, are you—'

'I'm behind you.'

He was standing at the service phone by the lifts. He'd thought to buy a clipboard; a man with a clipboard could go anywhere. He waved it. 'Took me ages to find you, girl. I came up through every department below. Now you've been promoted you won't want to come out with me tonight.'

'Where?'

'Trust me.'

He took her dancing at the London Casino and they had a wonderful time.

So Terry came back to her, and whatever he said, Victoria knew actions spoke louder than words. For all his pretence, he had come back and she knew where she stood. Sometimes she was busy at work, and he got back to Town less often in the winter, but his visits were longer, and the poor boy tried to make them last the evening. Victoria strung him along: she always had Lisa as an excuse to break off and get home. Her grandmother's continuing work as a District Commissioner in the Girl Guide movement meant that she was often out in the evenings herself and knew nothing of Victoria's increasingly regular Saturday night absences. The car had no heater and he took her to dance-halls to hold her, savouring her with his hands on her slim waist, her silky skin above her off-the-shoulder dress whispering to his finger-tips, warming her up as they smooched. When they were together allowances of three pounds of potatoes a week, rationing and austerity were very far away. Afterwards he took her to those picturesque pubs amid the Soho nightlife and warmed her up inside with brandies. They kissed goodnight in the byway of Little St James's Street, under the lamp at first, then in the darkness between the pools of light. Her lips, then her open mouth under his own tasted of the brandy he had given her, and his hand sliding on her hip glided to her breast. He could feel how close he was to getting her submission, though she twisted away with a laugh. But she knew what she saw in his eyes, she wasn't born yesterday, and she felt as he did.

He followed her earnestly. 'You know what you're doing to me.'

She glanced back and he saw the flash of her teeth. She knew.

He caught up with her and she stopped. He held her, his face in her hair, saying her name.

'You're so serious,' Victoria said.

'Don't you want me to be serious?'

'Much more than *that* serious.' A few squeezes in a doorway wasn't good enough for her.

'God, you're lovely,' he said hungrily. 'I want you and you want me too.' But the moment had gone and he knew it.

'You always get so boring at the end of the evening,' she said.

'It doesn't have to finish. Come down East with me.' He had never suggested that before, his home territory, and she shook her head. 'What's the matter?' he demanded roughly, frustrated. 'Don't you dare?'

Her mouth set.

'I will,' Victoria London dared him, 'if *you* will.'

## 2

'You aren't keeping anything secret from me, chum?' Vic said.

'Not me, Vic,' Terry said, leaning on the counter at the Old Bull and Bush. Vic rarely came here these days and Terry regarded the place almost as his own home ground, insofar as he had any home ground. He'd been brought up here in this pub and thought he knew it at least as well as Vic. As a child coming home here in the Vaudey School holidays he'd played alone for hours among the empty beer-casks awaiting collection in the side alley. During the evening he'd watched from the stairs, a small silent absence of a boy in short trousers, no mother to get him to bed early and tuck him in and kiss him goodnight: watching between the banister rods with his serious brown eyes, watching the customers filling the bars getting happier and louder and making fools of themselves as evening passed and the drink got hold of them. Sons and heirs down from Oxbridge slumming with their fine bright-eyed innocent girls, rubbing shoulders with rough types and sad old women with red grins. A boy learned a lot from watching people who'd had just a little too much, the young men who'd dropped their clean, classy girls home returning for cold lust, stolen goods, the meaning in a knowing wink, the interplay of marks and tarts; all this Terry observed. Sometime after midnight Vic would come upstairs and find him curled asleep between the risers and pretend surprise, saying, 'What, you still here?'

And Terry, like a sentry on watch, would claim: 'I wasn't asleep, Uncle Vic.' Vic would pat his head with his blunt fingers and tell him to get to his bed, and Terry would go at last, his duty done.

He was never quite part of that life downstairs, not like Vic was.

Vic sighed. Terry couldn't know there was something in him so like his father. Nigel had been an observer, a watcher of people, too.

Now Terry was a man, Vic saw less of him, but that suited Terry just fine.

*Come down East with me – or don't you dare?* he'd said.

To Victoria's sort of girl, Terry knew, a dare was a challenge – he had almost instantly persuaded himself that his frustrated slip of the tongue had been deliberate – a *dare* was part of the code of honour people like her lived by, as imperative as for any grubby boy who was dared to jump the gap of roaring water between the lock-gates. The upper classes never grew up – Terry had noticed that too from the pub stairs – they never gave up playing games even while the people around them were hungry and suffering in the real world. How he wanted her, body and soul, to show her how lucky she was. And he knew she'd come.

Victoria agreed and Terry was delighted. He'd bring her to the Old Bull and Bush. With a few drinks inside her and all warmed up, this time he had a place to take her, his room upstairs where he had spent his childhood beneath the sloping roof. Now it was outfitted for a man. To get her, he'd give a little, open her eyes to what things were really like, let her see him as he really was. It was a kind of pride, not only pride in himself but in his background. *This is where I am and who I am*. He gave Spike, Vic's man, the night off, and Jake the barman was in Terry's pocket. Terry arranged the ever-popular Cockney knees-up to be apparently spontaneous. Lil was happy to oblige, and Mimsy with her poor lick-and-spit face was always in for a bit of fun. But Victoria didn't watch the sad show. She had eyes only for Terry.

'I liked you as you really are,' she said.

'This is me,' he told her gently, the smoky bar, bare wood, beer and plush. She shook her head once, Victoria's way. He followed her outside.

The moon hung over the river. But then he realised *he* knew that, but she didn't. The river was invisible and all she saw was a moonlit, alien skyline of cranes and warehouses she didn't even know the names for, and he realised – really *felt* for the first time – the immense gulf between them.

'It isn't me, Terry,' she told him. 'And here, you aren't the Terry I know.' She shivered. 'Know and like.'

'Those silvery bits between the buildings,' Terry said distantly, 'that's the moon gleaming off the river.'

He now realised he couldn't exploit her, nothing he'd planned was going to work. He'd fallen in love with Victoria. He had denied it, but the more he denied it the more it was true, because all the time he was thinking about her, imagining her so vividly it was like sight.

Vic's probing brought him back to the present. 'Not even a little secret?' the older man asked again.

'You know me better than that, Vic.'

It was lunch-time trade and the bar was almost empty.

'Then don't look so bloody miserable,' Vic said. Terry finished his beer in silence. They said Vic had a girl going, and he wondered who she was. A man with something to hide quickly came to think everyone hid something. Terry tried to imagine Vic in love.

Strangely enough, it was easy.

# 3

'I love you, Victoria,' Terry admitted.

'Don't spoil it!' she laughed over her shoulder. 'All your women. Don't you kid me.'

'You're the first girl I've ever loved,' he called, knowing she'd never believe it. He shrugged, then looked at her honestly. She was wearing a mid-calf skirt printed with Dolly Varden flowers, plain white blouse and a soft waisted jacket with broad lapels. He'd brought her to Soho, to one of the good clubs serving moderately priced champagne. Reassuring her, wanting to be with her, to enjoy her attention. Trying to entertain her. They came outside into the beautiful Soho twilight, a spring evening with the coloured Chinese lights looped above them already brighter than the sky. It was warm enough to stroll. He wished he hadn't bought her the champagne. He'd had enough but the bottle was half-full and she wouldn't relinquish it. Victoria was merry but not drunk at all. She had insisted he bring the bottle with them, and he followed her tolerantly. 'Victoria,' he called. That was the moment, as she pulled ahead of him in the maze of alleys and courtyards, when he simply said he loved her. There in the narrow cobbled street, under the chains of Chinese lanterns.

She came back and he poured a sip of champagne into her glass.

'I live you,' he said, 'I breathe you. I've fallen in love at first sight.'

She sipped. 'Shall we dance?'

'Here!' he scoffed. 'I mean it, Victoria.'

She twirled.

'For God's sake,' he said. 'Stop. Stop it.'

She kept her eyes on his, then kissed his chin. 'What do you really want, Terry?'

He whispered, 'To love you.'

'Yes, I know exactly what you mean!'

'That's just it, Victoria. You don't. I just want to be with you.'

It was almost dark now and above them the lanterns glowed enormously, scarlet dragons' heads, golden tigers, little sparkly bells that tinkled softly in the breeze. A place neither of them was really part of. Neutral ground.

'Prove it,' Victoria said. 'Don't talk to me like you think I want to hear, like men think women talk, all that romantic stuff about love and hearts you're always trying to manipulate me with.'

'I'm not—'

'Prove it.'

He said in a deep voice, 'Go on.'

'I know a place where we can finish off that

champagne.' She opened her handbag and took out a bunch of brass keys.

'Jesus Christ,' Terry said.

'Don't you dare?'

'Yes, but—'

'Aren't I worth it? A minute ago you loved me, but that didn't last long, did it?'

'I meant it. I do mean it. But I don't like women who try and take over.'

She dropped the keys back in her bag and looked round for a taxi to take her home.

'All right,' Terry said, 'you've got a deal.'

He found the car and they got in. He drove without a word.

It was full dark when the MG pulled up in Old Bond Street outside the darkened Emporium, but the blazing display windows illuminated the pavement and the corner. The Food Hall was being heavily promoted and windows on each side of the plate-glass doors were given over to eye-catching promotions of delicious foods unavailable to most people for years: Suffolk hams, capons, a colourful display of Camp Coffee bottles held up seemingly in defiance of gravity by invisible thread.

Victoria crossed to the shadowy doors, selected the longest key on the bunch she had taken from Lisa's desk drawer, and slipped it in the lock. Terry got out over the car door and looked around him calmly, then followed her inside.

The store was a dim expanse of counters lit by a few low-wattage bulbs. Victoria locked the doors behind them, not letting him touch the keys. She paused at the top of the steps. Without floodlights the cosmetics' stands looked cheap and tawdry, their magic gone.

'Dogs?' Terry asked, drinking from the mouth of the champagne bottle.

'One old man called Mike who dotes on little Victoria.'

Her eyes were bright: what was she seeing? he wondered.

'Mike can remember my father carrying me in here as a baby.' When Terry tried to fill the glass in her hand she shook her head, remembering, going down one step. 'When I was old enough to walk I remember coming here, hanging from my father's hand, running as he walked. Everything seemed so huge in those days, cosmetics and perfumes filling the middle of the store . . . you don't see stock levels like those now, armies of shimmering bottles. I remember the women in black for the death of King George V.'

Terry followed her along the main gangway, watching the sway of her hair and hips. She turned suddenly and he raised his eyes explicitly to hers, tilting the bottle to his mouth. 'I live my life here,' she told him urgently. 'The store's been here all my life, wherever my parents sent me. I knew it was always here, better than I knew them. Knew I could depend on it. That they cared about this.' Her voice trembled with her passion.

He said calmly, 'I only care about you.'

She gave him a look that told him he'd said something cheap. He put down the bottle and held out his arms for her to come into. 'It's a pretty good dare, Victoria.' He'd kiss her and hold her tight with the darkened, motionless counters and displays around them for an audience, and always the danger that Mike or someone would come in and see them. But she shook her head, walking past the silent lifts to the stairs, and he followed her with his eyes.

'Where are you going, Victoria?' he called. 'Aren't you going to stay with me?' But he'd come this far, he couldn't turn back now, he was locked in.

He snatched up the bottle and went after her, hearing her shoes tapping on the main staircase above him. He took the steps two at a time. The third floor was under dust-sheets, grey ghosts. He caught her up on the fourth floor. His face made her stop.

'You forgot your bottle,' he sneered.

'Hold my hand,' she said. He saw she was trembling and regretted his ferocity. She used the keys to open one final door.

'What is this place?'

It was terribly silent and the lightswitch made a loud click under her fingers. Victoria closed the door behind them, her voice sounding deliberately casual, almost without care. 'The old apartment. My father met my mother here and fell in love with her. For years Ben and Pearl lived here in the twenties. But hardly at all after I was born.'

'Here you are pretending it's not important to you.'

She held out her glass and he filled it.

'It isn't,' she said. 'It's just a place.'

An immaculate place, he saw. The white carpet was kept cleaned and vacuumed, he guessed for occasional important guests of the company. A white sofa and armchairs, a black piano, long balcony windows holding the lights of London. Victoria pulled him after her, their footsteps gliding without sound on the thick carpet. 'George could have had it but he never liked what he called living above the shop. He has his own house.' It was the first time she had spoken of her half-brother. George knew Terry, though not as well as he knew Vic. All that was in the past, Terry knew, but there had been a time when George was in Vic's pocket.

'George?' Terry forced himself to give a baffled shrug, the first time in his life he hated himself for lying. 'Who's George?'

'My half-brother.'

'I thought we agreed not to talk about families,' Terry said, undoing his tie. 'I thought only us mattered.'

'Only us,' Victoria agreed. 'He never brings Cathy here.' It seemed a strange note on which they should themselves become lovers . . . but lovers was not quite what they were becoming, this prosaic business that left their bodies satisfied.

Victoria knew a little of what would happen, but Terry knew it all. His hunger making up for her inexperience, he took her on the floor, she could not stop what she had started, or control the urgent need in his eyes or hold him back, or his domination of her for the first time as he entered her quickly, despite her cries, urged on by them. She pinched her lips closed but he kissed them. She tried to share his enjoyment. He snarled her name as his moment came. It was wonderful for him.

'You can't tell me you don't love me,' he crowed. 'God, you're beautiful, Victoria. You feel lovely, I'd never hurt you. Every bit of you is mine.'

Then he slept, crouched over her on his elbows and knees, plugging her with his limp member. The carpet irritated her shoulderblades and Victoria put her arms around him to relieve them. He groaned in his sleep and began to move. She felt a little pleasure and set about conquering him. The second time was for her, but he thought he had done it all.

# PART IV

## The Waterfall

September 1949 – June 1951

# Chapter Nine

*'Why are you all blind?' Ben asked. 'Why can
only the children see?'*
*Roland turned his filmy eyes on him.*
*'Because it is the price we pay.'*

## 1

Every day during term-time for more than a year,
weather permitting, Ben walked with his shepherd's
crook from Clawfell to the village of Blane to wait for
Lola to finish school. Ria insisted on accompanying
him the first few times, but the blind man's walk was
not the feat it appeared to a sighted person to be, and
as always, though he loved her company, Ben got his
way. He needed and depended on Ria all the rest of
the day: the walk to Blane was his time alone – and
the walk back, with Lola, was just as important to
him. Getting to know his daughter.

He set out today as usual. The gravel driveway
looping from the Grange's porte-cochère crunched
loudly beneath his boots, especially the looser grains

345

undisturbed between the truck's smooth wheel-
tracks, and his ears constantly told him where he was:
grass was silent, gravel crunched, and as the drive
curved around the medieval ponds into the line of the
holloway he picked out the sound of the wind in the
trees. At Clawfell the moorland wind always blew.

And there was touch. The crushed, hardpacked
millstone surface of the track downhill towards Blane
was gritty beneath the special rubberised soles of his
boots; he was sensitive to every texture beneath his
striding feet, the vibration in his stick carrying its own
message. All this mattered. He told himself he had
never felt so aware. So alive. He had missed so much
before.

Ben's most reliable guide was the music of the
Rownslee leat running beside him, an old friend
chuckling its smooth course along the hillsides before
eventually running to waste beneath the derelict
mills. But first the stream followed the village street,
plunging muffled into a culvert beneath each side-
road, so that even silence told him where he was. On
the hard paving-stones the steel inserts cobbled into
the rubber heels clacked a bright rhythm, quite
different from the duller scuff of tarmac where he
crossed a road. He tapped the stick along the school
railing if he could not hear the children playing, and,
where the tapping stopped, he waited.

'Mr Trott' became a familiar figure in his long
tweed overcoat, waiting at the Leat Road school's
open gate for his daughter to come running out. The
council had upgraded the road and, with the
increased commercial traffic this attracted, the school

caretaker now doubled as a lollipop man, his heavy tread approaching the gates reluctantly, dragging the stick of his large circular warning sign behind him. The school was his kingdom, Ben knew. Corporal Macclesey was furious with the children for running, angry with them for being children, as though it was their fault and they should grow up more quickly. Their mothers who nagged him about the road throughout the summer were as bad as their bairns, in his opinion, and the corporal sought out the reassuringly masculine figure of 'Mr Trott' in self-defence. 'If their bairns rush out and get run down then it's not my fault, sir, but I'd get the blame. Is that fair, sir?' He spoke loudly and slowly because he was talking to a blind man. 'Stand there, careful-like,' he boomed solicitously this afternoon, 'I'll make sure yer bairn gets to yer.'

'She'll find me.'

'Only trying ter help, sir. You was an orsifer, sir?'

'Field commission. First war.'

'That were the one, that were. Could tell it from the way yer stands, sir. Lost yer peepers there an' all I bet, yer poor bastard.' His heels clicked and Ben realised the caretaker was saluting. 'Corporal Macclesey at yer service, sir. Eighth Battalion, the King's Own Yorkshire Light Infantry. The Somme, sir, Blighty Valley.' He screamed at the top of his voice: 'Yer silly bairns, yes, lassie, Jennie Housetree, I got yer name in me black book, get off the stupid road! Got ter sort 'em out, sir,' he told Ben in the same voice, 'got ter be cruel ter be kind.' He stamped off.

Lola suddenly slipped her hand into Ben's – and Ben hadn't heard a sound. 'You startled me,' he said. He no longer turned, instinctively looking for her as a sighted person would when startled.

'Nothing surprises you,' he heard her grin. 'Come on, race you home.' She had a lovely voice, lilting and melodious, and they walked hand in hand up Leat Road. He bought her some sweets at the Post Office, not giving her the money but going up the steps with her so they could choose the sweets together. 'You can have anything you like except humbugs.'

'Humbugs are my favourite,' she protested.

'Quarter of humbugs,' Ben ordered. A quarter of Wilkinson's licorice allsorts for Ria. Ria couldn't eat one without finishing the whole sticky bag, her fingers rustling guiltily to the last one. Strange, how much you could feel for someone and love them and still not know almost everything about them. He had noticed she sucked one sort noisily, and asked Lola.

'Those are the pink ones,' Lola confided, 'she likes them best.' Ben ordered a quarter of pink ones.

'Yer can't have just them,' the officious woman behind the counter told him. 'Yer can only have the allsorts. Take it or leave it,' she sniffed, 'it's all the same to me.'

'I'll take the whole box,' Ben said in the quiet voice of his that allowed no argument. 'I said I'll take the whole box, if you please.' Her mouth half open, the woman stopped her complaints. She looked round the other shoppers for support, then decided not to protest. Ben paid, feeling the edges of the coins with his thumbnail, then put the coupons down one by one on the counter.

In the street Lola said, 'You'll get yourself noticed doing things like that.'

'You're right.'

'But I love it when you're angry.' He heard her sucking a humbug contentedly.

Ben took the lid from the box of allsorts and popped one in his mouth. 'You've got to help me with all these.'

'Why should I, now I've got my humbugs?'

He laughed. She sounded so like Ria.

'Oh, you can't have that one!' Lola said, delighted. 'It's pink.'

It was a fine day and the buckle of her satchel, which Ben deduced she must be wearing slung from her shoulder, squeaked slightly as they walked from the village into the moorland summer he sensed gathering all around them: the warm sun bringing out the bergamot scent of gorse, dragonflies whirring above the leat's rippling waters, the rattle of wind in the rushes that lined the groughs, a distant cluck of grouse. With Lola's eyes to help them they returned home a slightly different way, up the remains of the steep track built by the Romans from Ilkley to Manchester, then striking out across peat hags where he would never have dared go alone. Why did he do this? Because of Lola. He loved to be with her, to hear her growing up, changing, developing, all that he had missed with Victoria.

'I can't wait for me mam's tea,' she said around her fifth humbug.

'You've lost your accent. You sound like a Yorkshirewoman.'

'Well,' she said sensibly, 'we have lived here almost

for ever, haven't we.' For a child that was true, he realised. For an adult the years flashed by.

How he longed to see her! Lola could not now be the little girl he had once seen. He could sense her transformed height from the angle of her hand in his, the rhythm of her lengthening stride, almost too tall for her age – but Ria said she was graceful, and Ben sensed the delicacy of all Lola's movements, hardly feeling her fingers helping him; he could easily have been unaware of her, become sunken in his own enforced, introverted silence. But she wouldn't let him. Suddenly just being with her filled him with tenderness. Had Edith Rumney, the woman who'd brought him up, felt what he felt now with Lola as the young Ben London skipped beside her down the streets of Whitechapel? Yes, oh yes. He remembered himself at Lola's age, remembered sound and touch and childish emotion as though he was still there, the days when everything was possible; no one escaped their childhood.

But he couldn't remember the pictures. The pictures, what it had looked like, were gone for him.

*I'm Vic Price. Remember me.* Vic's words came back to him.

'What's the matter?' Lola sounded alarmed and he realised he'd stopped so suddenly that she was several paces ahead of him.

'It's horrible being blind, Lola.'

Her footsteps came back. 'Dad. Please don't.'

'I'm forgetting my life, even the silliest things. I honestly can't remember pink. I can't visualise it.'

She hugged him.

'Sometimes in dreams, Lola, I can still see.'

'Don't hurt yourself, Daddy.' She sounded afraid.

'Love hurts.' He was afraid too. 'I dream of things from long ago and I see them so vividly. Yellow canaries hung outside the houses, the exact grey-green of the river, oranges piled up in the greengrocer stalls, Ria's cream and blue dress she wore . . . she wore when we were children. It's gone when I wake up, I've forgotten what my dream looks like. Even Pearl is almost gone, I can hardly see my wife, the woman I thought I loved. She was my life for twenty years. Gone. It's just words, Lola. Sounds, touch, that's all I am now. That's the worst thing. I'm even forgetting the sight I had.'

Lola gazed up at him curiously. He made her feel grown up. An adult crying was a terrible thing, but his not crying was worse: his dry, bright blue eyes without tears, and the hurt she saw in them. His fury. She watched his pain helplessly, but not wanting to look away, magnetised by his despair. If it wasn't for Ben London, everything here would have been perfect. Mum was contented here now, she wore a sort of smiling glow and she was gentle, the edge softened from her tongue as though her old life was a hard, itchy skin she had managed to shuck off. The three of them together. Lola passionately wanted it to continue always. The three of them having supper together around the table, Mum with her hair still tied up if she'd been doing her work upstairs, all laughing and joking and arguing, and there was always plenty of food. Even the arguments were fun together. Everything rotating around Daddy. But now as she

351

gazed up at him curiously Lola felt unsettled, as though he had lifted one corner of the carpet and revealed a frightening abyss beneath.

*Yellow canaries hung outside the houses. The river. Ria's cream and blue dress she wore.*

And now Lola heard her own Yorkshire voice claiming desperately, *'Well, we have lived here almost for ever, haven't we?'*

The sky was that perfect blue Miss Parkinson called 'azure'. Having said all she could say, Lola wandered away, dreaming of Miss Parkinson whose manner changed when the grown-ups were gone and only children were watching her, prisoners in her class-room, ancient make-up pinched into the lines that swarmed around her lips, her grey hair braided into a bun of such tightness and solidity that it must be very long. Lola imagined it uncoiling like a grey serpent every evening, Miss Parkinson wearing a shift in front of her dresser mirror, combing out its length like a secret. The boys all hated Miss Parkinson. Lola ran back to her father.

'I'm so happy,' she promised, her words tumbling out too fast. 'I'll be your eyes, I'll describe everything to you whether you want to know it or not, because I love you. The bracken's turning brown and the sprigs of heather are just showing purple, a bit. Will told me the names, he knows them all, and he can paint the colour of the sky. I don't want you to feel better, Daddy, I just want you as you are.'

'I wish I could see you, Lola.'

'I wish I was as pretty as the girls in Miss Parkinson's library books!'

He laughed and picked her up, hugging her fiercely. 'That's one advantage I have. It doesn't matter what you look like, to me you're the most beautiful girl in the world.'

'Are you really going to eat all those allsorts? You'll be sick. I'll sort out the pink ones for you if you like and put them in my humbugs' bag.'

'We're alike, you and I,' he said fondly, taking her for granted.

Just for that she let him eat a pink one without telling him. 'Oh!' he said, when he realised.

Ria was still house-cleaning. For her cleaning was no casual undertaking, it was a performance. First there were the proper clothes, overalls rolled up to the elbows, old shoes, her hair clipped back in a bushy ponytail. Then she assembled her props around her, buckets of soapy water, mop, sponge, brushes, rubber gloves, a stiff broom, a feather duster with a very long cane handle for winkling into the high corners and niches. And plenty of elbow-grease. Ria *attacked* dirt, it was impossible for her to dabble, to start all this just to stop for a cup of tea or lunch – when Ria was cleaning lunch was eaten on the job, bread in one hand and a chunk of cheese in the other, her eyes glinting determinedly to search out more cobwebs, more dirt. The more she cleaned the more she found. One thing led to another. She had decided to clean one room a day. She cleaned like an obsession.

It was a hopeless task. The house was designed for a different age, one with many servants and endless supplies of elbow-grease, and poor Ria couldn't hope to compete. Most of the place, she decided, had not been meant for living in at all, just for show. Almost the entire Grange, she realised gradually, was a façade, the rooms too large to enjoy living in and the bulky furniture impressive but uncomfortable. But the family quarters were human-scaled and cosy, a home within a house, and it was here that Ria was concentrating her efforts. It would be her surprise for Ben.

She walked her broom through the dusty warren of rooms and passageways, aware of the dark corridors for servants, to be neither seen nor heard by the posh folk, winding behind these walls. Lola played there, Ria knew. The happy games fortunate children played, growing up straight and tall with nothing to fear. It was not a bad achievement from a mother whose own childhood had been so different. She'd never forget her life in the grimy alleys and worming backways of London, all the secret ways she knew to get away from Vic, dreaming of marrying Ben, of escaping the filthy slums. She'd dreamt of him claiming some grand inheritance and of herself living like a lady. Ria had been no different from the other girls in Canary Warren, her competitors whose faces were old by the age of twelve. Ann, her best friend, had snagged men on the street to feed her baby, so she'd got another baby. Her fingers were blown off in the Silvertown munitions factory, so she was thrown back on the street without tuppence and no man would look at her. Ria had almost been her. A few lucky ones had found respectable men and lived unremarkable lives. But Ria had found Ben London.

Ria stopped by the open window, almost over-whelmed by the sudden feeling of love running through her. Ben and Lola were coming out of the trees and she watched them skipping stones across the pond, smiling at their laughing cries. Ben rubbed the stones between his fingers, sending them skipping with a flick of his strong wrists, and Lola called out the score, cheating. Good for you, girl! thought Ria, dabbing her eyes, enjoying herself enough to cry. She had achieved almost everything she wanted, though not in the way she wanted. Ben wasn't a gentleman, she wasn't a lady, and she didn't want to be. The Grange would never be a grand house again, but her children were happy and safe, and that was all that mattered.

Ben still gave his affection to Lola, not to Ria. Ria accepted this for Lola's sake. She no longer started rows at meal-times to force him to pay attention to her. They were too contented and quiescent to recapture the heat of their adolescence, she told herself, masking her disappointment. Watching them, she saw how much Ben meant to Lola, picking up stones for him, pointing him in the right direction. Ria listened to her squeaks of enjoyment, and her lips tightened with jealousy, despite herself. Those two spent so much time together that Lola often knew what Ben wanted before he did himself, what brand of whisky, whether he wanted a second helping at supper or nothing at all, reading his moods far better than Ria could. And yet there was so much Lola was too young to know about Ben and Ria.

She went outside. Had he really left his old life behind him? She didn't believe a word of it. Ria touched the capacious top pocket of her overalls, feeling the stiff bond envelope in there. Yet another letter. Earlier this afternoon Helen had brought it back – once a month she drove into Manchester and collected anything waiting for them from the poste restante of the main Post Office – and cheerfully handed it to Ria for Ben. Ria had been cleaning one of the front rooms, comfortable-looking armchairs piled resolutely into the corner, and Helen had seemed surprised by Ria's ferocious energy. 'You're a busy bee and no mistake! I didn't know you had it in you.'

'There's a lot you don't know about me,' Ria said belligerently.

'My! I must keep out of your way in this mood!' Helen laughed without looking Ria in the eye. 'I'm sure there's something I can do.'

'No thanks,' Ria said.

'I don't know why you work yourself so hard.'

Ria busied herself until Helen had gone.

How infuriating that woman was with her simple, caring love for Will, without curiosity or duplicity; Ria could hardly conceal her envy that Helen was happy with so little. Never hurt anyone, never did anything wrong, nothing for herself, wore no make-up, and that unglossy hair had never seen the inside of a salon. Her potential daughter-in-law was so genuinely sweet and unnervingly self-satisfied that Ria was angry with her. But it wasn't Helen's fault, nothing ever was. Anyway, Ria knew Ben would never marry her now. Ria Trott she was and must remain, her past living on in her name.

Ria studied the legal envelope as she walked. She knew Ben spoke on the pay-phone to Charlie Bookkeeper, his Holborn solicitor, and she suspected that was partly why he liked picking up Lola from school. The letters that returned were invariably these long legal envelopes, and their number had increased. Ria had given up everything for Ben, totally rejected her old life for him, but these letters were a constant reminder that he hadn't given up his own past.

But in that past Ria knew she had betrayed him twice. They could not possibly go back, because if they did one day Ria would have to face Ben and open her mouth and tell him that Lola was not his daughter. The weapons of Vic Price's hatred had always been the people Ben cared for most.

With a shock Ria noticed the changed address: c/o Post Office, Blane. So Helen had not been to Manchester after all, and Charlie was now sending direct to the village. Ria replaced it in her pocket with a frown, thinking of Vic.

Ben and Lola were at the waterside and she watched them from the shelter of the trees. They didn't look alike, the difference was obvious at a glance; dark-eyed Lola with her black hair and high-coloured cheeks. Almost her mother's eyes with those tawny flecks, and certainly Ria's vivacity, but God knew where Lola had got that thin gawkiness from, certainly not her grandmother Esther. Maybe her grandad, Dick? Ria had never seen a picture of him. The two of them were so involved with their game they still hadn't sensed Ria approaching. 'Four

. . . five!' Lola counted the splashes of her skipping stone.

'Rotten liar, girl,' Ria shouted.

'Not me, Mum!'

'Six,' Ben said. 'I heard. Hallo, Ria.' He touched her hand. 'I can't win, so she's trying to lose.' He seemed so at ease and defenceless, so *ordinary*, that Ria distrusted him at once. He was a fighter and anyone who knew Ben knew he never gave up. Her attempts to domesticate him had failed. He simply didn't understand her. Ria didn't want money, success, power, only to love him. And that was what he couldn't cope with.

'You've got your hands all muddy,' Ria scolded him, then squealed as Ben chased after her across the gravel. She dodged on to the soft grass, but he followed her by her giggles. Lola scavenged for stones at the water's edge, glancing after them: grown-ups.

When it had gone on for long enough, Ria let Ben catch her.

He held on to her. She felt how aware of her he was. He might even kiss her.

Ria kissed him instead. This time she didn't shiver. He did.

'Me too!' Lola rushed over to join in. They laughed and let her thin bony frame cuddle between them, but Ria, looking into Ben's face, had not imagined what she had felt. The change she saw expressed in his mouth and jaw, the tension in his muscles there.

She whispered, 'Another letter came for you.'

'I don't care about the letter.'

'But it must be about business,' she said, 'so it's

bound to be more important than anything else. Or shall I get Helen to read it to you as usual?'

'You read it.'

'You've let Charlie Bookkeeper know the name of the village, chum,' Ria said, tapping the address. Ben didn't answer. 'Is that safe for him? Is it safe for *us*? It wouldn't take a genius to add Blane to Clawfell and come up with four. Charlie isn't stupid. Suppose Vic—'

'Stop worrying about Vic. A lot of water's gone under the bridge, Ria. Vic's probably forgotten all about us by now.'

'Pull the other one, it's got bells on,' Ria said.

They sat on the grass, Lola kneeling behind Ria, reading over her shoulder. Ria opened the envelope and two smaller envelopes spilled into her lap, one from London House in Lisa's confident, rhythmical handwriting, the other in an unfamiliar hand, the '7' in Charlie's address written with a crossbar. Both had been marked *Please Forward* in the top left corner.

'It isn't business, it's family,' Ria announced. 'I'll read Lisa's first. She's well. Peggy's daughter, Anna, has got chickenpox . . .'

'I can read faster than you can,' Lola said. 'Turn the page.'

'Stop breathing on me, geroff,' Ria said. Ben lay back on the grass with his hands behind his head. 'Lisa's thinking of renting out London House,' Ria continued, 'she says it's much too big without a family to run around it.'

'Victoria might want it one day,' Ben murmured.

'Lisa thinks Victoria isn't interested in men or

children or families. All she cares about is the Emporium.'

'If that's what Victoria wants,' shrugged Ben, 'that's fine by me.'

'Poor girl,' sniffed Ria, 'I'd rather fall in love with something on two legs myself.'

'Don't come over all soft again,' Lola said, kissing her mother's cheek.

'David Jones has offered Victoria the radio department.'

'He's still hoping she'll fail,' Ben yawned. Ria looked at him without saying a word. He hadn't asked about George London. It would be easy for him to ring George for a chat from the village, wouldn't it? Ben kept his finger on the pulse all right. 'I think they're going to find out that Victoria has got what it takes. I believe in her. Maybe I should send her some shares. That would put the cat among the pigeons.' He added thoughtfully: 'I will do it. The shares are Victoria's birthright just as much as George's. And it will show him once and for all that I didn't steal Ralph's shares for myself.'

'You love it, don't you?' Ria accused him. 'All this business stuff, the gossip, the ins and outs of people struggling to get one over the next bloke. It's more real to you than this is.' She looked at the Grange, beautiful in the mellow Friday evening sunlight, someone else's dream. The air was hushed but still warm, and Ria thought how lovely the moment was, but still the seed of discontent itched away inside her. She couldn't stop herself saying something ugly. 'I wonder how much you really care about *us*, Ben.'

He touched her foot.

'No, don't,' Ria said weakly. 'You know I'd do anything for you.'

Lola wriggled between them. 'It says here George still hasn't asked Cathy to marry him. I should think she's getting pretty fed up with waiting.'

'Does it say that?' Ria demanded. 'Give that to me.'

Lola took up the next envelope. 'The writing's different on this one. The seven's got a funny mark on it.'

'What?' Ben sat up with a strange, hopeful expression on his face – for a moment almost boyish, the earnest look of a young man outdone, outfoxed in love. He sniffed the envelope as Lola discarded it. 'Nothing. I remembered—' He shrugged. 'A perfume. A scent is the most potent memory, isn't it? Chouchou always wore Chanel. And wrote the number 7 with a crossbar.'

'*Always?*' Ria said alertly. 'Every time?'

'I fell in love with her and she . . . she had her own reasons for using me.'

'And you didn't mind being used, as long as it got you into the hay,' Ria accused him.

'She was an extraordinary, indomitable woman who knew her mind. And it wasn't in the hay, we were at the Hôtel Crillon in Paris. I was seventeen years old.'

'So it's us women who taught you to use people, did we?' Ria said bitterly.

'You know the answer to that.'

'Even me?'

'Especially you, Ria.'

'I love it when you talk to me like this,' Ria said tearfully. 'So it's all my fault, is it?'

'Mum, don't start being unhappy again,' Lola said anxiously.

She was too late. 'Yes,' Ben answered Ria angrily, 'you, all of you except Pearl. She was an honest woman.'

'She was a nonentity,' Ria spat. There was a silence. 'I'm sorry. I didn't mean that.' Each of them knew she had.

Lola sat between them and read the letter with tears trickling down her cheeks.

'The Dowager Countess is dead now,' Ben told Ria in a low, angry voice. 'It was she who introduced Pearl to me.'

Ria laid her face against Ben's. 'Every time we talk, I mean really talk and say something, we hurt each other. But words are all we have.'

Lola finished the letter. 'It's from someone with a funny foreign squiggle under his name.'

'François, her son,' Ben murmured. 'François Benjamin Charles Enguerrand, Count of Coucy.'

'He hopes to visit England next spring,' Lola said, 'and he wants us to meet his wife Rachel. It's ever such nice paper. That'll be nice to see them both, won't it?'

Neither adult replied. Lola hung on to their arms on each side of her, as though her own small childish strength could hold them together.

Ria lay awake, all night it seemed, blaming herself.

Her blazing row with Ben had blown up out of the blue, the worst argument they'd had at Clawfell Grange, striking exactly when they had least to argue about. Ria had a short memory for tiffs; she turned to sunshine as quickly as to storm. She couldn't help sparking off people, it gave her life, and them too, she'd decided. But this awfulness – she squeezed her eyes shut, she really had said those awful bitter things – well, face it, it had been brewing up for a long time, fizzing up inside her all through her long, quiet, contented, utterly boring summer. She had everything she wanted, did she? Nonsense. She might be fooling everyone else, but she wasn't fooling herself. Ria's heart knew better than her head. *She was a nonentity.* She couldn't have expressed herself more plainly if she'd stood on her head shouting, *I love you*, the words themselves, it was so obvious. Instead she had gone much too far. It was the first time she had seen Lola cry from sheer unhappiness, sitting between them trying to bind them together, not understanding.

Ria was ashamed of herself.

She fell asleep at first light and it was only moments before the curtains were thrown wide. She sat up squinting against the light, dizzily awake after her thin, nervous doze. Lola's bed was empty, she was gone. Ben was standing by the window. Ria wondered if he would come out with the sort of reasonable thing they said in films, *We have to talk*. Instead his silence was devastating.

'I'm sorry,' Ria whispered. 'Ben, I didn't mean what I said.'

He stood as if looking out, his eyes turned somewhere beyond the sun, feeling its heat no doubt, but the whole vivid world beyond the glass was black to him. And so was she, thank God, kneeling on the bed in her least best raspberry-coloured nightdress with her hair messed seven ways to Christmas.

'You meant every word,' he murmured.

Ria couldn't deny it.

He turned suddenly. 'Wherever you like,' he said. 'We're going outside, anywhere. You choose. Lola's gone to Will at Home Farm for the day. You know how she loves being with him.' He held out his hand. 'You and me.'

'Ten minutes,' Ria promised.

'Five. Don't be late.'

Twenty minutes later Ria found him in the kitchen. She was still combing her hair. He was standing by the table as though he hadn't moved a muscle all the while she'd made him wait. She saw from the small wicker hamper on the table he'd raided the cellar; sticking out was the unmistakable gold foil neck of a champagne bottle, and he'd tossed in beside it a few rough lumps of bread and cheese, a couple of oranges. He said nothing. 'I could do better than this,' Ria fussed possessively, but he held his finger to his lips. She fell silent. He hefted the basket over his shoulder by its leather strap.

'Take me away from here,' he ordered.

So it was up to her. Ria was glad she was wearing her strong lace-up boots. They followed the stream feeding the ponds and, as they climbed, the house shrank beneath them, the millstone grit crags of Clere rose around them, but of course he could not know that. The house was no larger than a toy.

'Where are we going?' he asked.

'Anywhere,' she said serenely, 'as long as we're together.'

All his concentration was on Ria's hand leading him across the sheep-cropped slope, through the final gate into the tussocks and clumpy heather of the wild moor. The sun was hot now and his forehead was sheened with sweat, this was hard going for him. She found the stream again, roaring down the rocky bed of its deep ghyll, and they paused to eat the oranges.

'Do you remember—'

'I don't want to *remember* anything!' Ria said fiercely. 'It's all new. It's all fresh and new.'

'Long ago you taught me how to peel an orange,' he said simply. 'That's how little I knew before I met you.'

She stared at him, wishing with all her heart and soul that he could see her.

'How did we go so wrong?' she said.

She took his hand and again they climbed. Ria had a place in mind, her own place that she had discovered for herself, where she could be herself. The view was enormous, a sun-dappled panorama of the Dales. Sometimes she came here when her mood was saddest, scrambling up this steepening slope amongst the harsh rocks, came to this secret grassy knoll that a blind man could never find. She helped him up the last few feet. From above the waterfall plummeted into a deep, blue-green pool; occasionally she saw the flash of a fish down there among the quivering boulders and streams of shimmering bubbles. She needed to be away from him sometimes. But today she had brought him with her and it would never be hers alone again. She could feel the electricity between them.

'What do you see?' Ben London murmured.

She put his arms around her and closed her eyes. 'You.'

Ria was dozing. Ben lay beside her on the grass, her breathing playing across his face, the sun a warm cloak over their skin. Had he really laid Pearl's ghost to rest, or was he resurrecting her in his mind's eye? But Ria, cuddling him sleepily, believed love had won.

## 2

Vic slowed his car approaching Tower Bridge. On his left the crumbling yellow-brick warehouses of St Katherine's Dock caught his eye, but the nest of stone platforms where Ria had once seduced Ben London to escape Vic was still hidden by a mirror of smooth water, though the ebb had begun. High or low the river covered a multitude of sins. He gazed as though his eyesight could pierce the greasy surface, the traffic behind him hooting, one idiot van-driver trying to get round him, wheels spinning on the frost.

He drove on. He didn't take the Rotherhithe Tunnel, hating the thought of thousands of tons of water and mud pressing down on him. Even when he had taken Nigel's wife Arleen to the Greenwich Hospital in labour, her last journey, he had driven her round in the sun.

He never liked going south of the river. Crossing over Tower Bridge was entering foreign territory, his name carried no currency here. Vic turned left along Tooley Street, trying to keep the car off the tramlines. He could remember this area being famous as London's Larder, huge quantities of edibles – butter, flour, meat – supposedly shifted along here twenty-four-hours-a-day from the vast docklands dug out of the marshes ahead of him. On the skids now, couldn't handle the big ships. Everything going by road and rail was strangling the coasters that used to be London's lifeblood. Even in his lifetime the docks had been forests – forests of masts. There were only rusty smokestacks now, tramp steamers without pride.

He followed the rails into Jamaica Road, then turned left at Paradise Gate into Brunel Street and kept going east. These were mean streets, the road narrowing, twisting and turning between warehouses, switchbacking over swing bridges. Water roared in the ship-locks below. Alleyways showed sudden glimpses of the river curving round from his left, then to his right he saw the huge vistas of open water of the Surrey Commercial Docks, wastelands of rusty, derelict cranes, rotting Victorian pilings and seagulls quarrelling from the rows of mooring posts.

It was a rough but fair area, Vic knew – which was one reason, though not the only one, he had chosen

Cuckold's Point as his meeting-place. This was old London, disappearing London, from where the Pilgrim Fathers had set sail in front of the Mayflower pub, the London where children could go with God as easily as with vice, sometimes both. There was St Paul's school for girls almost inside the walls of Lavender Dock, any number of Wesleyan and Lutheran chapels, the St Pelagius Home for Girls of the Sisters of the Sacred Hearts of Jesus and Mary hard against the India Arms, and on the other side was the Holy Trinity school for boys, the children brought up cheek by jowl, in the battle for souls, with the hundreds of waterside pubs crammed between the warehouses. A safe district unless you wanted trouble, Vic knew. No shooters except the stuff brought home by sentimental old soldiers; the main discipline was fists or a razor-slashing, usually outside pubs. Vic didn't want trouble. That was why he'd chosen this place, both near to home and far. He was close to familiar territory, but his face wasn't known here.

These communities of Dickensian back-to-back terraces, with women putting out the washing and children only reluctantly getting out of the way for the car, were friendly, homely places – those streets that were left. Jerry had pounded Rotherhithe, whole rows had gone in a single stick of bombs, and nearly all were damaged. Hadn't broken the people's spirit, Vic saw. Scrap-metal dealers and corrugated iron fences had sprung up everywhere, small nasty fortunes made from the scrap looted from shattered property. Vic kept out of it: the police were always doing 'stops' under Section 66.

It was two in the afternoon, time for the street bookies to pack up their pitches at the start of the first gee-gee race. If here was anything like home they'd be out again in the evening to pay winnings and take bets on the greyhound racing. As he passed the Angel, a smuggling pub, a couple of bobbies were arresting one of Billy Hill's stooges, set up to make the statistics look right.

Rotherhithe Street followed the curving Thames on a narrow causeway raised between the river and Lavender Pond. Ancient steps with peculiar names led from gut-narrow alleys into the water: King and Queen stairs, Pageant stairs, the Swallow Galley public. Once this whole riverbank had been overhung with weeping willows but now warehouses almost enclosed the road, walkways criss-crossed overhead, smelling of coal and spices. Vic came to a narrow space cleared by bombs near an empty dry dock. He paused to check his watch – still too early, good, he always liked to arrive first. He drove across the rough ground, the car bouncing on the rubble beneath the spiky grass, then parked out of sight by the flood wall.

A windowless derelict house, a faded sign over its door proclaiming Half Moon & Calf's Head, had been left standing near the slipway of rough stone setts that slanted into the river. Once regular drinkers had a less romantic name for this place: it was known locally as the Outfall, after the stone outlet for raw sewage now hidden and supposedly disused beneath the river's mud. Within living memory the acid stink, on warm summer days, made eyes stream, watering the beer even more generously than the landlord. In the days before the bombs jarred its timbers to the foundations the Outfall had been more than just another pub for wharfies and stevies: for almost a hundred years it was a smuggling pub. Then between the wars, as the Half Moon & Calf's Head, it was prized as highly among the cognoscenti for its whitebait dinners as the Union in Greenwich and Wapping's Prospect of Whitby, which was how Vic came to know of it. Soho wasn't the only place he had been developing his property interests.

Vic made sure he was unobserved, then unlocked the thick door and went inside. There was no hall, only a narrow room not much wider than an ordinary living-room, but deep, running to the river, the 'front' of the building. It was heavily constructed, with only this single back door to defend against the Revenue men; fire regulations had succeeded in closing the place down where bombs had failed. Now the bar was converted to a simple kitchen, a couple of armchairs placed by the end window overlooking the river, though of course they mostly used the bed upstairs. Vic didn't sit, he stood looking out at the mud revealed as the tide fell, waiting. In the floor was a smuggler's hole leading to the boathouse below, flooded only at high tide, taking nothing larger than a longboat or a launch and probably not used for years.

From the foot of the nearby slipway a gravel 'hard', or track, with mooring dolphins at intervals, ran out a few hundred feet across the mud to Cuckold's Point.

The Limehouse Hole ferry would be setting over soon. He might have been recognised aboard, but Betty Stark would be safe.

Betty Dempsey, he corrected himself.

Herbert Dempsey, who worked in the import office of the Custom House serving the northern West India Dock, an import dock, was shielded from a view of the river and in fact the whole outside world by the high anti-theft wall of Limehouse Basin. Nevertheless, Betty kept looking over her shoulder as she hurried to catch the Limehouse Hole ferry, thinking up excuses as though her husband's eyes were fixed on her and his voice might suddenly say, 'Wh-hair do you think you are going, Mrs?' Part of the relief of having an affair was the possibility of being caught. She hated being called *Mrs*, she hated being called *the Wife*, but she couldn't tell him as he meant it kindly. To be caught would end it quickest, it would save a thousand words. Herbert was not an old man, a year shy of sixty, but he *thought* himself old. He moved like an old man and he reminisced forever about his first wife, calling Betty his 'young bride'. He was proud of her, not of himself, saying what a lucky man he was to have caught her. And he meant it. She was only ten years younger than he, but she had vitality. To her it was a marriage of convenience. She should have ruled the roost – he didn't have her strong personality – but at home Herbert shrank into himself like a tortoise, invulnerable in defence, tea at seven, something interesting on the wireless, bed at ten.

Today Betty wore a headscarf which she held over

her mouth as she walked. She might be recognised. Word might get back. If it did, and her marriage died completely, would Vic still be interested in her? Would she lose her fascination for him if she wasn't forbidden fruit? Yes, that was Vic through and through. She was wearing her saucy French knickers that he'd got for her last time, changing into them awkwardly in the ladies' loo in Emmett Street, and the itchy lace made her feel ever so guilty, ever so hot and, to be frank, full of anticipation, so that she knew Herbert would see right through her if he did happen by. The sad truth was that if he ever asked her, 'Wh-hair have you been, Mrs?' and she laughed in reply, 'Why, it's my day off, I've been to see my lover,' he'd never believe her. She might do it anyway, just to teach him. 'You get too many days off, Mrs. I don't know what the world's coming to.' But there was an animal inside her, and she was afraid of growing old.

Looking over her shoulder, she hurried down to Limehouse pier. The ferry was hardly larger than a whaler, with an old diesel engine that idled as slowly as a heartbeat. She sat alone in the bow, the only passenger on the vibrating seat as the heartbeat rose to a frenzy, sending the craft churning across the river towards the low skyline of Rotherhithe. The ferry-man bumped his boat alongside the hard, held out his arm indifferently, and she stepped down on to the gravel, muddy water still seeping like old brown blood between the stones. She waited while the boat reversed, watching until it was gone, then took off her headscarf and followed the causeway to the ramp. A thrill went through her. She was certain she was watched now, that Vic was eyeing her up and down from that big river window of the Half Moon & Calf's Head, though the glass reflected only the sky, but she made sure she walked with a swing, and she'd washed out her hair so that it looked nice. A gentleman would have come down to help her up the weedy slipway, but that wasn't what Vic was, thank God. She paused by the windowless side of the building to check for disasters in the mirror of her powder compact, adjusted her lipstick with the tip of her little finger, then smiled her eyes and knocked.

'When you walk like a tart you remind me of Ria,' Vic said, taking control of her effortlessly, guiding her inside, kissing her on the lips, spoiling her lipstick, smudging it over his own mouth. 'Shut up,' he said, 'don't talk.' He took her hand into his, they weren't even going to have a cup of tea. 'Don't talk until afterwards.' He pulled her upstairs, their shoulders bumping the walls. He'd drawn the curtains. That was a nice thought – they glowed with afternoon light – he must have wanted to please her. He took off his jacket, two tugs and his tie was off, he undressed in front of her while she wondered what she was supposed to do, then they both undressed with increasing speed. She stopped at the French satin camisole, posing, and he put her on the bed, not bothering with caresses or covering her with a sheet, and thirty seconds later it was over. He sat on the edge of the bed.

'It's my fault,' she said, putting her hand on his back. 'I do feel you.'

'What are you talking about now?'

'I can't show it. I do try. I must be slow or something.'

He shook off her cloying hands and opened the curtains, sitting with his elbows on his knees.

'I wish you enjoyed it more,' she said, frightened of losing him. 'You'd like me more, wouldn't you?' He didn't respond. 'If we were together more, you would,' she said. This was the bit she enjoyed, the talking afterwards, stroking his back, her hair against his skin. 'Oh, it's so complicated!' she sighed, 'being in love.'

Vic knew she wasn't in love. She was in love with her tongue and the words that came prattling off it, in love with the idea of love. They turned off their brains when they got between the sheets with a real man.

'I really feel I know you, Vic. After all, I've known you all my life. I might have been the girl you married. I mean, it could have happened. When I was Miss Betty Gobel and we had our lives in front of us, don't you remember? If only my Alan hadn't happened, it might have been you and me. Alan and I often used to see your little brother Arthur, him that died.'

'They all died. They were weak.'

'You're ever so strong, Vic.' Vic didn't argue with that, it was true. Her voice droned on, complimenting him, trying to form his opinions, the way they did, trying to make him obedient, as though men were like women.

'You didn't like me in those days,' he pointed out.

'But I noticed you,' she said. 'I was too good for

you. You were only interested in forbidden flesh.'
She giggled at her penny-dreadful phrase.

Vic didn't rise to the bait. 'Still am,' he said,
slapping her knee. 'Married woman, you are.'

From behind Betty put her legs around him, pulled
her arms against his chest, nestling her face in the
nape of his neck. She had no shame.

'I meant Ria,' she whispered. 'Do you still secretly
think of her?'

The woman was an idiot. 'Do you secretly think of
Nigel when we're doing it?'

That stopped her. 'That's different,' she said. 'I still
love him but it's different to loving you.'

'It bloody isn't.'

'Nigel and I had a platonic relationship,' she said
primly. 'We didn't do it.'

Vic laughed at that. 'The insatiable in pursuit of the
unattainable,' he said.

She sulked. 'It wasn't like that.'

'Don't sulk.'

'I'll sulk if I want.' Making him pay attention to
her. Then she said patiently, 'You've lost Ria. You
accept it now. She really is dead to you now.'

He didn't move at all. She kissed the lobe of his ear.

'So it's time for you to move on, Vic. I know what
you feel for me. A man can't lie in bed. Everybody
respects you, I respect you, but I know you . . . I
*know* you. There's a different Vic inside you, isn't
there? A gentle and loving man. But people never let
him be.'

They never changed their ideas. Once they got

something in their heads it took root for ever, however hard they tried to weed it out. She was talking about Nigel of course. Yet, could he not be? Vic closed his eyes for a second, part of him seeing her dream – although she was including herself in it. A change of identity, not to be Vic Price any more. Peace. Letting go.

'You're quite a man,' she murmured. 'I can help you.'

'You and your husband.'

'I know that Alan died somehow, Vic.'

He shot back: 'Got a postcard from the other side of the River Styx, did you?'

'And Ray Trott. And his dad, Ted Trott, some say.'

'They can say what they like if they can't show me the bodies.'

'Shush, shush.' She kissed his spine with the tip of her tongue and he felt the caress of her lipstick-sticky lips. She knew her danger, the dangerous things she was saying, but they were like that. Once they started they couldn't stop, it welled up inside. He could see she was confident in herself, confident she could bring him round, succeed in controlling him where Ria had failed.

'I am surrounded,' Vic said. 'I am surrounded by lies.'

'Leave home,' she whispered. 'Let go, Vic, and spread your wings.'

'With you?'

'Take me.'

He shrugged her off and went to the window. The lengths she was willing to go to intrigued him. When they fell in love, or thought they had, you could never be sure what they would do. They thought they knew you and then they thought they could own you.

Did she really believe he did this bed stuff because he loved her? He felt nothing but contempt for her, for her cheap perfume, for her dirty body, contempt for her wearing that silly French outfit, for letting him make her wear it, contempt for her desire of him.

*She'll never have a father.* Betty knew the truth about Lola's paternity, knew Vic's most precious secret. That was all that mattered. Betty could hurt him.

She sat on the bed watching him. Outside, evening was closing in quickly, the river was a ribbon of sky-coloured water between the huge muddy shores of Limehouse Reach at low tide.

'And the good, poor Mr D?' Vic said. 'Where does your darling hubby figure in your plans?'

'What's he to a man like you?'

'Nigel didn't deserve you,' Vic said.

Beyond his profile and the river she saw the Isle of Dogs, everything clear from the enormous warehouses of Sufferance Wharf to Island Gardens on the south extremity, and there between them, no more than half a mile away, lay the shabby rooflines of Havannah Street with tall construction-company cranes standing behind them like Martians. Vic's Mum's house. Couldn't he see it was all going? Couldn't he let go?

'Look at me,' Betty said, inhaling to lift her breasts beneath the tight red satin. 'Look at me, Mummy's boy.' She pinched him playfully, then ran the heels of her palms seductively over her red satin hips. Men were all the same.

He had her, angrily, wasting his spirit to prove her tongue wrong.

Afterwards she talked and talked. Night had fallen and the rising crescent moon hung over the Isle of Dogs like a piece of fingernail: she pointed it out to him as excitedly as a little girl. She caressed his muscular chest, murmuring, 'And everyone says you don't like women! I got you taped, I know how you tick. It's fear, aren't I right? You're frightened of us, yes you are. A big strong man like you.' She cuddled him. 'There's nothing to be frightened of with me.' She glanced up at his face. He didn't talk much but that was all right, it meant he was seeing things her way. 'After all, you have your own lovely daughter, Lola,' she prattled, 'you've created your very own girl, and she'll grow up to be a proper woman, don't forget.'

Vic didn't reply.

'What's the most important thing in the world to you, Vic?' Betty teased him affectionately, stroking him.

Vic's eyes gleamed.

'My daughter.'

He lay looking up at the ceiling and Betty talked, mistaking his silence for her dominion over him with her chattering tongue.

## 3

'I love you.'

In the dark they were equal, Ria had learned. She

was lying beside Ben in the dark and the dark was her friend. In the dark, perversely, there could be no secrets between them, only in the light. In the dark a blind man was not blind, the darkness of his days was an advantage to him. In the dark Ben's senses enveloped Ria so that black night with all its terrors was not to be feared, rather a warm womb that wrapped her round. In the dark Ben knew her better than she knew herself. In the dark (and it was always dark for him) he felt her every vibration, touched her, scented her, tasted her, so aware of each breath Ria took that he knew if she was sleeping or awake before she knew herself, knew everything about her. There was no point in trying to hide. Just being here was to share herself with him, intensely aware of herself through *his* senses, in the same way that during the day he sometimes, tragically, imagined he was seeing through *her* eyes – flashing glimpses that seemed to be of the kitchen where they were sitting, or the stairs she was helping him up, or the comfy family rooms she had cleaned and set the fires – as if sight could be shared between lovers, at least momentarily. As if she could give him even that. Ria knew they were deceiving themselves. These visualisations that seemed so real to him were just old memories surfacing, she was sure. All were of places he had been with Pearl and when Ria asked him to describe the rooms he had seen in his mind's eye it was all subtly wrong, the furniture had changed or she'd moved it. Did he see Pearl here? 'You don't have to get rid of her completely for me,' Ria whispered. 'Love never dies, I know. I'm not frightened of ghosts.'

For the first time in her life, Ria was at peace, and dared to hope that the bad things in the past really were behind them.

She pulled away from Ben guiltily as footsteps sounded in the corridor. Their bedroom door, always left half open, creaked wide, and Lola scampered under the sheets between them. She wriggled herself comfortable, her skinny frame wearing boy's pyjamas. 'God, your plates of meat are freezing,' Ria complained, remembering to tug down the hem of her nightdress. This was Ben's room, they'd moved the beds together, and Lola always liked to snuggle in on his side of the join. Before these early morning forays, Lola slept alone in the bedroom she had once shared with her mother, but in the school holidays she spent most of her days with Ben. In the night he belonged to Ria, but during the day he was Lola's.

She was nearly nine years old, not far off the age Ria had been when she first saw Ben: coming up to the age of obsession. Lola's early years had been without a father, and that must leave a mark. Ria knew Lola remembered some mental pictures vividly: she'd described Thumper the rabbit twitching his whiskers, Esther patiently rolling up curlers in her hair, and remembered Vic and the others vaguely, remembered Terry's car . . . but much of it was emotion, only the feeling of things seemed to remain, glimmering, shifting, half-glimpsed. Ria was glad of that.

'Your feet are icy,' Ben grumbled.

'They're not hers, they're mine,' Lola said.

'What are you doing in here so early? It's the middle of the night.'

Lola was delighted: even Dad got things wrong. 'It's five past six. François and Rachel are arriving today. They're actually coming here! You told them where we are.' She fell sleepily silent, dozing with her nose snuggled against Ben's pyjama-covered shoulder while light grew beyond the curtains. Her eyes flickered open. Both the adults were breathing deeply again. 'I had a dream,' she whispered, 'a lovely dream.'

She lifted her head. Ben had put his fingers against his mouth and he'd wake soon. Like most children she loved rules and routine, the sure and safe progression of bed, bath and breakfast that started every day, the thousand and one familiar talismans that made life secure: slippers, dressing-gown, toothbrush, steam condensing on the mirror, soap, the feel of fresh clothes and the smell of frying bacon. Mum was smiling in her sleep and Lola turned over and hugged her, knowing that life was wonderful. Mum often said different things from what the school said, but still Lola had to go. That was OK. She liked being told what to do.

She sat up. 'I remember,' she said, smiling, 'in my dream I saw white horses pulling a golden carriage, and it had lovely paintings on the doors . . .'

Ria woke with a shiver, and knew Ben was aware of it. Lola was remembering the night before Pearl's death.

'Come on!' Ria covered her dismay with her jolliest voice. 'It's a lovely day, draw the curtains! Let the sunshine in!' She chivvied them out of bed, shrugging on her dressing-gown first and beating them both to the bathroom. The two of them were her life and though she knew there were bad things in the world, she swept them under the carpet as thoroughly as her mother had done: out of sight, out of mind. Ria didn't want to know.

But Lola wanted to know everything.

Petrol rationing had ended, and their visitors would drive up from London by motor. It was bound to be a French car, Lola reckoned. Late in the afternoon she and Ben were carrying the fresh-caught trout for supper from Home Farm when a black Citroën – Lola recognised the make by the chevron on the grille – pulled up beside them. François, lean and active, jumped from the driver's seat and embraced Ben, kissing his cheeks first on one side then the other, while Lola watched round-eyed. 'It is the first time we have met since the night of the party!' François exclaimed. 'We set off at first light, we could not wait to be here.'

Lola observed him closely, not realising that she herself was observed with as much care from inside the car. François, now shaking Ben's hand, spoke smooth, elegant English. Lola guessed he was in his early thirties, with dark hair worn slightly long, and a white shirt: she fell in love with him immediately because his jacket was hung from a shaped wooden hanger in the open rear window of the car. He was now shaking hands with Ben: how alike they looked, she thought. Though François's eyes were brown he had Ben's straightforwardness beneath the flowery mannerisms, a streak of cold determination which she recognised. He did not miss much. She watched him until he noticed her, then held out her hand indifferently.

'I'm Lola,' she said.

He bowed and shook her hand, paying her all his attention. '*Enchanté, mam'selle.*' Lola would have died for him. 'She is most beautiful, Ben.'

'Thank you,' Ben said, surprised Ria never mentioned such a thing. What was Lola really like? What was really the colour of her eyes, her hair, her complexion? He could touch the clay of her, but he couldn't see the picture. 'That's why I wish I could see. To see Lola.'

'You must never give up . . . I was going to say hope. Determination.'

'I never do,' Ben said gently, but with that edge of iron in his voice, and again Lola thought how alike they were.

François took her hand. 'Lola, I would like to introduce you to my wife.'

He opened the passenger door, and the dark-haired woman inside gave a charming smile. 'Hallo,' Rachel said.

François turned to Ben. 'Yes. It is a miracle.'

Lola helped them carry their cases upstairs, following silently, seeing the Grange through the visitors' eyes: the house had been restored in bits and patches, Ria's work, as though Ben did not really care. Lola knew he did not intend to remain here for long, but Mum couldn't think of things that way. She had finished the stairs at last. All Mum thought of was herself: first Lola's happiness, then her own and Ben's. Ria's family. Ben had given her money for repairs to be professionally made. New curtains, whatever she asked for, he had casually given her. He didn't care about money. Mr Bookkeeper ensured that his bank accounts were kept topped up, and Pearl had been wealthy in her own right – the purchases poor Mum agonised over with such pleasure, stretch covers, a wallpaper with pale pink and pale blue roses entwined, little ornaments bought with Helen in the Manchester or Leeds street-markets or rescued from some dusty forgotten niche and lovingly spruced up, cost pennies by comparison. Of course Ben could not share in these little details that cumulatively built up warmth and a home. They had become Mum's private life.

Rachel was lovely. She was perhaps half a dozen years younger than François. Lola dreamed of looking like her, of moving with such grace, for Rachel's thinness had been filled out by her feminine curves and she looked exquisite. Lola sat quietly in the corner watching her unpack. Beneath her travelling coat, which she took off with a smile for the girl's intentness, Rachel was wearing a charcoal-grey dress, shot-silk, tightly sashed at the waist. Lola stared at her with longing. Rachel's black hair was drawn back like a ballet-dancer's from a face of strong yet delicately formed features, slim nose, high cheekbones and arched eyebrows, her slender neck encircled with a chain of pearls that were the largest Lola had ever seen – they must surely be false. Yet everything else about Rachel seemed so true. Her eyes were calm and deep, slightly slanted and dark as the sloes that could sometimes be found in valley hedgerows; yet there was something else in them too. Something that Lola had no way of recognising.

'Have you got a headache?' she asked, concerned, drawing the obvious conclusion.

'I have not,' laughed Rachel, 'though that might surprise you after such a long drive. Why do you ask?'

'Dad gets headaches sometimes and he's got some terrific red pills when he's got pain. He won't mind if I get you one.'

'I am perfectly well, thank you.'

'Are you sure?' Lola asked, fascinated to hear Rachel talk, watching her every movement, the unpacked clothes being hung in the wardrobe with the easy assurance of one used to travelling without a maid.

'Do I amuse you, Lola?'

'I thought countesses had maids.'

'I was not born a countess. François has always known who he is – he was born the Count of Coucy and that is all, one of the oldest and most distinguished families in France. But I, I cannot even know where I come from. Perhaps that is why François loves me as he does.'

Lola listened, entranced. No one had talked to her before of love as a thing you tried to work out: she had thought it was simply part of everyone. Rachel chose words like François, with a different rhythm from

English, but her accent was much more French than his.

'Why did François say that?'

'Say what? Do you want to help me unpack? This case is very heavy to lift on the bed. Perhaps together.'

They lifted, their faces close. 'About the miracle,' Lola said.

'The miracle is simply that I can speak to you. This is all François means. For many years I –' she touched her throat – 'I could not utter the words that were inside me. Only cries.' She smiled, as if such a terrifying condition must be made harmless for the little girl, a child could not possibly understand. 'Only cries like a little bird.' She tried to change the subject. 'I have some perfume here. I know you would like to try some . . . a dab on the throat, like this. Perfect!' But Lola was staring at the chain of pearls.

'They're real,' she said. 'They're real, aren't they?'

'Real and ancient. Some say they were brought back from the Holy Land during the Crusades. The setting of course is Fabergé.' She took them off and let Lola examine them, put them round her own neck in the mirror.

'Will you wear them tonight?' Lola begged. 'Please?'

Rachel had slipped out of her dress and was hesitating at the wardrobe. 'Yes, certainly,' she murmured absently. 'Which dress should I select, do you think? I never know.'

'The black one. And the pearls.'

'Yes, that is good. It shall be done completely as you say.'

'Did François teach you to speak English?' Lola grinned.

'Yes he did, as you well know, I think.'

'Theenk,' Lola said, and Rachel, dressing, laughed aloud.

'Well! You are a find.'

'Can I comb your hair? Tell me about your miracle.'

'That is François's Catholic word.' Rachel shrugged, glancing at the child's face above her own in the mirror. Her silky hair did not really need combing, but she kept still. 'No, it was no miracle. Only a medical condition. A psychosomatic medical condition. An English doctor treated me.'

'Did you have to have an operation?'

'Doctors cannot operate on something that exists only in the mind of the sufferer.'

Lola put her head on one side. 'Does that mean you were mad?'

They both looked round as Ben called upstairs. Will and Helen had arrived and dinner was served. Rachel jumped up, kissed Lola, and finished dressing.

'No, *ma petite chouchou*, I was not mad.' She touched the girl's shoulder with a kind expression. 'You see, some truths are too terrible to be spoken.'

Lola observed them sitting around the oval dinner table. She had been placed next to Rachel – not by chance, presumably, since Ben had decided where they would sit, fixing the seating plan in his mind so that he knew in which direction to turn through the babble of conversation. Opposite Rachel were Ben and François, Helen near Will. François, a diplomat on the Quai d'Orsay, was talking enthusiastically of his minister's proposal for a European Coal and Steel Community. Everyone but the British wanted to join. 'Of course it is not really about coal and steel at all,' he scoffed. 'The idea is to make another war unthinkable.'

'A united Europe has been the goal of every dictator for the last two thousand years,' Ben said.

'Peace is worth almost any price, surely?'

'I don't agree.'

'That's enough talk about politics, you men,' Ria insisted.

'Do you remember Fritzi Münchener?' François asked Ben with a smile. 'We had such happy times together at London House in the thirties! He is now an official with the German Foreign Ministry in Bonn. This is what old friendships are for – unofficial contacts! A Council of Europe is to be set up. Fritzi is working to promote our goal of a European Federation.'

'So did his father, Dolfo,' Ben said. 'His name for it was Greater Germany.'

'Things have changed,' François smiled.

Ria laid down the law. 'We're going to enjoy ourselves tonight. Sorry the food's rough and ready but you'll just have to lump it, that's the way we are here.'

Lola had never seen Mum decked out like this. She was radiant, showing off for their first guests, wearing a lovely shimmering evening dress she'd bought secretly on a shopping expedition with Helen. She'd lacquered her nails to match and taken the trouble to put up her hair beautifully, which was more than Helen had done; hers was straight as shears. Ria made the younger woman look dowdy, and Lola wondered how much more she didn't know about her mum. For the first time she realised, really *saw* it, that Mum had been on stage, a real star, and a nightclub hostess for years after that. Ria's tongue sparkled and she got everyone out of themselves. The nettle wine helped, then the trout Will had caught in the leat that afternoon, followed by cheese from Home Farm. Ria didn't forget Lola. 'Lola,' she whispered, leaning across the corner of the table, as the men argued about politics again, 'do you want to know a secret?'

'No!' Lola whispered excitedly.

'Then I'll tell you. I've put colour on my toenails too. Scarlet.'

'Oh!' said Lola with longing, trying to see under the tablecloth. 'Can I too?'

'Tomorrow.' Ria clapped her hands. 'You men, that's enough talking among yourselves.'

'The last time I saw Chouchou was at Coucy in 1939,' Ben told François. 'I was passing through just a few months before the outbreak of the war, as it turned out, on my way to find Roland. My half-brother had renounced his title, family, all I never had. His experience in the trenches, ordering men to die, had broken his spirit and he disappeared in

Africa. I wanted to save him, I suppose. Bring him back to – civilisation.'

'Coucy was a great castle for almost a thousand years,' whispered Rachel to Lola, 'with stone walls ten metres thick. No invader from the north, English or German, could reach Paris without breaking Coucy first. None did. Until General Ludendorff dynamited the towers, and now only ruins remain.'

'That's sad,' Lola said.

'Overdue,' said Rachel.

'Cheese,' Ria said, 'anyone for more cheese?'

'Chouchou was a fighter,' Ben was saying. 'Roland had lost faith in himself. But Chouchou was a woman. More, a Frenchwoman. She was made of sterner stuff.'

'She wrote to me that you had visited her, Ben,' François said, then explained to Ria, 'Monsieur London is an old friend of our family. In 1917 he flew my mother Chouchou – terribly illegally – to Deauville to be with my father the Count, an event without which I would not have occurred.'

Rachel touched her throat.

François sipped his wine. 'When you saw Chouchou at Coucy she knew she was dying, Ben.'

'What was she dying of?' asked Lola.

'Sssh!' said Helen.

'A cancer of the throat.'

'She was determined to beat it,' Ben said. 'She had tiger's eyes. She called the cancer "only a little one".'

'The doctors had given her only months to live.'

Ria stood up. 'Can't we talk about something nice? I'm sorry, François, but surely you can't be enjoying talking about these horrible things, and I did so want everyone to enjoy themselves tonight, I really wanted it.' She touched the back of her hand to her eye as if a speck of dirt had flown into it. 'You're our first guests here.'

There was a silence.

'I'll make the coffee,' Ria said. 'Lola, come.' She gestured her hand behind her as she went out, but Lola hung back.

'François is irrepressible, he runs away with himself,' Rachel apologised to Ben. 'I shall go after poor Ria and say I am so sorry for spoiling her evening.' She put down her napkin, holding out her hand to Lola, and followed Ria's footsteps to the servants' ante-room off the lounge.

'I've got to go to the toilet,' Lola said, pulling away.

But instead of going to the room beneath the stairs, she slipped back to the dining-room, and listened by the half-open oak door. Candlelight flickered on the dark panelled walls, and she crouched, pretending to lacquer her nails with her fingertips, while the men's voices murmured past her.

'I was sitting my degree at Oxford,' François was saying. 'I rushed home to Coucy as soon as I heard how ill Chouchou was, naturally. She refused to acknowledge that anything at all was wrong with her, but I could see she was very frightened. Obviously her greatest worry was me, hardly in my twenties, unmarried, with great responsibilities that must fall on me when she was gone. She defied the doctors, and she did not die, not then.'

'No one wins against death,' came Ben's voice.

* * *

'It's no good trying to talk me round, Rachel, I'm not sorry.' Ria was in the ante-room, making coffee in an unapologetic mood, banging the cups into a row of saucers. 'This room makes me feel like a servant!' she burst out.

'We are all ordinary people, Ria. Human beneath our skin.'

'Well, I'm sorry I blew up.'

'It is I who should apologise.'

'It's not you!' Ria gave Rachel's arm a squeeze. 'It's not you at all.' She smiled, then shook her head. 'It's Ben, I don't know what he's up to. No bloody port for him. Where's that girl of mine? I bet she isn't really in the airey, she's listening somewhere with her ears out on stalks.'

'You are trying to inject a lighter note into our conversation.' Rachel wasn't having it. 'Your dismay is François's fault, and I'm sorry he has upset you. But he is correct, Ria. This is something that must be faced.'

The kettle hissed steam cheerfully and Ria filled the cups. It was 'instant coffee', the latest thing, and she had been looking forward to showing it off. 'You see, Rachel, Ben's encouraging him. There's no need for them to rake over old wounds.'

Rachel hesitated. 'Evil exists in this world, Ria.'

'So does love,' Ria said. 'And that's all I'm interested in at my dinner party. I can get the rest from the newspapers.' Ria put down the kettle with a definite bump. 'What *is* François to him, Rachel?

392

Why should Ben trust François, a foreigner, with the knowledge of where he is when George and Victoria, his own children, don't know?'

'My mother's spirit was unconquerable,' Lola overheard François's voice continuing, 'and when the war came I joined, naturally, my father's old unit as a *poilu*. When the Nazis invaded France they rolled over us, outflanked us, drove us back; we had no orders and our confusion was total. I was trapped at Dunkirk, giving the British time to escape, but not ourselves. Forgotten, we watched the ships sail away. We threw away our guns, I was arrested by the French military authorities, escaped, captured by a Nazi armoured column, but they let me go with a bullet in my thigh. They were too busy racing for Paris . . . or wherever. It was all over for us. Doctor Lamprière took me into his family; it was months before I was fully well and returned home with papers to Coucy. The château had been taken over by the Gestapo. Many local people were shot. Today you see their stones set up on the roadsides, *Fusillés par les Allemands*. And my mother? She was gone. Chouchou, who had hardly the strength to raise a birdgun, had defied these killers with submachine guns. They dragged her down the steps of her home by her hair. A dying woman. To them she was not worth a bullet.'

'Coffee,' Ria said, bearing in the tray of steaming cups with a smile. 'Help yourselves to cream and sugar. Lola, where have you been?' she hissed by the sideboard, where she thought she could not be heard. 'It's time for your bed.'

'Can't I just stay up tonight? Please?'

'No, nor pretty please. Go to bed.'

'But I'll help you with the washing-up tomorrow.'

'You'll help anyway,' Ria said.

Lola set her mouth.

'It's time for Will and me to bow out,' Helen said. 'Really, it's been a fascinating evening, Ria. Thank you, François, for telling us your story.' She shook hands quickly, with a polite, distant smile, as though to put his words in their proper perspective.

'Ta, Mum,' Will said genially, 'I know how much tonight meant to you.'

Ria looked round her half-empty table. 'Well, you must all be tired. I'll just check Lola's in bed and kiss her goodnight.'

She went downstairs. Lola had left the light on in the bathroom as usual, and as usual Ria, yawning, clicked it off and went to tuck her girl up. Lola's clothes were thrown in a pile on the floor, as usual, and she put them neatly on the dresser. Ria sat on the side of the bed, seeing in the glow of light from the door that Lola was already peacefully asleep, her child's face framed by a mass of black curls, that luminous, perfect complexion. Ria kissed her, then rested her own head on the pillow for a moment, just a moment . . . Lola waited until her mother's breathing was even then wriggled out of bed, pulling on socks under her white flannel nightdress, and scampered upstairs through the secret passages, the hidden world once trodden only by servants.

'I never knew my parents,' Rachel said. 'I thought I did. My father, Salomon Blum, a watchmaker of Soissons, rented a small premises on the busy Rue Célestin, and was happily married to my mother Gabrielle. That they were not my father and mother never crossed my mind. Why should it? We were always poor, he was a kindly ineffectual man with no eye for money, and the landlord was always calling. This man also owned our little house in the backstreet. He did not knock on the door but walked straight in any time of the day or evening. My mother took in washing and sewing. She could never sit still for nervousness. That man, Monsieur Hulda, was a brute. He had a round red face with the features pinched into the middle of it, a burgher's face. Never drunk but always full of bonhomie, of good living, telling us we were lucky to have such a friend as he, and we believed him. This merry "uncle" with hairs in his ears looked at me with his glazed, crafty eyes and promised to send me to dancing school. Of course my father laughed about him, saying he was harmless. We children were undeceived, we four sisters and two brothers whispered under our bedsheets in our childish games, *Be silent, or the Hulda will get you*. He was always waiting around the corner, and he always picked on me, calling me Rachel Céleste. The lost one. The name caught on, Rachel Céleste, even to my uncle the butcher with his copper knives. Rachel

Céleste, because I was different, everyone could see it, except me. Except me.' She looked down at the table. 'A woman's enemies are not the inhabitants of hostile nations. Her real enemies live among her own people, and in her own family, and in her own mind.

'When I was nine years old – that was in 1933, the year Dachau was built – my parents confessed the truth to me, that they were not my parents, that no one knew who my parents were, that as a baby I was found lying in the Rue Célestin. They decided all was for the best, I might have been lost by accident, a careless nursemaid, or fallen from an open car, or perhaps crawled there myself from some fine house, so Salomon and Gabrielle took me in at first in hope of a reward. But they came to love me as one of their own – I became one of their children, and grew up. But even a woman's body can become her enemy, because she is coveted. I could not shake off the genial attentions of Monsieur Hulda, his kind glances, his small gifts. He brushed against me by mistake, he came to life when he saw me. He began to claim I made him unhappy. Why did I hate him? He became inconsolable. He made life very hard for the ones I loved. But I would not run away, and I would not submit to him. My "father" finally threatened that he would be reported to the gendarmerie. That was in June 1940, one week before the *blitzkrieg*.

'Under the Nazis, Hulda's Germanic name and widespread contacts in our community made him a man with the power of life and death. France was stood on her head, he *was* the police. We wore no yellow stars, not then, but we were classified, indexed, cross-referenced. Hulda made his offer. I need not be a Jewess. There were the papers ready on his desk, already filled out in the name of Rachel Céleste. All I need do was give in to him. And the Blum family? No one would ever know, they would be given a fresh start where rumours could not spread. He even held out the seven yellow rail warrants for them, my "father" Salomon, my "mother" Gabrielle, my "sisters" Suzanne, Ève, Faustine, and finally my two "brothers", Bernard, even little Édouard, all neatly typed: there would even be a holiday first, they must not forget to pack one suitcase each. So I submitted. Of course we know now what I had done.'

'You must not distress yourself,' François said, standing.

'I have learned to speak of it.'

He poured a glass of water and insisted she drink every drop. 'Ben, this is most distressing for Rachel. She will listen to you.'

Ben held out his hands. Rachel put her own hands in them.

'Please continue if you can,' Ben said gently. François made an angry exclamation and threw himself in the chair at the head of the table. Rachel saw the small pale figure of a child move from the curtain behind him, startled, then slip back again. A girl in a white nightdress – Lola. Rachel hid her smile, then realised there was no need. Ben could not see, and François was sulking. The fire flickered its warm shadows, and the little girl put her head out, held her finger to her lips. Rachel smiled. The two of them.

'So I became Rachel Céleste, with a comfortable room next to the Hôtel Foch, mistress of Hulda the collaborator. He had promised me that no one would ever know, but there is always a problem with this. *I* knew, and *he* knew. The pleasure men take in women, without love, is shortlived and quickly becomes routine, and routine becomes onerous. I was dangerous to him, the smallest indiscretion on my part could lead to his denunciation. But one night all his old ardour suddenly returned. He had signed the eighth rail warrant. One hour after he departed the soldiers arrived, and that was the end of me. I understood everything.

'But if evil exists – and we can see it does – so must love exist also, as inexplicable, as wonderful and terrible. Yes, Ben, wonderful, because a world without evil would be as soul-destroying as one without love. We have a choice. I am on the train, I am Rachel Blum the Jewess, one face in one thousand faces. With the dislocation of war no carriages are available, we are in darkened trucks, each jealously guarding a suitcase from our travelling companions, who guard their own suitcases from us. There is no cruelty from outside, locked doors prevent it, we are safe from anyone except ourselves, the strongest get the light. There is a dying woman and I hold her; the straw is thin, she cannot speak. At the halt I bring her a spoon of water. Suddenly there is shouting outside, something is wrong, the worst disaster that can afflict the Teutonic mind has occurred, an administrative mix-up. One of us should not be here. Soldiers are yelling, the heavy sliding doors are being banged open up and down the train. Nothing can save the dying woman . . . she presses something hard into my hand.'

'The Coucy pearls,' Ben said.

'With her other hand she takes my papers, and I am gone. I am a person of importance. I matter, I am identified. I am the Countess of Coucy.'

François came round the table and held her. 'It took me years to show Rachel that hers was really a very happy story. She had given the Blums years of happiness. That rogue Hulda might as easily have fixed upon one of their natural daughters, Ève or Suzanne or Faustine instead of her, such is the nature of obsession. Very probably the same dreadful fate that befell the family – the females died at Regensburg, nothing is known of the males – would have occurred just as tragically. Chouchou could not save her own life, but she saw how she could exchange her death for a life.'

'You could have denied Rachel,' Ben said.

'But I saw her, and loved her.' François kissed his wife's hair. 'She could not speak, but I saw her tragedy in her eyes. I had just arrived back at Coucy-la-Ville, my wound healed, when the Chief of Police turned up with Rachel. Yes, I could have denied her. The thought never crossed my mind. Everything about her was endearing me: her silence, her mystery, her suffering.'

'But your mother had not committed you to her.'

'I knew I could make her free,' said François, showing his determination. 'I vouched for her. The Bishop of Laon granted us a special dispensation to marry, and she was instructed under the Canon Law in the Catholic faith. There was nothing wrong with her intelligence or her handwriting, and she agreed that any children would be brought up in the Catholic faith . . . the children that are the most important blessing of marriage.'

Lola watched them. Ben said nothing, sitting with one hand on the table, staring in the direction of the fire. Rachel was standing near him with François, the firelight flickering over their faces, making their bodies shift and shimmer. Lola's curiosity brought her half a step forward. François was holding Rachel's hands in his own in exactly the same way Ben had held them, with the same intensity of emotion yet the same gentleness, even the same determination, because Lola was sure Rachel could not have got away from him. Lola stared. It was extraordinary, yet so obvious that she couldn't understand why she hadn't seen it from the very first moment. François was Ben's son.

She realised that even François did not know.

Lola must have made some very faint sound because Ben's head turned towards her.

'After the war,' François was saying proudly, 'I engaged the finest psychologists and speech thera-pists. They all advised that in cases like this, where Rachel's mind might be forced into general amnesia by relentless questioning, that time was the great healer. Then we lost our first child.' He kissed her hair. 'There will be others, lots of boys, to carry on the Coucy line. However, perhaps somehow that loss enabled her to face her wartime experiences . . . to talk about them. Yes, to talk. Rachel had to learn to speak all over again. It took years, her brain remembered but her tongue and lips had forgotten. The muscles had to learn to form the sounds, just as a baby's do. It was worth the wait,' he ended fondly.

'It was as easy to speak English as well as French,' Rachel said, then could not repress a yawn. She led François to the door. 'Ben, I am exhausted by my long day and I must say goodnight.'

'Goodnight, Rachel. Can you find your way?'

'Even without Lola to guide me,' said Rachel with a secret smile, glancing at the curtain where she knew Lola was hiding.

'Goodnight, Ben,' François said.

'Goodnight.'

The door was left open and a draught stirred the curtain beside Lola. Her father stared at it as though he saw a ghost.

Lola in her white nightgown turned away down the secret passage, the hem fluttering over her running feet, and did not stop until she was safely downstairs. Mum was snoring on Lola's bed, where she had dropped asleep still in her party clothes and shoes. Lola couldn't resist slipping the shoes off. Mum had not lied. Her toenails were painted scarlet.

Lola covered her with a blanket, then slipped in beside her, and did not wake until dawn.

In the early days of his blindness, sight-phantoms had been not uncommon for Ben, formless blots of light so dim as to be barely discernible, seemingly inside his eyes, impossible to focus on. They bloomed, sometimes ringed with a colour, a faint blue, or red, rotating perhaps like a beach-ball before fading again to nothing. Tormenting in their promise, he knew these visions weren't real, they were what doctors call cortical vision: seeing stars. Each display – and they were increasingly infrequent – lasted only a few seconds. Ria even had a name for them: the Sun Dogs.

But for almost five minutes Ben had watched that white blob. Sure, it changed shape, showing only part of itself, and sometimes it moved slightly, which made it appear much brighter, but even when motionless it did not entirely disappear.

His attention was distracted for a moment.

*Ben, I am exhausted by my long day and I must say goodnight.*

By an enormous effort of will Ben forced himself to sound calm and prosaic. *Goodnight, Rachel. Can you find your way?*

Every atom of him wanted to swivel and look behind him.

Rachel said something about Lola, and there was a secret in her voice. Ben glanced back. The white blob was still there.

Their voices came again, distracting him. *Goodnight, Ben.*

*Goodnight.*

Ben sat in the empty room. He could feel the fire in front of him, but its heat had fallen very low. He could not tell if any lights were on. He sat with his hands bunched into fists. He hardly dared hope. Finally he turned again, and looked behind him.

He was blind. The white blob was gone.

'Lola,' he cried, 'Lola, are you there?' But there was no reply. 'For God's sake, if you are, talk to me.'

Ben sat in the dark stirring the crunching embers of the fire with a poker, and each time a flame flared up, he stopped, staring. He did not go to bed at all that night.

# Chapter Ten

## 1

Victoria knew that David Jones had offered her Radio in the hope and expectation that she would fail. Her last department had broken takings records on three successive weeks during the summer sales, but that wasn't why he was offering her this plum job with such confidence. No, she was sure he wanted her to fail. Electrical Goods was a big and valuable department in the Emporium, with a large corner area at the front of the second floor, and it had always been the exclusive preserve of salesmen, not women. Women were well known to lack any natural aptitude for the baffling world of diodes and frequencies.

'Well, that's never a true one for a start,' sniffed Hilda in the canteen. 'Me sister Eth worked in Croydon as a solderer during the late war, see, she didn't 'ave fingers like sausages like mine. Lovely long nimble pinkies Eth 'ad. Yer don't see men doing fine piecework like what she did, not except at 'alf the speed. It's the sewing, see, it's in the blood. And don't think she didn't 'ave ter learn the difference between a diode and a triode neither. She married a policeman up Walworth Road, the Carter Street nick. 'E brings 'er 'ome fresh vegs from the nick's vegetable garden and she's got six nippers who all of 'em want ter be policemen. . . . Are yer listening?'

'An opportunity to fail,' Victoria said with determination, 'is also an opportunity to succeed.'

'Is it? Why'd yer fink 'e's so devious-like? Jones is not giving yer a chance because yer good at yer job, maybe?'

'Not him! You're such an innocent, Hilda. Their minds don't work that way. David Jones is out to get me and he has been right from the start, and he won't stop until we're finished. It's him or me. You don't understand, do you?'

'Jones 'as always played fair wiv us,' Wattie said. 'Christmas 'amper, always 'as a word friendly-like, an' looks yer in the eye.'

'So you're all on his side?' Victoria said.

'We aren't on nobody's side,' Hilda insisted patiently. 'Listen, girl. I remember when yer joined this place, yer very first day, 'ow young yer was. Give us yer smile what yer 'ad then, go on.'

Victoria couldn't help smiling, remembering her innocence about the store and its ways.

'That's it, yer can do it,' Hilda said. 'An' yer didn't know nuffink, did yer?'

'Did it show?'

'Now yer fink yer know everyfink. But don't forget us here in the heart of the place, will yer?'

They all thought they were the heart of the place, Victoria realised. Hilda really believed that the Emporium would fall to pieces without her quietly managing things here below. Old Wattie, pushing his trolley with the squeaky wheels and brown canvas sides to the lift, going up two floors and pushing it out again, really thought he was important. Bill Simmonds thought it mattered that he spent hours polishing that car, and he probably believed that the world would stop if he was late.

My father created this, she thought, and it lives on. Still living and breathing after he's gone. What a heavy responsibility it is.

'The Jones clique are all against me,' Victoria explained her attitude to them, 'all the old men who have done well under the old system and want things just the way they were – the store to be the way it used to be, like a gentlemen's club. Do you know they used to have a doorman to keep women out? The good old days! But these are modern times.' She insisted on the latter. 'Modern times.'

'David Jones is all right,' Hilda said doggedly, 'I knew 'im from the start. 'E's not yer enemy.'

'I'm afraid you're quite wrong.'

'Why'd yer 'ave ter 'ave enemies anyway? Life's difficult enough wivout inventing 'em.' Hilda was incapable of seeing the obvious, Victoria realised. The warm-hearted woman who had once seemed so motherly and wise to the young, impressionable Victoria she now saw was just a big fish in a very small pool. Victoria imagined a grouper or something equally shapeless and animate with a huge clumsy mouth gulping up all the available oxygen from her environment. Hilda knew nothing of the orderly world above her narrow horizon, Victoria knew, where the real decisions were taken and people's lives controlled . . . as Victoria had been controlled as a child, she told herself, denied, restricted; and her mouth tightened. 'Yer got ter 'ave somefink to fight against, don't yer, Vicky,' Hilda said, 'even if it's nuffink! Why d'yer fink everyone's against yer? Like it, do yer?'

'You don't have the faintest idea what I have to go through.'

'Cold, yer are. Cold tin-foil.'

'I have to be!' Victoria told the truth. 'I have to be.'

Bill Simmonds came in and dropped his peaked cap on the table. Hilda had got her gnashers into Victoria by the sound of it. He fetched a mug of tea.

'Listen, what about David Jones's daughter, Cathy, she's been a good friend to yer, ain't she?' Hilda demanded, ignoring Victoria's pale expression. 'That Cathy, she's a nice girl. Don't 'ear no complaints about 'er.'

'Fick ankles,' Wattie said.

'Shut yer face, Wattie.'

'That's right, Wattie, shut it,' Bill Simmonds said, so roughly that the others looked at him in surprise. He grunted, not meeting their eyes. He'd known about Cathy Jones and George London before any of them, but he'd broken the habit of a lifetime and kept this juicy titbit of gossip to himself. He liked Cathy, she was a sweet girl, with more genuine class than Victoria, and he liked her with George. They made a pleasant couple quietly holding hands in the back of the car while he drove, never arguing. Cathy always looked pleased to ride in the Rolls-Royce, appreciating it as the event it was and saying thank you. She was a real lady.

'Everyone's in a right mood today,' Hilda said, rubbing her hands, not with displeasure.

Victoria knew she could never explain to them. Cathy Jones, Victoria had decided, must be clever and ruthless – nothing wrong with that, Victoria admired it, a girl had to have something extra to make her way in a man's world. But at first Victoria had put Cathy down as simply the sort of quiet, businesslike girl who would do whatever Daddy told her to do. Certainly she enjoyed her work and was good at her job. Victoria had only realised how much more there was to the girl when Cathy started her relationship with George. She must be as clearsighted as Victoria, and Cathy, Victoria had now decided, had calculated her moves brilliantly. By bedding George she had one foot in each camp, she needn't be her father's creature.

Suppose Cathy succeeded in marrying George?

Victoria understood now how her father Ben had arranged the power structure of the store so that no other dynasty but his own should rule the Emporium. But with weak George in control – worse, George apparently helplessly in love with the daughter of his opponent – that was happening. George was being dominated by David Jones in the store, and in bed by Cathy. Day or night a Jones mouth was whispering in George's ear, Victoria told herself. George had even endured the humiliation of the Food Hall – David's successful project, enhancing David's prestige – with a smile, as though it didn't matter. Victoria knew it was in such tried and trusted ways that her father had moved against, and ousted – some said driven to his grave – old Georgy Leibig from power in the Emporium during the 1920s.

George was blinded by his love for Cathy, just as his mother had been for his father. The wool had fallen from *her* eyes too late for anything but self-recrimination. Victoria foresaw the same thing happening to George even if no one else did.

'You're all wrong.' She got up to go. 'Thanks for the tea.'

'Don't forget us,' Hilda called. 'We was yer friends.'

Each working day Cathy Jones arrived at the Emporium a little earlier than necessary. The bus from St John's Wood, where she kept her little flat and a whole family, it seemed, of cats who expected, insisted, *demanded* her to provide milk, stopped at the zebra-crossing by the Burlington Arcade.

Cathy jumped down. She wore George's ring on her finger. He had said it didn't mean anything, but that meant it did. Working in a store had taught her a lot about how men's minds worked. They were great deceivers of themselves, she thought fondly, and where their feelings were concerned hid themselves from even the most obvious truths. Cathy was in love with George. She knew better than to talk about it, and she never said 'I love you', or clung to him, or tried to force the pace. She had decided long ago that

George was The One, but he would have run a mile had she revealed how deeply she felt for him. He was a man of business, but a child in relationships. He treated her as just a friend, but Cathy darned his socks. George was almost incapable of looking after himself, and he didn't realise how much he needed her. They often went to a show on Saturday nights and it wasn't anyone else's hand he held. It was Cathy's.

She hung up her coat in the supervisors' cloakroom, brushed her hair and checked that she was presentable – no strand of hair on her navy-blue dress, seams straight – and went upstairs. She loved the Emporium before it opened, the bustle and life of the place, and she knew everyone and liked them just as much as they liked her. But this morning she didn't stop to pass a friendly minute or two with Miss Trant, and gave only a short nod to Mr Hull – if she stopped he'd chatter away at her for ages, his watery eyes not quite meeting hers, roving the ceiling then glancing across her bosom from left to right, then right to left, before not quite looking at her eyes again, his hands ceaselessly moving with little magic tricks meant to entertain or at least delay her: he was a member of the Magic Circle and performed at children's parties, but card tricks bored Cathy silly. She'd left it too late to tell him, and now she didn't have the heart. She'd laughed aloud in the ladies' loo when half the girls admitted they avoided him too. But this morning Cathy had an extra reason for not getting caught.

'Fooled you!' he called sadly. 'Queen of Hearts.'

Cathy went up to the second floor, her shoes

tapping a quick, regular rhythm, overtaking the men carrying up the decorations for the Grand Opening of the new Waterfalls Restaurant this afternoon, then slowed. The buzz of activity spreading through the store like a flame kindling paper had not yet reached up here. Victoria was alone. Her long blonde hair was tightly tied with blue ribbon into a ponytail, but Cathy imagined how pretty she must look with it fanned across her shoulders. Her skin looked so pale and clear that she must let it show, perhaps an off-the-shoulder ball-gown . . . Victoria's every movement was so graceful, so *taught*, that Cathy ached with momentary envy. *If only I was like her*. She had no boyfriend to enjoy such a lovely sight, so far as Cathy knew. Victoria in love would be very beautiful.

Cathy watched her turning on the televisions. The glowing test cards stamped their reflections across her features, monochrome squares and circles rippling over Victoria's cheeks, glinting in her eyes.

Cathy felt embarrassed about not being noticed; it looked as though she was spying. She cleared her throat and Victoria said, 'What can I do for you, Cathy?'

There was no doubt, Cathy thought, about who was now senior in their friendship. Victoria adjusted the horizontal hold distractedly, and Cathy kept her friendly smile on her face, but with less self-assurance. 'Actually I wanted to ask your advice,' she said honestly.

'I shouldn't have thought you needed my advice on anything.'

412

'What does that mean?' laughed Cathy.

'Ask your father. You and he will be running the place soon, won't you?'

Victoria was hurting. Cathy said gently, 'Victoria, I know you miss your own father—'

'I don't!'

'That's no reason to suspect mine of all sorts of devious plots and plans,' Cathy said defensively. 'Why should he be disloyal? He's got everything he wants.'

'People never get everything they want.'

'You're not seeing things as they really are.'

'I know what people are really like,' Victoria said coolly. 'They always want more. They're never happy.'

'Perhaps that's true for you.' Cathy came forward, uncomfortably realising things looked different through Victoria's eyes, yet hardly able to imagine it. Did this pretty girl really see herself surrounded by enemies, competitors, as though life was just a race? Perhaps she wanted it to be true. Victoria had never been in love. Cathy was, and being in love with George filled her life. She looked at Victoria with sympathy in her eyes, but Victoria didn't see it.

'Come and look what I've achieved,' Victoria said, taking Cathy's sleeve and leading her forward. Cathy just wanted to talk about George, the whole reason for her visit, not these *things*, but she had to admit that Victoria had transformed the Radio department – for a start, it was not called Wireless, as it had been under Amberson's rule. Cathy had liked old Amberson, 'Mr Frederick', a lot. 'He was your father's man,'

Victoria accused wickedly, 'and now he's retired at last.'

Mr Frederick had run the department since the days of steam wireless, and clients trusted his judgement because he looked scientific with his silk handkerchief plunged in his top pocket, his shock of distinguished grey hair, his professorial manner. He talked of rectifiers, carrier waves and heterodynes – 'In other words if two waves of about the same frequency are combined,' Victoria had heard him lecture a client, intimidating the poor man into nodding as if he understood a single word, 'then a third wave of a much lower frequency is produced, as in the *ruum-ruum* throbbing sound we hear, for example when we listen to the striking of Big Ben for the nine o'clock news on the BBC Home Service.' And the client's wife would say with relief, 'Oh, it'll pick up "Much Binding in the Marsh" then?' Victoria had seen at once how to succeed. She forsook technical jargon and kept her eyes firmly fixed on the woman, not the man – the woman was the one who mattered, her husband would go along with whatever she wanted in her home, and she wanted something that picked up 'Much Binding in the Marsh' and looked nice on the mantelshelf or in the corner. A nice-looking cabinet, Victoria realised, was a more important selling feature than the ability to pick up Hilversum. Television screens all looked the same, it was the box they came in that mattered. For the Emporium's top models she ordered gorgeous hard-wood cabinets from a firm of coachbuilders, but the tubes and electrical wiring were supplied as standard

by any of Britain's hundreds of small firms manufacturing televisions. The years of austerity were
ending.

'People believe in progress,' Victoria said. 'Next
year the Festival of Britain brouhaha will sell us an
extra ten thousand sets, and after *that*, there's the
Olympics. If anyone thought I couldn't succeed, I've
proved them wrong. I've turned the tables on them.'

'Victoria, can I speak to you seriously?'

'But I have been speaking seriously. I want you to
know, Cathy, that I can be as ruthless and nasty as any
man. I mean it. I'll fight you.'

'Why should you? I love George,' Cathy said. 'I
know you don't approve but I can't help it. He needs
me.'

Victoria cut to the nub of the matter. 'But does he
love you?'

'I want to please him but I can't get close to him,'
Cathy admitted wretchedly. 'I know I'm not rich and I
never went to finishing-school or Came Out as a
Debutante. I don't think he'll ever ask me to marry
him.'

'You can't get much closer to him than his bed,'
Victoria sparked, 'if you can't get him to do what you
want there, what hope have you got?'

Cathy bit her lower lip. 'You're quite wrong to
think so badly of me. I don't share his bed.'

'Oh, he can't love you much!'

'I'm afraid our relationship is too comfortable.
Somehow we've become just friends, not lovers. I
think he's shy,' Cathy said hopefully. 'I think he's shy
with women, do you think that's possible? I had to

415

talk to someone.' Cathy sat suddenly on one of the chairs by the record turntables. 'Does he think that if he asks me to marry him, I'll say no, and he couldn't bear it? He's so sensitive.'

Victoria crouched in front of her, looking kind. 'I don't think you ought to be too much in love with him,' she said in a low voice, picking a strand of hair off Cathy's shoulder. 'I'm truly sorry, Cathy,' she lied. 'I thought you were just head-hunting. After all, George is pretty well off.'

'You were bound to think that,' Cathy agreed subserviently, 'that's why I've kept so quiet about what I feel. But I – I—'

'Cathy, I think there's something you ought to know about George,' Victoria said authoritatively. 'He has a problem with women. His twin brother Ralph always had a pretty girl hanging on his arm, but for some reason George got absolutely left out. It was bound to have an effect.'

'He's shy,' Cathy said quickly. 'We need one another even if he won't admit it.'

'I'm afraid some men just fantasise about women. George fell in love with a black woman, we weren't supposed to know. It was his little secret.'

'Don't tell me,' protested Cathy.

'She was a minor actress,' Victoria said remorselessly, 'a gold-digger, you can imagine the sort. Her stagename was Natasha Cetawa. Took the part of slaves mostly, though of course she claimed she was a princess, daughter of Prince Cetawatunga of Oppidans Road or somesuch. I suppose George believed her, believed whatever she said. She was married, of course. George put her up in a little nest near Marble Arch. She treated him badly.'

'Poor George! He's afraid of making a fool of himself. Why didn't I see it? He can't believe I love him for himself. Just for himself.'

'I'm afraid George's relationships with women are a kind of revenge. His revenge over Natasha Cetawa. She was killed, a bomb, it was the war . . . he was never able to assert himself over her.'

'But why should he need to assert himself? I just want him to be himself, the George I know. I don't mean the George you're talking about. You seem to see a completely different man. I mean the man I *know*.'

'I'm sorry I had to be the one to tell you. You'll get over him.'

Victoria found it difficult to concentrate on her work for the rest of the morning. Was Cathy really so naïve? Victoria found it hard to credit: everything was within Cathy's grasp. All she had to do was work her wiles on George. Victoria knew that one way or another, between George and David, Cathy was at the fulcrum of power. Did the girl really not mean to use that lever? No, all she thought about was George and how sensitive he was and how much she loved him!

Someone called Victoria's name softly. She was dealing with a client, a skinny bulbous-nosed woman with a sniff, who only wanted to know how to keep the walnut radio cabinet clean. 'We recommend a fine beeswax polish,' said Victoria. The Shoe department sold shoe polish at over a hundred per cent profit with

417

nearly every pair of shoes, and people bought it because they didn't want the assistant to think them a scruffy sort who bought new shoes then didn't look after them. In the same way prospective purchasers, imagining the radio or television in pride of place in their living-room, often assured Victoria that they kept their homes spotless. 'Victoria . . .' Roger, one of the sales assistants, tapped his watch again. The opening ceremony for the Waterfalls was at midday. Victoria finished with her client, combed her hair and went upstairs.

The place was packed of course. George was holding court, his enthusiasm masking the shyness that sometimes made him self-important. 'It gives me much pleasure. . . .' A few flashbulbs popped. 'Old traditions allied with the most modern kitchens.' Lisa was surveying the guests with a flinty unimpressed gaze, but she stayed in the background, not spoiling George's day. 'He's shown he can do it,' she told Victoria. 'Don't underestimate George.'

'I couldn't possibly,' Victoria said sweetly, 'it would be so difficult.' Lisa drifted away and Victoria looked round. She had tried to persuade Terry to come but he wouldn't.

'I'm not having you showing me off in front of your fancy friends,' he'd said, kissing her neck. She'd had the strong impression he didn't want to meet George, wanted to keep their relationship apart from her life at work in the store.

'But I want to show you off.'

'I wouldn't fit in with that lot,' Terry had said.

418

'That's why you fancy your East End boy, aren't I right?'

'You're always right.' She loved it when he was assertive.

'That's good,' Terry had said, but there had been a gentleness in his eyes for her that made her purse her lips.

Victoria helped herself to a canapé, then a second. They were irresistible. The Waterfalls had been decked out like a gentlemen's club though, dark red leather, oak panelling, an incongruous chromium-plated tea-urn. David Jones circulated in the crowd, every morning-suited inch the professional, then saw Victoria and slipped through to her as quickly as a pike. That was what it came down to of course. She just didn't like him.

He made conversation for a moment, allowing her time to swallow her last canapé whole. 'White wine?'

'I will have a glass. Up to there.'

'You're looking well, Victoria.' Her eyes were bright and she had a cocky straightforwardness. They were standing almost pressed together by the crush, but he reckoned he'd have to be a great deal closer before he touched her. He doubted if anyone else ever got near her. Perhaps her father, she had her father's eyes, that vivid blue. But a child wasn't the sum of the parents. They were much more, and much less. Take Cathy. David saw so little of her mother in his daughter. Perhaps something of Harriet in their early years, that's all – but there was so much of himself. He had been very lucky the way things had

419

worked out for him, swept into a career that had been so much more successful than he could ever have dreamed, but he was desperately afraid Cathy would find life very hard. He still had not reconciled himself to letting her go, still sought her instinctively when he got home. She had been a part of his life for so many years but now he hardly saw her, his own daughter, even at weekends.

'You supported George's project, Victoria, but you don't approve of it,' David said.

'The roast beef and steak-and-kidney pudding brigade?' She shook her head and her hair moved, catching his attention. David felt a flash of heat in his loins. She was very attractive. She knew it too.

He laughed, finishing his wine, and she noticed how grey his hair had gone, almost white at his temples. The crowd swirled, separating them. George had finished speaking, and Victoria waited by a table until the numbers thinned, then came up beside him as he gulped his first canapé.

'Congratulations,' she said. 'I'm sure it will be very popular.'

'I know you hate it,' he grinned, 'but thank you for supporting me.'

'It's the least I could do. The next thing will be to open the third floor,' she suggested. 'All that wasted space. You've got to keep ahead of David Jones.'

'Let's not run before we can walk,' George said casually. 'These are good.' He was enjoying himself.

'I've been hearing about you and Cathy.'

'Good Lord, have you? What about?' He stopped with a frown. 'Who from?'

'Oh, you know. Gossip.' She shrugged. 'It isn't really love, is it?'

'Victoria, what I feel for Cathy has nothing to do with the Emporium.'

'Doesn't it?' Victoria said. 'What about her?'

That would make him think.

# 2

Vic was proud of himself. What with all the busy building works in the Havannah Street area on the Isle of Dogs, proper shops along West Ferry Road were getting hard to come by. All the little family businesses were going, ironmongers', chandlers', drapers', Mary Walker's Ladies Wear long gone, all the rest quietly closing down, and you hardly noticed until you wanted something, when you walked down and saw the place was just shut-up boards. The community was losing its heart. Behind Havannah Street – in fact chopping off the eastern half of it, bang, with walls of corrugated iron – demolition cranes with roaring engines had smashed the comfortable old houses down. That sound of falling rubble had haunted Vic's sleep. Nowadays it didn't seem that people mattered.

Now huge buildings were rising, council flats pushing rust-coloured girders into the sky, already six storeys high, cutting out the morning sun, the lower floors rapidly being clothed in slabs of pre-formed concrete. They would grow to ten or fifteen or twenty floors high, each little flat with its own cement

balcony, eight foot by three, instead of a garden.
When they were finished even the main road would
be in shadows, and the people all working out, not
living here except at night. No one would buy locally
so then the greengrocers' and butchers' would go, and
what would remain? Only the just-popping-out-for-a-
minute sort of place, sweet-shops for the kids, the fag
shop for Dad and maybe one of those classy
launderettes for Mum where she put her money in the
slot because she worked all week and didn't have time
to do it herself. It wouldn't be a working area, there
wouldn't be anyone in sight, except walking the dog,
and the council would probably ban them because of
their mess. People would be inside their walls, that's
where, Vic knew, where they'd never be seen. They'd
be watching the telly. A bit of washing drying on that
nice council balcony maybe.

Esther hung on. Of course she did. She'd been
hanging on all her life. She'd sit there in her front
room with the peeping-tom net curtains and it could
be a building site outside, but it wouldn't change her a
bit. She'd seen worse.

Esther didn't ask him where he was going tonight.
She knew Vic better than that. But she liked it when
he stayed home in the evenings and they listened to
the wireless. Often enough he slept up Cable Street at
the Old Bull and Bush, or didn't get back until early in
the morning. That was Vic for you. If you thought
about it you realised you didn't quite know where he
was.

'Just popping up to the Bush,' Vic said.

'But you haven't had your supper,' Esther fussed. 'It's the chicken.'

He knew better than to argue. 'Give me a leg to take with me.'

'You eat that,' Esther warned him, pressing the drumstick wrapped in greaseproof paper into his hand. 'Promise your old mum.'

'Promise.'

'Really, Vic, it's a huge chicken. It's not fair of you to bring a chook that big if you're not around to help me eat it.'

'I brought you a new fridge.' The almost-new Kelvinator dominated the kitchen with its white stare. 'Keep it in there.'

'I'll just have a sandwich,' Esther fretted. Vic pulled on his overcoat and kissed her forehead, then turned up the wireless.

Outside, the site workers were knocking off. There was Thames mud all over the roadway. A gang of kids were planning how to get over the iron wall when it was dark, he could see it in their eyes. Nick a wheelbarrow or two, some galvanised buckets, get into the hut for chippies' tools maybe, but Vic knew they'd need to find something strong enough to break the lock. 'You young scamps,' Vic said, 'buzz off.' They weren't Havannah Street kids, or even Malabar Street kids – what remained of Malabar Street – he would have known them. What offended him was they were Poplar kids, and they were bad news because they brought the police down after them. The police in their Austins and Wolseleys. There were so many rules and regulations that the police had plenty of room to make life hard for people. Once they got drawn into a street looking for some kid about a gone wheelbarrow, next thing they'd be doing the tax discs on the cars, defective trafficators, litter, harsh language, no end to it. 'Don't make me talk to you more than once,' Vic said. He knew which one was the leader now, and had him sized.

'We wasn't doing nothing!' complained the boy in a high voice. Too brainy, surmised Vic, and you should never complain.

'Buzz off home, sharpish,' he said contemptuously, 'this isn't your place.'

He got in the car and as he started the engine one of the kids piped up to the leader, ''Oo does 'e think 'e is?'

'That's Vic Price,' said someone, and the gang evaporated. Vic dropped the drumstick into the gutter where a dog would clean it up.

He frowned as he drove down Havannah Street. *Who does he think he is!*

At West Ferry Road he looked left, the Tooke Arms had a big sign hanging over the frosted-glass door, NO DIRTY BOOTS. He turned right, cruising past the shuttered shopfronts, most of them with broken glass leaking beneath the boards. He drove to the clothing warehouses of Commercial Road and parked outside the natty plate-glass windows of Aaron Levy's, one of the largest wholesalers of Dresses to the Trade. Aaron greeted Vic personally and escorted him back through the ranks of women's clothes. It was another sign of the times that old

Aaron Levy had his home not here but near the Golders Green Hippodrome in the same street where his three sons, none of whom had Biblical names, also had their houses.

'Cor, smells musty,' Vic said.

'Heavy materials, finest quality,' Aaron said. 'Winter wear. My ladies will not wear this until February, March.' There was nothing in his inner sanctum less than fifty years old. He sat in an hoop-backed office chair that looked as though it'd been bought secondhand from a school, and gestured Vic, his valued friend, into the comfortable, sag-bottomed armchair. But Vic sat on the arm, where their eyes were level.

'Have you got it?'

'It was difficult. Non-stock. It had to be specially made. I say made. Constructed. My man used genuine 1912 patterns he found firesale.'

'And your pin-money sweatshop girls knocked it up in half an hour.'

'Oh no, Vic, this cream material is a special order from Holland. And the attached navy-blue shoulder-cape was difficult, not my speciality. Who to turn to? Ha, to my sister's friend Michael, a purveyor of religious clothing to rabbis, Catholics, even the Church of England, those plain grey shoulder-capes they wear to look so impressive. Grey, black, purple, so why not blue?'

'Brilliant,' Vic said. 'Show me.'

'You'll love it,' Aaron said, watchful yet distant. Vic liked that.

'Show me, you old thief.'

Aaron slid a white card box from the shelf, laid it across his ancient desk. He lifted the lid and the sighing layers of tissue paper, then what lay beneath.

'That's it!' Vic said.

'Cream and blue.'

'Yes. Put it back.' Vic wouldn't touch the dress. 'Put it back!' He watched the old man carefully replace the dress, putting on the layers of tissue paper one by one, and finally the white card lid. 'It's beautiful,' Vic said. 'Tell me when you want paying.'

'Old times,' Aaron Levy said. 'It was a privilege.'

'Old friends,' Vic said.

He slid the dress-box across the rear seat of the car. The evening was still warm but already growing dark. He drove to Tower Bridge, and from there into the now familiar foreign territory of Tooley Street, turned left at Paradise Gate for the straight run along Brunel Street, then followed cranky Rotherhithe Street along the riverside to Cuckold's Point. No lights showed in the Half Moon & Calf's Head, windowless on the land side. By now it was night, and crossing the rough ground Vic's headlamps swung their beams across the figure of a woman in some old coat waiting by the floodwall, caught with squinting eyes and a cigarette to her mouth.

Betty was working nights.


This was the first time she had lied to her husband. Really lied, made up a lie that is, not just absent when he'd never notice because he was at work, and he never knew she'd been away. Thank God for automatic timers on electric cookers, so she could take his dinner out of the oven hot, that was all she could say. Watching him eat, a fit of the giggles had swept over her, thinking of what she had really been doing when Herbert thought she was faithfully putting his baked potato and bit of pie in the oven. She'd been between the sheets with Vic Price, rolling over him, biting his shoulders.

'Wh-hot's the matter, Mrs?' her husband asked with a frown, then a weak smile. 'Funny, am I?' Betty had been utterly unable to control her giggling.

'Not you, love,' she'd said. Then she'd come out with the big straightfaced lie. 'I'm working nights.'

'That's not funny.'

'There's so much sickness around. The staff are down with it, and of course hospital admissions are up. They need me, love.' She clinched it. 'It's my duty.' He sighed but his resistance evaporated. He was such a little man, married to his job, no fight in him at all.

'I'll miss you,' he said. 'The evening will be bloody boring without you, Mrs. That's a fact.'

'You go to bed early then.'

'I will but I shan't sleep without you.'

She looked at him with contempt, so confident in herself that she reached out and pinched his cheek, then smiled. She hated him for losing her so easily. It was his fault.

The afternoon she was supposed to start nights she left him a cold supper – no need to give away too many secrets about timers – and set off for the bus request stop, but as soon as she was away from the prying eyes of her own little neighbourhood, she turned left instead of right and walked down to the Limehouse Hole ferry. She wouldn't have to do this much longer. Vic was eating out of the palm of her hand. He was so like Nigel really. Beneath the surface he was a kind man, she knew, a misunderstood man, but she understood him. It was the ferry's last trip of the day, and she stood on the hard with darkness falling around her, listening to the heartbeat of the ferry's engine fading back towards Limehouse, then silence but for the lapping water. The stars were coming out. It was awfully romantic. She looked down in distaste as something cold lapped her foot. The tide was turning, and she started ashore. If only Vic would give her the key to the Half Moon & Calf's Head she could have cooked him something ready, and they could talk first, maybe even candles and a proper tablecloth. He kept himself too much to himself, but then they all did. It wasn't easy, being in love. It was the most difficult thing in the world.

Betty waited at the top of the slipway, smoking a cigarette, then headlights swept across her and she inhaled elegantly, losing twenty years.

'You're early,' Vic said.

'It was the last ferry,' she told him, and Vic nodded as though he hadn't known. 'You could give me a key, I could wait inside.'

'Feeling guilty?'

'Not when I'm with you, Vic.' She hugged his arm, looking up into his face.

'It's Herbert I feel sorry for,' Vic said as he unlocked the door.

'Yes!' she giggled. 'It's awful, isn't it? Sitting down to his cold supper like a good little boy.'

They went inside. 'You sit down by the window,' Vic said, not kissing her. This was better, normally he had her running upstairs by now and it was half over. Betty knew she was getting through to him. 'Take your shoes off,' Vic said, still not letting her kiss him. 'Drink? Gin-and-splash?'

'Nigel used to say it like that,' she confided, wanting Vic to know. Every time she saw him she'd wanted to tell him that and now she had. She sat barefoot. 'Vic.' She whispered: 'Vic, did you kill my first husband? Did you kill Alan?'

Vic laughed. 'You like not liking me, don't you?'

She leaned back in the armchair and toasted him with her eyes over the rim of the glass, her stockinged feet crossed on the seat of the chair opposite her. He gazed at them. She even lacquered her toenails like Ria. He turned away.

'Did you, Vic?' she whispered.

'No.'

He lifted her feet off the seat, sat in their place, stroked them in his lap. 'No,' he repeated gently, remembering the bubbles streaming from Alan's mouth.

'Vic, I wouldn't want nothing to happen to Herbert. He's a good sort.'

'Why should anything happen to him?'

'I want you to take me away,' Betty sighed. 'Far away from here. You've got plenty of money, we can afford it. It's not running from the past. To our future together, Vic.'

'That easy.'

'Take me with you. Let everything go, Vic. I want your love, I want to be with you.' She showed all of herself to him in these naked words, words which meant so much more to her than his caresses, her dreams so real now that they were almost within her grasp. 'Being together,' she said.

He knew she was thinking of the things that bloody women always dreamed up if they got the chance: shipboard nights, the Caribbean, islands and sunsets, escape. She must be desperate. They had heads for things like travel brochures, not for the important things. *She'll never have a father*, Vic heard again, her own words echoing through his mind.

'I'd like to do that,' Vic said.

*She'll never know her father.*

'You and me,' she said, 'and Lola too, maybe.'

Betty looked so eager. She didn't know him at all. Not the first thing about Vic. She was blind and deaf and ignorant, everything but dumb; she listened only to herself. She didn't see *him*. Gin-and-splash! They thought too much and when they got old, like Betty had let herself get old, in her head, they got too many memories. They got weighed down. Still good-looking though.

'Got you a present,' Vic said. 'Fix yourself another drink.' He went out to the car, coming back with a white card box which he laid carefully on the bar counter. Betty gave a little clap of excitement.

'Is it for me?'

'All for you,' Vic lied.

Betty lifted the lid, the layers of tissue paper

fluttering from her anxious fingers, then she pulled out the cream and blue dress with the old-fashioned frilly bits leading down from the shoulders to meet in the cleavage, a high frilly neck. You never saw anything like its quality nowadays. It even smelt special.

'Oh, it's lovely!' she gasped, holding it in front of her.

Vic's mind fled back to when he was a child. It was Christmas 1913, he and the lads had stolen the best goose on the island for Mum and they'd scoffed every last scrap, and the family were just off full-bellied to St Luke's church for the afternoon service Esther loved. Earlier Vic had given Ria an amazing present, the first time he'd ever bought anything for cash: a cheap'n'cheerful gaudy sparkle that suited her personality perfectly; it even had a bit of opal that matched her eyes. He'd been so proud of himself! Ria had ignored it. Later, Ben London, their serious-faced lodger a week shy of his fourteenth birthday, was giving Ria her Christmas present from *him*, and Vic was crouched jealously behind the curtain, excluded. It was a cream and blue dress.

He remembered how Ria's face had lit up.

Vic swallowed. 'And there's a cape too, that goes over your shoulders.'

Betty hesitated. 'Shall I put the dress on right now?'

'Do it,' Vic said hungrily.

'I know what you want,' Betty said.

*I'm Vic Price. Remember me.*

Betty slipped her coat off, Vic snatched it. She was

wearing a brown nonentity of a working dress, big black buttons; he threw it into the armchair. 'You have to wear petticoats,' he muttered, 'layers of petticoats.' He pulled them from the box, flouncy stuff, and a corset. 'They didn't have bras in those days.'

'Ooh, Vic. That's going too far. You're making me feel like a tart.'

'It was ladylike in them days.'

'If you say so.' She gave him a little peck, trusting him.

Finally she stepped into the dress, wriggled into it, petticoats and all. 'It's perfect,' she said.

'I know,' Vic said. From waist to frilly neck was done up with ten tiny navy blue buttons. He could see her fingers enjoyed doing them up. How they loved dressing up in fine clothes. Do anything for them.

'How do I look?' Betty twirled, her invisible bare feet making scuffing noises on the cheap carpet. She stopped. 'Do I look like her, Vic?'

He didn't reply. The only illumination came from a pretty table-lamp with a red shade; probably Vic had brought it down in a carload of stuff from the Old Bull and Bush. The end wall was the window overlooking the river but there was nothing to see, only the night; the glass was a black mirror on the room, herself standing there not looking at all like herself in a funny old cream and blue dress, Vic with his face obscure. A line of streetlights shining on the Isle of Dogs gleamed through the image, joining their figures like a necklace.

Betty giggled. She reached out for her drink. 'Well,

you wanted me to dress up. Men always do, don't you? You want to make us something we aren't. Well, here I am. Yours, darling.' She held out her arms, slopping the drink, just a drip. She finished it before she lost any more, putting the glass down carefully, her expression very serious. 'She isn't dead, is she?'

Vic waited.

'I knew you weren't telling the truth,' Betty grinned. 'Ria isn't really dead to you. Never. Now I look like her.' She put her hands under her hair, but it was the dress that was important. 'I'll take her place. . . .'

Vic seized her with terrible strength, his thumbs on each side of her windpipe, overwhelming her. She passed out almost at once. Her hands around his wrists relaxed. It was like a murder in a film, none of the horror of real life, her face didn't discolour or her tongue stick out of her mouth. He let her go. She fell limply and he stepped over her, did up his jacket and opened the smuggler's hole behind the bar counter, dragging her down the weedy steps before she stiffened. He knew all about rigor mortis, remembered how Ray Trott's hands stiffened around Nigel's neck . . . the look in Nigel's eyes staring up into his own. It was dark down here in the boathouse, the stink of the outfall was disgusting, and Vic's feet squelched in slime on the bottom steps. He lit a match, observing the slick surface of the mud that floored the place, probably fathoms deep. Illuminated by the wavering flame, he saw the end wall of wooden double doors like a lock-up garage's, but rotten and gap-toothed from the corrosive river-water, and the rising tide was already bubbling under them. He tied the body to one of the timbers supporting the rickety mooring platform lest it be swept away.

*A gentle and loving man who always wanted to be. But people never let him be.* Betty had been right about that at least. But not about Ria. She had long been dead to him. He had exorcised a ghost, that was all.

Vic dreamed of his daughter. Of course he didn't know what Lola looked like, he'd last seen her when she was only five and a half years old, but he imagined her as a young woman. Neither did he know where in the world she was, but it looked like Majorca or Bermuda or one of those far-off places. She was wearing a one-piece swimming costume that he'd bought her, swirly blues and greens. She knew she could have whatever she wanted. She was running on her long suntanned legs in the surf, like off the cover of a travel brochure, then she saw him in the deckchair and waved, turning towards him across the dry sand, digging in her toes for grip, racing towards him with the sand speckling her wet ankles, her shins. She skidded on to her knees beside him, wrapping a towel around her wet black hair. Obviously she knew him, they were great friends. 'Come on in, Dad,' she whispered, they were that close, 'the water's lovely.' Her eyes, those beautiful eyes like Ria's, opals spangled with tawny flecks of old gold.

*Dad.*

Vic woke smiling.

There was knocking under the floor. He got out of the armchair and fetched a broom from the cupboard, took it down below. The light was behind him as he descended and in his shadow Betty was crouched like an ungainly bird at the limit of the rope, two or three steps below him. He moved so that he could see her. The cream and blue dress was splashed and smeared with mud, dirty as sin. The rising water rinsed her bare grubby toes which stuck out beneath the hem of the dress; he glimpsed her lacquered toenails, dark red. He pushed her under with the broomhandle in the back of her neck and held her there with all his force until the water and the mud killed her.

*I'm Vic Price. Remember me.*

One day Lola would have a father. And she would know her father.

## 3

'This had better be worth getting me out from work,' Victoria said. She was sitting in the back of the Rolls with her hair still ponytailed – she had not undone it as she would if she'd stopped work – and Lisa noticed she kept glancing at her watch, making her point. Victoria lived her life at a hundred miles an hour. London traffic was too slow for her, though Bill Simmonds, his short white razor-stropped hairs showing neatly beneath the back of his chauffeur's peaked cap, seemed to cruise ahead smoothly and steadily whatever the traffic conditions. At crowded junctions he raised one hand to assert the direction he wished to take, and cut through in the sure knowledge that other cars got out of the way of a Roller. His head rarely moved to the left or the right. Such perfection was almost inhuman.

Victoria looked at her watch. 'You have no idea at all what it's about?'

'Victoria, all I know is that Charlie Bookkeeper rang and suggested a meeting at his office in Holborn,' Lisa murmured.

'Obviously it's about my father.'

Lisa shrugged.

'I never have asked you where he is,' Victoria reminded her.

'Such strongmindedness – or is it that you just don't care?'

'You know where my father's gone, don't you?'

'Yes, I think I have a fair idea.'

'I don't want to know,' Victoria said. 'I know he gets my letters, and I've spoken to him on the phone. I don't want him to interfere. It's my life and I want to show him what I can achieve. He left it up to *me*. Well, I know myself now.'

'Children usually think so,' Lisa said dryly, 'but you can't pretend your father doesn't exist. Or that your mother didn't. Their lives are your past. I haven't heard you talk of Pearl for – oh, for years.'

'I'm busy.'

'Is it worthwhile?'

Victoria laughed for the first time.

'Only later does one have regrets,' Lisa murmured. She was finally selling London House. It would go to

436

Lord Lancaster, a man she had never met and did not want to meet. This episode in the family's life was over at last, the place had become only a shell of the family home Ben had made of it in the thirties. Lisa's feelings had never recovered from that dreadful morning of the bomb and she was pleased, or perhaps just relieved, to be moving to a pleasant mews house in Mayfair without family connections, rented from the Grosvenor Estate. Victoria would be coming with her. In the smaller house, Lisa told herself, she would win back some of the influence over Victoria she had lost. Lisa was sixty-seven but she no more thought herself old than Victoria thought herself young.

'The traffic's heavy today,' Victoria said, pressing the intercom button. 'Simmonds?'

'Yes, Miss?' Like all chauffeurs Bill Simmonds had rewired the intercom so that he eavesdropped on the conversation of his backseat passengers, but it was impossible to catch him out.

'What's it about, Simmonds?'

'The King is reopening the House of Commons today, Miss.'

Victoria took her finger off the button. ' "Young" Bill knows everything that goes on,' she confided to Lisa.

'His father was a wicked man,' Lisa said. 'Mr Albert Simmonds. I well remember him.'

Bill braked heavily to avoid a van which had been quite obviously pulling out.

'I remember—' Lisa murmured.

'I heard on the radio that there's been a terrible air crash,' Victoria said, moving quickly to choke off another flood of reminiscences from the old woman, 'a British European Airways Viking. Heathrow, I think.'

But Lisa was unstoppable. 'After my baby – your father – was born alive . . . sometimes I felt that without him I hardly existed. I lost him with my own hands, left him on the tenth step of the London Hospital. I should have kept him even if we were freezing or starving. I know that now. Those dreadful childhood diseases – rickets, smallpox – perhaps awful things would have happened. Perhaps not. Kept him whatever the price. All the sadness and joy I missed. It can never be imagined into existence later, Victoria. It's simply not there.' She held out her hands. There was nothing in them.

'It's gone eleven o'clock,' Victoria said. 'We're late.'

'I was flabbergasted when he told me to sell London House,' Lisa admitted. 'Flabbergasted! The place where he and Pearl had been so happy, where he brought up his family. George. Ralph. Will. You. Surely it must have meant something to him? It's as if he's deliberately cutting his links with the past.'

'He must be very lonely.'

'The phone is not the best place to talk. I feel I *ought* to know him but I don't feel I really do. I told him he must consult the best doctors but he won't. Then I accused him of not *wanting* his sight back!'

'You were upset.'

'He didn't answer at once. "I suppose you might be right," he said. Then he simply said, "I *want* you to sell London House." Well, I've done it. But I don't understand him.' Lisa's cheeks were flushed red, her eyes hot, and Victoria noticed her left hand was clenched into a fist.

'You'll frighten Mr Bookkeeper,' she said.

'It would do you the world of good,' Lisa told her as the car pulled up, 'to find a nice young man.'

'Like you did, Grandma.'

'Don't be cheeky,' Lisa grumbled. 'Wait here, Simmonds.'

'Yes, ma'am,' Bill said, saluting, then closed the door after her. The two women went inside the chambers and he waited obediently. He didn't polish the car. He didn't stand by the warm radiator smoking a Harry Wragg behind his glove. *His father was a wicked man.* Bill Simmonds sat behind the steering wheel, though the veins in his legs were already hurting, thinking of his father.

The two women came out after half an hour and he knew at once something important had happened. Lisa looked shocked. Coming down the steps Victoria kept saying it made no difference. Bill opened the car door knowing the girl always slid across the seat to make room for her grandmother. This time Victoria sat where she was without moving, legs elegantly crossed. Bill dashed round to the other side and managed Lisa's door just in time.

'Where to, ma'am?'

'Home.'

'To the Emporium,' Victoria ordered.

Bill started the engine. The traffic was snarled solid going the other way, so rather than turn back along

Holborn, he cut down to the Strand. He glanced in the rearview mirror. Lisa's shock was turning to bafflement now, but Victoria looked very self-possessed and in control of her feelings. As always. Her lips moved.

'It makes no difference,' came her voice through the little loudspeaker in the seatback by his left shoulder.

'Of course it makes a difference!' Lisa snapped.

'Not to me. He is merely giving me the power to do what I want.'

'And what is that?'

'To be myself.'

'But Ben paid such a price for those shares!' Lisa's voice responded. 'Everyone said he stole them off Ralph. I never believed it, but—'

'Obviously I deserve them.'

Bill drove at a steady twenty-five miles per hour, trying to keep his thoughts in order. If Ben London had made over his shares in the Emporium to his daughter – the other half were held by George under the terms of Georgy Leibig's old Trust settlement – then Victoria would have real power in the store. Even Bill realised the difference they made. This was red-hot gossip, and he could hardly wait to show it off in front of Hilda in the canteen. He drove calmly and smoothly past the Aldwych.

'Ben went through hell for those shares,' Lisa insisted to Victoria. 'And now he's simply given them away, signed them over to you! What on earth does he think he's doing?'

'They're not worth anything. It's not as though I could turn them into money.'

'They were Ralph's half of the voting stock in the Emporium!'

'He's throwing away his old life. London House has gone—'

'I don't think you understand, Victoria. The sheer enormity of it, you can't imagine—'

'I don't care.'

'Of course you care.'

'Don't lecture me any more,' Victoria said. 'I don't want to know.'

'I can hardly believe he's in his right mind,' Lisa murmured.

'I won't be coming with you to Mayfair,' Victoria announced.

'Oh, but it's all arranged.'

'I'll move into the apartment above the Emporium.'

Lisa was silent. Then her lips moved sadly. 'What will George say?'

'It makes no difference,' came Victoria's voice, 'what George says.'


'Congratulations,' George said. He shook her long delicate hand, kissed her cold cheeks. 'Charlie Bookkeeper called me. Welcome to the Board, Victoria.'

She looked around his office. 'I'll be moving into the apartment. I trust you have no objections.'

'No, of course not.'

He should have objected, but he couldn't raise the energy to fight Victoria. 'Cathy's left me,' he said brokenly.

'Oh, George, I am so sorry,' Victoria said, and seemed to mean it.

To George, his relationship with Cathy had seemed so sure and subtle, so unacknowledged and mature that it must remain safe, their feelings kept so unexpressed that nothing could disturb or worry them, because nothing had been said or done. *They* knew what they felt for each other, it was their secret, and he had been content, content for the first time in his life.

Now it had all gone wrong, as though someone had poisoned Cathy's mind. Last Sunday morning she had come round to Primrose House as usual, a drink, he would finish reading the Sunday papers, lunch would be roast lamb with carrots, they'd take a walk in the park afterwards holding hands like lovers. But instead of one drink Cathy took two, though they were only exquisite little glasses from somewhere in France, and then he'd found her in the kitchen crying over the carrots. It had seemed so . . . basic. The raw carrots, her red eyes.

'People usually cry over onions,' he had reminded her gently.

'It's not about the carrots.' Had she cut herself? 'It's about us.'

'Thank God, I thought – never mind. Are you boiling or baking them?'

'George, if you're going to start off like that I'll leave right now.' He'd sipped his drink with an

442

understanding nod, letting her blow off steam. 'We're just friends,' Cathy had said miserably.

'Sounds like a favourable prognosis to me.'

'Oh, shut up. It's so friendly and companionable and nice and boring between us, and I like you so much.' She'd frowned at her glass.

'Good, then.'

'It's driving me crazy. Oh God, I hate these glasses, George. George? I don't want lunch with you or the theatre with you or a walk in the park with you, I just want you. I want you.'

'Well, I want you, too,' George said.

'Stop flying on automatic pilot, and look at me. *Look* at me.'

'I am looking at you.'

'What do you see?'

'You, Cathy.' She was wearing a belted woollen dress, she'd done something to her hair, but he couldn't remember how it had been.

'You're taking me for granted,' she said. 'You're taking *us* for granted.'

'You know what I feel for you.'

'No. I don't.'

'Well, you must know by now,' he'd chuckled.

'All I know is that we're living like a happily married couple.'

'Well, then.'

'Like we've been married for ten or twenty years and we hardly remember to look at one another, and the kids have left home and it's all behind us. It's all in front of us, George. At least it's supposed to be. How have I failed you?'

'Failed me? You?' He noticed the lines running from her nose to the corners of her mouth. 'You couldn't fail me, Cathy. Are you trying to bully me into saying something?'

'Why do you always think I want to bully you? Is there some difficulty you have with women? Why won't you admit it?'

'But we have a perfect relationship.'

'We have a perfectly awful relationship.' As well as her eyes, now Cathy's nose had started running, and she wiped it on a teatowel.

'There's nobody,' George had said.

'You've got to face it, George, you've got to face yourself.'

'There's nobody.'

'Then it's over.' Cathy didn't throw down the teatowel or drop it back over the rail, she folded it neatly and laid it on the kitchen table. He watched in silence. She added a pinch of salt to the boiled carrots he was going to eat alone. She glanced at him, then her expression hardened and she walked out past him, fetched her coat, and he heard the front door close.

George knew he loved Cathy. At any time when she was doing the business with the folding and salting he could have admitted it, touched her and uttered the saving words, *I love you*, except he couldn't. She would no longer have been unattainable, their emotions would have been public property. So he had lost her.

Victoria was saying, 'The private lift has its own key, I believe.'

'Yes.'

She looked at him patiently. He opened drawers in his desk until he found the brass key for her, held it out. 'You mustn't let Cathy get to you,' Victoria said without remorse.

'I don't think I can live without her,' George confessed. 'I've been such a fool.'

'I've seen her at work every day this week. Quite cheerful.'

'Doesn't she look upset?' George asked pathetically. 'It's very difficult to tell with Cathy unless you really know her. She's so professional.'

'No,' Victoria said authoritatively, 'she's not upset at all. She wanted you for your money, George. She's just a headhunter. But you're right,' she added thoughtfully, 'she is very good at her job.'

'I miss her so much,' George said, thinking only of his own hurt feelings. He couldn't help licking his wound. 'I feel so humiliated. I suppose what you say is true. It was there in front of me but I never saw it. It makes me hate myself.'

'I should take a holiday,' Victoria suggested casually.

'Not now.'

'The next full meeting of the Board is on Monday as usual?'

'I can't think of that now. You understand.'

'Yes, I do understand. I think the agenda should include that third floor, don't you? I know Clifford costed reopening the place. It's just darkness, it irritates me every time I come upstairs.'

'If you say so.'

'I'll have a look at the figures over the weekend,' Victoria said obligingly. She had no intention of doing more than glance over them, but it was important to chivvy George, even to the point of making him complain at her interference: he would be following her lead. 'Can we finance redecorations and stock from our own capital? Will we have to borrow from the bank? Who's the important person there? What's our credit rating? Should we expand present departments or open new ones?'

'I don't know,' George said wearily. He managed a smile. 'You're quite something, Victoria. You really do remind me of my mother. She always knew exactly what she wanted.'

'And did she always get it?'

'I'm afraid so.'

'I'll talk matters over with you before the meeting opens,' Victoria said. 'We don't want the family to look disorganised, do we?'

She left him alone in his office and leaned back against the door with a smile, then tossed the key in her fist. She'd won.

David Jones came up to her. He held out his hand like a gentleman.

'I've come to offer my congratulations, Victoria,' he said.

'Thank you,' she smiled. He must have known his days were numbered.

Bill Simmonds drove David Jones home to Wimbledon as usual. Nothing else was usual. It was a

Saturday mid-afternoon and shafts of wintry sunlight glared around the edges of fat black clouds hurrying across a cold, pale sky. Normally his passenger did not require Bill's services until closing time at five in the evening, more often six. But the summons had come out of the blue and caught Bill with a boiling hot mug fresh from the urn, and he'd been so surprised at the bell he slopped the tea down his front, and Spurs went one down on the radio. By the time Bill got himself shipshape they were level pegging. The commentator's starchy description faded behind him. 'Tell yer when yer come back,' Hilda called.

'Don't bother!' Bill cursed, slamming the car door and firing up the motor. He hated his uniform to be less than perfectly turned out for driving, even if no one but him would know about the cold trickling patch over his pot-belly, between the fourth and fifth buttons.

David Jones was waiting on the corner of Old Bond Street, the toecaps of his shoes stuck out over the edge of the kerb, standing on his heels like a man in shock. He still had his black hat and hardwood cane, he was holding his gloves in his left hand, and his brogues were beautifully polished as usual. The man bumped the door as he got in, then sat like a sack of potatoes. 'Are you all right, sir?' Bill asked in a low, respectful voice.

'Wimbledon.'

David Jones tried to pretend everything was normal on the ride home, but Bill wasn't fooled. David Jones had got the shove, everyone had seen it coming but him. He'd had a circle of friends, a lot of people owed David Jones plenty, but it was not the job of a manager to be loved.

Bill pulled up outside the front door. It was opened at once and the heavy figure of Harriet Jones, fluttering silks, blinking sleep from her eyes, anxiously descended the steps. The first conclusion a wife was going to jump to was a sudden illness, a heart attack. Fear and relief chased themselves across her face, then shock.

'Thirty years of our lives,' David Jones said.

Bill closed the car door quietly. He had left the engine running and its murmur was almost soundless.

David Jones reached out to Harriet. He had started at the Emporium at the age of sixteen, a willowy boy running errands in the Gentleman's department, working from seven in the morning until seven at night, sleeping in the male staff dormitory. Harriet had been a cheerful, ordinary girl working in the post room. Bill, watching, shook his head sadly. Those young people were inside them still, somewhere, he supposed. They knew no other life. David kissed Harriet but she turned her face away. Bill got in the car and drove.

Rain started, then hail came sweeping across Wimbledon Common like a white sheet, the windmill disappeared, and people walking back from the football started to run. Bill parked beneath a tree to save the paint and watched the fun, the same old London story: umbrellas blowing inside out, coats flapping, people holding newspapers over their heads sliding in the slush; one old man came a terrific cropper, turning in half a circle when he got up, then setting off again in another direction completely. He saw the fat lady with two terriers try in vain to disentangle them from their leads as they raced round and round her, yapping, winding themselves up until finally she grabbed them and tucked one under each arm, then sailed on before the storm like a ship under full canvas. One of the dads, hailstones bouncing on the back of his neck, bent down to his kid who was laughing about something and hit him across the head with his rolled-up newspaper, twice, three times, terrific soggy blows. That'll teach the lad, Bill thought approvingly, who had no children of his own.

Again Bill thought of his father. He didn't want to see him, he didn't want to feel old. He wanted to remember Dad as he was, a man to look up to, white shirt tucked in tight over his pot belly and that glint in his eye playing pitch-and-toss, 'Penny heads! Penny tails!' and all the children watching him, a vanished age. All gone and it would never come back.

*His father was a wicked man.*

Bill didn't want to know.

He realised that the hail had stopped and the sun had come out. The put-upon father of the naughty child was emptying hailstones out of his turn-ups.

'Young' Bill, an elderly chauffeur in his sixties still denying his age, started the engine then bought a bottle of whisky at the off-licence in the village and returned north of the river. He drove to Chelsea and parked in Collingwood Road. Once all this place had been slums, no doubt, but the Collingwood Road Estate was an experiment from the thirties, already old-fashioned but solidly built. The buildings looked a bit like wirelesses, some of them, and local lads had broken the curved windows which must be difficult to replace. Bill followed the sign along a paved courtyard to the old folk's home. Oh, it was nice. They kept them well treated and under control, early morning tea, afternoon tea, Horlicks at bedtime, and three square meals a day. They sat in rows of armchairs down the walls, looking like skinny brown chicks under identically permed hair. The nurses were cheerful and told him he'd come in the wrong side, the men's was round the other end of the building.

He didn't recognise his father. He stood right by him in the hall, looking, but he didn't see the old boy until the nurse pointed him out.

'Hello, Dad.'

Bert Simmonds was sitting in an armchair with a stretch cover. He was wearing a jacket, pyjama trousers with faded stripes, and cinnabar-red slippers held on by elastic. His liver-spotted hands were clasped in his lap and white strands had fallen over his face. He was asleep. Bill sat beside him and swore he was never going to end up in a place like this.

'Dad, I've brought yer a bottle of whisky,' he said loudly.

He put it in the old man's lap. The hands grasped it.

'Are yer all right, Dad?'

'Don't leave me,' Bert Simmonds said.

'It's me. Yer Bill. Yer looking all right.' They sat for a while.

'Don't leave me.'

450

'I won't leave yer,' Bill said, squeezing his eyes shut, 'but I got to go. I got the car with me and she's not mine. Not really mine.'

'Yer all the same,' Bert Simmonds said, 'ungrateful bastards. My best years for yer.'

Bill got up to go. 'Dad, 'ave yer ever done anything yer was ashamed of? I mean really ashamed?'

Bert looked at him as though he was crazy.

It was a relief to leave. Bill looked back from the outside, the paved courtyard, the bright sunlight, the hurrying clouds, and realised that one day he too would be old. He was that man. In his father he had seen what he would soon become.

He didn't come back to see Dad again, and old Bert Simmonds died two months later, in the New Year. The home sent notification to the wrong address at Wharncliffe Gardens, the old fourth-floor flat where no one had lived for years, so Bert Simmonds didn't bring his family back together even for an afternoon, even in death.

Terry slept all afternoon on his single bed in his attic bedroom at the Old Bull and Bush in Cable Street, the same cramped room he'd had since he was a child. He woke slowly, blinking his eyes open, very comfortable with his hands behind his head. Still with his trousers on, but his shoes off. Here he was safe.

It had hardly changed since those days, this room the schoolboy had come home to for holidays in his grey flannel shorts, Vaudey school cap and blazer, probably knocked about already and his shirt torn and splashed with mud balls by the village kids in Greenwich or Millwall, but it was a school rule that you had to travel home in school uniform. Terry liked rules, you knew where you were with them, you knew how far you could go. And when he got home Uncle Vic was here, open arms and a laugh, a good solid hug, and there were more rules, but they were different ones, Uncle Vic's ones, and the most important of them was that you didn't have to take any nonsense from outsiders. With Uncle Vic your enemies became the people who had been your friends, people at school maybe, and the people you were encouraged to look up to at school, the police, social workers, all the types who wanted to own your soul.

People who had such a high opinion of themselves that they didn't want to help you, they just wanted you to be like them.

This June afternoon he lay on the same bed with the same counterpane, same bedside table with a lamp on it, without a shade, and same battered old deal chest-of-drawers in the niche made by the dormer window. No one came in here, not even the cleaning lady. He'd repainted the room himself – white, you couldn't go wrong with white emulsion, and white gloss for the door and window-frame, matching guaranteed. Same old carpet, same old mess, the wooden Fairey Fox escorting an Avro bomber was broken but still faithfully on patrol, and the pile of yellowing newspapers and magazines remained in their place. It was a comfy room, too hot on a sunny day because of the south-facing black slate roof, but he had his ironing-board with neatly folded socks and coloured shirts sorted on one end; in the corner a classy trouser-press (purchased from the London Emporium, natch); and behind the door, where it couldn't be glimpsed by anyone outside, a photograph of Victoria London at a party wearing a streamer in her hair and a silly expression. It was overexposed and one of the streamers cast a squiggly shadow down her face, but it was his favourite photo of her and he never looked at it without affection. She was a wonderful girl, the girl of his dreams. She accepted him as himself.

Even Vic never came in here. Only Terry had a key to his room. This room was his personal property and Vic respected that.

Beneath Terry's chest-of-drawers was a loose board, and beneath that was a shooter, loaded, wrapped in oilcloth.

Because today was a Saturday Vic was downstairs in the bar, doing business with a swede, an outsider from the Cardiff docklands, so he was putting on the show. There was a touch of the impresario about Vic when he was gaining the confidence of customers. He seemed to love people round him, he got them going, he was the life and soul of the party. Terry grinned, hearing their laughter echoing up the stairs, then rolled out of bed and stretched. The sunlight had left the window. He began to prepare for the evening, the careful ritual of bath, proper shampoo on his hair, trimming his fingernails. Looking casual took as much effort as dressing up in starched collar, white tie – you needed a servant to do the knot properly – spats and patents, and he still saw young toffs come slumming dressed like that. But Victoria said they were daddies' boys, so Terry dressed to meet her as though he was just passing by, wool jacket swung over his shoulder, a good soft-collar shirt and a sports tie, flannel slacks, smart but very casual. He knew what she wanted.

He finished up and hooked his jacket casually from his finger over his shoulder, went a few steps downstairs. Here were the steps where he had hidden as a child in pyjamas, supposed to be in bed, watching the party below. There was something motionless about Vic's head even though he was laughing at the Welshman's jokes. Vic turned slightly, still without moving his head on his shoulders or his hand that enclosed a nearly full pint mug of beer, his mouth laughing, looking up at Terry with his eyes brown-black and motionless. The Welshman had started another story.

'Where are you off to?' Vic asked Terry, and all other voices stopped.

Terry grinned.

'Going slumming,' he said. He came down the last few steps.

'Do I know her?'

'One day all will be revealed, master,' Terry joked.

Vic gave him a push. 'Go on. And don't behave.'

Terry stepped into the warm evening air and his smile stopped. It wasn't a joke with Victoria. Being with Victoria was deadly serious, and he drove up West enjoying the setting sun lancing into his eyes, because he was coming closer to her. He was in love with her and it hurt. He hated not being with her, but he couldn't show her that. The trouble was, he'd started off with an act to attract her, leading her on like a mating ritual, and now he'd got her he dare not reveal himself. Yet he couldn't give her up. She was destroying him, tangling him up. There was nothing simple about being serious with a woman. He was living a lie, forced to hide himself from her when she was the first person he wanted to be open with.

Terry parked in Piccadilly and went round the corner to the private entrance, put the brass key she had given him in the lock, turned it. The same key operated the lift that whined and clicked four floors up to the small carpeted lobby. He combed his hair then tousled it engagingly. Jacket over shoulder, boyish grin, but the hardness in his eyes she liked. He looked confident and proud to be with her. He thumbed the doorbell, dit-dit dat, then used his key on the door and breezed in.

Victoria was working at the desk, evening filling the tall windows behind her, the desk-light slanting down her hair to the pen in her hand. She swept back her hair and looked up like someone who doesn't realise where the time has gone.

'Surprise,' Terry said.

'You make such a noise.' Victoria glanced at the art deco clock. 'Fix us a drink.' She went back to her papers.

He lifted her hair and kissed her cheek.

'I never know when you're going to be here,' she said. He knew she liked that, the way he came and went like a cat. That was why he did it.

'I want to be with you all the time,' he admitted.

'Liar!' she said, when he was being most truthful. She shook her head, freeing herself from his grasp. 'Fix that drink. Ten minutes.' Terry thought he never suffered as much as when he was with her. He mixed a couple of martinis, put hers on the desk, then stood at the open balcony window. He was never happier than when he was with her either. Listening to the scratch of her pen, the sigh of her breathing, the littlest things.

'You work as hard as a man,' he said.

'I like to arouse your competitive instincts.'

'And you always have an answer.'

She capped her pen and turned off the desklamp, came behind him and slid her arms round his shoulders. 'Say *daarlin*, darling.'

He kissed her mouth.

They walked down to the Troc and lost themselves in the crowd, dancing close among the other lovers, the language of legs. He wanted to hold her like this for ever, anonymous, close to her, no words needed. He wanted her so badly that he hoped they wouldn't make love tonight, he needed more. He needed to mean something to her.

But they went back and he knew what would happen.

Afterwards he pulled on his slacks, without underpants, and stood on the balcony. It must be the warmest night of the year so far. A few stars burned in the haze and over the curved glass spans of the Burlington Arcade. Terry reached out and with affection patted a gargoyle's head silhouetted against the streetlamps below.

'You're getting so serious,' Victoria said. 'It's very boring.' There was a light on in the bathroom and he could discern her by its glow, sitting in a mess of sheets and looking still very aware of herself. She was stark naked and she wanted to get him going again. All he could see of her was his. But he thought sadly: *only that*.

The girl he had first seen, first fallen for, was gone, leaving him sad that he couldn't make her love him.

'We're going to open up the third floor,' Victoria said, and suddenly Terry was aware of the darkened floors dropping in layers below them. 'Have I told you?' she said. 'Cathy has given George up. David Jones took early retirement, but he thought his friends would save him. But they don't, do they? I gave Cathy his job, faithful Cathy Jones following in her father's footsteps, and that kept the old boys quiet.'

'I thought Cathy loved George.'

'Never runs smooth,' Victoria shrugged.

'True love? He can't like her working here. Rubbing his nose in it, isn't she? Aren't *you*?'

'Cathy told him that if he didn't want her to do it, she wouldn't. I told George the Emporium needed her because she's so good at her job, so he came over, ever the gentleman, as I knew he would.'

'So you're keeping Cathy in the Emporium to keep George out.'

'Exactly. Killing two birds with one stone.'

Terry clapped slowly.

'You have your life, I have mine,' Victoria said.

'You've got a cute backbone, all curvy and knobbly.'

He looked round. 'I want you, not your job.'

'It is me,' Victoria said.

# PART V

## London's Daughter

August 1953 – January 1954

# Chapter Eleven

*'Look,' Edith said.*

*Peter looked cautiously. A dead baby. Pale as death.*

*'Where'd you find it?'*

*She sat in front of the stove, cuddling the bundle to her. 'Outside,' she said.*

*'I didn't see it.'*

*'You weren't looking.'*

Some stories are too terrible to be told.

Today Lola was alone. Three years and three months had passed since Rachel had revealed to them how she came to be the Countess of Coucy.

The morning was blazing hot, a rare enough event at Clawfell, so the house was empty as Ben and Ria enjoyed the sun outside, taking an inventory of the work that needed to be done: Mum's pet project, cementing Ben to her, making their lives at this house permanent. Lola had wanted to go with them, then when they actually asked her to come, she found herself claiming that she was busy.

'Suit yourself,' Mum sighed. *You're at the difficult age*, the sigh said. But she had brushed Lola's shoulder lightly with her fingertips, a loving expression in her eyes. She was the kindest woman in the world, but so out of touch.

Lola looked at Ben. He took Ria's arm and held his finger to his lips.

He knew Lola wanted to be alone. She had no secrets from him.

Lola crept behind the windows, pacing them from the shadowed rooms. She could hear their shoes crunching on the gravel as they walked around the Grange in the brilliant sunlight, with Mum prattling of course. Through the glass Lola saw that her mum's golden, streaked hair held a sunny glow. She was looking ever so lovey-dovey as usual with Ben, guiding him with her hand on his elbow, her eyes sparkling. Helen waved from the new Land Rover that had supplemented the battered truck, taking Will shopping in the village, then on to a church meeting – was there anything she could bring back? Ria shook her head, waving, and Will grinned and held up his thumb as the vehicle drove off in a cloud of August dust.

Lola understood now that Mum had always dreamed of this life, perhaps even to this moment cheerfully making plans in the sun, never telling anyone until they came true, not even the one man who could give her what she desired. If he didn't know what she wanted, she couldn't tell him . . . but now everything had come true for Ria, the slum child. Lola understood that desire, and envied it.

Lola understood secrets, that longing for something that could not be taken, only given. Why, for instance, didn't she carry her father's name?

She watched them, thinking: *Why isn't my name Lola London?*

Lola knew that Rachel's story – its truly dreadful conclusion revealed on a sunny day like today, and to Lola alone – had been bound to change her, and because she had never forgotten Rachel's words, they had come almost to haunt her. Then, Lola had been a naughty dark-eyed girl sneaking behind a curtain the night before to eavesdrop on the grown-ups' after-dinner talk. But now, following her parents from inside the house, she was in her thirteenth year, becoming an adult herself, changing however hard she tried to deny it, still clinging on to her childhood, her childish ways, sometimes leafing back through comics and books she had loved, revisiting old favourites . . . but she knew in her heart that she was slipping away from the youngster she had been. Her height was suddenly shooting up, she was acutely aware of her body changing even its shape, slimming and filling as though it lived a life of its own quite independent of her wishes. She noticed her ankles becoming shapely when she caught Geoff Lister staring at them in class, and heard him bragging lies about her and him to his pals as though she was an object, though they'd always been friends before. Some of the other grammar school boys were really cruel, knocking her books out of her arms in the corridor by the washrooms, or in the quad. Mr Parkinson, genially smoking his bloody pipe of Clan aromatic tobacco, its scent wafting in a sweet cloud downwind, his soft hands thrust in his tweed pockets, did nothing to prevent this. Lola already knew she wasn't pretty. Yet one or two boys were unusually kind, helping her pick her books up, giving her a smile.

'Look out for that one,' Jennie Housetree whispered, 'that's Charlie Trig, he's a little devil.'

'Why?'

'He's too friendly, that's why.'

For the first time in her life, Lola hardly knew who she was. Even the mirror told her she was different from the girl she had been.

*I'm Lola. I'm different.*

For Jennie everything was straightforward. 'You're Lola Trott, of course,' she'd say. 'One day you'll marry a farmer and change your name and have children. I'm going to go to university and be a doctor and never marry. But I'll still be your best friend if you like. Have you got a television? They're quite the thing to have.'

So Lola slavishly wore her fingernails long like Jennie Housetree, and Jennie whispered that she had a boyfriend, the awful Martin Breen who thought so much of himself that he was just silly, and Jennie's Mum had told Corporal Macclesey to hold him back a minute to let Jennie get home, but Jennie had developed a way of walking slowly, and getting caught. Alison Bassett, the formidable hockey captain, her face like a pudding basin overflowing with plum duff, the most appalling case of spots ever to afflict an adolescent, insisted that Jennie was a bad sort. 'You're quiet, Lola, and you're deep. You keep yourself to yourself, and that's the way to keep yourself. That's all I have to say.' She scratched a bruise and nodded reliably. 'Are you on for Friday's match? Run along then.'

And Lola obediently ran along.

She was good at running.

*I'm Lola Trott. I'm special.*

'You've got good long legs,' Alison decided, 'we'd better put you out on the wing.'

Once Lola had looked up to Alison, but now it seemed to her that everyone else was changing too. Even Mum had got difficult, because she didn't have any idea of modern clothes styles, content to wear last year's stuff or even the year before, embarrassing Lola at the school gates if her schoolfriends saw her: 'It's just my Mum,' she'd tell Jennie, and try to get Ria, who had never lost her London exuberance, away before her ways showed. But Ria always waved and cooed, turning Lola bright red among the hill-farmers' daughters thundering across Tom Tiddler's Ground. And Ria kissed her in public, and called out to her at the top of her voice, 'There she is,' waving her arms off as if Lola hadn't seen her quite well enough from the school building, 'there's my little girl!' Lola felt as awkward as Bambi crossing the quad, as though the tarmac was ice and a thousand miles wide, all arms and legs and achingly aware of herself, praying *Shush, Mum* . . . 'Wotcher, Lola!' Ria would call, waving her headscarf, and Lola stalked over with her head down and her cheeks burning, wishing the ground would swallow her up. Ria always greeted her with a splonking kiss. 'Wotcher, Lola!'

The boys picked that one up in no time, the cheery

London slang repeated in their flat Yorkshire voices. It was worse when the girls followed their lead. And suddenly Lola felt like an outsider here, where she had been brought up, among these people she spoke like, thought like, felt like, as average as any of them. Now that too was changed.

*I'm Lola*, Lola thought, *I'm special!*

Ben London knew.

Thank God when Dad picked her up from school, *he* didn't make a fool of her. Gratefully Lola drank him in with her eyes. Because he didn't encourage Jennie Housetree, she decided that she wouldn't either. Dad wasn't like anyone else. He had a way of saying, 'You'll be quite safe here,' that made her look around her with a frisson of danger. Dad knew the world was not a safe place and that was the way he liked it. At the school gate he was friendly with all the mums, and he could match their rough jokes. The corporal, hobbling out with his lollipop sign trailing behind him as soon as he saw Ben coming, almost worshipped him. Dad had a way of doing nothing, that commanded respect. He listened respectfully, too, and people knew they counted. And he made his own words count, saying little, but finishing what he started with unmistakable authority, so that often people turned to him first and last, waiting for him to speak.

Lola watched her father silently, observing him, wondering what his magic was.

And so she came to know him.

His magic was simply that he liked these people, he trusted them more than they trusted themselves – had more confidence in them than they themselves felt. They wouldn't let him down. He loved, she knew, to hear Corporal Macclesey and those grumbles about the weather and the children and his long, long stories of Blighty Valley. Dad found the man interesting. He could paint a picture in his mind from the touch and smell and sound of the large, once-impressive woman the corporal called Mrs Doctor Housetree, who collected her daughter Jennie only when her lunchtime aperitif would not be betrayed by her trembling fingers, which was not often. Mrs Doctor Housetree truly believed no one knew her secret – especially not the blind man, Mr Trott, waiting for his clumsy daughter.

At other times it was Mum at the school gates. *Wotcher, Lola!*

Today at the Grange, during the school holiday, Lola hid behind the windows, following them like an invisible presence, looking at Mum hanging all lovey-dovey on Dad's arm, as though she had fallen in love all over again. In her other hand, not that she was paying much attention to it, Mum held a notebook and she was pointing out to Dad the various repairs she wanted made, all the plans she had. They walked on and Lola darted to the next room and observed them come into view, standing back from the glass so she wouldn't be noticed. Mum was too busy enjoying herself anyway, not seeing the place as it really was. She was visualising the house of her dreams.

But Lola wondered if Dad was really so happy. He was wearing the sunglasses again. She couldn't remember exactly when he'd started putting them on but she did remember Mum had got worried about him staring at the sun because she said he didn't realise he was doing it, he was just turning his face to the warmth as far as he was concerned. Then Ben forgot to take them off, wearing them in the house, during the evening sometimes. Mum was always kidding him about his forgetfulness. In the winter months, togged up in overcoat, gloves, scarf and trilby, Ben did look like The Invisible Man, and Ria had a lot of fun with that, perhaps a little too much, elbowing Lola in the ribs and getting her in on the act too, before relenting to Ben and getting kissy. They had a good old laugh, but Lola didn't want to be got in on it. She felt apart even from the two of them. Even in joking she didn't want to choose one side or the other, and she wasn't really laughing. She pretended for Mum's sake. But really Lola just wanted them to be together.

On such a bright day as today the sunglasses looked perfectly normal and it was Mum who looked funny, squinting, holding the notebook over her eyes as she examined the cornices against the sunlight. Ben turned his head as though he was looking straight at Lola in the window.

Then Ria was saying something, her voice but not her words coming to Lola through the glass, and the moment passed, Ben nodding tolerantly. Whatever you say, dear.

Lola frowned. *She* could see he didn't care about whatever Mum was talking about. But he *always* cared, that was why they cared about *him*.

But Ria couldn't see it. Or wouldn't. Ben was getting ready to move.

Their time here was ending. Lola knew it, it was so obvious in the way Ben stood, listened so tolerantly, was so kind to the woman he loved. He knew none of this mattered. Ria didn't believe it because she didn't want to believe, and so she was making her plans for the house and the garden and Lola and she stuck as close to Ben as she could. But the signs were there broad as daylight if only Ria looked for them: Ben's increasing business correspondence through the solicitor, his order to Lisa that London House be sold, the painful gift of his shares in the Emporium to Victoria. Relinquishing all his links to Pearl, Ria doubtlessly told herself, and had wanted to understand *that* very well, of course, and cherished him all the more for it. Yes, love was sometimes blind.

Lola had the unwelcome feeling – and like all her feelings now, it was so *strong* – that Mum, growing closer to Ben after the troubles that had separated them, was rejecting her. The more Lola changed to be like her mother in feminine appearance and ways of thought, the more a veil seemed to fall between them. Communication seemed frustratingly muffled. Ria's lovey-doveyness seemed deliberately designed to exclude Lola. *I've* got him, she had seemed to Lola to be saying as she walked Ben outside the house, dragging him along by his arm as she did, concentrating his mind on her. Drainpipes, gutters, cornices – no, Lola realised, she was really saying Ria, Ria, Ria! That was Mum through and through, selfish to a degree, thinking only of herself. Me, me, pay attention to me.

Lola saw right through her mum. Ria dreamed of being married. She hadn't given a moment's thought to what the consequences of marrying Ben London would be, of course. Being Ria her head was full of wanting what she wanted and hang the consequences. So far Ben had saved her from herself.

They disappeared around the corner of the house and Lola cut through to the next room, the library, rows of morocco-bound volumes dusted by Ria but left respectfully unread. She opened the secret door and scampered up the stair inside the wall. She glimpsed their heads from an open upstairs window, and heard Ria complaining about a drainpipe.

'Put it on your list,' Ben said fondly. He was enjoying this time with her, stamping it on his memory as if it was the quiet before the storm, and Lola was reminded, not of the flashing thunderstorms that could come rolling excitingly across the wild moorland here, but of days of drab grey rain sliding across rows of rooftops and small dark streets between them . . . it was a childhood memory.

Lola could hardly remember where she had come from. She and Mum didn't go back to London because they didn't want to, because they loved him and that was a nice way for things to be, Lola knew. Mum was happy here, she had the man she loved, she had Will here, and she had Lola. Her family around her. Ben had given her this. What was he up to?

Lola crouched below the window. This side of the house was in shadow.

She shivered, listening to her parents' voices drifting, fading, until there was silence. She closed her eyes.

*Some stories are too terrible to be told.*

Lola ran through the rooms, her hands out in front of her, her skirt flapping around her long legs. She was wearing the shoes with heels Ben had let her buy on a trip to Manchester, ladylike shoes, so that she was afraid she might turn her ankle running like a panicky little girl like this, not really at all the young lady Mum wanted her to be. Ria had bought her lovely gold earrings on the same trip, supposed to be for special, but Lola wore them every day. When Ria had asked why, Lola had put her head on one side. 'Because every day is special, isn't it?'

'You're a funny one you are,' Ria had replied. 'You just want to wear them, that's what I think.'

Lola wondered if Mum had ever been this age. Mum had almost everything she'd ever wanted! Did she have to be so moody about anything Lola wanted, almost mocking? A kind of jealousy of youth, for the years Ria had lost that Lola had to look forward to. '*It's not my fault*,' Lola whispered, and pressed the earrings safely against her skin as she ran. She slowed, then rested her forehead against a cool windowpane.

She opened her eyes. It was the very place.

Lola remembered. She had come upon Rachel standing at this same window, bathing her face in the early May sun. It was the morning after Rachel's account of her childhood, of the adopted family she had unwittingly sent to their deaths, instead of saving them as she thought, by allowing the Nazi collaborator Monsieur Hulda to possess her. Much more than a monster to frighten children. *Be silent, or the Hulda will get you!* And he had. Lola had approached the Frenchwoman silently, a shy skinny girl reaching out for the adult woman who had known so much, suffered so much.

'Rachel Céleste.' Rachel had clapped her hand to her breast, gave a startled intake of breath. Her hair was curled into little licks under her ears.

'Oh la! You gave me such a fright!'

'I didn't mean to. Can I talk to you? It's such a lovely name, Céleste,' Lola had murmured.

'No one has called me it for years.' That day Rachel was wearing, not the Coucy pearls, only a plain skirt dark as spilled wine, and a white blouse nipped to her tiny waist.

'The lost one.'

'So you were listening,' Rachel had said without rancour.

'You knew I was.'

'Yes, I did.'

'You wanted me to. You wanted me to hear.'

Rachel had pointed from the window. 'Look, your father is walking outside. I told him how lucky he is to live in such a remote, heavenly place, to have escaped from the city. He has even built up his family around him. He has become successful at last.'

'He was always successful. He was a millionaire.'

'That is not a success. It is merely a number.'

Lola had leaned her elbows on the windowsill, watching the figure of her father, his back turned to them, walking on the white ribbon of the drive. Sheep were grazing the grass and he stopped, listening to them.

'He would do anything for you, Lola,' Rachel said. 'I mean it, nothing held back. A woman knows. He would die for you.'

They watched him walk on again, feeling with his stick on the grass, his feet following the white ribbon.

'He is a lucky man,' Rachel said. She had looked down at Lola.

'I think he makes his own luck,' Lola said.

'Lola, may I ask you a question? Why were you so determined to listen to such a history as mine, that I recounted last night?'

Lola looked up at the French girl, their faces, woman and child, almost nose to nose in the sun.

'Because you said it was a story too terrible to tell.'

'But—'

'But then you told it. So I knew it wasn't the worst. There is something worse.'

Rachel looked serious, then laughed. 'I see! One should never attempt to deceive a child.' She breathed a sigh. 'They are too logical. Yes, there is always something worse.'

'François doesn't know, does he? You can't tell François.'

'Even though I love him. Yes, that is the whole point. He was angry with me last night because he was trying to protect me. You may know that at the end of 1945 I was expecting a baby. He was born. He was born fully formed, dead. There is worse. I cannot give birth to another child, the doctors say it would kill me, and I have not told François. Because of me, *because* of me, he will be the last Count of Coucy. A thousand years . . . and I love him.'

'Rachel, I'm so sorry. It's so unfair on you.'

Rachel brushed Lola's hair out of her eyes. 'You must be cold in only that nightdress. I'll shut the window.'

'I'm not cold.'

'All right, then.'

Lola waited. 'What are you going to do that is so terrible, Rachel?'

'For me the decision is very simple. For his own sake I could pretend I do not love him, then there could be a divorce, but the church would never permit it. In the case of my death, of course, he could marry again, but I could not commit suicide. Therefore, when I fall with child again, I shall be exchanging a death for a life. Don't cry. It happened before, remember.'

'But she was an old lady! You're young and pretty, with your whole life in front of you.'

'I am the Countess of Coucy. I know my duty, Lola. I owe him a life.'

'But, Rachel—'

'You must say nothing.' She pressed the tip of her finger to Lola's lips. 'Say nothing. I am happy. I have found myself.'

Lola had realised how tough Rachel was – and how tough she expected Lola to be. Nature threw you away as soon as you'd had children. Rachel had dropped to her knees, hugging Lola to her, covering her face, Lola's high-coloured cheeks, the dark arches of her eyebrows, even the child's pale eyelids with remorseful, silent kisses.

Five months ago François had written that Rachel was expecting a baby. Lola had read the letter to Ben walking back from the post office after school. Her mouth had gone dry when she saw the envelope and she remembered exactly what Rachel had said. 'Dad, there's a funny-seven letter.'

'You've noticed!' Ben had been delighted at her keenness of observation, and if he noticed the dread in her voice, and of course he did, he chose to ignore it. 'His mother did them with a crossbar too, I remember.' He swung his stick as they walked. 'Open it up, it's from François.'

But Lola had hesitated. 'But suppose it's bad news?'

'Suppose it is, my love.' He stopped her with his hand on her arm. 'I know how much you liked Rachel. Good or bad, it has to be faced, doesn't it?'

'Yes, but Rachel is my friend. I wish *you* could read what François says.' She looked up at him with her dark gaze.

'It doesn't matter,' Ben said harshly. 'Sometimes bad things have to happen as well as good. And most often, Lola, they're all mixed up. Lola?' he called.

'Just then,' she said, standing quiet as a mouse, 'you sounded very cruel.'

He turned back to her. 'I couldn't help myself,' he said. 'I'm sorry if I frightened you. I was angry with me, not you.'

'I'm never frightened when I'm with you.'

Lola opened the letter. 'Rachel is expecting a baby within the next six months or so,' she said. Her lip trembled.

'You worry about things too much,' Ben said gently. 'Rachel is determined not to fail. Either way now, whether by her life or her death, she wins, and that's all that's important.'

*Oh*, thought Lola, *what an awful place the world can be.*

Ben took her hand and squeezed her lightly. 'You saw François. Does he look like me?'

'Yes, he does, Daddy.'

'Does he really?'

'I saw it at once!'

'Then everything is a bonus. You see, Lola, I have no secrets from you.' He walked on, and she ran to catch him up, matched his stride, then slipped her hand into his.

'I love you, Dad.'

'I love you too, Lola. Very much.'

They walked. She looked up. 'Not one?'

He chuckled. 'Go on, ask away.'

'Do you really love Victoria?'

He looked surprised at her choice of question. 'Yes, I do.'

'I saw her once,' Lola said wistfully, 'it was in the hospital, and she was ever so pretty, I thought I'd never seen anyone as pretty as she was. I wished I could grow up to be like her. She wasn't that much older than I am now.'

'I like you as you are.'

'I'm glad really. When you talk to her on the phone you don't sound close to her. You make me feel cold.'

'Lola,' Ben confessed, 'when she was a child I treated Victoria badly. I was too kind, her mother doted on her, and we gave her everything she wanted. We thought that was love. But it isn't. It isn't nearly enough.'

'What do you want her to –' Lola searched for the word – 'achieve?'

'Herself.'

Lola walked beside her father in silence. 'It's so hard to believe you're blind.'

They sat on a narrow footbridge over the leat, Lola swinging her legs over the edge, Ben sitting motionless as a statue. He wrapped his hands around his walking stick, his knuckles standing out white. Then he reached out to Lola and pulled her very gently to him.

'I've been blind almost all my adult life, Lola,' he whispered. 'I was blind since that spring morning in 1921, in Havannah Street, when I let your mother go. I should have stayed with her, held her tight, kept her whatever price I had to pay. Everything that ever happened to me after that has been wasted time, because all the time I loved Ria. But I couldn't admit it. I mean *really* admit it, give up everything for her. All those years, Lola, I hardly saw her – once, or twice, by chance . . . but because her love never wavered, she held my life together like a thread.'

Lola rested her cheek on his shoulder.

'I think that's lovely.'

477

'I was a failure, Lola. Remember that. Because I failed Ria.'

The smooth surface of the leat slid beneath them. Lola brushed the water with the toe of her school shoe, pulling out a long vee of ripples.

'She gives me life,' Ben said.

'I wish I had everything I wanted,' Lola said enviously.

He laughed. 'You wouldn't go to school, you'd be one of those flippin' kids lying in bed all day listening to the Goons. And I'd look like Jack Hawkins.'

'Why won't you marry her now?'

His grin died. He didn't reply.

Lola warmed to her subject. 'A big church wedding with bells, and everyone happy and thousands of people. You know how Mum loves showing off! I'd wear a long dress covered with flowers, pinks, yellows—' She stopped as he pulled away from her a little.

'It wouldn't be that easy,' he said. 'There wouldn't be anything easy about marrying Ria.'

No, Ben thought, as he sat with Lola on the footbridge, his eyes closed behind the dark glasses. There would be nothing easy about marrying Ria, acknowledging Lola as his daughter. The heavy tortoiseshell frames hurt his nose, as always, but he had learned to live with that. He was almost sure Lola knew he could see. And even if she didn't believe it now, he knew he couldn't keep his secret from her for more than another few months, perhaps a little longer if he was lucky. Without him realising it, his blindness had actually become a kind of refuge, a place to hide away. They were living comfortable lives in a loving home, and he had become the willing prisoner of their happiness. Seeing changed everything. He saw that he must hurt the women he loved.

No, that wouldn't be easy.

*Not running from. Running to.*

He remembered his long trek into Africa in search of Roland, his half-brother, who had renounced war and Western civilisation, even his family, to hide himself away in the bend of the river, Bula Matari, and find a life worth living. A kind of white man's heaven, bringing peace and agriculture to the natives so that they laid down their spears for hoes. But when Roland cut down the trees to make fenced and irrigated fields, the stagnant waters brought river-blindness to the community. Ben had arrived at the native village to find the elders led out with sticks to their day's work by children too young to be blind, but who would grow up to fall blind. '*This is a good war*,' Roland, himself losing his sight, had told Ben. Ben did not believe in good wars. He believed in winning.

Without winning there was no love, only dreams that evaporated in the morning light. He held Lola tight against him on the bridge.

'It's all right, Dad, I'm here,' she whispered, 'I'm here.'

Lola was the ghost he had seen. The girl in the white nightdress. Not that at first he *saw* her as such, the mystery of sight did not work that way. For several minutes the pale, upside-down blur printed on the backs of his eyes seemed of no importance, mere cortical vision. Ben had been more aware of the touch of his fingers on the tabletop, the feel of the stem of his wine-glass, even the heat of the fire on his face had seemed more real than that hazy visual phantasm. The familiar creak of his chair as he sat back, François taking angry breaths as Rachel continued with her story in her lilting voice, the complex emotions Ben sensed in her accents and pauses, her occasionally clumsy English. The vibration of François's footsteps coming from the end of the table to comfort Rachel by the door. All these things were more real. But the blur did not fade.

Ben had tried to fix his eyes on whatever it was, and of course he could not. But he became aware of the pale blur until it dominated his attention.

It changed shape, he lost sight of it for a moment, but it came back and still it did not fade.

François was speaking. 'There will be other babies to carry on the Coucy line . . .' The sound of a light kiss, on Rachel's forehead perhaps. 'However, perhaps somehow that loss enabled Rachel to face her wartime experiences . . . to talk about them. Yes, to talk. She had to learn to speak all over again. It took years, her brain and lips had forgotten.' Ben hardly heard him. François's voice seemed to trail into a vast distance. '. . . the muscles had to learn to form the sounds, just as a baby's do . . .' Then his voice said, 'Goodnight, Ben.'

Ben forced himself to reply calmly. 'Goodnight.'

He listened to their footsteps depart.

Alone, all Ben's concentration centred on the white blob. He had felt a draught from the doorway, heard the curtain move, and the ghostly blur changed, grew larger. Then suddenly it flashed to one side and was gone.

He almost cried out with the sadness of it.

There came the click of the servants' door closing in the wall, then a faint pattering sound in the corridor. The sound of a child running back to bed.

Suppose his sight was beginning to return? Ben was very frightened.

He knew he had 'seen' Lola, yet her shape had been incomprehensible to his eyes. He had understood not one single thing about her, whether he was looking at her standing on the far side of the room, or at her face close up. He had no concept of scale or perspective, everything was flat and without meaning. He sat by the fire all night, sensing its flicker but seeing nothing he could recognise as flames.

He was afraid that if he slept, when he woke in the morning everything would be dark again. But 'morning' turned out to be worse than darkness. What he sensed was without form, a dim and exhausting luminescence that pulled his eyes this way and that. He saw only a very small area – like peering down twin tunnels, or the barrels of a shotgun. Any movement that crossed this double-sighted binocular area stood out vividly from the almost featureless background, but the reactions of his eye muscles were slow and uncoordinated. Movement was a dire and meaningless carnival that he caught only in glimpses, whirling around him when he turned his head, and he had to close his eyes from nausea.

He fumbled his way down to his bedroom and found his dark glasses in a drawer, slipped them on with a sigh of relief. Even so he stumbled giddily in the doorway, his other senses confused by his returned – he could not call this *sight* – his returned light-sensitivity. It could go as easily as it had come.

But right from the start, he dared to hope.

'Lola darling,' Ria's voice called from the kitchen, 'I don't want any coloured stuff from you today, what with I turned everything red with your socks last time. Just chuck us your nightdress and I'll bung it in the wash.'

A white nightdress. The ghost had been Lola wearing a nightdress. Obviously she had been hiding in the room last night – what else had he missed? Ben heard Lola's footsteps and only by a conscious effort did he not flinch as something passed in front of him. 'Hallo, Dad.' Yes, he recognised her voice.

'Hallo, Lola.'

A paler flash, perhaps her face – or perhaps the light on her teeth, if she was smiling. Did she have a toothy smile? He didn't know. He realised he was seeing as a baby sees, an unfocused riot of confusing light reflections, though for him everything seemed to be shades of grey. Even colours seemed to be shapes, and everything seemed to be not solid, as though people were fluid, constantly changing. His brain must learn again its old, disused skills. Even to see the right way up seemed an almost insurmountable challenge. He saw upside-down.

But if he could somehow learn to see properly, that would change everything.

To see was not enough. He must make sense of what he saw.

Because if he could see, he must make choices, and he must make the right ones.

'Are you all right, Dad?' Lola's voice asked. Her face was a riot of shapes and colours like a modern painting.

'A hangover, that's all.' Ben held his head. 'I think I had one glass too many of Will's nettle wine last night.'

'Old boozer,' called Ria.

'I'll get you an aspirin,' Lola said. 'You look awful.'

'He always looks awful,' Ria called fondly, 'don't tell him.'

'I remember Uncle Vic telling me about his pub—' Lola said.

'Never mind your Uncle Vic,' said Ria sharply, her voice coming close. 'Get along with you!'

'What was his pub called, Mum?'

'I don't remember,' Ria said doggedly. 'I've forgotten.'

Lola snapped her fingers. 'He called it the 'Bush,' she exclaimed, remembering, 'and it was in, oh, I think it was Stable Street.'

Ben said: 'Cable Street.'

'Anyway, whatever it was, he told me he sold his best customers The Hair of the Dog What Bit Them.

It was French brandy with an oyster in it and a raw egg, and a good shake of Bertie Wooster sauce.'

'That's your Uncle Vic for you,' Ben said.

'That's enough about Uncle Vic, both of you,' said Ria.

'He was very kind to me,' Lola said. 'I miss him.'

'Shut up!' Ria said. 'You're not too big to feel the flat of my hand.' Lola's footsteps scampered into the bathroom, where the medicine cabinet was kept. 'That girl,' Ria confided, 'is getting to be of an age when she's trying to wind me up.'

'Then don't worry.'

'I'm not worried.' Ria hesitated. 'You don't think she really misses him, do you?'

'Yes,' Ben said.

'You're as bad as she is,' Ria snorted, going back to the kitchen. 'What d'you reckon those French people want for breakfast?'

'No hairs of no dogs,' Ben said, and Lola laughed. Rachel's overheard story had obviously left her unaffected. Lola pressed the aspirin and a glass of water into his hand, then asked if she could run off and find Rachel. 'OK,' Ben said around the pills, 'but I don't know where she is.'

'I do,' Lola said.

Alone, Ben closed his eyes. He must get to know Lola, really know her. He thought best on the move, and went outside for a walk that Rachel and Lola witnessed from the upstairs window. It would be terribly hard to keep his secret from the child, she was so observant, but he knew it must be done. If Lola knew, so would Ria. Ria would understand at once that their life at Clawfell was finished. No one ever escaped their childhood.

Lola woke.

She was cold and stiff, in exactly the same position in which she had fallen asleep spying on Ben and Ria from that very same first-floor window. Her long legs were tucked under her where she had slumped, her head was cradled in her arms on the windowsill. The wooden edge made a painful line across her breasts. Mum had been prattling about cornices and drain-pipes, making her cheerful inventory of work to do on the house of her dreams. Work that would never be done. Lola was suddenly quite sure of it. A thousand details swarmed together in her waking mind, the dark glasses, his sixth sense, everything.

How well did she know her father? She loved him, but that wasn't the same: every duckling, even an ugly duckling, imprinted itself on its parent and swam loyally after it through the reed-beds. Mum had led her here for her own reasons, but Lola had trusted her. Now, growing up, she questioned everything.

Earlier that day, Dad had looked straight at her. Lola awoke convinced of it. He wore the dark glasses not because he was blind, but because he was not.

How little she really knew of him.

Lola blinked. Outside, she realised, everything had changed, shadows were thrown across the grass, and the air had softened with evening. Mum and Dad had probably come back into the house. Mum would be starting supper, Dad sitting at the table in the way he had, his wrists on the veined wood and powerful fingers working the knife, obligingly peeling potatoes by touch, or carrots, or whatever damned Home Farm vegetable it was. The sound of the returning Land Rover's engine carried to her and Lola put back her hair then went downstairs, waiting on the gravel as Helen pulled up. 'You look as though you've been sleeping,' Helen scolded her. 'I dropped by the post office for your father.' She handed over a bundle of letters, then the parish magazine, patting that like a special treat.

'Thanks,' Lola said. Helen beamed and drove off.

Lola sorted the letters going back into the house, the usual ones from Charlie Bookkeeper in legal envelopes doubtless containing enclosures, a few local bills addressed to Mr Trott, and a letter from France. It was postmarked Coucy-la-Ville and Lola recognised François's handwriting well enough by now. A cold hand squeezed her heart. She knew the letter contained the news of Rachel's death in labour, and the birth of a new heir for the Coucy dynasty. For a moment Lola hated François, hated all the things that destroyed people, what people did to themselves for pride and duty and love.

'What's up with you?' Ria stopped her in the corridor. 'You've got a face as long as a Monday morning.' Ria's little bit of London in Yorkshire. 'Give us a smile, darling!' She was carrying out the old scuttle, fetching more coal for the range.

Lola tried to get past. 'Helen brought some letters for Dad, that's all.'

'Oh, those,' snorted Ria. 'I hate those bloody things. They're never good news. I'd be happy if we never had any letters, wouldn't you? You sure you're all right?' Mum had her antennae up. 'You do look peaky, ever so. It's not the curse, is it?'

'Mum, don't.'

'You're not to keep quiet from your mum if there's anything worrying you. You keep too much inside yourself, you do, my girl.'

Lola put her head down. 'And nobody else does.'

'Oh, I expect I did when I was your age, love,' Ria said with such sadness that Lola wondered how deeply she knew her mother. 'Oh, my poor little Lola.' *Little* Lola – and Lola was easily as tall as Mum! She was all too aware from school that her skinniness and black hair made her look even taller. When had Mum last looked at her, really looked? *How well do you know your daughter?*

'I never want to grow up,' Lola said.

She watched Mum carry out the scuttle then went into the kitchen, where her father was sitting just as she had imagined him, his wrists on the table, wearing his red and blue check lumberjack shirt that had a small tear in the stitching on one broad shoulder. The overhead bulbs reflected chains of light across his dark glasses. By his left hand were piled dirty potatoes, the clean peeled ones floating in a pail on the floor. He turned towards her footsteps, the knife still working on the potato in his hand.

'Hallo, Lola.'

'You needn't pretend,' Lola said. 'I know you can see.' She put the letter on the table without a sound. 'It's from François. I'm sorry, I can't bear to read it.'

He wiped his hands on the front of his shirt. 'I've

been meaning to stitch that for you,' Lola said. She put her hands in her armpits and sat opposite him.

Ben reached up and slowly removed his dark glasses, squinting at once against the sting of the lights. Tears showed under his eyelashes. He slid his hand on the table until his fingers found the envelope, then lifted it and opened the flap in front of his face.

'It isn't a letter,' he said. 'It's a photograph.'

'Then you *can* see!' Lola cried.

'Rachel is holding her child in her arms.'

'She's had her baby?' Lola hugged herself. 'It's wonderful! I'm so pleased,' she sniffled. 'It worked out for the best for her after all. Let me have a look,' she begged.

'No snivelling, then.'

'I promise.'

'Wait, François has written something across the corner.' Ben peered close. 'He says, "Mother and daughter are doing well."' He gave a sigh, then began to chuckle.

'Mother and *daughter*?' Lola said, wishing she could see his face.

Ben laughed aloud. 'So much for the plans of mice and men,' he said. 'And women. What an irony. A daughter! So François is the last Count of Coucy after all.'

'Then they'll have to love her for herself,' Lola said. She reached out with her fingertip and pushed down the photo to reveal his face.

'Yes,' Ben said. His eyes stared directly into her own, piercingly blue. 'I can see you, Lola.' He reached out, as though touch was still his most powerful sense, but then he stopped, gazing wonderingly at her with those brilliant eyes, an examination so close that her cheeks flushed. His gaze traced the shine in her black hair, the curve of her eyebrows over her long lashes. 'Your eyes are so large,' he murmured, 'that deep blue . . . ultramarine blue. And the flecks of gold. Your mother's.'

'Not too much of disappointment then,' Lola said shyly.

'You're beautiful,' he said. He wrapped her in his arms, enclosing her. She hugged him tight.

There was a silence. 'Who's beautiful?' Ria said from the doorway. 'Oh my good God,' she said, 'oh no.' She dropped the scuttle and it rolled on its side, coal-dust flew out and lumps of coal scattered, rattling across the tiled floor.

'He can see,' Lola said. She added, 'It's just suddenly come back.'

Ria put her hands to her face.

'It's a miracle,' Lola said.

'Look at all this bloody coal-dust,' Ria fretted, 'and I just washed this floor this morning.' Her fingers trailed black streaks across her face. 'We're nearly at the bottom of the bunker, it's almost all dust,' she complained. 'Tomorrow I was going to order coal to see us through the winter. Now I don't know whether to laugh or cry.'

'Ria Trott, come here,' Ben said.

She held out her hands. He went to her.

'The three of us!' Lola said, half questioningly.

'He doesn't need us any more,' Ria said. 'It's a declaration of war.' She was crying openly now.

'What a bastard you are, Ben London. You're leaving us.'

Ben kissed her.

'No don't,' she said, 'don't lie to me again.'

'Ria,' Ben said, 'marry me.'

# Chapter Twelve

## 1

Cathy had eagerly accepted the challenge of her promotion to general manager, which had been her father's position for so many years, offered her by Victoria. It was a time of opportunity, they told themselves, for women who made their opportunities. Harriet, Cathy's mother, made no secret of her envy. 'If only I had been born twenty years later,' she informed her daughter, 'I should have been where you are now, with a career and my independence.'

Swept along by Victoria's enthusiasm, Cathy had no doubts she could do the job. She had nearly ten years' experience in the Emporium, knew everyone, and knew the web of traditions and relationships that came together to make the life of a great store.

When the nine o'clock bell sounded and the plate-glass doors started swinging open to admit the growing throng of clients – that was the moment she enjoyed. By mid-morning the salesfloors were a humming and buzzing swarm of excitement, cash tills ringing, ladies from Berkshire and Tunbridge Wells bumping into one another, saying, 'Well I never!' and greeting each

491

other as old friends, hats of every shape and size, a child crying for his or her mother being taken in hand by staff specially trained for such routine emergencies, a lady from Bath who knocked over an entire display case of fine St Gobain crystal leaving no fragment larger than a piece of tinsel. The usual three or four clients who collapsed, quite often from exhaustion, to be cared for by the Emporium's own nurse; the ten or fifteen more with minor sprains or ailments or just a wish for attention, even if it was only a glass of water or a whiff of smelling-salts, who made it to First Aid by themselves. The baby who threw her milk bottle from her pram, which then exploded like a milky bomb across a pile of antique Aubusson rugs, trickling down through more than half a dozen layers before the frantic assistant, impeccably polite, dealt with the matter. The shoplifters, forgetful or cunning or stupid, occasionally stylish with poacher pockets or false arms that left their fingers free to work through the front of their coat. The clients who complained. The clients who returned clothes that they had worn. Cathy dealt calmly and efficiently with the one hundred and one crises of the average working week. The job was in her blood, having observed for so long how her poor father coped, and the sort of work he brought home. And of course she had her mother's advice.

'Look,' Cathy told Victoria, gazing through one of the observation windows at the bustle and activity of a particularly busy Saturday, 'don't you love it?'

'Yes,' smiled Victoria at Cathy's naïve enthusiasm, 'the sound of cash tills ringing.'

As well as the day-to-day matters, Cathy had also to make plans for the longer term, developing the Emporium's selling strategies for the next twelve or eighteen months, in January bringing forward detailed plans to Victoria for the July sales, even an outline for the July sales after that. Cathy was intelligent and coped well with her busy, varied tasks. She told herself that with her very long hours of work, often past midnight then up at six, she repaid Victoria's faith in her.

However, to Cathy there was much more to this than ambition. Cathy had taken the job partly because she was angry at her rejection by George, and this kept her in his eye. Cathy was unrepentant. In her heart she blamed him for not having the guts to make an effort for her, and though her first instinct had been to fly away and get a job in another store, in Oxford Street perhaps, she found an unexpected ally in Victoria, keeping George on the defensive for her own purposes, who persuaded her to stay. 'If you run away, my dear, George will simply convince himself he was in the right all the time, and he'll be unbearable.' So Cathy wouldn't back down from George. It was her job to report directly to him when Victoria was away. George, of course, had no choice but to pretend there was nothing personal between Cathy and himself and never had been, and they covered the order of business coolly and correctly. Had he found another girl? Cathy was sure she would have known. Eventually George tried to make a joke of these businesslike visits, Cathy with her elbows at her sides and her sharp, unrelenting features, her agenda and notes on a clipboard clasped in front of her. He kept her back after their last meeting.

'You really don't like me, do you?' he said, leaning back in his chair.

'I like you very much. That makes no difference to how I work with you.'

'But you know the real me, and this is tearing me apart!' He laughed, then tried to make a big deal out of it. 'Hell hath no fury like a woman scorned, is that it, Cathy?'

'You didn't scorn me, George. You disappointed me. May I go now?'

'You know what I felt for you.'

'You didn't show it.'

'Should I have gone down on one knee?' he joked.

'If you really meant it,' Cathy said, leaving, 'yes.'

Victoria was right, Cathy decided in the outer office – as Victoria was usually right. George was taking his revenge on women; he was the sort of man who pretended to be involved and charming and accessible then backed down. It was so obvious when Victoria put it in her straightforward words. His mother had been a strong personality and he had never got over the trauma of her death when he was a child.

'He's frightened of admitting his feelings for another woman,' Victoria said over lunch, patting a Waterfalls napkin to her lips. 'For you.'

'Are you sure?'

'Of course I'm sure. That's George through and through, and he'll never change.'

'Well, I suppose you do know him better than anyone,' Cathy admitted.

Victoria permitted herself a small smile. 'He is frightened, in fact, of feelings. Men are cowards. Don't blame yourself, Cathy. Now,' she rustled the papers, 'let's go over the ten-day preliminary returns and the thirty-day forecasts.'

Cathy said miserably, yet still in her bright, loyal voice, signing the lunch account for Victoria, 'But I do blame myself.'

Victoria patted Cathy's shoulder, knowing better than to pay heed to such pangs of self-doubt. The reality was, Victoria congratulated herself, that Cathy had at last got a grip on herself. In the past Cathy, mooning in love with poor foolish George, had become hopeless at work, but Victoria discovered that Cathy spurned had a motivating edge. The department heads and buyers straightened their backs now when she came by, the floorwalkers tipped the wink to the section managers, and the section managers cracked the whip to keep the sales staff and stockkeepers on the *qui vive*; everyone was busy. Victoria was pleased that she had made the right choice. She had put not her own man, but her own woman, in the position of power, and it was working. By making Cathy general manager she had both pacified the Jones clique and finished them as a force in the Emporium, and best of all Cathy was the loyal type, never the stuff of which rebel leaders are made. Another benefit for Victoria was that the appointment had marginalised George. Obviously Cathy's presence made him uncomfortable, yet as Victoria had anticipated he had not opposed her choice, so engrained was he in thinking only of the good of the Emporium. This meant, Victoria knew, that George had given up against Victoria. She had her father's determined mouth and he'd learned by now that she would get her way in the end.

Victoria was pleased with herself. She had her hair taken up and waved by Mr Teasy-Weasy himself. The shorter, immaculate hairstyle accentuated her face and piercing eyes, giving her a less voluptuous, more businesslike look. Another benefit was that it took less time to look after. Terry hated it and always complained, and that was another reason Victoria liked her new hairstyle, because of course he still came round, scowling and desirable but faithful as a lap-dog, and she knew she could make him do whatever she wanted. When she provoked him it made him react with a hardness, almost a carelessness, that she liked, because even so he couldn't leave her alone.

During the run-up to Christmas, of course, all stock was full price. Victoria went with Cathy on a tour of inspection through the store, walking with small steps in the departments she was less than satisfied with. Gradually it occurred to her that Cathy's mind was distracted. 'Don't you feel well?' she asked.

'I need to talk,' Cathy said. Shoppers hurried around them laden with awkwardly shaped gift-boxes, crying children, wrappings and decorations, in exhausted voices asking the way to Father Christmas's Grotto even though the arrows were prominently displayed on the direction boards. People turned their brains off when they were spending money and wanted to be led by the hand. It was all part of the service.

'Talk away.' Victoria paused at a display. 'Cheap leather looks even cheaper under bright lights. Couldn't these bulbs be softened, or coloured?'

Cathy made a note. 'I mean in private.'

'I'm very glad that we opened up this floor. We could get more selling space from closing down some of the departmental forward stock areas, and cut pilfering too. Or would the extra room be better used for escalators? Have you seen that American study?'

'There's something I have to tell you,' Cathy said.

'It's important to get people moving between the floors, maximise their opportunity to buy, their exposure to helpful information. Advertisements on the escalators to remind them of goods they didn't know they wanted, pretty underwear, gifts, season's fashions.'

'I'm back with George,' Cathy said.

Victoria put out her arm. 'Come with me. We can talk in my office.' They went up the final flight of stairs and Victoria opened the door for Cathy, motioned her to the chair, then walked around her desk and sat behind it. She put her elbows on the wood and clasped her hands with a smile. 'You and I know one another well enough, Cathy. You must get over this obsession. It's making a fool of you.'

'I'm sorry to let you down. I tried to be the woman you wanted me to be, but I'm not like you.'

Victoria picked up a paperknife and put it down.

'You haven't thought this through. You could go far in the Emporium. You know we have plans for expansion and perhaps another store—'

'I'm not interested in it,' Cathy said. 'I used to be, but now I'm not. I don't care about what you're offering me any more. I'm wasting my time. Soon I'll be thirty years old.'

'But you can't be serious about giving all this up for George. You don't actually see yourself as a housewife, surely!'

'All I know is I love him, and he loves me.'

'He proposes and that's it? You're going to chuck it all in. Be sensible, Cathy.'

'He got down on one knee,' Cathy said.

Victoria stared across the desk with cold, pale eyes. 'You're a fool. Look what I'm offering you.'

'I'm formally handing in my notice.'

'Then good riddance to you,' Victoria said and, turning her back on her, let Cathy go.


Rumour travelled faster than light in the Emporium. 'Cathy's jumped ship,' Hilda said. 'I'd never've thought she was a one ter do that.'

'She crossed madam once too often,' Wattie said. 'Like 'er dad. Jumped, or was pushed.'

''E's taken on that little department store in Wimbledon, I 'eard,' Hilda said glumly. 'And now old Mr Ford's jumped too.'

'Pushed,' said Wattie.

'And 'e was a real gentleman.'

'With Cathy it's love,' said Bill Simmonds without

looking up from his magazine. 'It's love, and yer all fools.'

'Yer dirty old man,' Hilda said. 'I've 'eard about blokes like yer.'

'Bill's burning the candle for Cathy,' Wattie said. 'Yer old enough to be 'er grandad.'

'Dad,' said Bill.

Kevin, the new loader, came in peeling off his leather gloves. 'You blokes still arguing?'

'Cathy's better off with George than staying 'ere, I reckon,' Bill said, ignoring the newcomer.

'I'd give George a kiss an' a cuddle if it'd get me out of 'ere,' winked Hilda.

'Cathy has given it all up for love,' Bill insisted.

There was a pause. 'Suppose Bill's right?' asked Wattie.

'Nah, don't pay no mind to young Bill,' Hilda said, ''E 'asn't been the same since 'is dad kicked the bucket.'

For the first time Victoria phoned Terry just to hear his voice. 'Do you want me to come over?' he said.

'No, don't bother yourself.'

'Half an hour,' he said, and he was as good as his word despite the evening traffic, *dit-dit dat* on the doorbell and breezing in, dropping his overcoat over the back of a white armchair. He didn't bother to kiss her hallo, just went into the all-electric kitchen and came out with coffee. Only then did he lean over the back of the sofa and kiss her precisely in the sensitive hollow between her jaw and her ear, feeling the shiver run through her.

'Oh darling,' she said.

'Evenin', daarlin. Still can't get used to your hair,' he said, sitting beside her, blowing the steam from his coffee.

'Now, don't be a bore.'

'What's it all about?'

'Sometimes it feels,' Victoria sighed, 'as though I don't have a friend in the world.'

'You got me.' *But you'll never love me*, he thought. *You don't see people as people, only as tools*.

She ran her finger down his cheek, fond and rejecting.

'Cathy's gone, after all I did for her.'

'Poor pussycat.'

'I don't have anyone to take her place. I shall have to do much of her work myself, at least until a replacement can be found.'

'I thought you liked a challenge.'

Victoria was silent.

'Cathy's gone back to George. She looked really happy. I wondered why I hadn't seen George at the Emporium for weeks.'

'So they've left you all alone,' Terry said. 'Better pick up the phone to dear old Terry, he always comes running when you give him a bell.'

She squeezed his hand. 'I do appreciate you much more than that.'

'I wonder if you know how you hurt people,' he said quietly.

'I hate it when you pretend to be weak and . . . and something you're not.' She stood up, went to her desk where, for the first time since he had known her, her mail lay unopened, and put down her coffee.

'You know Clifford Ford,' she muttered, 'the financial man who's been with us for yonks. I had to let him go, he was so old. Probably the last person left from my father's day, of any importance. It's just me. It's all mine now.'

'Just what you wanted.'

'I suppose so.'

'So what's bothering you?'

'I don't know.'

'I'm the one person you can tell, Victoria.'

'It's just that if Cathy and George have been talking, they know I tried to set them against one another.'

Terry grinned. 'I've got to admire you. You did really?'

'For their own good, of course.'

'Of course,' Terry said, straightfaced. 'First tiny pang of guilt, is this? You're growing up, Victoria.'

She picked up an envelope and fiddled with it. 'It was in the best interests of the Emporium.'

'Yeah.'

Even Victoria blushed faintly. 'I told no lies.'

'Yeah, I know what you mean,' Terry said.

But Victoria didn't reply. Her eyes widened, looking at the card that had fallen from the envelope she held.

'Oh my God,' she said.

'It's stopped snowing,' Cathy said, 'I can see the moon.'

'The moon over Primrose Hill,' George murmured, putting his hands on her shoulders.

'Let's go out!' Cathy turned excitedly into his arms.

'Do you know what time of night it is?'

'That's the whole point!' She ran to fetch her coat, returned wrapping her muffler round her face. 'There will be no one else there. No kids pushing toboggans. No poodles. No nannies. Only us.'

'Your voice is muffled, my love.' He pushed down the muffler and kissed the tip of her nose. 'We'll probably get arrested by a policeman.'

'Yes, let's!' she said fiercely.

'I can tell you're going to be very good for me,' said George with resignation. 'Now, where did you put my wellies?'

He chased her out into the snow, his torchlight flashing around her figure running ahead of him into the pale night. The snow took all sound, lying deeper over the grass. Primrose Hill rose above them, blue and smooth in the moonlight, and Cathy let him catch her as they climbed. She grabbed his hand, he'd forgotten his gloves. 'I'll have to get you sorted out,' she panted.

'Look at that,' he whispered.

They sat on the bench at the summit with the lights of London spread out like a map below them and the moon above. The river gleamed, narrower on their right than to the left, where it seemed they could see clear to France.

'Have you done the right thing?' George murmured.

'You're freezing.' She blew on his hand, rubbed it,

held it between her own. 'Stop flashing that torch and be romantic.'

'Leaving the Emporium.'

'There'll be times when I'm sorry.'

'Oh dear.'

'When I'm up to my knees in dirty terries and the babies are screaming—'

'How many?'

'*All* of them, and supper's burning in the oven—'

'You'll say, Thank God I chose George.'

'Where's your other hand? Now put that one in your pocket.'

'You've got warm breath. It's awfully exciting.'

'That's enough of that.'

'Gosh, I've found something in my pocket.'

'It's Victoria I feel so sorry for. She tried so hard to split us up because she hasn't got anyone. Only that store, and it's her life now. I feel so sad for her.'

'Victoria is more than capable of looking after herself, Cathy. She's going to be one of those coping women.' George frowned at the envelope he had taken from his pocket. 'I must have put it there this morning and forgotten it in all the excitement.' He opened the flap. 'I wonder if it's true that one can't quite read by moonlight,' he said, squinting.

'Don't hurt your eyes. What does it say?'

'It isn't a letter, it's a card. No, it's no good, I can't read it.' He flashed the torch. 'Good God! It's from my father.'

'Are you sure? George, what's the matter?'

George put back his head. 'He's beaten us to it.' His laughter echoed across the snow. 'He's beaten us to it!'

\* \* \*

'He must be senile,' Victoria said. 'That's the only thing that explains it.'

Terry crossed to her desk and lifted the card from her fingers. 'It's an RSVP,' she said, adding as though he wouldn't understand, '*Répondez s'il vous plaît.*'

'I'm not that stupid,' Terry said. He kissed her on the lips deliberately, making her look at him, then read the card casually.

> *The pleasure of your attendance is requested at the marriage between Mr Ben London and Mrs Ria Trott, only surviving daughter of Mrs Esther Price of Havannah Street, SE14. The wedding will take place at St Luke's Church, Havannah Street at 12 o'clock noon on Saturday 23 January, 1954. RSVP Mr Charles Bookkeeper, Holborn Chambers.*

Terry struggled to hide his amazement. Ria must be mad.

'The shares are mine,' Victoria said. 'A marriage makes no difference.'

'For Christ's sake, do you always have to think about yourself?'

She looked interested at his outburst. 'SE14, that's the East End, isn't it?'

'Yes, of course it is!' She hugged his elbow, and as always it surprised Terry how much this assertive, soft-centred woman loved him to be aggressive, loved to think she tamed him. She didn't feel threatened by him. She had no idea what he was really like, yet he loved her.

'Then you must know these people, Terry Price,' she murmured, 'this other Price family.'

'The East End's a biggish place you know, even the Isle of Dogs.' Terry sounded very calm. He was wondering how he could hide the news of this forthcoming attraction from Vic. Terry still vividly remembered that trip with him and Vic chasing the Roller down to Brighton, the fog sliding in across the sea, the look on Vic's face when he realised that Ria had finally given him the slip. That look was not quickly forgotten. And according to this she was coming back to Vic's territory of her own will – Ria must be out of her mind to rub Vic's nose in it like this – getting married a few doors up Vic's own street!

Vic would explode.

'The Isle of Dogs,' mused Victoria. 'I've never been there before.' He realised that she was determined to attend – of course she would, that was the point of the invitation, women were attracted to wedding bells like bees to honey. 'Is it near Cable Street and your Old Bull and Bush?'

'Not very far as the crow flies.'

'I suppose there are thousands of people called Price in the East End, it must be a very common name.'

'It's a very close-knit community . . .' Suddenly Terry saw how he could use this situation to his advantage. 'In fact we are related. My father Nigel, who died when I was very young, was Ria's half-brother. I never knew her, she was considered the black sheep of the family. Ran a nightclub, I think.'

'How exotic.' She looked at him in surprise.

'You'll enjoy it. You can meet some real people, be free for an hour. Don't worry, we don't spit on the carpet and we don't allow any rubbish in our gardens.'

'You're so proud of yourself and you think I'm so ignorant, don't you?'

'Yeah.'

'Stay.'

'I got to get back.' He was thinking about Vic.

Victoria pointed at the window. 'It's been snowing,' she said, and he saw Piccadilly stretched out white beneath the streetlamps. 'Now you'll have to do as you're told. You don't mind, do you?'

'When I was a tiddler,' Hilda said, 'I was very partial ter snow. Remember them snowballs where if there was someone yer didn't like yer slipped a few road-chippings in the middle and it socked 'em in the mush like grapeshot? Them was the days. Very fond I was of shoving snow down people's backs when I was young, and I remember I liked sliding on the ice and falling on my bum and pretending I was 'urt, and if there was some silly old geezer came ter help yer up, yer'd 'ave a look-see what 'e 'ad going in 'is pockets. But now I'm old.' She took off her galoshes, revealing two layers of football socks in Millwall colours, and dug congealed snow morosely from the toes. ''Ow I 'ates snow.'

'Yer 'aven't 'eard the big news then?' Wattie called.

'Not now, Wattie, I'm suffering, there's a luv.'

'Ben London's coming 'ome!'

'He's never.'

'Ben London? Thought he was dead,' Kevin said, passing through.

'Before your time, luv,' Hilda called after him insultingly.

''Orse's mouth,' Wattie promised, nodding at Bill Simmonds. 'Alive and kicking.'

'Wedding invitations 'ave been sent out,' Bill said. 'I drove George ter the solicitor's this morning, and they was talking about it in the back of the car. Everyone's getting one.'

'Who's the poor unfortunate girl?' Hilda said.

'There's only ever been one,' Bill said. He remembered that first night after the bomb, seven years ago, the woman coming out of the dark with her tattered suitcase, shaking his hand like a man. He'd recognised her at once, Miss Ria Price, the singing Star of the Stage. He'd seen her sing for the boys once, Poplar-way, when he was a driver in Kaiser Bill's war, and he'd hung about the stage door after, to call out 'Wotcher, Ria!' with his pals. That windy night in Piccadilly, no longer a starstruck young Tommie, he'd nerved himself beforehand to greet her with that same famous catchphrase. But alone, he didn't have the guts. He was a professional man with a job to do and he'd come over all gruff. And there had been her daughter trailing behind her, a lovely little girl, but born out of wedlock no doubt, and no doubt Mr London's. She'd put her grubby feet on the Connolly hide seats, too, while he drove them to London's Hotel on Park Lane. Bill had never told anyone about that night: gossip was a recognised perk but ultimately a chauffeur's loyalty to his guv'nor was absolute. The first written rule a fine chauffeur lived by was to arrive on time, but the first unwritten rule was his absolute discretion. Mr London had sworn him to secrecy, personally, blinded and lying on a hospital bed. Mr London had a way of holding your hand, and Bill had never betrayed that trust.

'What more d'yer know, young Bill?' Hilda demanded.

'Only what I told yer. There's only ever been one, and Ria's the one.'

'Come on, we're yer pals,' Hilda said.

'No, yer aren't really.' Bill got up, fitting his peaked cap carefully over his short white hair.

'Where yer going?' Hilda demanded.

'Just following orders,' Bill said, and left.

Wattie sat down next to Hilda and, alone, put his arm around her. 'Looks like it's back to the good old days for us, old girl. Mr London'll sort this place out, bring Ford back, and Jones. And Kevin and his union types'll have us out on strike over these bloody awful working conditions. Interesting times.'

'A wedding,' Hilda said mistily. 'I can wear my 'at.'

Bill Simmonds cruised his Phantom III slowly along the salted black tarmac of Piccadilly and turned her carefully on to the snowy sidestreets of Mayfair, entering the warren of exclusive streets around Shepherd Market. If London House had been a monument to her son's vanity, and he had overheard her call it that in her blunt, dismissive voice, then Lisa's choice of house here signified lost hope. She had leased it insisting that Victoria would join her here, this covered archway barely wide enough for the Rolls leading into the cobbled mews. The house, converted from stables, took up one side of the courtyard, which was too narrow to turn the car. Bill reversed in. He never wanted to come here, and he liked Lisa as little as she liked him. Whatever he did to be obliging, he knew, she never was going to like him; it was one of those women's things, instinctive, nothing he could do about it. Serve her right Victoria wouldn't live with her, leaving Lisa with four empty bedrooms, each of them with a bathroom, Oake the butler, Peggy the housekeeper, too many yappy dogs and no one to interfere with.

He saluted and she walked past him into the car like he was a piece of dirt. 'The Emporium.' She was tapping the card with her fingernails.

'My felicitations and best wishes on your good news, ma'am,' Bill said, sounding fawning and hating himself for it.

She stopped him closing the door, and for the first time he heard warmth and kindliness in her voice. 'I'm a very lucky old lady, I know. Perhaps it really is the best of all possible worlds, after all.'

'Yes, ma'am.'

'Thank you, Simmonds.'

Lisa leaned back and closed her eyes as the car whispered through the streets. Her bones ached – the tuberculosis which had afflicted her joints had been cured, but her bones remembered their pain, and she supposed she would have to use a stick soon. The Rolls pulled up on the corner of Old Bond Street, outside the private entrance to Victoria's apartment. A young man came out, throwing a scarf around his neck, crossing the snowy pavement in soft Italian shoes. He glanced at her incuriously, unlocking a parked car with snow on the convertible hood and the bonnet. Parked there since last evening, then. Simmonds prompted her, 'Shall I wait, ma'am?'

'Yes, I shan't be long.'

'Right you are, ma'am.'

Lisa watched the Jaguar sports car drive away, first gear whining, the snow flying off the bodywork in a miniature blizzard as it accelerated towards Piccadilly Circus.

Lisa used her key to get into the lobby and summoned the lift. At the top her shoes made no sound on the carpet. She knocked on the door, but lightly, then unlocked the door and went in.

Her initial thought was that everything in the apartment had been changed. What immediately caught her eye was a bottle of brandy fallen over on the white carpet, obviously put down carelessly by someone leaning over the end of the sofa. Two balloon glasses stood beside it. Lisa put her handbag over her wrist and picked them up, held them against the slit of daylight from the half-drawn balcony curtains. Lipstick on one glass. She placed them carefully on the table and hunted down a strange stale smell, the unpleasant aroma of a couple of dirty plates of eggs not washed up – not even put into the sink to soak.

Lisa realised that *this* was the sort of thing that had changed – only these details, the coffee grains on the formica, the air of dirtiness, of indifference. Lisa gradually realised that all the important things, the carpet, the desk, the white Syrie Maugham armchairs and art deco lamp-standards and mirrors, all these were unchanged from when Ben openly lived here with Pearl, to the shock of Society, before they were married. But at least they had been in love, or thought they were. They knew what they were doing, there had been nothing casual about their relationship: it was definitely between adults. .Lisa tripped over one of Victoria's shoes lying discarded on the carpet.

Her mouth pursed into a severe line.

The heating was set very high. Lisa wished there was someone to take her coat, and her hat seemed pinned on very tight.

She knocked on the bedroom door and it swung open. Here was the bed where Ben had made love with Pearl; the same bed, quite possibly, where Victoria had been conceived. Victoria lay on the pink satin covers, naked as the day she was born, her toes pointing away from her, one hand folded over her tummy. Her mouth was open and she was snoring. Two stiff, lacquered curls stuck out from her hair on to the pillow. How sad she looked. Lisa could hardly bring herself to move; she knew she should leave, leave right now.

But something was very odd in here. Of course Victoria had added all sorts of little knick-knacks to this room: in theory it was so much more feminine with these pinks and whites, the pink satin valance softened with pink chiffon, the bedhead in matching pink velvet; yet she seemed unaware that so much remained as it had been. The heavy brass handles on the cupboards, the ugly modern painting over the bed, a fine copy of a Mantegna mother and son opposite it, and the naval chest of drawers in dark mahogany, with brass-bound corners, looked plainly incongruous . . . at first. It was not, Lisa reckoned, as much Victoria's room as Victoria thought.

Even Victoria looked different. This was the face of the girl that normally only a man would see, her make-up rubbed off, her lips and eyelashes almost disappeared. Victoria was lucky: her face was still given identity by her dark eyebrows, a straight, simple line, almost a frown. That was all. Lisa put the sheet over her.

'Terry?' Victoria murmured. Her eyes flickered open. 'What are you doing here?' She sat up, outraged, then calm. 'I suppose you want to talk about this wedding business,' she yawned.

'A young man left in a hurry,' Lisa said, 'perhaps he overslept too.'

Victoria didn't bother with recriminations. 'How did you get in?'

'I used my key. The key you once stole.'

'That doesn't give you a right to come here now.'

'Do you love him?'

Victoria laughed and swung her legs over the edge of the bed. Her shins were shaved so finely that they were glossy even without nylons. She wiggled her toes in the carpet.

'So you do,' Lisa said.

'No.'

'Baby, baby, please.' Lisa held out her hand.

'I can't tell you,' Victoria's voice shook with

emotion, 'how much I resent your interference in my private life.' She put her elbows on her knees and the miracle happened. Victoria cried. Her body trembled with sobs. She rocked back and forth from her toes, her hands over her mouth, the bed creaking. Lisa found the dressing-gown and draped it over her shoulders.

Victoria shifted along the bed, making room. Her grandmother sat beside her.

'Baby, how well do you know the man you love?'

Victoria sniffed, making a terrific snotty sound in her nose. 'I don't love him,' she breathed out through her mouth. 'Could you pass a tissue?'

'He doesn't mean anything at all to you?'

'He's fun.' Victoria blew, looked, blew again. 'We have fun.'

'You've never let go, lived from day to day, hour to hour, for love?'

'I've no time for love.'

Lisa tapped the wedding card with her nail.

'That makes no difference,' Victoria said.

'I learned the hard way.' Lisa sighed. 'You see, I was in love with Ben's father, Charles Cleremont. I was a child until he took me, and I loved him ever after. He was a complete bastard who hurt me terribly. That's the worst kind of love, because I could only stop loving the pain your grandfather caused me by running away. I always ran away. All those years ago yet they've made some sort of mark, even on your life. Although the young always deny it. It's always for the first time, isn't it?'

'I don't love Terry.'

'It's obvious to me.'

Victoria made herself grin, though her eyes were still overflowing. 'I don't think you understand modern relationships. Marriage is not an option. It's just love, grandmama. Terry's OK. We'll work it out.'

'Victoria, you are an adult now and there is one question that a woman in love must ultimately ask herself.'

'Is that the time?' Victoria laughed. 'I've got to get to work.'

'She must ask herself how well she knows herself. How well do you know yourself, Victoria?'

Victoria stopped in the act of selecting a dress. She turned uncertainly, then rubbed her hand, remembering her father's grip, and she remembered his voice. *You.*

To be herself. But how could you know who you really were? You just got out of bed in the mornings and did your best.

*You.*

## 2

Esther had received the envelopes in the last post yesterday, the two of them clattering together through her letterbox. She had been dancing in the front room, not that she let on about the dancing to anyone, more it was conducting, and sort of swaying her upper body a little to the rhythm. The BBC did put on such nice light music. Once you'd had to go out to be entertained at the penny gaffs, music-hall or theatre – those were the days before dancehalls – and mostly you were standing so you could dance in the crowd anyway, every night if you could afford it, some of the places not much bigger than people's houses, and you might go through the boards if you bounced too hard, like some of the singers did. And everywhere you went you got the street musicians of course, lots more barrel-organ men than nowadays – Lord Reith had killed them off properly – and the Italians busking on big thorough-fares in the better areas, looking like brigands with their long moustaches, and sometimes a fat woman waddling round to take the money, and no thank-you from them either, them being Roman Catholics. But now the BBC brought it into your own home, endless entertainment for the twist of a button: Henry Hall, Edward Heath; from big band sounds to chamber music to 'Listen With Mother' in a breathless, ecstatic rush that was difficult to stop. Even though she hated the news, she had to listen to it, she couldn't bring herself to turn that black bakelite button off, and there were some terrible comedy programmes they put on that weren't funny at all, but you had to listen to them because it was the BBC, and they knew best. But then the letterbox clattered and the shadow of the departing postman crossed the net curtains, and Esther nipped into the hall between programmes (they gave you a decent interval to put the kettle on) to find the two identical envelopes lying on the mat.

She picked them up.

The first was addressed in fancy flowing script to *Mrs Esther Price, Havannah Street, SE14*. She opened it with her blunt fingers and pulled out the card. *The pleasure of your attendance. Mr Ben London. St Luke's Church. Havannah Street.*

'Oh my good God,' Esther said. She went back into the front room, reached for the bottle, then put it down and turned off the radio. It suddenly seemed very quiet. She read the card again. *Mrs Ria Trott*. For a moment her mind was totally blank on the name, she couldn't think who it was. The only surviving daughter of Mrs Esther Price, that's who. Ria. Esther had another go at the bottle, wiggling the cork out successfully this time, and remembered to find a glass from the sideboard. She put the glass on the polished wood, not bothering about a mat, filled it, and drank it. The more she drank, staring at the card in her hand, the worse she felt.

*Whatsoever a woman soweth, that shall she also reap.*

Esther re-read the invitation a hundred times, each time more vividly as the sweet oloroso sherry lubricated her mental processes. She re-read the envelope also. The second envelope was written in identical arty loops and coils to her own. The only difference was that it was addressed to Mr Victor Price. She had no doubt that it contained the same invitation.

Vic had been invited to Ria's wedding.

Ben London was coming back here to the Isle of Dogs where he had started in order to marry the girl he loved, Ria, in St Luke's Church. The place as a child Ria had dreamed of being married to the man she loved. She had refused point-blank to marry Ray Trott there.

*A proper wedding*. Esther was as keen on proper weddings as proper funerals. But this wasn't a dream wedding, it was a nightmare.

What would happen this evening when Vic walked in the door and opened his very own invitation to the wedding of a lifetime? Esther shuddered to think what he would do. He might hurt himself. This had always been her worry with Vic, even as a little boy he was the sort who took things to heart, and at the back of her mind it had always been her fear: Vic might hurt himself.

Ria had kept Vic on the rails. But you know what brothers and sisters were like, they were always fighting.

Poor Vic! He'd never done anything wrong. If only Ria had never brought that little workhouse boy home! The worst of it was that none of this was Vic's fault – it was Ria who brought Ben home, Esther who welcomed him with open arms. Vic must have felt it was the end of the world.

Esther blamed herself. In the end, she told herself, Mum was to blame for everything because Mum created everything: home, children, family. Esther began blaming herself, tearfully starting another bottle, for the way in which she'd run slap into the arms of that worthless second husband Tom, a deal-porter with a kind heart but without a thought in his head. Labour though Tom might, he'd never been able to give his family the one thing they needed from a man: cash. He was soft and always let himself get pushed to the back of the lump when the ones at the front got chosen for work, never had the sense to play the game and use his muscle. Vic had looked after the family since he was eight years old; he'd never had a childhood.

He'd grown up too quickly, but that wasn't his fault, it was his Mum's fault. 'My fault,' Esther confessed to the mirror.

It was true Vic had touched Ria, but you couldn't blame him, what did you expect with them sleeping five to a bed in the Canary Warren days, healthy boys and girls, bound to be curious, not Vic's fault. Men were expected to be like that. It was Ria's fault, of course, because she was a girl. Ria had been no more capable of suppressing her sexuality than Mum, and like Mum would doubtless have birthed half a dozen brats by the age of twenty-five if she hadn't had Vic to look after her. Vic had never married, but his life had been ruined by the two women in his life. Esther bumped into the back of the armchair and almost fell arsy-tipsy. It had grown dark, and still Vic hadn't returned.

Esther sat in the armchair and waited up for Vic.

She couldn't help sneaking thoughts about the wedding, wishing St Luke's was more grand, imagining all the people there, wondering what Ria would wear. Scarlet, probably.

Still no Vic. Esther thought how little she knew about what he really did, and realised how little she saw of him here. He was a good boy, but how much did she really know about her son?

She recoiled from that question. Whatever it was, she might see it in herself.

'You're asleep, Mum,' Vic said, waking her. 'Go up to bed.'

'Vic, something terrible's happened!'

Vic stood in the open door illuminated by the streetlamp, and behind his parked car she saw the lighted windows of the council's four huge tower-blocks rising into the sky: Cuba Block, Havannah Block, Malabar Block, Glengall Block. He came inside, closing the door. 'Now calm down,' he said.

'Ria's marrying Ben London!' Esther told him.

Vic's face did not change. 'Has it happened?'

'No, dear, we'll have to wait until next month. I suppose the banns have to be read.'

'Where will the wedding be held? In this country?' Esther pointed.

'Here? That can't be right,' Vic said. 'He wouldn't dare.' She handed him the envelope with his name on it. Vic grunted, turning it over in his hands. 'He knows I hate being called Victor.' He tore it open.

'I'm sorry, dear!' Esther bleated, as though it was all her own fault. He took her shoulder in his hand, reassuring her.

'St Luke's,' he murmured, 'you always wanted that.'

'Now, Vic, promise you won't do anything silly.'

'Don't worry, Mum,' Vic said mildly. 'I know what he's up to.'

Esther waited, hanging on Vic's every word.

'He's throwing down the gauntlet,' Vic said. 'Revenge. He can't get me out of his mind. He doesn't care about Ria, Mum, he only cares about me. He's coming here to finish it one way or the other.'

519

'I don't like it when you're so calm,' Esther said.

'You go up to bed now, Mum,' Vic ordered. He kissed her cheek. 'Off you go, no more arguing.'

'Are you sure you're all right, darling?'

'Don't worry about me, Mum,' Vic grinned. 'I'm looking forward to seeing her at last.'

'Well, you know Ria. I don't suppose she's changed much.'

Vic closed the door behind the old biddy, then flicked on the light. Reply to Holborn Chambers. With a rapid movement he picked up the phone to the Old Bull and Bush, but Terry was out.

Vic turned off the light and sat in the net of shadows cast by the streetlamps and the lights of the tower-blocks. On the fourth floor, above the ragged black silhouettes of the chimney-pots, a woman in a dressing-gown was doing her ironing. Above him the sounds of Mum getting ready for bed ceased. It was very quiet.

*I'm looking forward to seeing her at last.* Mum had thought he meant Ria, but Ria was dead. It was not Ria he wanted to see with all his heart and lungs, not Ria he had all the dreams for; she was floating at the bottom of the river in her cream and blue dress. It was Lola he would see.

Vic's daughter was coming back to Havannah Street.

In the morning Vic drove to the Old Bull and Bush in Cable Street. As he got out, Terry pulled up his white Jaguar sports car with a scream of brakes. Terry jumped out, elegant-looking in those Italian loafers and the very casual tailored jacket, but his face was tough. 'All right, Vic, what d'you want done?'

'Take it easy,' Vic said.

'Then you haven't heard. Ria—'

'I heard,' Vic said, putting his arm around Terry's shoulders. 'I want you back at the centre. I want Mr Charles Bookkeeper watched day and night.'

'I'll do it.'

'Too bloody right you will, and no cock-ups this time.'

'I won't let you down again, Vic.'

'The banns will have to be read, and that means our friends are supposed to be resident in the parish. Get Spike to find out what address they're using as a front.'

'Right away, Vic.'

'One more thing. I am particularly interested in the girl, Lola. Is that clear?'

'Yes, Vic.'

'You see, I know how a woman's mind works,' Vic said quietly, almost to himself. 'Ria will make sure her little girl is there to see her married, even if it's only for a few minutes.'

Terry looked at him. Vic in a rage was a frightening sight. But Vic so calm as this, grinning and chummy, was absolutely terrifying.

Ria walked slowly. Everything along West Ferry Road seemed boarded up and decaying; the familiar places remained, but not as she remembered them, cheerful and full of life. The people were gone. The docks were motionless and no sailors staggered across the road to the pubs – half of them were closed. A couple of black women wearing beads in their hair chatted on the corner in a language Ria could not understand. Half of Havannah Street was knocked down. The houses that were left were in shadow, their windows grimy from the spray thrown up by passing cars on rainy days. Rubbish lying in the gutters, a kid's overturned soap-trolley, its broken steering rope repaired with sashcord but now its axle broken. The other half of the street, once cheery houses, was a bare paved area stretching in front of the block of flats. Bits of paper circled busily in the wind and a woman hurried across the empty space holding on to her hat, her child running head-down beside her. There was a council sign provided for the adults at one end, *No Parking*, and at the other a sign for the children, *No Ball Games*. They passed Ria without a glance, hurrying out of sight.

Ria walked along the row of front doors until she came to the one she wanted. There was a doorbell, but she knocked. She waited a few seconds, then knocked again.

'Hallo, Mum,' Ria said when the door was opened, 'I've come home.'

# Chapter Thirteen

## 1

'Will you come?' Ria asked.

'Of course I will, darling,' Esther said, hugging her, 'couldn't miss my little girl's church wedding, could I? My social event of the year, you are.' She pulled her daughter into the hall. 'Come and have a cuppa. You haven't changed at all. You're too skinny in the tummy and your bust's too big. Sit down, it still don't cost extra.'

'You haven't changed anything,' said Ria, looking around the little kitchen. 'You've got one of those Kelvinator fridges.'

Esther was miffed. 'You haven't noticed the new kettle, then.' It was electric and turned itself off when it had boiled. They sat watching it begin to steam. 'You're staying for a little while then.' Esther hovered over the kettle. 'Wait. It's going to do it any minute.' The kettle clicked off and Esther pounced on it victoriously and filled the pot. 'I've spoken to the minister, he's a new man. He's so tall his clerical gown has had to have a bit sewn in, otherwise you could see him from his knees down, and I suppose it wouldn't be dignified. I've had a word with him and told him I want personal bits put in when he talks about you and what a happy day and a special day for us all it is, as though he knew you, and you was friends, and he was a friend of the family. St Luke's is awfully small, dear.'

'Those who can't get in can watch from the streets. Ben doesn't do things in a small way.'

'Vic was a bit frightening about it when he opened his invitation.'

'We're well looked after,' Ria said. 'No one makes a cup of tea like you, Mum.'

'What a kind thing to say, ever so. You're not letting Ben make you soft, are you?'

'I don't think so.'

'Who's doing the looking after?'

'About a dozen of Billy Hill's boys from up West.'

'Vic don't like Billy overmuch,' Esther warned.

'That's exactly what Ben said.'

'I hope you haven't brought Lola with you, in case there might be trouble.'

'Ben says there won't be any trouble.'

'He's always the one to start it,' Esther grumbled, 'and you're the one what encourages him. I know your feminine wiles, my dear, I've practised them myself, in my day. Where are you staying, exactly?'

Ria took her out into the yard. The ramshackle airey remained hunched by the back wall, but its slanted roof had been lifted by the wind on one side, the nails showing, and it looked disused. Esther wasn't keeping potatoes any more, and she'd let the frost get to the tiny rose bed. Thumper's hutch, its door hanging off, had not been turned to firewood probably because of the wire mesh. Ria pointed up into the sky.

'We're staying up there,' she said. The concrete and glass façade rose high above them, by this time of day finally illuminated by the sun on this side, so that the windows reflected the afternoon sky. The pre-formed concrete looked unnaturally white, but dark streaks and stains had already appeared beneath the balconies and windows. 'Top floor, the corner flat.'

'It's looking right down on us. You can see everything we do.'

'That's what Ben wants,' Ria said. 'He doesn't want Vic to forget him.'

'I'll stand by you, because you're my daughter,' Esther said. 'But I'll be standing by Vic too, mind, because he's my son.'

'Ben believes that Vic killed Pearl, Mum,' Ria blurted.

Esther went back inside and Ria followed her, biting her tongue.

'Did he?' Esther said.

As always Ria had to tell the truth to her Mum. 'No, he didn't. In this case Vic was innocent. It doesn't matter anyway, Mum. Only me and Lola matter now.'

'Vic was innocent in every case. I never believed Vic hurt anyone, though people say he did, but it's that sort of a world isn't it? I do believe in love, darling. You look so happy. I mean, I know it must be a worrying time and all, but you do look so very happy it makes my heart ache. I haven't seen you look joyful like this for, oh,' she said with overflowing eyes, 'you're my little girl again, my little Ria.'

'Big bust,' Ria said. She wasn't going to let her mother off that one.

'Big bust, big heart, and always noisy, yet you always kept yourself to yourself, didn't you? My very own Ria.' Mum heaved a sigh. 'Do you know who did it?'

'Yes, Mum, I do.'

'I thought Ben was blind. I suppose that was just a clever story put about.'

'It was true.'

'And you love him.'

'That's true too.'

'You see, I have to be on Vic's side, darling, because he's my own flesh and blood.'

'So am I, Mum.'

'Yes,' Esther said, 'but you're a girl.'

For three weeks in the New Year Ben London and Ria lived 'resident in the Parish' at the top of the tower-block overlooking Havannah Street. Technically they were not living together because Ben had rented two adjacent flats from the council, with different numbers, and though a couple of workmen knocked them together – the walls were plasterboard – the proprieties had been observed. Ben arrived by taxi, a tall figure wearing working trousers, check shirt and donkey jacket. A couple of broadshouldered men followed in the car behind as he paid off the cabbie and walked up what was left of Havannah Street. No expression showed in his face at

the changes that had occurred, and the dark glasses
hid his eyes. Once the area of slums very close to
here, between the docks, had been called Canary
Warren. *That* has gone, his slow, long-striding
footsteps seemed to say; now this is going too. He
looked at the uncared-for little houses without
affection. Only once did he stop.

'Where are the people?' he called.

The two men from Billy Hill's glanced at one
another. 'Let's get out of the daylight,' one said.

Ben went into Havannah Block. The lift was
temporarily out of order so he took the stairs,
building rubbish thrown down the central well, the
concrete landings rising above him. The heavies
coughed and one of them climbed with his coat over
his arm. 'Don't worry,' Ben said, 'no accidents are
going to happen.'

Even so, when he reached the top floor, the flat's
hardboard door had been replaced with one lined
with steel, and a Chubb deadlock. The men went in
first, then nodded and waited outside. Ria had gone
for a chit-chat over a cuppa with her mum, as she did
most afternoons, when Vic went out: Ben went on to
the balcony where he could see the foreshortened
figures of the other two men keeping an eye on
the Havannah Street premises, one lounging in
Commons Street, hardly wider than an alley, the
other where he could keep an eye on the back.
Esther had made a big to-do of saying she guaranteed
Ria's safety, an offer not in her power to make. Ben
frowned. Vic had made no effort to contact Ria, not
one.

527

The wind, which seemed to circle perpetually around the flats, blew Ben's hair over his glasses. He took them off, blinking. The Judd Street specialist had examined his eyes and pronounced his vision almost as good as it ever was; the physical injuries to the sclera and those tiny but agonising scratches to the corneal lenses had healed long ago, scarring was minimal, and Ben had grown used to the small blank areas that distorted his sight. 'But be careful,' the specialist advised. 'I suspect it was not physical injury to the eyes, or the traumatic flash of the explosion, that caused your loss of sight. It may simply be that you banged your head on that marble floor.'

'You mean,' Ben had murmured, 'that what has been given may be taken away.'

'You understand.'

'I may go blind again?'

'Anyone may. It would be best,' the specialist advised unctuously, 'to avoid violent games.'

Ben braced his hands on the balcony railing. From here the rooftops below, puffing white smoke into the sunlight, seemed more important than the gloomy web of streets separating them. The talk of a smokeless zone was still just talk. He sniffed the air, loving the rich smell of it, smoke and the river. The broad Thames made a vivid green curve, silhouetted with cranes, from the dark jungle of Wapping on his right to Greenwich rising into the hills on his left. Ahead of him he saw Rotherhithe, toy buildings dotted along the muddy foreshore.

'For a start,' Esther said, 'I don't like what you're

wearing. That red jacket doesn't go with your eyes, you used to have lovely eyes. And that skirt is too tight.'

'It's the fashion.'

'You're not as young as you were.'

'But I feel young,' Ria said.

'You always contradict me,' the old woman grumbled. 'You won't even tell me where you've been hiding.' She was up to her old game, trying to play Ria off against Vic.

'For obvious reasons,' Ria said.

'Oh, Vic couldn't care less about you! It's not surprising, the way you treat him. I want to see my granddaughter.'

'She has to attend school, it's the regulations. Don't worry, she's being properly looked after.'

'Who by?'

'I can't tell you that.'

'She's probably missing her mum,' Esther said spitefully.

'I'm sorry, I'm upsetting you.' Ria stood up to go.

'I'm so afraid.' Esther gripped Ria's hand so tight it hurt, probably deliberately. 'You're all I've got.'

'Except Vic.'

'That's what I meant,' Esther said. 'You and Vic.'

Ria kissed her mum goodbye and went to leave the dark little dwelling with a feeling of relief. After her long absence it seemed so changed, so full of Vic's presence instead of her own – he had taken over her old room apparently. Ria paused in the hall, no longer feeling it was the house she had once known, and could hardly imagine back to when she had lived here with Lola. She sensed so little of Mum in it now, the Mum she thought she had known so well. She missed all the little things that had made Mum so special, Mum's humour, her wide-ranging laugh that brought all the kids in, her deep kindness. Now Mum's personality was stiffening into old age, growing stronger and simpler, though she self-consciously tried to act herself the way she had been. When the layers fell away it wasn't Mum Ria sensed, it was Vic. Vic in these homilies on the sideboard, Vic in the new curtains, Vic in Esther's choice of clothes. Vic wasn't a mummy's boy, it was the other way round, he forced his mother into his own image. The kitchen door opened.

'Don't go,' Esther said, hobbling through. 'You could have your old room back, we could all live here again, the way we were.'

'What about Ben?' Ria said. 'Don't my feelings have any say in this?'

'Look at you!' Esther said. 'You can't keep living between your legs. You'll be old too! Ben doesn't love you. He just hates Vic.'

'You're wrong.' Ria opened the door. 'He doesn't hate Vic. He loves me.'

'Have you told him Vic didn't kill Pearl?'

Ria stopped. She shook her head. 'Why make it worse?'

'Have you kept any other secrets from him – the man you love?' Esther jeered.

Ria slammed the door from the street.

She stood on the pavement for a moment, trembling, so that one of the men waiting across the street started over. Ria stopped him with a shake of her head, everything's all right. The door behind Ria opened for the last time.

'You'll never be free of where you come from, Ria,' came her mother's voice.

A knock warned Ben that Ria was leaving her Mum's. He saw her in the street below. She looked up and her tiny figure waved. Ben waved back.

He gauged the time it would take her to climb the stairs and opened the door at the exact moment she reached the top. He kissed her on the concrete landing. 'You're sweating.'

'I hardly say hallo to my mother and already I've had enough of her.'

'I hoped for a reconciliation.'

'She's not a very receptive audience, Ben.' Ria went into the flat and he closed the door behind them. 'I pulled out all the stops with her.'

'Wotcher, Ria,' Ben laughed.

'She's more of an actress than I am.'

'Maybe she's where you get it from.'

Ria threw a cushion at him. 'You know, I think it's me. I don't think she's ever loved me.'

'Come off it, Ria.'

'Because I had a different father and it caused all the trouble. And then I was different, I didn't do things *her* way. It's Vic she loves.'

He crossed to the window and took her in his arms. 'What's really the matter?'

'I'm doing this for you, Ben.'

'I'd better be worth it.'

'Do you love me? Do you *really* love me? Or are you just doing this because you hate Vic more?'

'All for you.' He held her to his chest, stroking the back of her head.

'God, I hope I can live up to your picture of me.'

'Got to be better than that,' Ben said, pinching her playfully. She dodged behind the black PVC sofa and chucked another cushion. 'Don't half fancy you in that skirt,' Ben said.

'You've only got your mind on one thing,' she said, pleased. 'Actually, this is a pretty fair place, don't you think? Got a bathroom with a proper bath and hot running water, and an airing-cupboard. I wouldn't mind living here. The rooms are quite nice really.'

'It's a pretty good place with the door locked and bolted.'

'Do you really think Lola's safe with Will and Helen until the wedding?'

'Safe as houses,' Ben said.


## 2

Vic parked by the blind side wall of the Half Moon & Calf's Head, went up the steps and unlocked the door. The long room inside struck cold, dampness emanating from the boathouse below no doubt. He clicked on the electric fire but kept his overcoat on until it was warm. He sat in the armchair by the picture-window that filled the end wall, a pair of binoculars on the table beside him. As the place warmed up he became more aware of the smell of the outfall below him. The mud went out for hundreds of feet here at full low tide, slick and slimy, pecked by seagulls for worms. Other birds perched fastidiously on the gravel banks here and there, and he knew some of the older buildings were built of sand and gravel dug from the river, mixed into mortar, binding bricks of Thames mud. Vic knew the river went down a long way, generations of sewage and rubbish going down into the mud. Nigel had found a Roman coin once. Two thousand years of faeces, the river was. People never thought about what was going on around them.

Vic lifted the binoculars.

From the other side of the river the Isle of Dogs rushed near, looking enormous in the eyepieces. Here were the cranes and rooflines of the place that had been his home, and he focused on the concrete and glass block rising amongst them. What a dreadful thing it was, without a soul, without life, a vertical slum with all mod cons instead of the advantages of a real slum. The setting sun made the windows glare like the sunset. He saw someone moving on the balcony. He thought it was Ria. She went in.

Vic put the glasses down and rubbed his face wearily. For him it was all the past. He couldn't think of Ria. None of this mattered. All he could think about was his daughter. It was a father's love, uncomplicated and unselfish, for his own male flesh and blood transformed miraculously into the feminine shape. To show her who her father was.

He went out to the telephone kiosk and rang the Old Bull and Bush. 'Where's Terry?' he asked Jake.

''E just got back, 'e's taking a kip I should fink.'

'Get him, then!'

Terry's voice came on the line. 'I was in the bath. Charlie Bookkeeper's been in the magistrate's court most of the day. I got the roster, he's booked up and he's not going anywhere. He left his car at home this morning. Spike's in the public gallery just in case.'

'Keep on it,' Vic said.

'One more thing. I happen to know,' Terry said, not letting on how he came by this information, 'that Miss Victoria London will be one of the bridesmaids.'

'Got him,' Vic said.

'So it looks as though his two daughters will be the bridesmaids.'

'Yes,' Vic said. 'Ben London's two daughters.'

'You all right, Vic?'

Vic grinned. Terry had a shooter hidden beneath his bedroom floor, and he didn't know Vic knew.

'I'm feeling fine,' Vic said. 'I love weddings.'

Vic hung up. It was time to talk to a man about a boat.

# Chapter Fourteen

## 1

Saturday 23 January dawned bright and clear, but very cold. St Luke's, a low building constructed of grey-green Thames brick like the houses that once surrounded it, was completely dwarfed by the blocks of flats. The cats were coming home; the dogs were being put out. Roads and pavements were shiny with ice as the milkman's float slithered by. Quiet did not fall again.

As soon as the milk-float was gone the first workmen appeared, gangs of men with spades and brooms hefted over their shoulders. Wearing dark blue work-jackets, caps turned backwards and baggy trousers, they made the streets ring as they worked along them in squads, breaking up the ice with shovels, sweeping the leftover snow into dumps which were then loaded into open lorries and carted away. After tea-up, vans arrived and bags of gritted salt were thrown down to prevent refreezing. Shortly afterwards technicians arrived and hung OB lighting units from lampposts and whatever trees they could find. 'Look at this,' Ben called from the balcony. He was wearing only an unbuttoned dress shirt and slim black trousers, impervious to the cold.

'I'm supposed to be getting ready,' came Ria's voice, but she nipped out, her hair tangled where the hairdresser had been interrupted. 'Bloody hell,' she said. 'All for us.' She dashed back in.

A film-unit generator was parked on the paved area in front of Havannah Block and made a test-run, its heavy, glamorous rumble thrown back between the high façade and the warehouses, echoing through the morning air over the little rooftops below. Housewives opened their windows and stuck their heads out, still in curlers. Suddenly the lights went out and silence returned. Delighted small boys escaping breakfast followed the technicians around, picking up whatever was left lying about amongst the cables now snaking along the pavements, and dogs cocked their legs on the electrical connections. Brand-new galvanised braziers were set, primed full of charcoal but unlit, at intervals along the centre of Havannah Street. Three policemen appeared and stuck together, then drifted off as though they had somewhere important to go. Billy Hill's lads kept an eye on the kids and made sure things ran smoothly. Because they'd been lucky with the weather the marquee wouldn't be needed, but a pantechnicon arrived with the name of a famous circus arched in huge gilt and scarlet letters on its side, and a ramp was let down at the back. Coaches disgorged men in shirtsleeves who unloaded what seemed like endless supplies of trestle-tables and benches from the pantechnicon, laying them out in lines along the street. There was a major-domo with a whistle: men were running everywhere, as tightly organised as a military machine; banners were unfurled, a sign unrolled across the street from chimney-pot to chimney-pot, BEN as if drawn in child's crayon, then a heart, then RIA – her face was going to go red as a brick when she saw that, the sort of thing a small boy might dream up, and maybe hold in his mind for many years.

Ben went inside and dressed carefully in his grey cravat, grey waistcoat, black tails and black patent pumps. He left the grey beaverskin topper in its box. Through the thin walls of the flat next door he heard Ria's raised voice to the hairdresser, 'Leave it alone! What are you up to now. You haven't got fingers, you've got bananas, you have.' She was looking forward very much to today and everything had to be perfect. She didn't really believe Vic would come. Ben knew he would. He glanced at his watch. It was almost time Lola was here. It wasn't like Bill Simmonds to be late.

'It's too tight!' cried Ria, panicking. Frantic shuffling sounds from the dressmaker. Ben grinned and returned to the balcony. The caterers had arrived below, a row of Emporium delivery vans parked along West Ferry Road. Dapper men in dinner suits pointed and gave orders; London's Hotel waiters in tight white jackets, white gloves and, no doubt, warm woollen underwear, set out trays of glasses with that smooth hurry, not haste, for which they were famous. The Rolls-Royce turned the corner. Ben ran downstairs, a couple of Billy Hill's mob falling into step behind him, and met it as it pulled up at the steps. Bill Simmonds helped the young lady out.

'She's grown since I last saw 'er, Mr London,' he said.

'Do I look all right?' Lola asked her father shyly. 'The train was delayed by iced points and I had to change in the loo.'

'I thought it best to bring the young m'lady straight 'ere from Marylebone Station, sir,' Bill said.

'That's perfectly right,' Ben said, and Simmonds saluted. Will climbed out from the car, his innocent pink face wreathed in smiles.

'Good morning, Father.' They shook hands and Will nudged Lola gently. 'All the way from Manchester—'

'Ssh,' Lola said.

'She was worried about her bridesmaid's dress being crumpled in the suitcase—'

'My dress of flowers.' It was indeed a fine gown, and Ben admired it on her: mostly pastel shades, but enough bright touches to set fire to Lola's complexion and her eyes. 'And then I worried about it getting crumpled while I was changing, I could hardly turn round . . .'

'We should get inside, Mr London,' one of the heavies said. 'All right?'

'We have someone special to do your hair,' Ben promised, kissing his daughter's cheek. He held out his arm and they went up the steps. 'If,' Ben added, 'he hasn't lost his bottle after Ria's finished with him.' Lola took the steps two at a time in her nervousness.

Someone had persuaded the lift to work and Lola pecked Ben's cheek as they rode up, then wiped her lipstick off him with a large man's handkerchief.

'Ria will think I've been kissing strange women,' Ben said.

'Do you think I'm grown up?'

'One day,' Ben said. 'No hurry.'

'It was so strange driving along West Ferry Road. I used to know these little streets so well. It was like driving back to my childhood.'

'I know the feeling.' He gripped her hands. 'You can't come back, Lola. You are so very beautiful.'

The lift doors opened and he handed her in to Ria without looking, then returned to the balcony. Bulky grey television cameras marked BBC in white letters were being set up on dollies by men in suits and ties. The Pathé News had mounted their camera on the roof of an estate car, were panning well above the heads of the gathering crowd. By midday, as the sun swung around Havannah Block, St Luke's would be free of the shadows. A few warbling oompahs came from the brass band tuning up.

'Not long now,' Ben said.

'My dress won't fit if you want to know.' Above Ria's voice came the sound of Lola laughing.

Victoria arrived and Ben hugged her. 'Careful,' she said, 'you might crack me.'

'We have a lot of time to catch up,' Ben said. Victoria was wearing the bridesmaid's dress identical to Lola's, but in a very different way. Victoria really was a grown woman.

'Unfortunately I came with Lisa: she hired a car since you appropriated our Mr Simmonds, and the driver was an idiot.'

'It doesn't matter now.'

'He put us out in some frightful street where the people looked at us. I had to ask them for directions and my shoes are dirty.'

'Victoria,' he said gently, touching his fingers to her lips. 'Don't be silly.'

'All those years,' she said, and he could feel her lips trembling, 'you didn't even tell me you could see. You make me feel such a fool.'

'I hear the Emporium is doing very well.'

'I haven't let you down,' Victoria said.

Lola came in. The two girls looked at one another, Lola as tall but a gawky adolescent, still awkward in her bones, her black curly hair falling carelessly as she ran her hand through it in her nervousness. 'Hallo,' she said.

'You must be Lola Trott,' Victoria said.

'Not from today on,' Ben said. 'Victoria, meet your half-sister.'

'We're wearing exactly the same dress,' Lola said. 'Daddy wanted us to. I've got the posies and there's a lovely circlet of flowers to wear in your hair.' Ben watched them stand together. Apart from the similar dresses he had insisted on, the difference between them seemed complete, Victoria with her tightly curled blonde hair, her educated poise, an adult woman confident in herself. Or that was the impression she had learned to give.

Ben left them to look at the posies in the next room. From the balcony he saw that the street was now rapidly filling with people, the women in their best overcoats, drawn to the promise of the tables with their white linen cloths and the brightly coloured balloons hanging in nets above them. George and Cathy arrived in a taxi and strolled in the sun with their faces upturned. He waved, but they didn't see him. More coaches were arriving from the Emporium and the babble of voices reached up to him. He couldn't see the road surface any more, it was a steady swirl of hats and shoulders down there. Almost time. He put his hat under his arm and knocked on the wall. 'Mr London presents his compliments to Mrs Trott, and he's going down now.'

'Not ready!' came Ria's muffled voice.

Ben went down in the lift with Will. 'Never seen you so smart, Will,' he said.

'I keep wondering what Helen's doing. I hope she remembered to milk Gladys.' Will's heart was still at Home Farm.

George was waiting outside; Ben could see exactly how it lay between him and Cathy. George kept his fingers crossed. 'I hardly dared dream it would go so well.'

'The more people the better,' Ben said. Lisa was talking to a circle of children. She saw him and came over, using a stick, and they embraced. Guests were drifting into the church, and Ben escorted her to her seat. Outside, the little churchyard was full, sunny now, and laughter rose into the still air. Ben had a

541

word with Charlie Bookkeeper in the quiet corner by
Nigel's headstone, which had no flowers on it. Betty
Stark must have come to terms with her love, or
found another man. 'Is everything in hand, of
course?'

'Of course. Bill Simmonds will drive you to
London's Hotel afterwards, as arranged, in the Rolls.
No one knows my car,' Charlie confided in a low
voice, 'it's parked in Cuba Street, and I'll pick up Lola
at the flats' back entrance. Will too, it'll be a long
drive. A couple of your . . . gentlemen will accom-
pany us in their own car, at least as far as
Northampton.'

'All the way to Clawfell,' Ben said.

Charlie grunted with amusement. 'I really think
you're taking these precautions to an extreme, you
know. I won't let you down.' He inhaled through his
nose. 'What a lovely day.'

Ben spotted Esther coming out of her doorway into
the street. As was a mother's right, she was dressed to
arrest in a large scarlet hat with a blue band, blue
neckscarf setting off her scarlet coat with its very wide
lapels and a silver brooch. Beneath it she wore a calf-
length skirt of the same scarlet, and lipstick that
matched. A Daimler pulled up among the people,
driven by Spike, and Vic got out, followed by Terry.
Grinning, Vic shook hands, pleased to be here, the
perfect guest, making smalltalk. The Daimler reversed out of sight through the people. Vic took
Esther's arm and led her into the church while Ben
shook hands with the minister.

Ben nodded to the man by the door and in the

church a couple of big men flanked Vic. 'Easy, boys,' Vic said as they frisked him.

'You won't find anything,' Terry warned them.

'Don't make trouble, Terry,' Vic yawned with equanimity. 'This is a happy day, after all.'

'It's consecrated ground!' Esther said, outraged. 'Don't you *touch* me. Hold your head high, Vic.'

'Come on, Mum, there's our seat,' Vic said, leading her to it. He glanced back at Billy Hill's boys with contempt. Their glinting eyes were all show. They were soft. If he'd been intending anything, it would have been hidden in Mum's handbag, or up her skirt. These West End casino types had no idea of the way things were done in Vic Price's territory.

Outside, Ben was chatting with the minister. 'She'll be late,' he promised.

But for once in his life Ben was wrong about Ria. Ria got to the church on time.

They walked up the aisle. 'Electric blue,' Ben whispered as their hands were joined. 'I never guessed. Your hair looks wonderful. You're spectacular.'

'Have I said yes?'

'You said *I do*, Mrs London.' He glanced round at the bridesmaids, winked at them, and Lola winked back. In the posy of orchids she held, she still had her thumb sticking up for good luck.

'I get an itchy feeling between my shoulderblades with Vic looking at me,' Ria whispered.

'He's quiet as you please. He's looking after his mum,' Ben said, glancing round. 'He knows he can't do anything with all these people here. And if he doesn't do anything now, he knows he never can. He's lost you.'

'Sometimes I think you and Vic know one another too well,' Ria admitted. 'I just want to get away from here.'

'Let's make sure Vic gets the message first. It's over, loud and clear. It's over.'

'Are we signing the register now?' Ria fretted. 'Quick, before I forget how to spell my name.'

Outside, the low midday sun struck bright across the rooftops of Havannah Street into their eyes. Ben and Ria pushed slowly through the crowd of well-wishers, shaking hands to each side, followed by Lola, laughing and radiant, and Victoria who looked embarrassed by the young girl's enthusiasm. Ria called out to people at the top of her voice and somebody yelled back, 'Wotcher, Ria!' Others took up the chant, then the shouts broke up in roars of merriment, none laughing harder than Ria in her electric blue dress. Vic turned away for a moment, his face like thunder. Esther ignored Ria, brushing aside her hand and kiss and going straight to Lola.

'D'you remember me?'

'Of course I do, Gran!'

'Oh my God, they've even taught you to speak different,' Esther said. 'You're not the little girl I knew.' She turned her back and walked away.

'Don't worry about what that sour old puss says, love,' said Ria, hugging Lola to her with one arm. 'She'll come round.'

During the marriage ceremony the braziers had

been lit, the air above them quivering with clean charcoal heat, people gathering gratefully round to warm their hands. The tables were piled with plates and food in long steaming dishes on warmers; a roast baron of beef was being sliced by a big-bellied chef wearing a tall white toque above his jolly red face, sharpening his carving knife on a steel with long, sexual strokes like a showman. Waitresses wearing frilly aprons, black dresses and leggings against the cold weaved amongst the crowds with shimmering platters of brazier-hot sausage rolls, all sorts of good hot things on sticks, piping hot pies and dainties. There were glasses of iced champagne, hot toddy, tumblers of ale. People who hadn't met for years were renewing friendships with backslapping greetings, ancient ladies watching the proceedings from chairs placed near the braziers, old soldiers with leaden medals across their chests, nodding in memory of the Boche over their beer.

'It's awful,' Esther whispered to Vic, 'it reminds me of the street party we had when Nigel came home from the trenches. "Welcome Home, Nigel." Vic, I don't think I can hardly bear it.'

Vic followed Lola with his eyes.

Victoria saw Terry and almost waved her hand off her wrist. 'I wish I was with you,' she whispered.

'I wish you were, too.' Terry looked around him, a man at work, his eyes never still.

'Give me a kiss,' Victoria said.

'The wedding's made you feel naughty, hasn't it. Your grandma's looking. The one with a stick.'

'Lisa. Who cares?'

'She knows?'

Victoria kissed his lips on tiptoe, crushing the posy between their bodies. Ria turned away. 'What's the matter?' Ben asked her. 'You look white as death.'

'Nothing!' Ria laughed. 'Someone stepped over my grave, that's all.'

Ben snagged a waiter and held out a sausage roll on a cocktail stick. 'With all my love,' he said solemnly, then nodded to George pushing past him. 'Enjoying yourself?'

'Wonderful time,' George said, red-faced with champagne and looking thoroughly at home, as always, in white tie and tails. Someone else claimed Ben's attention and George grabbed Victoria's elbow. 'Who's that I saw you kissing?'

'George, you're so old-fashioned. I can kiss who I like.'

'There's kissing and kissing.'

'How would you know? Thank you for your concern, big brother, but I'm quite capable of looking after myself. I always have been.'

'He's terrifically handsome,' Cathy said.

'Isn't he?' agreed Victoria, delighted.

'His name is Terry Price,' George said. 'He's a thoroughly bad type.'

'Now I like him even more,' Victoria said, then added insultingly, 'at least he isn't boring.'

'How long have you been in love?' Cathy asked.

'He's simply my boyfriend. It's nothing serious—'

Cathy gasped: 'He's not the same one?'

'Didn't you guess?'

'What's this?' George said.

'Victoria told me years ago that she had a boyfriend, but she was always saying that – a pilot, or someone who'd asked her out for a drink—'

'Now you believe me,' Victoria said. 'You were always so patronising.'

'So it's serious after all,' Cathy said.

'Dear Cathy! Everything always has to be serious with you, doesn't it?'

'Victoria,' said George, 'I think you really are playing with fire. You can't possibly have anything in common with Terry Price. Believe me, I *know*.'

'You live your little life, George, I'll live mine.'

'For your own good—'

'Don't come over all missionary on me, George!'

George threw up his arms. 'If that's the way you want it.' The wedding party moved on. George helped himself to a sherry, then pulled a face.

'I feel so sorry for her,' Cathy said. 'Now I'm gone she doesn't have anyone.'

'Except Terry,' said George, and tossed down the rest of his drink.

Lola found the door to the little Havannah Street house open.

'I wouldn't go in there, Miss,' said the leader of the two men who followed her everywhere. Lola called them the hillbillies.

'I used to live here,' she told him, slipping inside before they could stop her. They folded their arms and guarded the door, looking out with eyes both sleepy and violent.

Lola took a few steps down the hall where she had

played as a child. It was so tiny! The front room had shrunk, cluttered with armchairs, yet she remembered hiding under the sideboard, peeping out between its legs – she must have been tiny herself. She glanced up the stairs, her hand resting lightly on the newel-post, which she realised she had never been tall enough to touch before. The kitchen also had shrunk, there was a big new fridge so you couldn't have the door open at the same time as the fridge door, and there was a kettle with a switch on it, and an electric toaster. The grill of the gas cooker didn't look as though it had been cleaned since she last saw it.

'I should clear off out of there now, Miss,' called the hillbilly. 'Mr London's getting ready to move on.'

'I won't be a minute.'

Lola went into the back yard. She knelt in front of the empty hutch, remembering feeding scraps of lettuce and greens through the chickenwire, the rabbit holding them between his paws to nibble them, his bright eyes. She remembered taking him out of the hutch and holding him to her thin chest, suddenly saw herself: a skinny girl sitting on the cold brick wall around the potato patch, stroking that old black and white rabbit for hours, never going to let him go.

'Where's Lola?' Ben said.

'You didn't half give me a turn,' Ria scolded the returning girl. 'It's all right, Ben, she's here.'

'Everyone's here,' Ben said with satisfaction. 'We're having a spree.' The calliope mounted on the back of a circus lorry, its organ-pipes shining brassily in the sun, shrilled and tooted with frantic gaiety. At

548

the other end of the street the brass band pomp-pomped steadily, and a row of perspiring drum-majorettes twirled their sticks and showed their legs. Urchins wandered between plates of jelly and cakes, unbreakable melamine lemonade cups impossible to prise from their clenched hands, and stared in wonderment at the attractions that Ben had laid on: the smooth-chested fire-eater in his sooty yellow leotard and, on a specially strengthened platform, the Strongest Man in the World strutting with his ferocious moustaches, tight white swimsuit and codpiece. There was a Punch and Judy stand, with the crocodile eating up the baby and the children squealing with excitement, and the clown whose hair lifted into the air when he laughed, his eyes squirting real tears. Wattie punched someone to get the seat next to Hilda, dropped his lunch, then stepped in it and fell over. 'Yer a bloody clown, Wattie,' Hilda said.

'I'm not a clown, I just 'ad too much ter drink,' said Wattie, offended. 'Sorry, mate,' he told the man he'd punched. Bill Simmonds sat beside Mike, once the nightwatchman, now replaced by automatic alarms and a security firm. Ben came round to talk to them all. Bill went over to drink lemonade from the children's table, pouring it from the melamine cup into a gin glass so as not to look stupid. Moira was making eyes at a very nice young man with a perfectly straight Greek nose, and Jeanette had got stuck with Mr Hull and his magic box o'tricks. Mrs LeHaye wrapped chicken legs in napkins and slipped them into her handbag. Ben had tried to think of everyone:

even the disgraced Maeve Feynton was there, complete with her two seemingly identical toddlers, except that one was dressed in blue, the other in pink. David and Harriet Jones had arrived, sticking rather on the fringes, but Mandy Harthfirth marched up to them determined to talk about the intricacies of stock control. Babs, saucy and lustrous, danced with Roger from Electrical Appliances with his wavy blond hair and dark blue pinstripe. Daisy sat quietly with her new husband, and Miss Trant couldn't get away from Miss Purves.

And Vic followed Lola with his eyes. Mr Bookkeeper had looked at his watch and walked off towards the flats. There was no sign of Terry. Good boy.

One of the hillbillies tapped Bill Simmonds on the shoulder. 'Time.' Bill finished his lemonade, urinated against a wall in a quiet place round the back of the church, then drove the Rolls to the arranged point on the corner of Havannah Street and West Ferry Road. The Pathé News was there and the lights came on. Mr and Mrs London and the bridesmaids broke free of the crowd and walked to the car.

Vic came out in front of them and instantly half a dozen broad-shouldered hillbillies surrounded him. It was impossible not to feel sorry for the man. Ben twitched his hand and the men fell back, leaving Vic alone.

'You've lost,' Ben said. 'It's finished.'

Vic didn't look at Ria; not so much as a glance. 'You're welcome to her,' he said. 'I wish you all the happiness you deserve.' The cameras whirred.

Vic held out his hand to Ria. She accepted it, starting up a little on her toes. Her hand lingered in his, her fingers slipping out slowly, then he let her go.

'This is my daughter,' Ben said, bringing her forward, his eyes not moving from Vic's. 'May I introduce Lola London.'

'She's growing up,' Vic said. He took her hand very lightly, almost clinging to it, as though all his strength was turned in against himself.

Finally Vic held out his hand to Ben, not in reconciliation but in acknowledgement that reconciliation was impossible. He knew Ben wouldn't take his hand, but still he let the moment stretch out, publicly losing face.

Ben and Ria got in the car. Vic was hustled away. Two hillbillies moved Lola smoothly through the crowd, and Victoria found herself alone. She looked around for Terry, but he was nowhere to be seen.

# 2

It was so bloody obvious: a truly amateurish piece of campaigning, but what did you expect from a West End mob? They whisked the girl, gawky creature that she was, through the crowd slick as you like, a couple of men left behind to discourage anyone from following. But Terry was already ahead of them, knowing Charlie Bookkeeper was the key. He always had been, and so it proved now. The solicitor had his car waiting at the flats' back entrance, engine idling, another dead giveaway, looking at his timepiece every twenty seconds. These big men made Charlie uneasy. He had no sense, Terry thought contemptuously. Even Vic wouldn't make his move here.

Charlie Bookkeeper's face lit up when Lola was brought to him. He wanted to take the posy but the girl hung on to it. Will arrived. He held open the passenger door for Lola then got in the back. Charlie drove. Just the three of them, but Will was strong.

Terry nodded to Spike in the Daimler.

A couple of Billy Hill's big boys got in a Humber and followed the solicitor's car, close. The solicitor did no barging, waited politely for a break in the traffic along West Ferry Road before turning in, the Humber behind almost touching his bumper. No bloody idea. Spike let a van pass then slipped the Daimler after them.

Terry ran for his Jaguar XK. He caught Spike before the Commercial Road then fell back, keeping a good distance. He had a full tank of petrol, a tube of mints on the passenger seat, a bottle for calls of nature, and a car radio that worked well as long as he kept below fifty miles an hour, after which the wind started making too much noise around the canvas hood. He helped himself to one of the mints, tapping his fingers on the thin-rimmed wheel, content. Occasionally he pulled forward enough to check that Spike kept Bookkeeper's staid Wolseley in sight through central London, not too close but not too far. The Saturday traffic was fairly light – there was a big match on – so traffic lights were no problem. A woman dashed across in front of Terry and he ran over her shopping. He didn't stop.

The cars turned on to the Great North Road at Bignall's Corner but the solicitor maintained a sedate forty, so Terry kept the radio on. Spike fell back on the three-lane section south of Hatfield and Terry took over for a while. The sun was a flat glare across the fields to their left, then the light began to fail. Terry waited before putting on his headlights, then kept his distance, any lights three hundred yards back looked pretty much the same in a rearview mirror, especially if they moved around a bit. A stroke of luck: one of the Humber's red tail lenses was cracked, making it easy to distinguish from the others as the convoy proceeded north.

Near Stamford there was a moment of panic as the Wolseley pulled into a lay-by, the Humber weaving then pulling in behind it. Terry drove past, then shot into a side road, waving Spike on to the next lay-by. He three-pointed and waited with his lights out. A couple of minutes later the Wolseley droned past without an escort. Terry waited five minutes to make sure: that silly big-headed bastard of a solicitor had sent his helpers home. What a kind-hearted employer he was. Get your beauty sleep, boys.

Terry pulled out with a squeal of tyres and hit seventy-five, catching Spike up, faithfully following the Wolseley almost half a mile behind on the empty road. People were safely indoors ironing their suits ready for church tomorrow. One of the Wolseley's number-plate lights was out. Like most people, Charlie let his speed rise as the hours passed, his passengers probably asleep, and Terry gave up on the radio.

In the middle of the night the solicitor turned west through the sleeping industrial towns of the Midlands, and picked up petrol. 'I'm bushed,' Spike said, pulling up at the pump behind Terry afterwards, 'I'm not as young as I was.'

'You've done enough. Finish filling up the Jag and take her home. How's the Daimler off for juice?'

'I don't reckon he's going much further.' Spike handed over the keys. 'There's another couple of gallons in a tin in the boot if you need it.'

Terry took his mints and relaxed in the quiet luxury of the Daimler driving through the night. He reckoned they were making for Manchester, but the glow of the city fell behind them as the Wolseley turned on to a side road into the hills.

Before dawn, they came to journey's end.

Ria kissed Ben London's face. He stirred and said: 'Ria!'

'It's all right,' she whispered, and he settled.

'Whumph,' he said. 'Arrmph.' She waited until he was breathing deeply again, his hand on her thigh, then gently disengaged his fingers, kissed them, and slid out of the bed holding her breath.

Ria crossed the hotel room and slipped behind the curtain, pressed her face against the glass. The lights of London were pale globes, the sky over the East End was pretty, and Green Park was just starting to look green.

Vic had let her go. He didn't care about Ria any more. She was married, properly married this time –

but only because Vic had let her go. Billy Hill's nancy-boys wouldn't have lasted thirty seconds if that had been the way Vic willed it. But he hadn't lifted a finger. Goodbye, Mrs London.

It was cold at the window and Ria hopped to warm her feet by the radiator. Seven years ago she and Lola had been brought to this suite, or one very similar. A few hours before that, Terry had murdered Pearl. That was the first secret Ria had kept from Ben. Had she wanted him to hate Vic so much? Yes, because *she* hated Vic. She wanted the whole load of guilt on Vic. Everything, except his real guilt. Their lovely child. The one secret she could never tell Ben.

She had used Ben to get her revenge. She remembered Ben telling Vic, *This is my daughter. May I introduce Lola London?*

Vic's daughter was London's daughter now.

But of course, that was a lie. Ria lay beside her husband, telling herself it made no difference.

Terry parked among the trees near some ponds. There was a big house but it was empty, no smoke coming from the chimneys. The Wolseley stayed by the farmhouse all day, probably they were catching up on their sleep. Terry caught up on his, not minding the discomfort. In the late afternoon a slamming door woke him and the figure of Charlie Bookkeeper crossed to the Wolseley, tossed an overnight bag in the boot, got in the car with a wave goodbye and drove off. Lola crossed the yard to the barn, but Will was with her. A cow lowed. A woman with straight black hair and a red birthmark on her face came out and called them. Terry didn't recognise her. Then Will called back, 'Coming, Helen.' They returned and lights came on in the farmhouse. There was only the one track to the place, so Terry let the Daimler freewheel downhill to the road, then parked by a small, smelly stone building with sheep grazing nearby, where he could keep an eye on anyone using the track. Not one vehicle passed the whole night. First thing in the morning Terry drank from the stream: the mints had left a bad taste in his mouth.

A Land Rover came down the track at eight-thirty, driven by the woman with black hair, Helen. Lola sat beside her wearing a school uniform. This was going to be very easy. Terry followed them to Blane, watched Lola go in through the school gates. There was a tough-looking old boy who was very protective of the girl, and altogether too many people hanging around.

Terry filled up the car's tank with petrol and asked the attendant for the phone. Vic told him exactly what to do.

# Chapter Fifteen

## 1

The phone rang in the middle of the night. Ben sat up and turned on the bedside lamp. Ria lay awake beside him, her eyes narrowed against the temporary glare. So she had been awake for some time. He sat looking down at her. 'I don't see so well in half light,' he said.

'There's quite a glow from the streetlamps when you're used to it.'

He let the phone ring. She looked at it, then back to him. They had not discussed where they would be going for a honeymoon, but she knew they would not be returning to Clawfell, their life there was in the past. She was not sure in what direction their future lay.

*Darling, there's something I must tell you*. She imagined herself mouthing the words.

'What's the matter?' he said.

'For God's sake answer the bloody thing!' she cried.

He lifted the earpiece. 'Yes, it's me. Hallo, Will.' He covered the mouthpiece. 'It's Will. He's calling from Dr Housetree's surgery in Blane, which has a phone.'

Ria looked at the bedside clock: past midnight. It was Tuesday morning. She knelt beside Ben, trying to overhear. 'What is it?' she hissed.

'Yes,' Ben nodded at Will's voice. 'Calm down.' He listened, then spoke soothingly. 'You couldn't have done anything. No, take the truck back to Home Farm and stay there. You can't do anything until first light anyway. I'll be there, don't worry. No, don't involve the police. Try and get some sleep. Bye, Will. Bye.'

He put down the phone.

'I'm afraid it's bad news.'

Ria said: 'Lola's run away, hasn't she?'

'Why should you think that?'

Ria thought of the way Lola had looked at Vic as he held her hand.

'Nothing,' she said.

'Darling, Helen and Lola have both disappeared.'

'I'll have to go and see Mum,' Ria said dully. 'I'll give my girl such a spanking when I see her.'

'Will was working and he didn't notice they were late at first. Then he thought the Land Rover had simply broken down. He took the truck out to look for them but found no sign. Corporal Macclesey at the caretaker's lodge swore that Helen brought Lola to school, and picked her up too. Will's been frantic. You know what he's like without Helen.'

Ria clung to any straw. 'Maybe there's been an accident – rolled down a glen—'

Ben held her shoulders firmly. 'I think we both know that didn't happen.' Ria was too frightened to say anything.

'I'm going up there,' Ben said decisively. He got up and started pulling on his clothes.

'I'm the one to blame,' Ria said wretchedly.

He stared at his wife, then kissed her and went out.

Fifteen minutes later, 'young' Bill Simmonds sat up, white-haired and naked, his face as wrinkled as a monkey's, as a loud knocking came on the door of his Wharncliffe Gardens flat.

Bill drove gently to let her oil warm through properly. A Phantom III was very choosy about her oil temperature and pressure, and he didn't want to risk blowing any of her exquisite gaskets made of silk thread. He glanced in the rearview mirror. 'It's a pleasure to have yer back with us again, sir.'

Mr London sat with his eyes closed and one finger across his mouth. He didn't look like a man who cared much about the intricacies of silk gaskets, although Bill knew how fascinating they were: the enormous pressures contained by surfaces polished mirror-smooth and mating so finely that a single thread made them perfect. Mr London opened his eyes. 'Faster,' he said without thumbing the intercom. Bill pretended not to hear. 'Faster!' Mr London said. Bill drove faster, wincing at the heaviness of the gear-lever stirring the thick, cold oil.

'Lola's gone,' Will said. It was first light. 'Helen's terribly shaken. If the truck's headlights hadn't caught the gleam of the Land Rover's windscreen where it was hidden behind the bothy—'

'I'm not shaken,' insisted Helen.

Will sat beside her in the kitchen at Home Farm, holding a bandage to her head. 'I'm quite capable of looking after myself, thank you,' Helen said irritably. 'I was an idiot. I should have known better than to play the good Samaritan nowadays.'

'I'll look after you,' Will said. His hands were shaking. Helen patted his arm.

Ben was standing by the fire. From here, through the little cross-paned window of the cottage, he could see Simmonds raising both flaps of the Rolls's bonnet, waving his hands at the heat shimmering visibly up from the engine.

He turned to Helen. 'Tell me exactly what happened.'

'It was so silly really. I fetched Lola from school at four-thirty in the Land Rover. She wanted to go home with Jennie Housetree – to tell her all about the wedding, I suppose. You know what girls of that age are like, empty heads waiting to be filled,' she said severely. 'I said no. Then just as we were coming home, where our track turns off, a car had broken down with a puncture. Or so it appeared. Completely blocked our way. Such a personable young man holding the jack, very apologetic he was.'

'What sort of car?'

'I'm afraid I don't notice them very much. But quite big. The radiator had a sort of fluted top to it.'

Ben called Simmonds. 'Fluted?' Bill said knowledgeably. 'That's one of yer Daimlers, that is.'

'Thanks, Bill.'

'Can I clean the car now, sir?'

'Whatever you like. You drove beyond the call of duty last night.'

'Yes, sir!' Bill said proudly, flapping his chamois-leather at his hip.

'Anyway,' Helen continued when the door closed, 'I don't remember what happened. When I woke I found my own handkerchief in my mouth so that I could hardly breathe, tied tight with another handkerchief, a man's. Clean, I'm relieved to say.'

'Suppose she'd had a cold?' Will interrupted, trying to make them understand how nearly something awful had happened to Helen. 'She would have suffocated.'

'I suppose that young man just didn't think,' Helen said.

'He didn't care,' said Ben.

'He tied my arms and legs together with the tow-rope, and left me there in the back of the Land Rover, behind that little stone bothy. Thank God Will saw the windscreen gleam. He would never have seen me by daylight.'

'Do you think Lola escaped?' Will asked hopefully.

Ben shook his head. 'She was bundled into the boot of the Daimler the moment Helen went down.'

'If only I'd woken sooner.'

'Helen, you wouldn't be here if you had.'

Ben watched Simmonds fill his bucket from the spigot in the yard, patiently cleaning the filthy Rolls.

Will said: 'My own uncle. That's what hurts.'

Ben turned to Helen. 'You kept calling him a young man.'

'In his twenties, I suppose.'

'It was Terry, wasn't it?' Will said dully.

'Then Vic is still in London,' Ben said. He opened the window and shouted. 'Bill!'

'But I haven't finished cleaning her,' Bill Simmonds said.

When the phone rang at four in the morning, Vic was sitting in the front room at Havannah Street, waiting. He snatched it up on the first ring, pressing the receiver tight to his ear.

'Is she safe?'

He listened to Terry's voice.

'Drive safely,' he said, and hung up.

It was time to put it all behind him.

He went upstairs. Esther called out sleepily from her bedroom. 'It's only me, Mum. It's nothing. Go back to sleep,' he said, without even looking at her door. He heard her turn over, muttering.

Vic went to his room and closed the door behind him.

His suitcase, not a large one, was already lying on the bed packed with what he would take with him. Not much. Few mementoes, no bad memories. Vic was ending his life, or rather, ending his old life.

Soon Vic Price would not exist.

On the dresser was the photograph of Ria and Lola he'd kept all these years: Lola aged about five, a studio portrait taken by the arty bloke in Poplar High Street as a favour to Vic. Vic took it out of its frame and tore Ria's face off. The other half, his little daughter smiling shyly under her dark lashes, was so like him it stunned him. Vic put it with the clothes he was taking. Only enough to see him by for a few days, shirts mostly. He'd buy new stuff on the ship. He took a single passport and glanced at it, father and daughter travelling together, Lola's up-to-date photograph sneaked at the wedding by the same bloke. Plenty of photographers at weddings. He slipped the tickets in it and dropped it in the case, which he closed. He hefted its weight and went downstairs. He put his doorkey on the mantelshelf in the front room, then without looking back went outside, shutting the door silently behind him. The Yale lock clicked for the last time.

Spike had returned with the Jaguar yesterday. Vic put the suitcase in the shallow boot, where it just fitted, and drove to Cable Street. The Old Bull and Bush felt quiet and dead, smelling of spilt beer and stale smoke. Vic climbed the stairs to Terry's room at the top, felt for the spare key where Terry hid it, and went in. Crossing to the dresser set in the dormer window, he stopped. Behind the door Terry had a blown-up photograph of Victoria London. Vic shook his head. People never ceased to amaze him.

He pulled the dresser aside, then lifted the carpet and the board beneath. The shooter was wrapped in cloth smelling of machine oil, an officer's Webley, and it was loaded. Vic slipped it in his overcoat pocket, replaced the board, flapped down the carpet. He spent several seconds aligning the dresser exactly as it had been on the sun-faded pattern, then went into the corridor, locked the door, replaced the key, and departed.

It was time he drove to a place he had come increasingly to dislike.

Terry kept strictly to the speed limits. He knew it was

never the big things went wrong, it was always the little details that let you down, usually several arriving together: only five miles an hour over the speed limit, but a tail-light out too, and a policeman with a headache who wanted to spread it around. Terry checked his lights and cleaned them, made sure he had enough fuel to do the journey in one, no bumping noises from the boot to attract a curious petrol station attendant. 'Got a bag of ferrets in there, chum?' No one wanted to deal with that sort of question at five a.m. on the North Circular Road.

Traffic was building up as Terry crossed Tower Bridge and turned left into Rotherhithe. In the quiet streets off the main commuter routes nothing was moving. Terry missed Rotherhithe Street and had to look at the map. He went left until he found the river and followed the curve of it south, knowing he was near when he saw the Jag parked, reasonably enough, outside the premises of a scrap-metal merchant. Spike could collect it later, while Terry slept.

There it was, the Half Moon & Calf's Head just as Vic had described it, an apparently windowless building standing on its own, its front overhanging the misty river, on stilts maybe. Terry turned off the headlamps as the Daimler bumped across the rough ground, then got out into the grey morning light. He went up the steps and knocked on the door. Vic was waiting.

'If you've hurt one hair on her head, I'll kill you.'

'Take it easy,' Terry said.

'Get back in the car.'

'Hey,' Terry said, 'this isn't the welcome I expected.'

'You won't see me again,' Vic said. 'Don't talk. You live your own life now, Terry. No more Uncle Vic to hold your hand.'

Terry stared at him. 'Sure!' he said. 'Sure, if that's the way you want it!' He got back in the car, obediently, but slammed the door, and sat with his arms crossed. He'd sleep all day and be awake all night.

Vic opened the boot.

He held out his hand, offering it very gently to the frightened girl. Again it was impossible not to think of Vic's great strength turned inward against himself.

'We've got a lot to talk about,' he said, and her hand slipped into his own, almost clinging to him.

## 2

Ria couldn't bear to stay in bed. When the room service waiter, Luigi from Firenze, as he informed all his ladies in the hope of increasing his tip, brought her breakfast – two, she had forgotten to cancel Ben's – he found the bride dressed and pacing the room. With a shrug he placed the two bed-trays, with their silver covers, in front of the empty pillows on the bed. It was not his fault if a little marital discord had changed arrangements. It was not uncommon. He waited for his tip.

Ria sat by the phone, nibbling a piece of bacon.

When Ben rang she dropped it guiltily back on the plate. Lola had definitely been taken, probably by Terry. 'Terry?' Ria said.

'I didn't think Nigel's boy was capable of it,' came Ben's voice from Blane.

*Darling, there's something I must tell you.* Ria covered the mouthpiece with her hand.

'Obviously he is,' Ben went on. 'I'm coming back, I can't do any good here. See you this evening. Love you.'

'I might be out, Ben.'

He paused. 'I'll know where to find you.'

Ria knew too. She put on her hat and coat, but just as she was about to go out the phone rang again. It was Lisa. She wanted to speak to Ben about something that was bothering her. Ria wanted to shout, *What have you got to bother about? You abandoned your baby! What right have you got to interfere now?* Instead she forced herself to sound calm. 'I'm afraid Lola's gone missing.'

'Is this something to do with you?'

'Yes,' Ria said, 'I'm afraid I think it is. I'm just going over to Havannah Street now.'

'You must find Lola,' Lisa said authoritatively, 'you must hold her and never let her go.'

'When I find her,' Ria promised, 'I'm going to give her bum such a tanning that she'll never forget.'

'You sound very angry with yourself.'

'Of course I'm not going to hit her. I'm going to give her the biggest cuddle she's ever had in her life; if only she'll come back, I'll never let her out of my sight again.'

They promised to keep in touch, then Ria took a taxi to Havannah Street. It looked dull and drab after the wedding festivities. The pavements were so deadly with ice, what with it being in shadow all morning now because of the blocks of flats, that she walked in the road.

She rang the bell. Esther took one look at her face. 'What's happened?' she said, glancing down the hall behind her.

'Something awful,' Ria said. 'I'm to blame.'

'You haven't left Ben, have you?' Esther said, talking in the doorway like a conspirator.

'It's worse than that. I thought it would be happy-ever-after when we were safely married, but it isn't like that.'

'What?'

'Being in love. Ben knew.'

Esther relented. 'I was a bit brisk with you the other day. It was for Vic's sake. You'd better go now,' she whispered. 'He's asleep in his room.'

'I bet he's not,' Ria said. She led the way upstairs, opened his door without knocking. 'His bed hasn't been slept in.' She checked the wardrobe. 'He's got more clothes than this, hasn't he?'

Esther peeped in. 'He keeps his suitcase under the bed.'

Ria crouched briefly. 'No he doesn't.'

'Of course he does, you aren't looking properly!' Esther got to her hands and knees in a businesslike way, going to show Ria up. 'It's not here.'

'He's gone,' Ria said. She helped Esther up, then followed her mum around the room as the old woman checked the wardrobe again and again, pushing the hangers back and forth as though there was some perfectly sensible explanation. 'The dry cleaners!' Esther exclaimed.

Ria pulled open an empty drawer. 'Does he have all his socks done at the dry cleaners too?'

'What's happened?' murmured Esther. She tidied up the torn photograph on the floor. 'Here's your face.'

'I think you know what's happened,' Ria said. 'He's taken Lola.'

'I swear to God I'm innocent,' Esther muttered pathetically. 'He can't have gone. We had tea last night and he was himself. The last I heard of him he was up in the night and I said, "Is that you, Vic?" and he said, "It's only me, Mum. Go back to sleep." So I went back to sleep and I've been creeping around quiet as a mouse this morning, because I thought he was sleeping late. And all the while I needn't have bothered. He never even said goodbye.'

Ria slammed the drawer and went downstairs to the front room, held up something glinting. It was Vic's Yale doorkey. 'Mum, this is his goodbye note. He's never coming back.'

Esther sat. She placed her hands in her lap, then looked up. 'Is there something you want to tell me?'

'Lola is Vic's daughter.'

Esther stared at her for a moment. 'I suppose I've always known it,' she said. 'It's so obvious that you don't see it, you just don't see it. I'm to blame as much as you are, darling.'

'*Vic is to blame!* Not us. We never did anything

wrong. It was all Vic. He overheard you tell me that I was Dick's daughter. That was when I was still living above Trott's Nightclub on the Strand, just before the war. Vic came and raped me there, and Lola is his child. Not your fault, not mine, not hers. *It's all Vic's fault!'*

Esther gave her a lost look.

'I could not face what he had done to me,' Ria said economically. 'I pretended to seduce Ben, to make the child his, to make Lola a love-child. It was the only way I could cope. Ben was innocent. The only people who knew were me, Vic, Pearl, and Betty Stark.'

'She turned out badly,' Esther said. 'She left her husband and ran away with a Polish seaman. Vic told me. But I always thought Betty was a good sort. There was something strange in his eyes when he told me.'

'I don't think Betty ran away with any seaman,' Ria said. 'You can't make excuses for Vic any more, Mum.'

'Vic let Nigel drown,' Esther said wearily. 'He let him go. I knew that.'

'And my poor Ray Trott. And Ted Trott. And Alan Stark.'

'It's the blood, you see,' Esther said without tears. 'Don't you feel how terribly strong it is? Lola is Vic's own blood, she is his only family. Yes, I understand exactly what Vic is going through. Don't you?'

# 3

'You're my daughter,' Vic said. 'I love you. I would never hurt you.'

'Ben is my father,' Lola said.

'Of course, you would say that at first. But believe me, you'll come to see the truth of what I say.' He followed her down the long room, past the kitchen units and the old bar counter. When she stopped and pulled aside the curtain hung over the stairwell to keep the draughts out, he almost bumped into her. 'That's upstairs,' he said.

'Can I go up there?'

''Course you can, princess.'

Instead, she walked to the picture window overlooking the river, standing between the armchairs with her arms folded, her back to him. He tried to see her face.

'It had to be done like this,' Vic said. 'That's the Isle of Dogs,' he pointed out. 'We had happy times there, didn't we?'

'I can't remember.'

'He's changed you, hasn't he,' Vic said flatly. 'You even speak funny. Yorkshire, is it? I suppose he's told you all sorts of stories.'

She said, 'How would I know?'

Vic tried to laugh. 'Cor, smell of petrol, you do. That school uniform's no good. Am I speaking too loud? Have you got a headache?'

'There was a spare can in the boot. It smelt awful. And the car rocked and rocked. I thought I was going to die.'

'But you're with me now,' Vic said. 'It's never easy.'

'Was Helen hurt?'

'Not her! I had to get you to me, darling. Everyone else only tells you lies. Trust me.'

'Can I go now?'

'Trust me,' Vic said slowly. 'I got you togs upstairs, a selection. I didn't know your size, but I'll learn that sort of thing, won't I? I just said you were sort of long and stringy,' he tried to joke. 'Of course you're ever so pretty really, you're a dream. You can go upstairs alone.' She wondered what would happen if she tried to escape. She looked at him but he didn't understand what she was thinking.

'What happens if I try to escape?'

'It's in the roof,' he said blankly, 'it's got no windows. Why should you, anyway?'

Lola went to the stairs, let the curtain drop behind her and climbed with loud footsteps. There was no sound of him following. He had locked the heavy main door of the place, but unobtrusively. There *was* a window in the bedroom, but it was in the end wall, thirty feet above the mud, and anyway she saw it was stuck closed with generations of paint. There was a secondhand-looking bed with some clothes thrown over the patchwork coverlet.

*You're my daughter. I love you. I would never hurt you.*

Just words, but he believed them, and so she believed them. There was nothing frightening about Vic, he simply wanted her belief. Lola chose a pair of dark blue slacks from the clothes, putting them on before lifting her school dress over her head, then quickly buttoning on a sailor-style top with a white stripe. He'd even thought of shoes, but they were far too small, as though he still secretly, without being aware of it, thought of her as the child she had been. Lola kept her school shoes on, took her comb from her satchel and flicked through her hair quickly in the fly-specked mirror. The face that looked back at her told her no lies.

She strung out her time upstairs until she heard him moving around below, then went down. 'Hallo, princess!' Vic greeted her with false joviality. 'You look cracking, you do.' She still thought of him as Uncle Vic, what memories she had of him were of Uncle Vic, but they were just pictures really. Uncle Vic dressed up as Father Christmas. Uncle Vic carving the turkey, the big social events. She had no particular memories of him with Mum. So much of the adult world was hidden from a child.

'Have you told Mum I'm safe?'

'I want to get to know you. I want you to know your real father. Give me a chance, Lola. All these years it's been hidden inside me. For God's sake have a heart.'

Lola went to the window. The tide was far away, almost no traffic on the river she could signal to even if she could think of a way. Seagulls strutted on the revealed mud, fighting over tidbits with sudden flurries of wings and beaks.

'I'm your prisoner.'

'I'm the prisoner,' Vic said with terrible feeling, and Lola felt the depth of emotion, the rage of it, that made him attractive. 'I am your father.' He held out his wrists as though he were handcuffed. 'We'll escape.'

'You poor man,' she said.

'The *Mauretania* sails from Tilbury tomorrow afternoon,' Vic said. He lifted up a hatch in the floor. Lola looked down the steps leading downward, then held her nose. 'It floods at high tide, it's not so bad. Twelve horsepower, lovely polished wood, I got the launch in with no trouble. That's the way they used to do it, see. The smugglers.'

## 4

Ben drove the Phantom III south and Bill Simmonds, who was supposed to get some sleep in the back, watched in horror as the speedometer climbed towards ninety miles per hour. This in a car weighing almost three tons. Bill was unable to rest and hung miserably from the straps. He could even hear the engine, Ben would blow the cylinder-head for sure, and Bill was certain that he hadn't pressed the lever that pressure-lubricated the suspension once in the last two hundred and fifty miles. The man had no mechanical sympathy.

But Ben couldn't drive in the dark. Bill took over gratefully.

'Suppose she dies?' Ben said at the roadside. 'Suppose she dies because of me?'

'You weren't to know what would happen, sir.'

'Wasn't I?'

\* \* \*

Ria and Esther had nothing to do. They sat in the
front room like plaster statues, pale-faced. Esther
couldn't face laying the coal fire; she brought down
the electric bar-fire from Vic's bedroom. 'I found
these,' she grunted as she plugged it in. 'Thomas
Cook brochures. Everywhere under the sun.'

'He's taking her away.' Ria covered her face.

'Now, calm down,' Esther said with rough affection. 'That sort of thing won't do no good. He's trying
to escape himself. He wouldn't hurt her. Trying to
find himself in her, he is, his own flesh and blood.'
Esther shrugged. 'Now, Lola's no softie, is she? Got a
head on her shoulders. I feel sorry for her, but I feel
sorry for them both, too.'

Both women jerked as the doorbell rang. 'Too
early for Ben,' Esther said. She picked up the
poker.

'I'll go.' Ria opened the front door. Lisa was
standing there.

'No news,' Ria said. 'We're waiting.'

'It's a lonely vigil,' Lisa said. The streetlamp
gleamed on her white hair, and her eyes were as
piercing as ever. Then she blinked, leaning on her
stick. 'I have been alone in my house all day. It's not a
time to be alone. I, too, know what it is to lose a
child.'

'Come in,' Ria said. 'She isn't lost yet.'

They waited without saying much, Ria in the
armchair, Esther and Lisa on the sofa. Each time the
clock on the mantelpiece chimed, which it did very
prettily every quarter-hour, with the full works every

574

hour, the three women looked at its cheerful face then settled back. 'Vic brought it back from the market,' Esther said apologetically. 'He was a good boy that way. You don't notice the racket it makes normally.'

'Ben's late,' Ria said. 'He phoned that message from Blane Post Office before midday to say he was coming straight back. We're only an hour off midnight, for God's sake.' They all looked at the clock. 'He should have been here by now.' She split the curtain and looked out. 'That's done it. Foggy. Can't hardly see to the end of the road. Wait a minute.' Glowing headlamps turned into sight, and there came the murmur of an engine pulling up outside. Ria ran to the door. 'Ben!' Climbing out of the passenger seat, he dropped the packages wrapped in newspaper that he was carrying and lifted her up, kissing her.

'Fog,' he said. 'Bearing up?'

She nodded and tried to smile. The street smelt of fog and smoke.

'Wotcher, Ria,' he said, and picked up the scattered packages. 'Fish'n'chips. Got them in Commercial Road. You haven't eaten, have you?'

'We couldn't eat,' Ria said, following him inside. 'Your mum's here. And mine.'

'This is Bill Simmonds. Tuck in, Bill. I reckoned the right number of portions. Still warm.' He kissed Lisa, then Esther. 'All forgiven?'

'I still say Ria was the dangerous one,' Esher said fondly, 'bringing in outsiders.'

* * *

Ben sat on the arm of the sofa, eating out of the paper. 'It's a London pea-souper,' he said. 'Clear as a bell until Hendon then it shut down. I walked in front of the car with a torch. Any news?'

Ria shook her head.

'Terry kidnapped Lola,' Ben said. 'That's where I got it wrong. I thought he was just a clever boy like his dad, Nigel. That was my mistake.'

'Ben,' Ria said, 'it was Terry who made the bomb that killed Pearl. Vic had nothing to do with it.'

'Terry!' Ben said. He spread his hands. 'But why? I spared his life.'

'You knocked him down. You threatened him with a pistol.'

'But—'

Ria shrugged. 'To prove himself. To make himself a man. To get out from Vic's shadow.'

'But he hasn't,' Ben said. 'He hasn't.'

'The games men play,' Lisa said.

Ben stood up. He wiped his hands on his handkerchief. 'Where will I find him?'

'The Old Bull and Bush, like as anywhere,' Esther said. 'I could phone, if you want. It isn't the sort of place that closes.' She slipped on a pair of reading glasses and started dialling the number. When she finished Ben took the phone. 'It'll be Jake,' she whispered.

'Hallo, Jake,' Ben said heartily, 'Terry there, is he?'

'No, Terry's not 'ere. 'E's gone aht. D'yer know what time it is? I'm just cleanin' up.'

'Where's he gone, chum?'

'I've no bloody idea, mate, this isn't the London Zoo and I'm not 'is keeper.' The line went dead.

Ben put down the phone.

'I know where he is,' Lisa said.

The Rolls pulled up outside the Emporium and Ben got out.

'Wait here, Simmonds.'

'Yes, sir.' Bill stayed where he was, his hands on the wheel, not looking round.

Ben stared up at the great building. The windows were brilliantly lit, of course, the enticing displays stretching into the fog on each side until they faded to no more than a misty glow, then darkness. Above him was also darkness, everything above the second floor hidden in the glare thrown back from the streetlight above him. He took his mother's keys from his pocket and used them in the private entrance.

The lift was at the top; someone was at home.

Ben pressed the button to call the empty lift down, then took the marble stairs two steps at a time. The upstairs lobby was carpeted, his shoes made no sound as he crossed to the door and slipped his key in the lock. The lights were out in the lounge. He put them on one by one as he went through. He turned on the bedroom lights and pulled Terry out of bed by his feet.

Terry screamed, then struggled. He broke free, slipped on the satin sheets that had followed him on to the floor, and Ben tripped him. Terry crashed, then wriggled under them and came up the other side. He backed to the door. 'Where's Lola?' Ben said.

Terry whimpered. He had hurt his head.

'What is this about?' Victoria demanded. She sat up in her nightdress, holding the coverlet around her, looking both pathetic and elegant. Her bare feet stuck out below the fringe. 'What are you doing? We've done nothing wrong. How dare you!'

'Stay there, love.' Ben pushed Terry into the lounge. '*Where did you take Lola?*'

Terry ran. Ben caught him in the lobby. Terry hammered on the button for the lift, then dodged aside. The machinery whirred softly as the lift commenced its tedious journey upwards. Terry banged on the doors, then slid along the wall and ran into the corridor. Ben heard the fire door knocked open, then thud shut on its springs. Terry's bare feet slapped on the lino of the darkened salesfloors as Ben followed him. There was a cry as Terry fell down a motionless escalator, tumbling down the metal steps from this floor to the one below, then silence.

Ben turned up the lights.

Terry lay among the framed advertisements he had knocked from the walls on his way down, women's lingerie mostly, Visit the Waterfalls Restaurant, Gloria Fox lipsticks for the Smile that Smiles.

'It's my leg,' Terry said.

'I'm not going to hurt you.' Ben knelt beside him. 'We're going to go and see Vic. You're going to show me, Terry.'

Victoria came down. Her face was streaked, her hair everywhere. 'He hasn't really done anything wrong, has he?'

'You haven't. Terry has.'

She put her face close to her father's. 'I'll never forgive you for this. You and I have nothing in common. You're worse than that man you hate.'

'I have to be.'

'I've done everything you wanted,' Victoria said in a small voice. 'What did you really want of me?'

Ben smiled. 'To be you.' He squeezed her hand lightly. '*You*.'


'Turn left along Piccadilly,' Terry said. He looked back at Victoria standing in the doorway. 'I love you,' he called from the window of the Rolls-Royce, 'remember that.' The car moved off and he looked back until her figure could no longer be seen, then turned and put his hands on his knees with some of his old cockiness. 'She's where I went wrong,' he said. 'I fell for her.'

Terry was wearing a check work-shirt and a grey flannel suit, one size too large, which Ben had found for him in Menswear by the escalator.

'Where now?' Ben said.

'Tower Bridge.'

It was the early hours of the morning and now that most people's fires had died down the fog was thinning somewhat. The Strand was a slow crawl, almost impenetrable with fog, but they found Tower Hill clear, the battlements of the Tower and the tall bascules of Tower Bridge jutting into the moonlight from the mist below. Ben stopped at a telephone kiosk and phoned Havannah Street.

* * *

'It's Ben.' Ria listened, then said, 'Be careful, love.'
She put down the phone. 'He's got Terry. They're
going south of the river. Ben thinks Rotherhithe.'

'South of the river!' Esther said. 'I would never
have believed it.'

'I'll make another pot of tea,' Lisa said. 'It's a long
night.'

'I'll do it,' Esther said, 'it's my kitchen, I know
where everything is.' All three of them ended up in
the kitchen, Esther squeezing between them to the
various cupboards. 'I don't know what I'm doing,' she
confessed, getting the cups but not the saucers.

'One just has to live from day to day,' Lisa said.

'I wish my baby had never lived,' Esther said,
putting down the cups and picking them up. 'If Vic
was born now I'd kill him myself. It would have been
kindest. Lisa, pass me the saucers would you, I don't
think I'm up to it.'

'Listen,' Ria said. 'It's an engine.' She went to the
front room.

'It's Vic!' Esther said.

Ria peeped through the curtains. 'It's Terry's car.'
She went to the door.

Victoria was standing on the step. 'Can – can I
come in?'


The Rolls-Royce drifted almost soundlessly through
the mist along Rotherhithe Street, the swing bridges
creaking beneath its weight as it passed. The huge
expanses of open water on their right attracted the

580

mist, as did the river on their left, the mist swirling upstream as the tide rose, but between the ware-houses the air was still and dark.

'Turn off the headlights,' Ben said. 'Sidelights only.'

'Gorblimey,' Simmonds said.

Moonlight glowed on the vapour ahead of them. 'It's there,' Terry said.

'Pull off the road,' Ben ordered. He wound heavy-duty fabric tape from the carpet department around Terry's wrists. 'What's the picture?'

'There's quite an area of waste ground,' Terry said. 'Bombs, I guess. Standing alone you'll see a building, an old riverside smuggling inn I think. No windows on the land side. That's where I delivered her and that's all I know.'

'Out,' Ben said, pulling Terry out by his arms. He opened the boot. 'In you get.'

'You're not going to put me in there,' Terry said.

'You put Lola in a place like that.' Ben waited. Terry got in. 'Stay with the car,' Ben ordered Bill Simmonds, closing the lid. 'I won't be long. Just having a look round.'

'Very good, sir.'


Vic's daughter lay in the dark. Lola had never felt so alone. The double bed was quite comfortable, though rather saggy. Everything was all wrong – all the little things. Because Vic was staying up all night he evidently expected her to do so. 'I don't need much sleep,' he'd told her jovially. Neither should you, was his obvious inference. 'Come on, we can talk, I know what you young people are like. Talk, talk, all day and all night. We've got a lot of catching up to do, Lola, we'll get to know one another and make up all the time we've missed. Yes?'

'Yes.'

'Yes!' he laughed, but when her eyelids drooped he left her feeling guilty to be so tired, as though she'd let him down. Her yawns were an insult to him, she wasn't keeping up her side of the relationship. Maybe he was right, she ought to stay up with him, talk to him, keep him calm. 'Go on then, go to bed,' Vic said roughly, dismissing her.

'I'm so tired,' she said.

'Don't worry about it!' He kissed her forehead. 'Off you go. Up the wooden hill. Don't forget your prayers.' It dawned on Lola that she was a complete mystery to him, he didn't know how to communicate with her at all. When she spoke he wasn't really listening to her. 'Up early in the morning!' he said heartily.

'Why?'

'High tide, of course.'

There was no toothbrush in the little bathroom, another thing he'd forgotten, and no proper night clothes. She took off her shoes and got into bed dressed, feeling more comfortable like that, pulling the sheets up to her chin. Vic came up, knelt by the bed and clasped his hands in front of him.

'You are mine,' he said. 'You're just like me, you are.'

He unscrewed the lightbulb and shut the door. His footsteps went downstairs. She heard him moving around down there, a constant presence. Lola's eyelids drifted closed. She slept.

She awoke confused, with no idea of what time had passed, everything absolutely silent. She swung her feet on to the floor, still in her socks, and crossed to the faint glow showing through the cheap curtains. It wasn't dawn, it was moonlight: blue vapour hung over the black waters rippling upstream, the moon glaring in a pale sky with a star or two. The Isle of Dogs was hidden below the fog, except for the four blocks of flats showing like a row of sentinels. A single window was lit, for a sick child maybe, the parents worried whether to call out the doctor. Maybe the sky was slightly lighter behind the flats, she thought, and went back to bed. Vic's footsteps came upstairs, very soft, not at all like he'd gone down. The bedroom door creaked but the darkness didn't change.

'Lola, darling?' came his voice.

She murmured sleepily.

'Are you asleep?'

'I'm awake now.'

'Was that you I heard moving round?' The window went dark, he must be standing in front of it. 'Tide's nearly up,' he said. Suddenly he turned and came back to her. 'Can you hear them?' He pushed her down on the bed, grabbing at her until he found her wrist. 'There's somebody moving around outside.'

They listened.

'I can't hear anything.'

'They're out there,' Vic said.

He took both her wrists in his one hand; he was terribly strong. He pulled her off the bed and pushed her shoes against her. 'Put them on.' Lola put the left shoe on her right foot. She forced herself to concentrate and put them on properly. He pulled her to the stairs and they went down. The picture-window illuminated the long living-room with moonlight.

'I can hear their feet in the mud,' Vic said.

He opened the hatch in the floor and pulled Lola down after him.

Ben crossed the waste ground. His sight was poor in the colourless moonlight, and twice he almost turned his ankle on broken bricks. The swirls of mist confused his sight, the outline of the building that appeared in front of him appearing to shift and distort, several times to disappear altogether. He passed his hand across his eyes and pressed on. Soon he was close enough to see that the walls were blank, no windows on the land side. Terry had told the truth. There was enough light for him to make out the faded sign, Half Moon & Calf's Head.

Ben trod lightly up the steps to the massive door. One glance was enough. He turned back and walked under the shadow of the floodwall to a raised ramp. A gravel causeway stretched across the mud beyond. The tide was already flowing over it, showing small lips of foam around the mooring posts, sluicing across the mud.

Ben crossed the ramp in a quick, crouching run, and dropped down on to the mud.

* * *

Back at the Rolls-Royce, Bill Simmonds was getting worried. The man in the boot wouldn't stop knocking. He must be using his feet, and Bill thought of the damage he could do. 'I can't breathe,' came the muffled voice again. Bill put back his peaked cap with his thumb.

'Give it some 'ush,' he said. Bang, bang with the feet again, setting the car rocking. 'Hey, that's enough of that!' Bill hissed, knocking on the boot with the flat of his hand.

A moment of quiet. 'I'm suffocating. Let me out, for pity's sake.'

A Rolls-Royce was well insulated, every hole faithfully plugged with a rubber grommet to keep out wind and road noise, the doors and boot snug-fitting on rubber or velvet seals.

Bill bent down. He could hear the bloke panting, then there was more kicking. 'Hoi!' Bill said, alarmed. Drumming noises. 'Hang on a mo', I'll open it a crack, but you got to promise to lie still,' Bill said. He turned the catch and Terry knocked the lid down with his feet, barking Bill's knuckles. 'Ow!' Bill said. Terry butted him with his head and Bill sat down. He saw the look in Terry's eyes and stayed down. Terry ran off into the dark, his hands still taped behind him.

Bill got up. The boot light swung from its electric wire, the carpet was ripped away from the sides.

Ben froze, the mud seeping over his ankles, as a light appeared not in the Half Moon & Calf's Head but rather in the boathouse below, as though a naked bulb had been switched on in there, its glare streaming through the gaps in the rotten wood and between the doors, casting long shadows across the mud. He heard a hollow sound like feet thumping down wooden steps, sloshing noises, then the light went out and there was silence.

Ben didn't move. He knew Vic was looking out from the gap between the doors; it was what he would have done. Ben's calf muscle cramped, caught half between steps, his left foot sinking deeper because it had happened to be taking most of his weight as he moved forward. He didn't shift, well aware how sensitive an eye was to movement. Something glinted in the gap now. Did Vic have Lola down there with him? Ben tried to remember if there had been a lighter footstep alongside Vic's on the stairs. Of course he had her with him, and perhaps she was wearing jewellery and it was glinting.

But the only bright jewellery Lola possessed was her gold earrings, which she was not allowed to wear to school. Anyway, this was not a golden glint, it was smooth, blueish, like a gun.

Vic had a gun.

Ben wondered how long he could keep still. He looked round, moving only his eyes, as a pair of distant headlights glowed through the fog. They illuminated the silhouette of a running man.

Terry fell and ran again, disappearing from Ben's sight behind the floodwall. He could hear the breath whining in Terry's throat. Moments later Terry reappeared, going up the steps to the door with awkward strides, his hands strapped behind him making his balance ungainly. Such was his desperation to get to his Uncle Vic that Ben thought he might actually beat on the door with his head. Instead Terry began kicking the door, and Ben could hear him sobbing as the headlights drew closer.

Terry's nerve broke. He half dashed, half fell down the steps, limping now on his bad leg. He disappeared behind the floodwall, then reappeared on the ramp gasping for breath. He plunged down.

'Terry, stop,' Ben said.

Terry's shadow staggered through the mud towards the boathouse. He reached the doors.

'Vic!' Ben shouted.

A gunshot rang out. There was no flash. Terry fell shot through the head.

'Got him!' Vic said. 'Stop crying. *Stop your bloody noise!*'

Such was the depth of fury in his voice that Lola's sobs stopped.

'You bloody women,' Vic jeered. 'You're all the same.'

Lola drew a quivering breath. 'That's Terry. You've shot Terry.'

'Nonsense,' Vic said. His face close to hers smelt of burnt powder. The rising tide gleamed in the gap between the doors, already lapping the jagged shape of Terry's head. 'Shut your bloody nonsense.' He turned, splashing through the muddy floor of the boathouse and tugging at the launch as though it would already move.

A call came from outside. 'Hallo, Vic.'

Vic shook his head. He grabbed Lola.

Ben London's voice echoed from the shadow of the floodwall. 'Terry's gone the way of the others, Vic.'

Vic pulled Lola back to the door. He stood a little back from the gap, hidden, moving his whole body from side to side to get the angle on Ben with his cunning eyes.

'He needed you,' Ben said, 'so you destroyed him.'

Vic looked at dawn brightening the sky over the Isle of Dogs. 'I can't see you,' he said.

'You hurt me by getting me through Lola, not Ria,' Ben called. 'I thought you were capable of love. At least a little. I was wrong.'

'I love Lola,' Vic said.

Ben was silent.

Vic said: '*I* am Lola's father. She's mine, not yours.'

A pair of headlamps, yellow in the growing daylight, appeared on the causeway ramp. Ben turned to wave Bill Simmonds back. Vic saw the movement and fired.

Ben heard Lola scream. He scrambled to his feet. Everything was gone, everything was dark. He clapped his hands to his eyes and gave a terrible cry. He could smell gunsmoke and there was pain in his head. He knew Vic would fire again. The worst thing was the return of his blindness. He stumbled back, banging into the floodwall behind him, then scraped his hands along the crumbling brick until the gravel of the causeway crunched beneath his shoes. Another shot rang out. Ben fell from the far side of the causeway, arms flailing, and rolled into the slime below.

Vic grabbed Lola, wrists in his hands, arm around her waist. He lifted her up though she was kicking, the mud flying off her shoes spattering them both. He splashed to the launch and heaved her over the stern.

'That's settled,' Vic said.

She lay sobbing on the boards, then looked up.

'You don't half look a sight, princess!' he said jovially. 'Look like a bloody dalmatian dog, you do!' He wiped the muddy spots affectionately from her cheeks with his thumb, then looked down at the river rising around his knees.

'Reckon there's about enough water to float the old girl now, don't you?'

He pushed open the doors, admitting a greasy stream of water, then untied the ropes from the mooring rings and let them drop. Splashing to the steps, he jumped into the stern of the boat, picked up Lola and half carried her past the engine housing, also of gleaming wood, into the narrow wheelhouse. Barely with standing room, the wheelhouse was open to the rear, containing only the helm and engine controls; he seemed to fill it. He opened a double-jointed hatch she had not noticed and thrust her into the tiny cabin below the foredeck.

'We'll have to get you cleaned up,' he said. The starter motor whirred as he pressed the button with his thumb, her eyes level with his knees, and he smiled at her with genuine gentleness. The engine fired and he throttled back, then crouched down to her.

'You and me. We're a team. Like father, like daughter.'

'I'm nothing like you,' she said.

'You'll learn.'

Bill Simmonds ran down the ramp in front of the Rolls-Royce on to the gravel causeway. The rising tide lapped its raised banks, the river sliding on each side of him now, the last fifty yards submerged and visible only as a disturbance in the water flowing upstream. Ben London lay with his head on the stones, the tide tugging him. His face was covered with mud and blood. Bill knelt, heedless of his uniform, and cradled Ben's head in his lap. 'Sir? Make it back can yer, sir?'

Behind him, the doors of the boathouse opened.

Bill scrambled up. 'Come on now.' He got his hands under Ben's armpits and heaved him back with all his strength. Bill's cap fell off and the river took it. ''Elp me if you can, sir!' Ben moved his legs weakly and Bill dragged him backwards on to the ramp.

Ben groaned.

'Sit up if yer can, sir.' Bill grabbed the duster from the Rolls-Royce and supported Ben's shoulders, wiped the slime from his eyes. 'Yer let me handle it, sir, it's only dirt. The bastard's winged yer, yer going have to have stitches I daresay.' His voice quivered with outrage. 'Look what that one did to my car, sir!'

The sound of an engine being started carried to them from the boathouse, then it was throttled back to engage the propeller. The bow of the boat nosed through the doors, already gaining speed.

'He's getting away!'

Vic gunned the motor, keeping close to the sunken causeway where he knew the river bed was clear of obstructions, heading for deep water. The windscreen buzzed with the vibration of the motor and he pressed his hand against the glass to quieten it. He looked over his shoulder. Ben London was sitting on the ramp, already getting smaller, his head in his hands. Then the Rolls-Royce moved off past him. Vic stared as it bumped down on to the causeway, picking up speed, spray flying up on each side of it like silver wings. Vic slammed the throttle open. The car turned to ram him, but plunged immediately from the causeway into deeper water. When the disturbance subsided the roof reappeared. The short, white-haired figure of a uniformed man wriggled from the driver's window and splashed towards the shore.

Bill Simmonds sat down beside Ben on the ramp. 'Worth a go, sir.'
    'Don't worry about the car,' Ben said.
    'I'll tell yer what, sir,' Bill said with satisfaction, staring at the rippling, vacant waters. 'That's one thing, in all 'is years of being a chauffeur, that my dad would never have done.'

The engine was very loud in the cabin. Lola sat on the narrow bunk with her hands over her ears. Through the porthole she saw the sun rise like a red ball over the Isle of Dogs, then the river swung round and the launch turned towards the east.

'You can come up now,' Vic said.

It was a lovely day, Lola saw. Mist clung to the marshy shore and the river-valleys winding down from the hills, thc river Lea looping between Hackney and Wanstead on their left, Vaudey and Holywell making a steeper slope into the hills on their right, but the air was clear above. Vic stood at the helm without looking at her.

'Why wouldn't you let me help him?' she called.

'Obvious reasons.'

'Are you going to kill me?'

Vic laughed. 'Why should I?' He opened a leather case and scanned the shore with binoculars.

'You know you're not going to get away,' Lola said. 'You've got to take me back.'

'I can't let you go.' Vic looked round at her, trying to make her understand. 'You're all I have, darling.'

'Take me back. You don't own me any more than Ben does.'

He piloted the boat in silence. Lola's hair blew in the wind. The river was becoming much broader, its grey-green waters choppy. A big cargo vessel passed them, its wash lifting the little launch and twisting her round on its surge. Vic cut the throttle. He was sweating.

'I'll tell,' Lola said quietly. 'I know you've got it all planned, you can get me on the ship somehow. But you can't hide me for ever, and sooner or later I'll find someone.'

'Don't sound so bloody sure of yourself! You sound just like your mother.' The boat rocked in the heaving waters. Vic noticed the ropes trailing across the foredeck and turned off the motor. 'I'll have to take those in before they get round the propeller.' He braced his legs, pulling the wet, slimy ropes out of the water with an expression of disgust, half coiled them, then let them flop on the boards. Without the engine the sound of the river slapping at the sides of the boat seemed very loud.

'I'll talk,' Lola said, 'to anyone I can find.' She put her head on one side, just like Vic.

He knew she meant it.

'I'm not yours,' she said, 'I'm not his, I'm myself. I'm my own person.'

The boat rocked. Water from the ropes ran from side to side across their feet.

'Take me home,' Lola demanded. A ship's siren hooted, then its steel wall slid past behind her.

Vic held out his hands to grab her.

'I'll jump!' she said from the very edge.

'You'll have us both in,' he cried. 'Look out!'

'Touch me and I'll throw myself over,' she said, and he knew she would. Her hair was flying in the wind and there was a certain light in her eyes. But she couldn't see the waves from the ship rising up behind her, breaking foam.

'Lola!'

He tried to save her. Tottered. Confused, he found his feet tangled in the ropes. He fell. The cold shock of the water. He couldn't find her down there. The ropes slithered around him and water filled his mouth. One of his hands caught the side of the boat.

Vic hauled himself up on breaking fingernails, hanging there at the limit of his strength. Lola was safe in the stern. Her clothes weren't even wet.

'You see?' Vic croaked, 'You're just like me.'

He tried to reach Terry's gun in his pocket, but its weight dragged him down. He looked up into Lola's eyes, his fingers relaxed their claw-like grip on the boat's side and, for her sake, finally he let go.

## 5

Nobody noticed a ferryman. All his life his job had been to ferry people across the waters, and changeable waters they were, what with all the traffic going up and down and the weather always being different and the wind blowing hard or soft, onshore or off, and it was a real work of skill to bring the old bitch alongside sometimes. The name of the Limehouse Hole ferryman was Fred, though he was often called Hoi You or Hurry Tup, not that people looked at him when they cursed him. People on a ferry were always going places. You saw a lot of interesting people as a ferryman, but they never saw you.

Fred's moustache was grey and his eyes were wrinkled by years in the sun and wind. When it rained he wore black oilskins. On sunny winter days, like today, he wore a fisherman's jersey, very warm, never washed, smelling of diesel. He stood on the edge of the Limehouse Hole Pier squinting at the falling tide and sniffing the fickle wind, balancing them in his mind. He climbed down.

The whaler contained as many passengers as he was going to get: a woman with a baby, not her own; an impatient young man; a workman with clean hands and a lunchbox already raided for the cheese and pickle. No one looked at the ferryman. The whaler's engine idled as slowly as a heartbeat.

He cast off, leaned on the tiller, and set the little engine hammering with his seaboot on the throttle. The tide was ebbing fast now, so he kept an eye out for traffic coming down. Instead, he saw a launch coming up against the tide. No one else noticed this strange phenomenon, foam high at the bow but moving slowly against the fast water. He snorted to himself at the ropes left trailing over the side, the landlubbers. As he came closer to Cuckold's Point he saw the launch was piloted by a girl. Nobody else had noticed her. Cheese and Pickle ate another sandwich. The baby was crying and the old woman shook it, then stuck her finger in its mouth and the baby sucked.

Fred brought the whaler alongside expertly and landed them on the causeway. His passengers got out, he lent the woman with the baby his arm but she didn't say thank you. His passengers walked past a man sitting on the floodwall ramp without looking at him.

Fred could hear the launch's engine, suddenly close. The girl grounded the vessel on the causeway where it would soon be high and dry. She ran to the man sitting on the ramp and threw her arms around him.

Fred lit his pipe. Some sort of disturbance in the

water caught his eye. While he waited for a new batch of passengers the falling tide revealed a Rolls-Royce sitting on the mud, dirty water squirting out around its doors. He puffed his pipe phlegmatically. Amazing what you found in the river sometimes.

# Epilogue

Even Victoria was smiling. It was dark outside and the store was closed, but the ground floor of the Emporium was a busy swirl of people enjoying themselves. Models paraded the new season's fashions along a catwalk, the excuse for the celebrations. Ben London, watching from the stairs, was back at the head of his family. 'Happy?' he whispered to Victoria.

'Yes, I think I'm happy.'

'Good,' he said, 'because you're the one with the money, so you're picking up the tab.'

Lola hopped from one foot to the other. 'Can I go down now?' she hissed to Ria.

'You're not to talk to any boys,' Ria said.

'Off you go,' said Ben. Lola, wearing her bright new dress of sunlight yellow trimmed with blue, chosen from the Emporium's racks, ran down the steps and greeted her friends. François had arrived from the Embassy with a smiling Rachel and their baby daughter, asleep in a flounced white crib, very French, placed in a quiet corner. Rachel squeezed Lola's hand: their secret. Cathy was there with George, making sure he was introduced to the right people, and the glass in his hand contained only mineral water. Esther's glass held a generous measure of sweet sherry. She fiddled a piece of dressmaking material between her fingers.

'I don't think much of this quality,' she told Lisa.

'Isn't it amazing,' Lisa murmured, 'how everything comes a full circle in the end?'

Bill Simmonds had acquired a lady on his arm, whom he introduced to everyone as Mrs Alma Hoblin, a widow. She steered him away from the girls parading on the catwalk. 'I was just looking,' he grumbled.

'I know your looking,' she said.

Will and Helen had come down from Clawfell, Will with a clutch of paintings in a new style to try on the London dealers. He had discovered he was quite capable of doing this on his own, and Helen looked a little sour about it.

'What are they going to do?' she asked rather petulantly, nodding at Ben and Ria on the stairs.

'The first thing is, they're not staying here,' Will said wisely, 'and the second thing is, they're not going back to Clawfell.'

'I think that scar on his forehead rather suits him,' Esther said.

'It *is* rather exciting,' said Victoria.

'I'm glad you've arrived, Vicky,' Esther said. 'Some of this stuff here is not up to scratch, you know . . .'

From the staircase, Ben and Ria looked back.

'Where's Lola?' Ben asked.

'She'll come running when she sees us go.' Ria

stopped, not taking the next step. 'It's all over, isn't it?'

'No,' Ben said, 'it's just beginning.'

'You know the truth, don't you?'

'What about?'

'No more games, Ben. About Lola. You know about Lola.'

'Oh, that truth.' He put his finger to her lips.

'I *want* to tell you.'

'Some truths are best never told.'

'Did Vic tell you?'

'I knew the moment I first saw her at Clawfell. Vic was right. It's obvious.'

Ria said: 'No, you knew all along that Lola wasn't yours, didn't you?' She shook her gorgeous hair, looked up at him and blinked her eyes, blue and gold. He put his face close to hers. Nothing had changed since the first moment he saw her, a girl in a tattered yellow dress in the fog outside the Queen's Theatre, as old as she'd got fingers on her hands.

'You could never lie to me, Ria.'

She breathed, 'Why not?'

He kissed her.

'*Because* I love you.'

# A selection of bestsellers from Headline

| | | |
|---|---|---|
| THE LADYKILLER | Martina Cole | £5.99 ☐ |
| JESSICA'S GIRL | Josephine Cox | £5.99 ☐ |
| NICE GIRLS | Claudia Crawford | £4.99 ☐ |
| HER HUNGRY HEART | Roberta Latow | £5.99 ☐ |
| FLOOD WATER | Peter Ling | £4.99 ☐ |
| THE OTHER MOTHER | Seth Margolis | £4.99 ☐ |
| ACT OF PASSION | Rosalind Miles | £4.99 ☐ |
| A NEST OF SINGING BIRDS | Elizabeth Murphy | £5.99 ☐ |
| THE COCKNEY GIRL | Gilda O'Neill | £4.99 ☐ |
| FORBIDDEN FEELINGS | Una-Mary Parker | £5.99 ☐ |
| OUR STREET | Victor Pemberton | £5.99 ☐ |
| GREEN GROW THE RUSHES | Harriet Smart | £5.99 ☐ |
| BLUE DRESS GIRL | E V Thompson | £5.99 ☐ |
| DAYDREAMS | Elizabeth Walker | £5.99 ☐ |

*All Headline books are available at your local bookshop or newsagent, or can be ordered direct from the publisher. Just tick the titles you want and fill in the form below. Prices and availability subject to change without notice.*

Headline Book Publishing PLC, Cash Sales Department, Bookpoint, 39 Milton Park, Abingdon, OXON, OX14 4TD, UK. If you have a credit card you may order by telephone – 0235 831700.

Please enclose a cheque or postal order made payable to Bookpoint Ltd to the value of the cover price and allow the following for postage and packing:
UK & BFPO: £1.00 for the first book, 50p for the second book and 30p for each additional book ordered up to a maximum charge of £3.00.
OVERSEAS & EIRE: £2.00 for the first book, £1.00 for the second book and 50p for each additional book.

Name ......................................................................................................................

Address ...............................................................................................................

.............................................................................................................................

.............................................................................................................................

If you would prefer to pay by credit card, please complete:
Please debit my Visa/Access/Diner's Card/American Express (delete as applicable) card no:

| | | | | | | | | | | | | | | | |
|---|---|---|---|---|---|---|---|---|---|---|---|---|---|---|---|
| | | | | | | | | | | | | | | | |

Signature ......................................................................... Expiry Date ...........